CARVED IN STONE

FRAN MARIAN

Red Hills Press

Carved in Stone

Copyright © 2012 by Fran Marian

Published by Red Hills Press

Tucson, AZ 85748

ISBN-10: 0978784820
EAN-13: 9780978784829

Printed in the United States of America

First Edition August 2012

Cover art by Terry Medaris

This book is dedicated to my grandchildren: Scott, Brittney, Michael, Jacob and Evan.

CHARACTERS

ANGULLI	Horse trainer and close friend of Prince Takana
AZZIA	Mother of Ras, wife of Hapati
BROCAS	Assistant to Master Palla
ELIN	Daughter of Lord Odepinu
GILLE	A Royal Guard
HAPATI	Personal scribe of King Suldana II
IBIRANU	Chief of the Royal Guard
INARA	Wife of Master Scribe Palla
JERAN	A Royal Guard
KING AMILLA	Sovereign of Kazaram
KING NARAM-SUEN	Sovereign of Luwadna
KING SULDANA II	Sovereign of Hittite Kingdom
LORD ODEPINU	Lord of Vassal State of Harmesh
MASTER PALLA	Head of the *eduba*, the scribe school
MUTWALLI	Unsuccessful student of the scribe school
QUEEN ALINA	Wife of King Naram-Suen, sister of Queen Patupa
QUEEN PATUPA	Mother of Prince Takana, sister of King Suldana II
QUEEN RESAT	Wife of King Suldana II
PRINCE SETMEL	Son of Queen Resat
PRINCE TAKANA	Nephew of King Suldana II, son of Queen Patupa
RAS	Son of Hapati and close friend of Prince Takana
URHI	A Royal Guard, son of Ibiranu

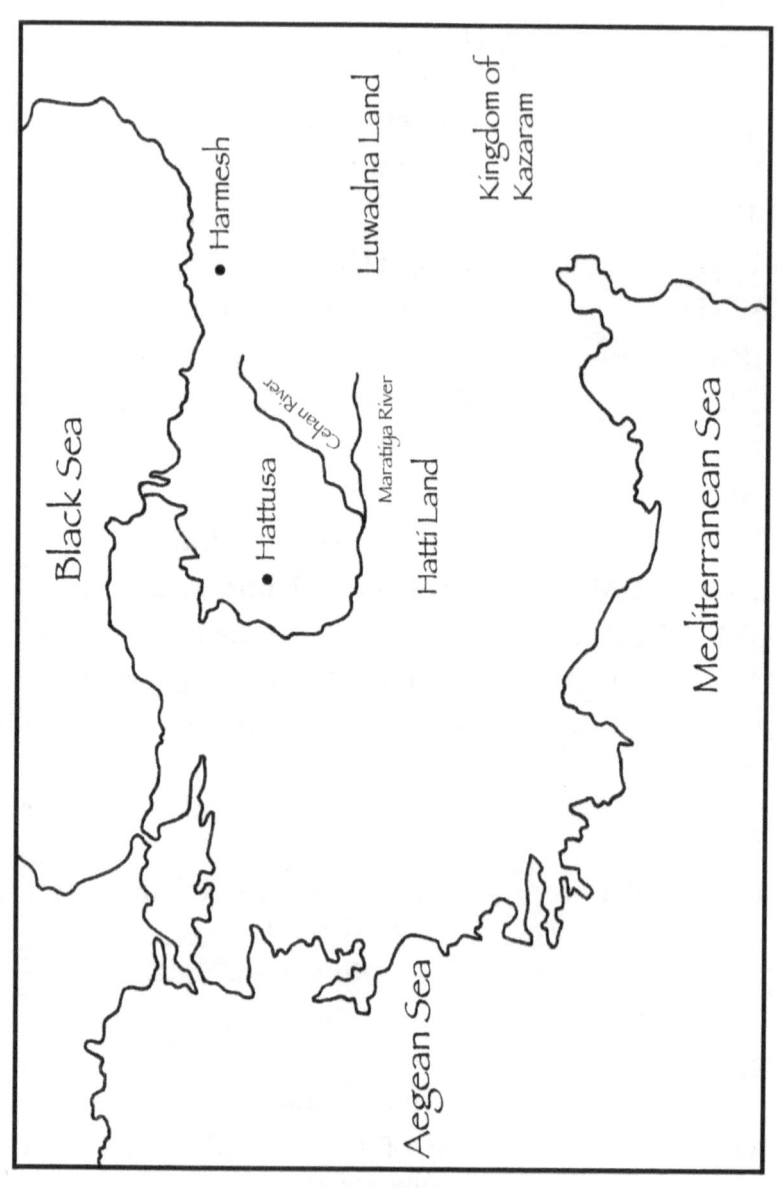

The World of the Hittites

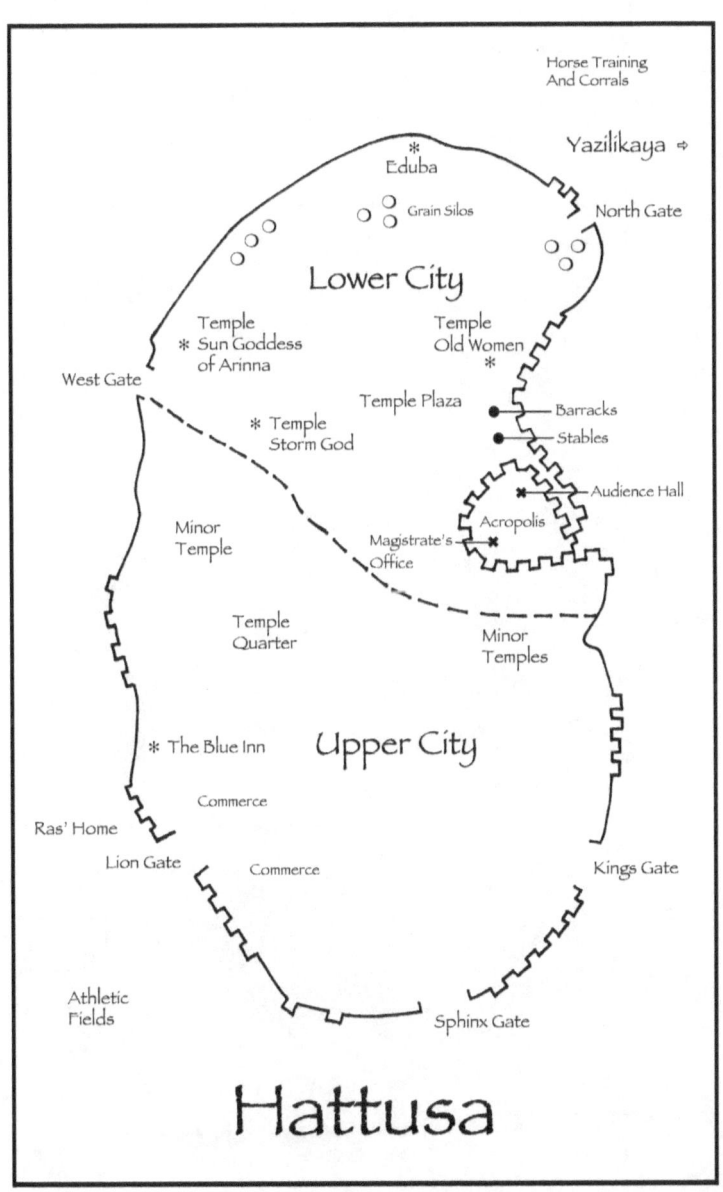

Horse Training
And Corrals

Yazilikaya ⇨

*
Eduba

Grain Silos

North Gate

Lower City

Temple
* Sun Goddess
of Arinna

Temple
Old Women
*

West Gate

Temple Plaza

Barracks

* Temple
Storm God

Stables

Audience Hall

Minor
Temple

Acropolis

Magistrate's
Office

Minor
Temples

Temple
Quarter

* The Blue Inn

Upper City

Commerce

Ras' Home

Lion Gate

Commerce

Kings Gate

Athletic
Fields

Sphinx Gate

Hattusa

CHAPTER ONE
Hattusa, Capital City of the Hittite Empire
1460 BCE

TAKANA

The king's bedchamber stank. It struck Prince Takana's senses like a physical barrier and he paused at the door to pull a mint leaf from his waistband. He crushed it under his nose before he followed his mother, who was moving deliberately through the packed room to her brother's bedside, looking neither left nor right until she locked eyes with Queen Resat, the *tawananna.*

"Queen Patupa, Prince Takana," the queen said with a slight nod.

"Is my brother in any pain? He looks . . ."

"He's been faithfully cared for," she said, with no little resentment coating her words. "Moments ago the physician gave him a draught of mint and cannabis."

Takana placed a reassuring hand on his mother's back. He wanted to believe his uncle slept peacefully, but the lingering odors of potions, poultices and sacrificed animals spoke volumes about the frantic healing rituals that had taken place. He bit his lip. Nothing in his twenty years had prepared him for this parting. When was the last time they'd spoken together? He could still hear the king's bass voice, complimenting, inspiring, challenging. Then the king gave Takana the ultimate vote of confidence when he sent him to the vassal state of Harmesh to restore order. He gulped when he realized that was the last time they'd spent time together. Takana's few visits to the capital city were brief, leaving time only to pay his respects and report to the authorities.

At his side, his mother fumbled with her cloak, filthy with the dust of eight day's travel. He caught it as it slid off her shoulders, folded it over his arm and stole a quick glance at her face. He'd never known his regal mother to lose her composure, but there was more than death at stake. Deep sadness merged with the worry she'd expressed while they traveled. *I'm afraid if the king dies, the Kingdom of the Hittites will change and our future along with it.*

Although he'd tried to counter her arguments, Takana knew power could shift, loyalties might dissolve and lives of status could fall in an instant. But for the moment, looking at his uncle's pale face, his thoughts and prayers were for a miracle of restoration.

Just behind the royal family, white-robed high priests and representatives of the Hittites' multiple gods formed a halo around the king. The king's chief scribe, Hapati, was bent slightly forward over the king's head, ready to record his words should he speak.

Takana, taller than most in the room, stretched to survey the assembled dignitaries. He rubbed the stubble of his beard. The *mešedi*, the king's elite bodyguards, were posted at the massive chamber's several doors. His cousin, Prince Setmel, standing behind the queen, had yet to acknowledge him. He was the crown prince, the *tuhkanti*, but the title fit him like a robe fit a dog. He had thick, wet lips and a narrow face that held a scowl like an official seal. They'd shared the same warrior training, religious duty instruction and athletic training, but never friendship.

The High Priest of the Storm God stood at the foot of the king's bed, presiding over the traditional healing rites. At his side was the *hasawa*, the Old Woman, interpreter of the Divine Will. At that moment the priest turned to whisper in her ear. When he finished, she stepped forward, raising a flask-shaped bottle covered with rings—holy symbols to prevent profane use. Her unearthly voice issued forth from the depths of a white hood:

"Lords and Ladies of the Court, I have stood on the bank of moving water to watch the flight of birds. I asked the wind, the trees and the water to use their voices to carry my words to the gods. The gods answered through the birds. I saw them fly together in the same direction. From this we know that all our healing efforts have been correct.

"O, My Lord, Most Powerful Storm God, gather together all the gods of the heavens and save our beloved King Suldana II. His service to you is not ended. He has more to give. He praises your goodness to him and to the people of Hatti Land. Restore him and you will reap our gratitude in gifts of succulent foods and obeisance. Your temple will overflow."

She flicked her hand and her temple servants entered the room, pulling a full-grown black ox. Once again her voice vibrated the stale air: "O, Mighty God, we offer you a sacred ox, into whose body all offensive words and deeds will enter. Be pleased with this substitute, we implore you. Restore strength and power to our beloved king."

A servant drew a knife smoothly and deeply across the ox's throat. For several moments, the animal moaned and pulled at the restraints. Thick, dark blood poured into a wide bowl, undulating until the smell filled Takana's mouth and he tasted metal. Several servants stepped forward to take the sacrifice and its life force from the room. As ritual prescribed, both would be burned in the Storm God's temple. When the door closed behind them, the room grew tense with anticipation. A moment later Takana's head dropped, knowing the substitute sacrifice was a ritual of last resort.

A collective sigh seemed to punctuate the court's acceptance. The king's physician stepped to the side of the bed. There was no hiding his hopeless expression or his mechanical movements. All treatments had failed. The gods had been petitioned and the Divine Will had been invoked. Nothing more could be done. Takana released a long-held breath. King Suldana II would die.

Fabrics rustled and leather squeaked. Takana had the sense that the room's occupants were fixated on the rise and fall of King Suldana's barrel chest. Even Takana found his breath synchronizing involuntarily with the king's—shallow, uneven, suspended—as if his youthful strength might be transferred to his beloved king. He shifted his gaze from the king and swept the room. Most of those present were genuinely heartbroken. Others, Takana knew, couldn't wait to get on with a new order predicated on power and greed. Once the king was dead, they'd line up behind the queen and the son she'd been grooming for the throne long before the king fell ill. Nothing would stop them once the prescribed fourteen days of mourning ended. He shuddered. It was his mother's worst fear.

Behind Takana someone whispered that Thutmose III of Egypt had sent his personal physician, a towering, ebony figure with coal black eyes that, some said, could see into the body and vaporize the evil within. Someone else, of a more cynical inclination, said they feared a rival kingdom might use the Hittites' moment of weakness to their own advantage. When Takana and his mother approached the city, he'd noted the additional soldiers. Now he understood why. Takana winced at the thought of anything interrupting the procedures it would take to escort the king to his place among the gods in the Afterworld.

His mother tapped his arm and slid her eyes left. There, against the wall, was his close friend, Ras. He, too, stood next to his mother, his curly hair showing above the crowd like a nest of spun copper. Takana willed him to turn around, but his friend was intent on his father, the king's scribe. Though the scribe stood ready, his ear inclined to the king's lips, Takana held little hope the king would ever speak again. His throat constricted and his eyes fell on the clay tablet and stylus in Hapati's hand that would never capture King Suldana's wisdom and kindness again.

He turned to the only window in the room where a thin slice of morning light entered through the heavy draperies. Like the inexorable hand of a sundial, it moved across the room and crept along the bed linen to the king's face. His eyes moved beneath their lids. The queen gasped and reached for Prince Setmel at her side. The touch brought the *tuhkanti's* face to life. Eyebrows peaked over close-set eyes, nostrils flared below a narrow bony nose and his fleshy lips formed an oval. His expression lasted no more than an instant before it settled back into boredom.

Setmel as king. It was beyond imagining. Takana knew the king's son better than most. As members of the royal family, they'd been raised together in the palace, competed at games and at strategies of combat and leadership since they were boys. Setmel bested through trickery and treachery, never with intelligence or skill.

Somewhere in the room a voice cracked the silence. "Look, the Sun Goddess of Arinna holds out her hand to receive our beloved king."

Heads swiveled to the crack of morning light falling across the king's face. Suddenly the king's lips moved and Hapati's stylus jabbed at the soft clay tablet. Several moments later the scribe straightened his back, covered the tablet with a damp cloth and cradled it against his chest.

When Takana looked back at the king, he was inanimate. His mother convulsed with sobs. He wrapped his arms around her. Slowly, the room's occupants inched toward the bed, drawn by the gravity of death. Only Queen Resat remained erect, more intent on the crowd than the king. Their eyes met and for the briefest moment he wondered if she was in shock. He felt he should give her a comforting smile, but couldn't. Years of her cold stares and suspicious looks, which in more recent years became openly hostile, were hard to dismiss, especially in the presence of the weakening king.

When the king ordered him to Harmesh, Takana and his mother speculated he might have two goals in mind: personal growth for Takana as a leader of men and peace in the palace. But at that moment, standing at the deceased king's bedside, bitterness overshadowed the benefits. He tore his eyes away from the queen and saw that Ras had spotted him and was crossing the room.

As they tried to close the distance between them, the *mešedi* moved in and formed a protective wall around the king's bed. It was a signal to clear the room so the Storm God's High Priest and the Old Woman could begin to prepare the king's body for the Afterlife.

"Where's Queen Resat?" Takana's mother said. "I must not leave without paying my respects."

He scanned the room and shrugged his shoulders when there was no sign of her. By then Ras had reached him. "I'm so sorry. We have lost a great king." He grasped Takana's shoulder and bowed to his mother.

"I'd like . . . Do you have some time?" Takana said. "Do you mind, mother?"

"No, I want to rest. You two have been separated for a long time. I'll be in our apartment when you return."

His mother's voice had been light, but there were times fear formed a sheen over her warm brown eyes. This was one of those times.

They accompanied her to the door, just one terrace level under the king's, where other members of the royal family were quartered for King Suldana's final days. They'd come from vice royal states and surrounding kingdoms, knowing accommodations awaited them in the towering palace.

It was an imposing structure, stretching nearly one hundred and ten yards from side to side. Nine tall terraces, each embellished with heavy columns of gleaming white stone, were joined together by a sweeping staircase in the front and a ramp for horses and chariots at the back. The acropolis rose majestically in the northeast corner of Hattusa, where the Upper City crowned and leveled off north into the older Lower City. In descending order under the king's level of elegant rooms, were apartments for royal family, chief military commanders, the chief scribe's family, tablet archivists, bureaucratic officials, medical consultants, royal bodyguards and household staff, including cooks, domestic slaves, doorkeepers, pages, heralds, prayer reciters, barbers, cleaners, craftsmen and grooms—a city within a city.

Takana and Ras walked briskly through the plaza and acropolis gate, receiving a sober nod from the royal guardsmen on duty. Suddenly Ras turned to him.

"It's good to have you home. I know how close you were to the king and I'm so sorry . . . sorry for all of us." Takana nodded and Ras threw his arm around his shoulder. "I know Angulli wants to see you too. Let's see if he can join us."

A lump in Takana's throat prevented anything more than another nod. He not only craved the comfort of their friendship, he also knew he could express his worries to them without fear. Maybe he could learn something to ease his mother's and his concern about the kingdom's welfare.

They walked north along the eastern city wall to the horse stables, purposefully located a distance from the acropolis to prevent contamination. Moments later they were mounted on two horses. They left the city, trotting evenly without talking. The image of the king's body was still imprinted on Takana's mind and his chest felt heavy. At least the rush of fresh air helped to clear away the smells of the king's bedchamber. He ruffled his sweat-matted hair in the breeze.

At the edge of the forest, north of the fortified wall, Takana and Ras slowed their mounts. The rising sun dangled just above the horizon, casting long tree shadows across the road. They kept to the shaded edge of the large land reserve set aside for the king's horses. Somewhere ahead the herd was milling around the corral, perhaps moving toward the feeding troughs in anticipation of the first meal of the day. As Takana and Ras drew closer, the barest outline of five stone cottages formed in the distance. These were the homes of several generations of horse trainers—their friend Angulli was one of them.

Takana had turned to listen to the sounds of the herd when he heard a shout. Angulli burst through the door of the largest cottage and ran toward them. Takana jumped down and Angulli crushed him in a bear hug.

"Will you ever give up tears?" Takana said, as his friend stepped back and rubbed his eyes.

Angulli's ears glowed scarlet. "Maybe when I reach your old age!" He grinned and lowered his head. "I heard you were here for . . . I'm so sorry. We've lost our beloved king and you've lost your uncle. But, I'm very happy to see you. You, too, Ras." Angulli used his arm to swipe his freshly shaved cheeks before he stepped back and placed his hands on his hips. He was a year younger and a head shorter than both Takana and Ras and sported the clothing and tanned skin of an outdoorsman. His dark eyebrows were canted alongside pale green eyes. They gave him a look of empathy and kindness that suited his character. His hand-woven cotton tunic strained across a broad chest and hung down almost to the tops of his high, mud-splattered, soft leather boots with upturned toes.

"We've come straight from the acropolis. How did you hear so quickly?" Ras said.

"We *peasants* on the outside have our ways," Angulli said good-naturedly. "Actually, my oldest brother was in the city all night, so . . ." His head dropped. "The only king I've ever . . . feels strange . . . But now," he said, looking at Takana, "he's our powerful protector in the Afterlife, right? I'll never forget his goodness to me."

Takana nodded. How typical of Angulli, he thought, to feel at once the loss and almost immediately recognize the gain. It reminded him of one more happy memory: the day the king visited the corral and Takana introduced Angulli as his friend. The king promptly invited Angulli to join the games. *I suspect those shoulders might bring strong competition to our spear throwers,* the king had said. Angulli was delighted and proved the king right many times over. Having his horse-trainer friend take part in the games also deepened their friendship.

"Can you come with us? I'm starving for talk," Takana said.

"Me, too. Wait here. I'll get rid of these filthy boots."

Moments later he returned on his own horse and followed Takana's lead toward the distant hills. They followed a trickling stream bed that twisted between high rock walls on either side. The land sloped downward, ending in a wide muddy wallow with a narrow ribbon of moving water at one edge. Soft emerald grass grew in abundance around the area, and the horses, when freed, immediately began grazing.

"When did you arrive in Hattusa?" Ras said.

"Not more than four or five hours ago. We left Harmesh right after a messenger arrived with the news of my uncle's condition. Considering the ruts in the road, we did well to get here in eight days."

They found dry ground near the rocks where they could sit and watch the horses. Takana hadn't been aware of his tension until he leaned into the warmth of the black rock and felt his body sag. He'd given it little thought, but neither he nor his mother had slept the last night in their anxiety to reach the acropolis. He hoped his mother would sleep, but being with friends was what he needed most.

Bird songs and wind filled the quiet. Ras, stretched out on the ground, chewed his lip and crossed one long, lean leg over the other. His free leg moved constantly and he drummed his fingers on the grass. Angulli watched the sun's light creep downward on a wall of jagged black rock that formed the other side of the narrow canyon.

The tightness in Takana's chest loosened. Sadness lingered but it was held at bay by the pleasure of sitting with friends. He was grateful nothing had changed between them.

"Tell me, what have you heard about the people's mood? What's going on? What do you think is going to happen?"

"Ask me in fourteen days when our kingdom falls into Setmel's hands," Angulli said, shaking his head. "Have you spoken to your father, Ras?"

Ras emptied his lungs with an impatient blast. "In a way, my friend, I envy you for what you *don't* know about my father's work. He'll be in seclusion, working on the king's Proclamation and protected by guards. When the mourning period ends, he'll take the tablet to the Temple of the Storm God. I'll see him when *you* do, when the High Priest reads the king's tablet naming Prince Setmel as king."

Takana lowered his head. Missing his friends wasn't the only downside of living in Harmesh. He and his mother missed the vitality of the capital city, the daily exchange of fresh information and gossip with those who ran the kingdom. Though he knew the king had his reasons for sending him away, some days it felt like a punishment. As time passed, he and his mother speculated about the queen and her influence on the king's decision. Most royal families nurtured their nieces and nephews. After all, they supplied the leadership for the outlying regions of the kingdom. Blood relatives were usually more reliable than others, although there had been exceptions.

But that wasn't all he missed. Fresh produce, handmade tools and household goods flowed into the city daily, not only from vice royal kingdoms and vassal states, but from foreign kingdoms. Exotic products gave the people of Hattusa a window to what lay beyond the vast land of their kingdom.

As a child Takana felt welcomed by the queen. His mother sensed otherwise, although there was nothing she could do when the king specifically asked for him. But when he and Setmel began warrior training together, Queen Resat criticized Takana and complimented Setmel, making sure her voice was overheard by everyone.

Nevertheless, Takana considered his time in Harmesh valuable. He'd been challenged to find his own strengths and shape his own course without the king's help. The

11

work he accomplished in the vassal state gave him a better understanding of the kingdom's rural villages and small town life than most men who'd lived all their lives behind the city's walls.

While Hattusa and its people enjoyed the privilege of ample food and the protection of the royal guard and the army, life outside was governed more by security issues, innovation and self reliance. In truth, he might never have chosen to leave, but admitted he felt more experienced because of it. He raised a prayer of thanks to the gods for the wisdom of his king.

Takana looked up to see his friends staring, waiting. "Sorry, I get a little nostalgic when I'm here. I was just thinking about the things I miss about the city—you, of course, but knowing what's going on, too. We get official messages but . . ." He ruffled his damp hair with his fingers again.

"I want to hear about Harmesh," Ras said, sitting up and crossing his legs. "Word was you put down a rebellion."

Takana coughed, took a deep breath and exhaled slowly. "Not exactly, I mean, that's what the king thought my task would be, but . . . I've had two years to think about this. My mother and I believe the king had more than one reason to send me away."

"No battle?" Ras said, sticking to his point.

"I was prepared for one. The king gave me a hundred armed warriors and two chariots to command. When we were barely in sight of the city walls, I divided the men. One chariot and half of the men were to wait hidden at that point and the rest, except for ten, were to wait at a closer spot. Then, while I approached the gate in a chariot with the remaining men, a single warrior watched nearby to alert the others. They were to attack in waves if there was trouble. But as we came within sight of the gate, it opened and Lord Odepinu and his royal court walked out and bowed with respect."

"Ha! A trick," Ras said. His body was taut with energy and his green eyes danced.

"No, not at all," Takana said, noting Angulli's relief and Ras' disappointment.

"So why did you stay? Two years is a long time," Angulli said.

"My uncle had been misled. The Lord of Harmesh wasn't rebelling, he was just a poor administrator and unable to keep the vassal state solvent. They'd fallen behind in taxes owed to King Suldana and in their frantic efforts to make restitution, they failed to communicate. My guess is they were embarrassed.

"I stayed on to help them organize their farming, record keeping and other things. Before long, visitors from vice royal kingdoms and other vassal states were coming to learn from our successes. Mother and I actually were beginning preparations to leave for Hattusa when we received word about the king's failing health."

Ras kicked up a clod of damp earth. "All the time I was envious of your challenge and you were doing boring administrative work. I can't believe it," Ras said.

"All right. Not your cup of tea. I get it. But it was satisfying to me—helping people do their best, increasing efficiency and productivity. Look at it this way, our kingdom's taxes are restored and everyone's happy."

"Yeah, I guess," Angulli said. "But your place is here in the capital of the kingdom. Somebody else could have taken care of the problems in Harmesh." Angulli flushed. It wasn't like him to speak his mind, especially about political matters. He looked like he was ashamed of his outburst.

"Probably," Takana said, placing a hand on Angulli's shoulder. Gratitude spread across his friend's face with the gesture. "But he knew it would be a good experience for me and it was. The queen's hostility toward me was a factor too."

"Ha! Politics," Ras said.

"Yeah, the stuff I'm glad I know nothing about," Angulli said, throwing a pebble into a spot where the water had formed a small, swirling eddy.

"That's not smart," Ras said. "With that attitude you'll be caught watching some horse while an arrow comes at your back. I suppose you think the disappearance of two of our running mates is nothing to worry about, eh?"

"Huh?" Takana said, sitting up abruptly.

"They made some unflattering comments about Setmel. Seems he took an illegal shortcut during a cross-country run. Their allegations were true, by the way, but hardly safe, at least not close to Urhi's big ears," Ras said.

"Urhi?"

"Yeah. Royal Guard Chief Ibiranu's pride and joy. Urhi likes impressing his father with such tidbits," Ras said.

"I *do* think it's something to worry about, Ras. I just believe he'll make an ass of himself soon enough." Angulli sighed and twirled a blade of grass around his finger.

Takana shifted and rose on his knees. "What do you mean, they disappeared?"

"Gone. Haven't seen them at the athletic field and they're dedicated to the games. There's a rumor they're being held somewhere, waiting for Setmel to accuse them of treason. Nobody's talking about it anymore. They're scared."

"And you wonder why I want no part of the city's politics?" Angulli said, tossing another pebble. "At least horses have no hidden agendas."

They sat in silence again, but Ras' words troubled Takana and he frowned. If it was becoming dangerous to speak, that could only mean the *tawananna* and the *tuhkanti* felt threatened. And that meant forces would be rallying on two sides—those who wanted Setmel on the throne and those who didn't. Furthermore, Takana knew fear wouldn't stop those who opposed the crown prince. They had nothing to lose. Living under Setmel would be as good as death to them. What would that mean for his mother, for him?

"Did you see my father capture the king's final words?" Ras said. "What could have roused the king so urgently, I wonder?"

The frown on Takana's brow deepened.

CHAPTER TWO

IBIRANU

Royal Guard Chief Ibiranu stood at Queen Resat's side as the king took his last breath. He watched with disapproval as some of the palace royals pressed closer to fawn over Prince Takana and his mother, Queen Patupa. His face flushed, thinking their behavior was inappropriate, even disgusting. His queen ought to be the object of everyone's attention. He could feel the words waiting in his throat like a flaming arrow, held tight on the bow. But as he considered his options, Queen Resat grabbed his tunic and pulled him into an adjacent dressing chamber.

"Did you hear what the king said?" she hissed. Dark stains marked the back and underarms of her brown silk gown. She pulled at the cloth to free it from her skin and ran her pink tongue across wine-stained teeth.

Ibiranu cleared his throat and pushed a dank coil of hair under his helmet before he spoke. "My queen, how could I? Hapati hid my lord's mouth. If we'd been alone, my blade would've provided a snack of his tender ears for the royal cats."

He looked down at her hands, clutching his sleeves with such force her flesh whitened. She trembled and stared into his chest. A jeweled comb lost its hold on her auburn hair and it cascaded to her shoulders. He wanted to grasp it and let the silk slide between his fingers. But he stood motionless while she mumbled.

"What did the old fool say? Why did he not take me into his confidence? Men and their exclusive sodality! He and his scribe! I was his *wife*. I deserved to know his thoughts. If he'd given me some assurance, I wouldn't have had to take things into my own hands. I felt alone . . . but I thought of Hatti, only of Hatti."

"What? You must never think you're alone. I'm here," Ibiranu said. He struggled to understand, to keep up with her thoughts. She was impetuous, unpredictable and so strong. He'd heard whispers here and there about her secret meetings with other kings, of alliances being formed. Was she that bold? She thought the king lacked ambition and had missed opportunities to increase the kingdom's power and wealth. He agreed completely on that score and assured her his warriors were ready to fight. Had she moved on her own?

She suddenly pushed back and looked at him fiercely. "Damn him," she said. "The king never said he had confidence in Setmel. He complained, right to the very end, he complained."

"Yes, my queen, but he respected tradition above everything. Remember how he rallied the people to observe our celebrations and rituals. He said they were the mortar that held us together as a kingdom. Prince Setmel will be king, you'll see."

She paced from one end of the dressing room to the other as if his words were never spoken. Her voice rang with mockery and bitterness. "Setmel didn't love the people enough. Setmel was hard hearted."

She stopped and planted her fists on Ibiranu's chest. "I tried to convince him of Setmel's strength. I assured him the kingdom would thrive under his guidance. But, damn him, I think he wished our son was more like Takana. Can you believe that?"

Suddenly, she listened at the dressing room door and dropped her voice lower. "Listen, Ibiranu, maybe the king followed tradition, maybe not. I must know what the king dictated on that tablet. I don't trust Hapati and I'm not the only one. Others agree when I say he's too smug, too confident of the king's total trust. It doesn't stretch the imagination to believe he abuses his position. I wouldn't put it past him to forget Setmel and I are the king's immediate family. Actions against us are treasonous! Find Hapati quickly."

Ibiranu had never seen her eyes so wild, so feral, but then they softened to green flecked with gold, the color he loved. She let her hands slip from his chest, ran them along his thighs and pressed herself hard against him. "Setmel *must* be king!" she said. "Our kingdom has seen enough of weakness. How many times did the old fool answer aggression with strengthened trade treaties or other diplomatic rubbish. The kingdom could be twice as rich. You know as well as I, Ibiranu, our Hittite warriors could have conquered territory beyond imagination. My Setmel can do it. *You* must see to it that he has the opportunity. Do what must be done and quickly!"

Ibiranu whispered. "But what's to be done? Hapati is the only one who . . ."

"Must I think of everything? Just get me the tablet so I can be sure. No one must be allowed to stand in my son's way, certainly not Hapati, a mere scribe. And certainly not that weakling Prince Takana and his mother. They'll cause problems for Setmel if they have the chance, I'm certain of it. Why must I be burdened by any of them? Find a way, Ibiranu, a way to send them someplace where no one will *ever* find them. But first, the tablet. Get it."

He kissed her hand, moved his lips to her neck, but she turned back to the bedchamber. Alone in the dark, he replayed her words in his head. Had his clever queen already formed an alliance behind the king's back? Was there truth to the rumors? He would ask her later, after he'd taken care of Hapati.

When he passed through the still half-full bedchamber, he saw the queen had collapsed across the king's body. "My king, my beloved," she cried. He saw Setmel place his hand on her shoulder. She topped it with her own and wailed again. Ibiranu lowered his head to hide his smile and strode through the crowd. She would keep the room entertained and give him time to carry out her wishes.

Dashing from the king's quarters at the summit of the acropolis, Ibiranu descended four palace levels and through an equal number of long, graceful colonnades to the Tablet Archives where Hapati worked. Royal guards snapped to attention on each terrace as he passed. He prided himself on their discipline, particularly around the acropolis. No one could question his management inside the city. He recalled with some bitterness that the king had never warmed to him. Only the queen provided ample praise for his abilities. This business of Hapati was another test of his loyalty to her. His body quivered thinking of how she would reward his success. Someday she would admit his body was created for hers, but that was a thought he kept to himself.

He entered the terrace level where the tablets were stored in seven large rooms. Hapati's workroom occupied the terrace corner, where light filtered in from two sides and guards had an open view of anyone approaching. Ibiranu nodded to the posted guards and stepped inside without knocking.

"Wha...? Ibiranu, what are you doing here?" Hapati said, automatically covering the tablet before him with a cloth.

The stone room was cool. Red embers were banked in the fireplace, ready for rekindling against the autumn chill if needed. A small, roughly-hewn table and stool stood alone in the room's center, testimony to the scribe's solitary work. Three walls supported wooden shelves, separated by stone columns. One set of shelves held freshly-formed clay tablets wrapped in cloth to preserve their moisture. Others held King Suldana's archives—the annals, letters, decrees, and treaties of his reign.

As chief of the royal guard, Ibiranu was familiar with every chamber in the acropolis and knew the wooden shelves would provide sufficient heat to harden the clay and preserve the precious documents in the event of fire. In any emergency, two members of the guard had responsibility to report immediately to the scribe's chamber and protect the archives, if not from fire, from unscrupulous villains.

"You have no business here."

Ignoring the challenge, Ibiranu pressed on. "Do you have everything you need?" As he spoke, he glanced around the austere room. He thanked the gods for choosing him to lead men and be recognized for his stature wherever he went in the kingdom. A scribe's life was no better than a mole's.

"All but the privacy to complete my work. The High Priest of the Storm God is counting on me." He edged toward the door.

Ibiranu blocked him. "Yes, of course. My only wish is for your protection. If you need an escort, send the—"

"My orders are to take the tablet to the High Priest. He'll safeguard the king's words until the proper time when the burial rites are completed. You don't need *me* to tell you these things, Chief Ibiranu."

The chief saw Hapati shiver, a reaction that pleased him. After all, men who challenged him often vanished, even important men. He enjoyed his second smile of the day as he walked to the door. But when the metal lock clicked, the queen's voice echoed in his head. *I must know what's on that tablet.* He swung around so fast, his sword hit the side of the wall and he addressed one of the sentries.

"Go to the barracks and . . ." His mouth slammed shut with his next thought. Would *his* sword draw Hapati's blood? The idea repulsed him. In the heat of battle he was as ruthless as anyone, but this was different. Could he kill in cold blood? Yes, if ordered by the king. Was it the queen's order that troubled him? He shook his head involuntarily as another thought took the forefront. Would it not be better to keep his sword clean? The kingdom was unsettled. Who really knew how the powers might shift?

Ibiranu breathed deeply and turned his thoughts to the royal guards. Who might relish such a daring assignment? Who, among his guards, possessed the desire to rise in the ranks? His mind fell on Gille, a steady, intelligent officer who was dependable and experienced, yet never placed himself in the limelight. Yes! This would be Gille's debut. He turned again to the posted guard.

"Tell Gille to recruit two other guards and meet me in the stables. Tell him to prepare one additional horse and be mounted and ready to leave when I get there. Quick now!" He looked left and right. When he was sure the corridor was clear, Ibiranu pushed back into the room.

"Don't argue further with me, Hapati! The queen has entrusted me with your safety. Bring your tablet and come with me." He drew himself up and placed his hand on the hilt of the crescent blade hanging from his waist.

Hapati tried once more. "You've placed extra guards outside my door to protect me while I do the king's work. Why is this time different from all the others? I'll have the message sooner if I work here where I have everything I need." His hands were trembling and sweat ran on his neck. "I don't understand why I must be moved." He tried again to reach the door, but was blocked.

"Now! Collect what you need. Don't try my patience. There are treasonous activities at work in Hattusa. It's my job to keep the kingdom safe."

"Treason? What's that got to do with me? Go root out the traitors. That's *your* job. *My* job is to record the king's words. Let me be."

Ibiranu heard the desperation in Hapati's voice. It would not do for him to draw attention when they left the acropolis. He sighed before he spoke, this time in a slow, measured tone.

"Hapati, believe me, your safety is my concern. It's my responsibility to know the city and I say you are in danger. Please, come with me."

Hapati clutched the tablet to his chest with both arms. "But . . ."

Ibiranu ignored him and pointed to the door. Moments later they had reached the ground level corridor. Ibiranu placed his hand in the middle of Hapati's back, nudging him forward at a fast pace. They moved together to the rear of the acropolis, down a long ramp designed for carts and chariots to access the apartments, and finally through the fortified palace wall and along the city wall to the stables.

There, Gille and two other royal guardsmen were mounted and ready. An additional horse was brought and Ibiranu signaled with a snap of his hand that the scribe should mount. Ibiranu took the lead. Hapati followed, surrounded by the three guards. They left through a rarely-used portal north of the barracks. Ibiranu allowed himself another smile as he wondered if Hapati knew this would be his last time in the palace.

Ibiranu struggled with his horse to maintain a slow pace. It wasn't the first time and, to be honest, it pleased him. He had chosen the powerful, challenging beast after hours of watching its intimidating behavior in a herd of newly-broken horses. Commanding such a beast verified his own power each time he mounted.

Still Ibiranu had no desire to attract attention, even if there was nothing unusual about guards moving through the city. Patrols routinely perused the cobbled roads that crisscrossed Hattusa's three-quarter-mile width and two-mile length. It was their responsibility to inspect the temples that honored the gods, as well as the homes and shops that served the roughly ten thousand people living in and around the capital. A keen observer, however, might question why the chief of the king's royal guard was fulfilling such a menial task when only times of pageantry and displays of military readiness warranted his appearance.

While he rode, Ibiranu considered his mission and his queen's wishes. Clearly, Hapati was the only one who could read the king's words. The *hasawa* and the king's physician were the only others in the bedchamber who could read, but it would have been Hapati's duty to prevent that. How wise his queen was! She understood the great harm Hapati could do to the kingdom if he so desired. She didn't need to express every little detail of her order. It was enough to know Hapati was a threat and needed to be removed. It was his responsibility and he would fulfill his duty.

The land sloped downward along the north side of the acropolis and, while the palace terraces offered a panoramic view of the Upper City in the south, the Lower City in the north could be seen only from the palace roof. Guards were posted on the roof when activities were planned in the plaza. This was not one of those days. Ibiranu led the way along the least populated streets. He turned once to see Hapati looking from side to side, perhaps hoping to catch someone's attention. Ibiranu, with no little satisfaction, saw that the streets were barren.

At the North Gate, the guard on duty swiftly removed the wooden bar, swung the heavy doors aside and ran ahead through the connecting chamber to repeat his actions at the outer door. Outside, Ibiranu smacked the stallion's rump with his hand and the eager horse quickened its pace. The other horses moved forward behind him, beating a dignified trot in the hard packed earth.

Well beyond the wall and a good distance from the nearest building, Ibiranu turned his horse into the surrounding forest's heavy curtain of green. Tall, dense Aleppo pine and heavily branched plane trees formed a canopy overhead. Even the sun lost its view of them. Suddenly, Ibiranu stopped, turned and pointed to the two guards.

"Return to the palace and resume your normal duties. Gille and I will return before nightfall."

Gille took a position on Hapati's left and Ibiranu shot forward again but not before he noticed Hapati rubbing the back of his neck. Ibiranu, too, felt a prickling sensation. Such feelings had been reported in the area approaching Yazilikaya, the Hittite sacred burial grounds. It was said the fingers of ghosts came out to warn the living to stay away or face death. But Ibiranu pushed aside his discomfort and concentrated on the path. The sun, strong enough to cast deep shadows, dropped shafts of light on the forest floor, thick with broom bush and tall, dry grasses.

He spurred his horse on to the northeast, dodging the trees. Soon large outcroppings of jagged black rocks replaced the trees. They were in the area people only whispered about—the burial ground inhabited by gods and ghosts. He'd heard the rocks in this area were the spit of angry *Harkassoss*, the white mountain, which rose to a frozen peak. It was silent now, but could be roused again if offended.

Ibiranu felt a change in his mount's energy. Instead of the usual eagerness to push forward, the horse became skittish, stepping sideways, snorting and pulling at the reins. Yazilikaya had an aura unlike any other place in the kingdom. Even those who gave little attention to spirits and ghosts felt the effect of the jagged black rocks and the soft earth that rose like a mist with the lightest breeze or footfall.

Ibiranu distracted himself by repeating the queen's words under his breath. But even as he replayed her order, other voices emerged in counterpoint: *To be in Yazilikaya for any reason other than worship, ritual or festival is an offense.*

"You will bring the gods down on us! Even the horses know better," Hapati shouted.

Ibiranu pulled back until he was alongside Hapati. "It is *you* who upset the natural order. I obey the orders of the queen and in a few moments you'll face the gods of the Underworld and learn the penalty for your treason." He turned quickly to Gille to be sure the young guard realized the seriousness of their mission. Gille's face registered surprise, but he said nothing.

Hapati's hand rose to his throat and he urged his horse to Ibiranu's. "*My* treason? Underworld? What sort of insanity is this?" The scribe kicked his horse and tried to turn back, but Ibiranu lashed out and grabbed Hapati's reins.

"In the name of the holy gods, Ibiranu, what are you doing? I have a sworn duty to prepare the king's final words. You are sworn to protect me. The queen has no part in this and you know it."

Still holding Hapati's reins, Ibiranu kicked his horse forward into an area with many footpaths. One more turn and a towering rock formation rose before them. Where the rock was deepest, steps had been carved upward leading to the many chambers Ibiranu had been told were inside. Soon King Suldana's bones would be placed there in a *hekur*, his stone tomb. The sooner the better, he thought, though he knew the gods would require many sacrifices and supplications before then. And when all was completed, his queen would reward him for ensuring Prince Setmel's name appeared on the tablet when it was read to the people.

They continued among the rocks beyond Yazilikaya until Ibiranu pulled his mount to a stop and dismounted next to a mound that appeared to be the remains of a small stone house. He walked back and whispered into Gille's ear. The young guard nodded and dismounted. Ibiranu walked his horse a short distance away to watch from the shade of a lone tree. Hapati clutched the tablet against his chest as Gille pulled him awkwardly from his horse and walked him behind the rocks.

No wind stirred the trees or lifted dust from the baked soil. The horses stood like statues, though their hides twitched. Nothing shattered the quiet until sounds of digging came from behind the rocks and a flock of crows rose together in a flurry of black feathers. The crows circled and settled with their necks stretched out to better view the disturbance. Moments later a sweating Gille stepped into the open. He scraped his sword several times over a jutting rock with a smooth edge, remounted his horse and joined Ibiranu. The heat of the midday sun on the black rock dried the blood before it could spread.

"The tablet?" Ibiranu said, pulling himself up on the stallion.

"Crushed to bits and buried with him," Gille said, shaking the dirt from his uniform.

Ibiranu worked his jaw. "Huh? Well . . . all right. Good. It's gone." He turned his horse and they retraced their steps back to the city, where they returned the horses. When they'd washed their hands and faces, Ibiranu pulled Gille to a dark corner of the stable and grabbed the back of his neck.

"This day we have secured the kingdom. In the eyes of the gods we are heroes. Let that be your reward and speak to no one about what you've seen or done. Do you understand? Blessed be the *tuhkanti*, Prince Setmel! He will favor us many times over.

"Now, quickly bring me a scribe who can be discreet. I will wait here."

When Gille left, Ibiranu checked the area for workers. Seeing none, he slipped into an open stall and pulled the door closed to wait. He paced back and forth in the small space, replaying his actions and finding no flaw. He whispered "Yazilikaya" to himself, almost daring the spirits to touch him. When nothing happened, he understood it as confirmation that the ghosts had rightfully claimed Hapati for themselves. He felt giddy and lightheaded, until footsteps sounded and, seeing Gille, he stepped out of the stall.

Gille, not too gently, nudged a man ahead. His head was bowed, narrow shoulders curved forward and his hair hung in greasy hanks.

"Mutwalli is a capable scribe," Gille said.

"He'd better be. Your career depends on it," Ibiranu said. He moved closer and noted sweat beading up on the man's face.

"Do you know who I am?" Ibiranu barked.

"Yes, yes, of course. Chief Ibiranu."

"Good. I have an order from the queen for you. You will produce a tablet that decrees Prince Setmel as King of Hatti. Do you understand?" Mutwalli blinked spasmodically before he nodded. Ibiranu instantly grabbed his tunic and moved his face so close to Mutwalli he could smell the scribe's breath. "You would dare to produce a false tablet! Dare to defy the words of the king who will soon be a god?"

Mutwalli stepped back and his whole body seemed to take on a new aspect. "With pleasure! I might as well already be dead. Years ago the king and Master Palla chose Hapati over me when I was his senior. I should have been the king's scribe! They conspired against me for reasons they never explained. My family status suffers because I was denied work as a scribe. Oh, yes, sweet revenge! I will produce a table that wipes out the words of King Suldana II, gladly."

It was the response Ibiranu hoped for. "Excellent! Do it quickly and bring it to me. Tell no one and let no one see you." The scribe nodded again. Ibiranu sent him off, watching until he disappeared before he and Gille walked to the Temple Plaza.

As they approached, horns were blowing from the roof of the Storm God's temple. The people were dutifully filling the area around the bottom of the steps. Merchants had closed their shops and women had set aside their household chores as word of the king's death spread throughout the city. All eyes were fixed on the central door. Ibiranu and Gille joined the flow, working their way to a spot near the steps. A stone carving of the Sacred Bull commanded one side of the portico and above the high, brass-covered door was a carved relief of King Suldana's Coronation ritual. Ibiranu stared at the figures, substituting King Setmel, Queen Resat and himself at her side.

29

Like a vision come to life, the royal family stepped through the temple door, already looking like the throne belonged to them. Members of the royal court followed and, by the time the temple portico was filled, the plaza below was packed with the city's people. When the shifting and whispering stopped, the Old Woman, interpreter of the Oracle and representative of the Divine Will, stepped to the front and pulled her white hood forward until her face was hidden in shadow. Her voice thundered from the dark hole.

"Hittites! King Suldana II has begun his journey to the Underworld. We ask the gods to prepare a place of honor and importance for him. He was a good king. While he lived among us he loved the gods and worshipped them on our behalf. With equal devotion he loved us, his people. Now, we commit ourselves to help him on his path to the Underworld.

"Hittites! Dedicate yourselves to the required Fourteen Days of Mourning. Pray to the gods for his safe journey. Cleanse yourselves in word and deed. Bring your sacrifices to the temples. Let there be no doubt our king led a worthy kingdom.

"Though we will not see him, his power and protection have already begun to grow. Soon our great king will be stronger in the Afterworld than when he was among us. His ancestors are gathered around him. He is not lonely. Tomorrow is the First Day of Mourning. In fourteen days his successor will be proclaimed. Then our blessed Day of Coronation will be here! Then we will dance and shout for our new king! Until then let each citizen look to his own cleansing and ritual obedience."

Ibiranu caught the queen's eye and nodded.

CHAPTER THREE
THE FIRST DAY OF MOURNING

High Priest of the Storm God prays:
"Life is bound up with death and death is bound up with life.
A human does not live forever.
Make our King Suldana II welcome at the gate to the Underworld."

QUEEN RESAT, THE *TAWANANNA*

The climbing sun touched the highest points on the acropolis walls, while the High Priest of the Storm God droned on in the king's bedchamber. As he spoke, another slaughtered plough ox was carried in and placed at the king's feet.

"Our king now becomes a god. Accept, O gods, his sins." He turned and addressed the king's body. "What *you* have become, let *this* become. May your soul descend into this ox."

Queen Resat, standing by the king's bed, could barely keep her eyes open. She'd slept fitfully, imagining the body and the *mešedi* surrounding it all night in the adjacent chamber. She fought to listen to the priest but her eyes wandered across the room to Prince Takana and Queen Patupa. Suspicious thoughts rolled over her consciousness. The king's sister and her irksome son were like two woodpeckers hammering against her skull. What would they do when Setmel became king? What plans were they hatching?

Wine was poured out and the vessel smashed. Finally, a male goat was swung to and fro over the corpse. With this final act of purification, the king was ready for the next ritual at the Storm God's temple. Six additional *mešedi* entered the bedchamber carrying a richly draped bier. They lifted the king's body and transferred it. At a signal from the Old Woman the group filed out onto the terrace, followed by the bier. The streets below were already lined with silent citizens. Their heads followed the movements of the royal procession. Queen Resat kept her eyes on the back of the Old Woman's head and forced herself to listen, not to the voices in her head, but to the sound of soft felt shoes shuffling on the cobblestones.

Finally she bent her head and watched her sandaled feet peek and retreat beneath her gown. What were the people thinking? Did they pity her in her loss? She'd never felt the affection of the common citizens, nor did she crave it like her husband had. Did it matter to them that she was the forward thinking one, the one who had ambitions for the kingdom? No, in their ignorance they preferred to gossip and spread rumors about Setmel. That's why they were the peasants and she was the queen. Let them cry tears for the king and for the past. Setmel controlled the future and it would be glorious.

By the time she reached the Storm God's temple, her spirits had lifted. The bier was placed beneath the altar, under a statue of the Sacred Bull. The High Priest offered a

First Day of Mourning prayer, after which the room quickly emptied of all but the bodyguards and priest.

A waiting chariot whisked her back to the royal apartment, where she staggered to a lounge and called out: "Fill my bathing pool." She pulled at the combs that held her hair high on her head and waved aside the servant girl who sprang to help her. The funerary odors escaped from her tresses as they tumbled free and though she covered her nose with her hand, the pungent odor, to her disgust, seemed to have become a permanent part of her body.

Other women fluttered around, reminding her of hungry hens, pecking for favors. Fortunately, she reminded herself servant girls were easily replaced by others eager to leave their lives of impoverishment for the luxury of the acropolis. "Perhaps a warm bath will soothe the ache in my broken heart," she said. "And oil, my favorite oil." The servant girls dashed to fill the pool with steaming water, to draw down the reed shades, close the wooden shutters, light candles, sprinkle the water's surface with flower petals and, finally, to add the contents of a small vial of oil.

Sometime later, with the scent of cedar hanging in the air, the queen, wrapped in linen, sat propped on pillows. A servant fanned her hair while another separated the strands with a fine comb. She sniffed both arms and was satisfied at the pleasing aroma of the forest.

"Send for my son," she said when they'd finished, "and bring me a dry robe . . . the green one. No, wait, I will dress." She turned to a young girl tucked in the corner of the room amid threads and cloth. "Have you finished the embroidery on the blue gown?"

"Almost, my queen," the girl replied.

The queen threw up her hands, a movement that caused the needle worker to flinch. "Where is the other one who does stitching, the red-headed one?" The girls looked anxiously from one to another. "Well?"

"She is not well, my queen." The voice was firm, unwavering, and came from the most mature of the queen's servants.

"Not well? She did not ask permission to leave my service," the queen said. A memory jumped forward, one she had dismissed as normal. She remembered seeing Setmel whispering to that very needle worker. She was attractive and Setmel had normal appetites. It didn't matter at the time. But now her eyes narrowed with suspicion. "What does the palace physician say?"

"My queen, she will be fine after a few days of rest. All of us can fulfill her duties, I assure you."

The queen, already holding a frown, added a scowl. The girl might be pregnant. Why should Setmel be concerned with an unwanted child, or worse, a common woman who might want something from him?

"Send for the physician and leave me." She pulled the linen robe tightly across her waist and stood by the lounge, picking at the fringe of a thick crimson throw. At a soft knock on the bedchamber door, she called out, "Enter."

"How may I serve, my queen?" The physician was tall and bony and he bent his frame almost in half to speak. He wore a colorful wool cap that covered the dome of his oversized head to the tops of his large ears and almost controlled his bush of black hair. His face was unreadable, an irritation to the queen.

"I'm well enough, but one of my servant girls is not available to me. The others are covering for her. I suspect she is distracted by other things, a pregnancy perhaps."

"What's her name?"

"Should I know everyone's name? She has red hair. Ask one of the other servants."

"Ah, yes, I believe I know the one."

"These girls owe me their complete attention. Do I need to remind you of funeral rites, of the Coronation? I am worn out with grief and need their undivided attention."

"What would you have me do, my queen?"

"Well, I'm not a monster, minister to her, of course."

"Yes, my queen. Unless her condition is serious she should be ready to serve in a few days."

The physician turned to leave but the queen moved and walked with him to the door. "Keep her in your infirmary until you hear from me. Is that clear?"

When the doctor left she walked to the window facing the plaza below where the people milled about. Her mind mulled over several options before she settled on the one that would offer Setmel a future free of entanglements. As soon as time permitted she would summon Ibiranu and ask him to have the young woman exiled for dereliction of duty. Then she sighed deeply. She wondered if the people understood the breadth of skills it required to keep the kingdom running smoothly. She called for her servant girls.

A flurry of activity ensued until the queen settled on a finely-woven gown of pale yellow, a color leeched from golden field flowers. Trays of lapis lazuli bracelets, gold and amethyst earrings and necklaces of turquoise from the Nile Valley were placed where she could choose what suited her. She chose gold disc earrings and a heavy gold chain, which she lifted over her head and adjusted over the swell of her breasts. As a finishing touch, she asked to be misted with a favorite perfume from the island of Crete. By the time Setmel arrived she was dressed and waiting on a richly upholstered lounge. The issue of uncompleted needlework and an inconvenient pregnancy were long gone from her mind.

"Ye gods, mother. It's like night in here. Why are the shades down?"

She ignored him. He'd never exhibited empathy of any kind so there was no reason to expect his sympathy. He hadn't spent the night with a dead body in the next room and the muzzy sounds of endless prayers. In a way, she concluded, his attitude would serve him well as a leader. He would not be distracted by emotion or whining petitioners. She turned her thoughts to why she'd sent for him, stalling for time by picking at the folds of her gown. Finally, she fixed him with a stern look. "The people are watching you, Setmel."

"Watching me? Don't make me laugh, mother. Father is dead and he's all they think about. They haven't a whole brain among them." Angry red blotches spotted his narrow face and his lips glistened. "And *you*, you left me standing alone next to him while you disappeared with Ibiranu yesterday. Did you think I didn't notice? I've never felt so uncomfortable in my life, standing by his *dead body*. I swear I could smell the decay. It was disgusting. No one spoke to me. Am I invisible? By the gods, I'm their future king. This morning I hoped you'd at least say you were sorry, but not a word, *not a single word of sympathy for me.*"

"You're right. But be patient. As soon as the days of mourning are over, you will be the center of everyone's attention. That's when you'll learn who your allies are. As for the others, don't worry, they'll quickly learn the consequences of disloyalty."

Setmel's mournful face reconfigured a sneer. "I'll tell you who's at the top of my list—Takana. For years he's been a hair in my mouth. How I'd love to spit him out, his friends, too. When I'm king, I'll show them what real leadership is. They've kept me from their inner circle, but soon they'll have no choice but to accept me. *Inheritance* wins over their silly competitions. How quickly?"

"What?" The queen had walked to an open window.

"Even *you* ignore me, mother. Perhaps you need reminding as well. I *said*, How quickly can I be rid of them? Aren't they still needed in Harmesh? Maybe another vassal state needs help. Put him to work increasing our coffers instead of prowling around Hattusa." He stuck out his chin and delivered a downward dark-eyed stare.

The queen averted her face and ran her hands over her hips. When she looked back at Setmel, she smiled sweetly. "I've raised you to be a magnificent king. But you should remember that a king has his advisers, and not only will I be your wisest counselor but also your strongest supporter. While you played with baby toys, dearest, I learned many things about the politics of the acropolis royals and others . . . yes, many others. You'll soon be grateful for such knowledge."

"Then what *do* you suggest I do about Prince Takana?"

"Ah, our minds are working together already. I—"

A high-pitched scream sent the queen and Setmel to the window. In the plaza below, women were screaming and pointing at the sky. Others in the plaza gaped and raised their arms as if to protect themselves. Neither the queen nor Setmel could see the object of their fright because the terrace roof obscured their view. They left the room and walked outside to the far edge of the terrace. A blast of wind forced the queen to wrap her arms around a column. When she'd steadied herself, she sucked in her breath at the sight of the sun. A dark shadow had fallen across the disc on one side. Setmel, pressed against her back, placed a trembling hand on her arm. She turned to look at him and was sickened by the sight. He was cowed. His knees were buckling under him. She pulled her arm away.

At that moment, a chariot arrived on the terrace, arriving from the ramp at the rear of the building. Ibiranu, flushed and breathless, jumped down.

"My queen, the High Priest of the Sun Goddess of Arinna is asking for you."

"Give me a moment," she said, returning to the apartment. She leaned against the closed door to calm herself. Whatever the Sun Goddess was doing, no harm would come to her. She was sure of it. She forced herself to breathe steadily to shut out her fear. She reminded herself of the special bond she had with the Sun Goddess. Wasn't that one of the reasons she was chosen to be King Suldana's bride?

Her story was a legend among the people. Her father, a distant cousin to the king, had been king of a far-west vice royal kingdom until the Storm God withheld the rain from their land and the state was in danger of defaulting on their tribute to Hattusa.

Her pious parents ordered prayers and petitions and offerings to no avail. Finally in desperation they ignored the Hittite law and surrendered to the ancient belief that the gods would respond to human sacrifice as a way to appease the Storm God. They took her, then a cherubic two year old, to the farthest corner of their land and left her there with a prayer to the Storm God to accept her as a living gift. The following day, red from the sun's flames, she was found by a nomad and carried to town where she was identified and taken to her parents. At the moment of recognition between parent and child, a thunderbolt split the sky and the rains began. Her parents announced she was blessed by the Sun Goddess of Arinna who'd persuaded the Storm God to send the rain.

It made perfect sense to her that the temple priest, the earthly voice of the Sun Goddess, would want to use her special bond to intercede. Brimming with confidence, she lifted a woolen cape from a hook, but before she could fasten it around her shoulders, Ibiranu's voice at the door asked to speak to her. She let him in and watched with curiosity as he closed the door and looked around the room.

"Why are you causing a delay?"

"My queen, I thought you should know how I have carried out your orders," he said.

"Yes, but be quick."

"Hapati and his tablet have been buried and I have ordered another tablet made—all very discretely, of course."

"What? You killed him?"

"You said, 'Send him someplace where no one will ever find him.' Is this why your patron god is abandoning us? I never meant . . . forgive me, my queen. I will make a sacrifice at the temple."

Queen Resat turned away from him. Was the Goddess angry? Was it not a mother's duty to protect her son, to secure his future? She had done what any mother would do. She would pray, pray earnestly to make her patron understand. She climbed into Ibiranu's chariot and another came forward for Setmel. They tore through the streets to the Temple of the Sun Goddess where people were already gathering. They quickly surrounded the chariot when it stopped, begging her to save them, to restore their precious Sun Goddess. The temple guards ran forward to clear a way for her.

The wind whipped from every direction and a sudden gust caught her cape and lifted it into the air. For a brief moment it floated high and spread behind her, a glowing opalescence. The people gasped and clutched their chests. "She is a goddess come to save us," a woman said, before falling on her knees.

"Put your trust in me," the queen answered, reaching out to them with both arms. She climbed the steps to the temple portico where the High Priest was waiting to escort her and Prince Setmel inside.

"No, wait," she said turning. "I must calm the people."

The High Priest looked surprised but he bowed and stepped back.

She looked at the half shadow of sun and said: "O Sun Goddess, My Lady, Lady of Hatti Land, Queen of Heaven and Earth, I am your servant, a calf of your stable, a cornerstone of your foundation. You picked me up, My Lady, and gave me to King Suldana, who is on his way to you to live and protect us.

"We will purify ourselves before you. We will carry out your wishes. We will be faithful to observe your regulations and rituals. We plead with you. Do not turn away, My Lady, Sun Goddess of Arinna. Come back with your warmth and life-giving power."

She saw with satisfaction that her words soothed them, although the heavenly orb continued to diminish. She turned and nodded to the High Priest who followed her into the temple. Before the door closed she saw one of the temple guards bar Ibiranu from entering. She gave the slighted Ibiranu a sympathetic nod before he disappeared from sight.

The inner chamber echoed with the sound of a metal lock slipping into place. It seemed to repeat endlessly down the long corridors that fanned outward into darkness. The queen clutched her cape against the cold fear of her guilt and lifted her chin. It did nothing to stop her body from trembling. She raised her eyes to the high centered altar where a carving of the Sun Goddess of Arinna stared down in stony disinterest. Had she always appeared so cold?

Her frequent visits to the Sun Goddess throughout the seasons were marked with celebration, praise and joy. At those times she was surrounded by attendants adorned with colorful flowers and the people would flood the plaza, dancing and singing to lively music. The High Priest would address her with respect and humility. This time was different. His expression could neither be called respectful nor humble. He quickly glanced around the chamber before looking at the queen.

"When someone arouses a god's anger, is it only on the offender that the god takes revenge?" the priest said.

The queen staggered backward as if she'd been struck. "What do you mean? Who has offended the Sun Goddess of Arinna?"

"I have consulted the Oracle. Listen and judge for yourself." He stepped back to a spot directly under the altar and raised his head. "Thus spoke the Oracle, 'Look to the one closest to the sun, for the offense has caused the Sun Goddess to withdraw herself.' "

He walked forward and faced her squarely. "Are *you* not the closest to the sun, *tawananna?*" His eyes bore into her for a long moment before shifting to Prince Setmel, who had slowly inched his way back against the door. Now he turned away and fell to his knees.

The queen's eyes fluttered. Her body swayed. She considered throwing herself at the feet of the Sun Goddess' image to beg for understanding, but thought better of it. The people might see such action as guilt. Ibiranu, she decided, was the key to a wiser strategy. He alone knew about her order and he was her protector, her loyal servant.

A noise in the far corner of the temple drew her attention—Setmel lay curled on the floor. She raised her head, breathed deeply and turned to the priest. "My strength comes from the Sun Goddess. Whatever I do comes directly from her. She guides me in ways that make the kingdom strong. You interpret the Oracle incorrectly."

For a long moment the priest surveyed her face, which she made sure showed him nothing but firm resolve. "We'll see," he said, grabbing his white robe and turning away.

"We must go to the Great Temple of the Storm God and seek his High Priest's counsel. Order an ox for sacrifice!" he shouted to the temple servants. "Order the people to surround the Storm God's temple and pray for our salvation!"

He walked to the door, but the queen stood looking at the Sun Goddess. She turned, walked to the base of the altar and knelt. "I must pray."

She lowered her head and silently allowed her mind to sort through the chaos of unspoken feelings. *I am the servant of the Sun Goddess of Arinna and together we serve the Storm God, the greatest power in the heavens. O My Lady, if I have offended, I ask you to forgive me. I did not order Hapati's death. I was misunderstood. Do not leave us. Restore your life-giving presence to us.*

She left the altar and followed the High Priest to the portico where it seemed night had come, stars filled the sky and a chill traveled on the wind. She ploughed through the frightened crowd. They tore their eyes from the heavens to watch her leading the way to the Temple of the Storm God and fell in behind her. At the temple, she hesitated before the gargantuan statue of the Sacred Bull. "Give me your strength, O Sacred One," she whispered, as the guards opened the door.

Just inside, the Storm God's High Priest stood waiting. At the top of the elevated altar, a huge black ox was restrained by several slaves. Minor priests ran around tossing finely crushed herbs into the air. In the next instant, the priest signaled the slaughter and, while the blood ran along a shallow channel and flowed into a large stone bowl, the queen and the others knelt. He raised his voice:

"Hear your people, O Mighty Storm God, Supreme Overlord, Protector of the Hittite Kingdom. Why have you neglected us? Have we failed to fulfill our duties? Have we forgotten to ask for your life-giving rain? No! If we have offended and caused you to withhold your power, enlighten us. We will perform every necessary act. Come now to our aid. Are you distracted? Defend your companion in the heavens, our Sun Goddess of Arinna. Are you not more powerful than the one who attacks her? Awake." The walls echoed his words.

The queen gasped and a shiver worked its way through her body as she listened to his interpretation, his perception of the god's province. But then, she reasoned, he was the earthly voice of the Storm God, the mightiest god of all. It must be that the Storm God spoke to him.

"Come, kneel, we must pray together," the High Priest said.

The queen breathed a sigh, her body slowly filling with inner peace and understanding. How could anything happen unless the Storm God willed it? The kingdom's most powerful god had wrapped her in love and security. It was a message everyone in the kingdom would soon hear. She allowed herself to bask in the priest's petition.

Suddenly the people outside were shouting. The High Priest ordered the doors opened. They saw brilliance burst from the dark disc and push itself free. Moment by moment the temple's details sharpened and shadows deepened. The queen, closing her eyes, stepped into the sunshine to let the Goddess' warmth surround her.

"The Storm God has defended our Sun Goddess of Arinna and he has won," the High Priest shouted over the din. "Go to your homes and give him your grateful thanks with prayers and the foods he loves. The Hittite Kingdom is safe. Our *tawananna* is beloved by the gods."

Later, alone in her bedchamber, the queen lay naked on silk sheets the color of clouds. She had ordered her servants to burn every piece of clothing she'd worn that day. She asked to be washed from head to toe with fragrant soap, toweled with soft cotton and rubbed with cleansing eucalyptus oil. When they finished, she stretched out on a lounge and pulled a silk sheet to her waist, ordered the shades lowered and the room emptied. All she wanted to do was to pray, to thank the gods, she told them, and when the last servant disappeared she stroked her breasts with oiled fingers.

In the quiet room she replayed the day. It had begun in fear and ended in enlightenment. The Sun Goddess' High Priest might be clothed in spotless white, but he was stained with imperfection. Still, as *tawananna*, she could be forgiving. The poor man suffers from seclusion, from spending too much time alone, she thought. It would seem that his solitude produced fear and irrational thought. Furthermore, King Suldana had not yet left the Underworld. When the days of mourning were complete he would lend his power to the gods who protect Hatti. No wonder the Sun Goddess was attacked. It was a moment of weakness for Hatti. It had nothing to do with her. She hadn't ordered Hapati's death. It was Ibiranu's doing. And, perhaps the most significant lesson of the day was that the Storm God was "closest to the sun" and, as impossible as it seemed, he was to blame for the Sun Goddess' vulnerability.

Every young child in the kingdom learns the gods' relationship with their mortal worshippers is like that of the king with his subjects, the master of a household with his servants. Like the kings on earth, the great gods lived in their own magnificent palaces with a staff to assist them in their duties and to attend to their every need. But, just as servants are dependent on their king, so, too, is the king dependent on his subjects. A god who neglects his responsibilities to his servants can become the victim of his own negligence. Yes, the Storm King was to blame.

Her thoughts moved to the army of gods who surrounded her, of her ancestors in the Underworld who looked after her, of her husband who was waiting in the Afterworld for his place among the gods. Euphoria surged through her body. She remembered the king as a young man, his eager hands on her body, his words of love, his desire to please her. Soon her body pulsed with glorious sensation and she dozed.

She was vaguely aware of the soft tapping of rain against the roof. In her dreamy state they were the adoring, clapping hands of her subjects. Three loud thumps startled her. She raised her head and saw one of her servant girls rushing to the door. Ibiranu burst in.

"My Lady, I'm appalled at the High Priest's behavior. He must be censured for accusing you of . . ."

Queen Resat rolled onto her back and sighed. "Take care, Ibiranu." She settled her head back on the lounge. Her auburn hair cascaded over the edge. "It's not your place to criticize the gods' appointed representatives. The High Priest of the Storm God alone can overrule the other priests, and this he has already done. The Sun Goddess' priest knows he misinterpreted the Oracle. He acknowledges I had nothing to do with the sudden attack on my Sun Goddess of Arinna."

"Forgive me! I am too quick to protect you, but . . ."

The queen slipped her legs over edge of the couch, allowing the sheet to fall away and expose her naked side. Ibiranu swallowed.

"There *are* a few things you can do for me." She slowly wrapped the sheet tightly around herself while watching the eagerness on his face. "First, the people need to know about your diligence regarding Hapati and how you saved the kingdom from his treachery." Ibiranu snapped to attention as if expecting a medal to be pinned to his chest.

"Make arrangements immediately for an official announcement of Hapati's treason and his execution. And when that is accomplished, see to it that Hapati's wife, Azzia, and his son, Ras, are removed from the royal apartments. Hapati was a traitor. For all I know, they are complicit."

"*Remove?*"

"Outside the city would suffice, I think . . . wait, I will seek the will of the gods. After today, I feel the gods understand my frailty and how much I need their protection. They will tell me what to do. They alone know the hearts of those who oppose me. If they order their . . . deaths, I cannot save them. Is that not so?"

"Indeed. I will await your command." He bowed and turned to leave.

"Second!" she said.

He spun around.

"One of the servant girls has proved unsatisfactory and might cause problems for Setmel. You'll find her in the physician's infirmary. Remove her. Someplace very far from Hattusa should do it."

Ibiranu seemed ready to question her, but she gave him a stern look and sighed impatiently. If only those who served her would do so without needing long explanations. One day soon, when she stands behind Setmel on the throne, Hatti's citizens will realize how valuable and effective her opinions are.

"And one more thing, my strong Ibiranu . . ." She sat once again on the lounge, arranging the folds of the silky sheet until he had walked back to her side. "Don't you agree that our new king must have nothing less than complete loyalty from the people?" She paused only to draw in a deep breath, not to wait for Ibiranu to respond. "Of course you do, I know you do. During these days of mourning the people are restless. I believe some might think they can change destiny."

"Destiny?"

"Prince Setmel is the *tuhkanti*, yet some dare to criticize him. You must be especially alert to anyone who can't give him their complete loyalty. You agree?"

Ibiranu nodded. "Of course. You are the prince's greatest ally but I would like our *tuhkanti* to think of me as his second greatest. Do you have names? Suspicions?"

"Takana comes to mind."

When Ibiranu left, she walked to the window where her guardian Sun Goddess of Arinna was reclining on the horizon, sending shafts of red, yellow, and purple to say "goodnight."

CHAPTER FOUR
THE SECOND DAY OF MOURNING

The Old Woman, the hasawa, prays:
"O Mighty Storm God, Sun Goddess of Arinna, gods of
the heavens and earth, spirits of our King Suldana's ancestors,
send us your blessings as we prepare him to join you in the sky.
Await him as one who was powerful, obedient to your wishes,
kind to his people and who comes to add his mighty spirit to
yours. Attend the flames that seek his bones."

TAKANA

Thick grumbling clouds concealed the stars throughout the night. Watching from the acropolis terrace, Takana imagined the Storm God raging in the heavens. It was a night when only innocent babes would find sleep; the rest of Hattusa trembled with each growl. What were the people to think? Takana himself was shocked when the Mighty One's own High Priest accused him of neglect. Since no rain fell, was the Storm God expressing displeasure? Taka-na whispered a prayer to the Mighty God to show mercy.

No one dared question the Storm God's High Priest, but Takana believed the benevolent gods, with their all-seeing eyes, might be agitated over the people's suffering. Yesterday their king died, many sensed evil in the kingdom and feared the future under Setmel. These were reasons enough for unrest among the gods. Yet Takana believed the gods expressed their displeasure toward the people by casting down violent storms, or by withholding life-giving rain, or by shaking the earth beneath their feet. That one god would attack another was beyond his understanding. It seemed there were mysteries and wonders locked in the heavens yet to be revealed.

He imagined the same thoughts might be in the minds of the people. Their lamps remained lit all night and from time to time he heard voices shouting from windows and doorways. Then, as morning drew near, the moaning clouds drifted away. People ventured cautiously outside to look east for the first sign of light. At last, the sky began to glow and a great shout rang out. People poured from their homes and fell to their knees to thank the gods.

Takana watched the citizens building fires in the streets. They peeled off their clothes, purging anything that might be a reminder of what they'd witnessed the day before. It was a common ritual, healing and cathartic. Then house by house, after the night-long vigil, the city grew quiet and the people slipped away to their beds, exhausted but pleased their efforts had satisfied the gods.

As columns of smoke twisted upward like supplicant arms, Takana knelt to thank the Storm God. The sun's rays fell on his face and with it the fear and chaos of the dark day and night lifted. He yawned and felt the pull of his own bed, but as he moved toward the door to his apartment the blare of trumpets sounded. The apartment door banged open and his mother stumbled out and joined him.

"Is that the summons to accompany the king's body to the place of cremation?" She fastened a cloak at her neck.

"I don't think so. Too early." They hurried down the terraces, glancing occasionally at the exhausted people staggering from their homes and spilling into the plaza. To their surprise the sound came from the two-story Magistrate's Building, west of the palace. The Magistrate, guardian of The Law and voice of justice in the absence of the king, stood on the portico, flanked by the High Priest of the Storm God, Chief of the *Mešedi*, Royal Guard Chief Ibiranu, the *tawananna* and *tuhkanti*. The Magistrate nodded when Takana and his mother took their places. He stepped forward to address the people.

"Citizens of Hatti, Royal Guard Chief Ibiranu uncovered a crime of treason and fulfilled his duty with an execution. The king's scribe, Hapati, was seen escaping from the palace with the king's Proclamation Tablet. He was spotted by our diligent royal guards six miles east of the city. He resisted capture and was executed and buried without honor. May the gods forgive this interruption of the Second Day of Mourning our King Suldana."

Takana was stunned. He looked around for Ras and his mother but couldn't see them. His mother grabbed his arm.

"This is unbelievable. What's happening here? Hapati's no traitor."

Takana hustled her away to their apartment. His mind ricocheted from one question to another as they climbed the stairs of the acropolis. Who decided Hapati was a traitor? The only one who could order Ibiranu to . . . The queen, yes! She wanted him out of the way . . . must have thought Hapati could do her harm. How? Why? That viper! He was hot with anger but felt stabbed by cold thoughts.

As Takana closed the door of their apartment, he paused. "Ras and Azzia need to know we don't believe this for a moment! I won't be long," Takana said, moving to reopen the door.

His mother grabbed his tunic. "But cautiously, my son. I'm afraid the *tawananna* is already exerting her influence. Hapati may be just the first of those beloved by the king to be eliminated. We may be next."

Takana nodded and acknowledged his mother's keen perception. Too, it was a reminder that sheltering her might be well beyond his ability, if the need should arise. But as he moved away, she grabbed at him again.

"Remember the mourning rites. An hour or so."

"I'll be there on time but first I want to talk to Master Palla." The old scribe had been increasingly on his mind. With recent events, it was imperative. He needed to talk to someone he trusted, someone who understood the various pathways within Hatti's government and someone who knew how to move along them without leaving footprints.

"Yes, good," his mother said. "He may know more than what we've been able to see for ourselves. But be watchful." Her voice cracked but there was no time for Takana to comfort her.

Two terraces down, he raised his hand to knock on Ras' door but whirled around, taut with tension, when he heard a sound. "Master Palla! Ye gods, you were my next stop. Have you heard the outrageous announcement? It's absurd. What's happening here?"

"More than you can imagine, Prince Takana. I took a chance you'd come here. I need to talk to you. Can you . . .?"

"Yes, they need to know we don't believe a word of what was said about Hapati. But I can come back later. I need to talk to you too."

They descended the acropolis steps together. "I have urgent information for you," Palla said. "But not here. This move against Hapati is a message for all of us who don't like the direction the queen is taking. She's becoming bolder with each day. Let's go to my office."

At street level they walked around the back of the Magistrate's offices where a horse and chariot were tethered to a pole. With the litheness of a younger man, Palla took the reins and followed the heavily fortified wall to the Acropolis Plaza gate that led into the Lower City. He held the horse to a slow walk until they'd passed through the gate and then trotted evenly past the storage silos, minor temples and homes.

The *eduba*, the scribe school, where Palla had his office, was situated against the northern wall of the city at the end of several major streets, surrounded by large, heavy-branched plane trees. Although Takana's schooling revolved around warrior training and left no time for learning to read and write, he'd always liked the look of the place. With the greenery and wide walkways, it seemed peaceful, like a sanctuary. Later he understood it was Master Palla who provided those feelings. When the old scribe visited the king and Takana happened to be there, he included him in the conversation. Takana felt safe expressing himself and taking advice and criticism from such a learned man. More than once, Takana noticed the king sat off to the side smiling while he and Master Palla talked.

For as long as Takana could remember, Master Palla ran the kingdom's scribe school. His clients were the men who worked on every level of government and commerce in the city and beyond. His reputation was such that it was not unusual for royalty and wealthy landowners outside Hattusa to seek his counsel in choosing a scribe.

When King Suldana needed a personal scribe, Master Palla recommended Hapati, an exemplary graduate and, perhaps more important, a man without political connections or aspirations. It caused some clamor among the royals for a time. Some had put forth other names for the king's consideration—a relative or a favorite. What an advantage to have the ear of the king's most intimate servant! In the end, the clamor morphed into resentment and jealousy—hidden from the king but followed closely by the canny old scribe.

Palla's work required knowledge well beyond superficial information. In addition to his work as administrator of the *eduba,* he took a personal hand in matching scribe with master and task with skill. At this particular time, it was Master Palla's political astuteness that Takana needed. The old man had his ear to the kingdom's heartbeat and Takana's need for information had reached a critical point.

The moment Palla's office door closed, Takana spoke. "I've little time. My mother expects me at the funeral rites. But you know as well as I Hapati was incapable of treason. What's going on? Do you think that's why the Sun Goddess hid her light from us? Are the gods telling us something is wrong? We must—"

Palla threw up his hand and motioned Takana to a chair. "Sit down." He brought his face within inches of Takana before he spoke. "Hapati is *not* dead."

Takana drew a sharp breath and was about to speak when Palla held up his hand again.

"I don't doubt the gods are angry. They know more than any of us and I can barely hold myself together with the things I've seen and heard. But listen to me, there's more to tell you, so much more."

Takana had stopped breathing. His eyes blinked and his lips moved but without sound.

"You want to know how I know these things, yes? First, I'll tell you *why.*" The old man's eyes filled and overflowed. "Salvation, Takana, and . . . love." He swayed, reached for a chair and sat heavily.

"Are you all right?" Takana reached out to steady the old scribe. When he could wait no longer, he said: "If you can, just tell me about Hapati before I leave. I'll come back after the funeral rites for more."

"It's the *tawananna.* She wants to purge Hatti Land of anyone who might thwart her agenda, which is to move aggressively against our neighbors. She wants power and riches and she's infected the *tuhkanti* with her poison. You haven't forgotten how this city whispers, have you? She spread slanderous rumors about Hapati, and Ibiranu who acts on the queen's behalf like a male dog in heat does her bidding unquestioningly."

"Hmmmm, I'd heard rumors but . . . the uncertainty and fear . . . it's growing," Takana said.

"Just so. I believe she moved against Hapati because of his closeness to the king. But Hapati isn't the only one who's disappeared without due process of our laws."

"Two of my running teammates?"

"Yes. They're being held. There's more to tell you, but for now this will have to suffice. Listen, I know Ras is your friend, but he mustn't know. He's . . ."

"I understand how he is. It'll be terrible to keep this from him, but I will for now." Takana moved to the door. His head filled with questions, but they would require calm to elicit the right answers.

"One more piece of information," Palla said. "I said Chief Ibiranu is loyal to the queen but not all of the royal guardsmen are."

"What? Impossible. They've sworn their allegiance." Takana stepped back.

"Sworn to what? To whom? Sometimes we must risk our lives for justice. We must stand up for truth." A vein throbbed at the old man's temple, his voice cracked with passion and he swallowed several times before continuing. "At least half of the royal guardsmen disapprove of the queen's actions. That's how I learned Ibiranu removed Hapati from the city and why he is still alive and the tablet bearing our beloved king's final words is safe." Again he paused, looking as if he wanted to say more. "Well, for now I want you to know these same brave warriors are sworn to protect you, your mother, and others who disagree with the *tawananna*."

"What is she afraid of? What does she think I will do? I may not respect Setmel, but I'm no threat to him. If I don't like what he does as king, I have other options."

"Let's not discuss this now."

Takana sighed and nodded. "I hate keeping this secret from Ras. How long do you think?"

"The timing must be right and for the safety of the people these treacheries must be revealed before the Magistrate and the High Priest of the Storm God. They safeguard The Law, and they alone can control the people. If the people knew the full extent of Queen Resat's agenda . . . No! Nothing must reach their ears. But soon, hopefully soon.

"Now, you must go. I'll wait for you to return when you're able," He stood and placed his weathered hand on Takana's shoulder. "You've been trained as a warrior to be alert to danger. This is a time to test your skills."

When the sun reached its apex, the royal families, temple representatives and city dignitaries gathered in chariots at the King's Gate to follow the bier to Yazilikaya. Takana and his mother rode directly behind the *tawananna* and the *mešedi* bearing the king's bier. The long line traveled north on the road that paralleled the eastern city wall and then east into the forest, where the air carried the moist richness of the earth.

At the place of cremation, royal guards led the horses and chariots away while the *mešedi* placed King Suldana's body over a pyre. The *mešedi* then surrounded the mountain of logs. The Old Woman, pulling her white hood forward, addressed the dignitaries.

"O Most Powerful Storm God, lend me your ear and listen to my words. We bring you the most precious of our bounty and give all honor and thanks to you. As you savor our gifts, look kindly on us and prepare a journey of ease for our King Suldana."

They walked to their seats, servants circulated with food and drink and the funeral banquet began. Food offerings of roasted lamb, boiled chickpeas and lentils, apricots, cherries, figs and almonds were piled high on round brass platters. Temple servants hoisted them first to the tables of the gods, then to the people. Others poured *walhi*, a ritual beer, and wine for the gods and the spirits of the king's ancestors who waited to receive him. Slaves, conscripted from their owners throughout Hattusa, worked behind the temple servants to provide whatever was needed and remove all traces after the ceremony.

Around the perimeter of the tables set for the royal family and other dignitaries, two rows of tables had been arranged for spirits to whom the Old Woman prayed, plus one for the deceased himself and another for the Day of Death. Until well into the late afternoon, the people carried their individual offerings to the gods' tables. Then as the sun set, the Chief *Mešedi* carried a torch to the pyre. With a roar, flames leaped up the sides to engulf the bier bearing King Suldana's body. Everything—the rock towers, the priests and the people—became a silhouette against the darkening indigo canopy.

They watched the flames flicker yellow, red and blue, finally ending in a twisting gray spiral toward the nostrils of the gods. When the *tawananna* and the *tuhkanti* rose and climbed into their chariots, the others followed, leaving the *mešedi* to protect their beloved monarch.

CHAPTER FIVE
THE SECOND DAY OF MOURNING

RAS

The moment the Magistrate announced Hapati's execution for treason, heads swiveled to see Ras and Azzia's reaction. Ras felt their stares but he had turned to stone, trying to make sense of the words. A moment later his mother, standing in front of him, swayed and fell back into his arms. He swept her up and ran to their palace apartment, slammed the door and bolted it. They stood frozen together.

"How could the gods let this happen?" The words spilled from Ras like he'd been punched in the stomach. Then, in a burst, he said, "Of course! Yesterday the Sun Goddess of Heaven, our Sun Goddess of Arinna, was threatened. She witnessed the death of an innocent man and suffered for us."

Three sharp strikes against the door brought their conversation to an abrupt halt.

"Lock yourself in your room, mother, quickly," he whispered, slipping the bolt from the door.

A royal guardsman stood well beyond the door, his eyes looking not at Ras but a spot above Ras's head. He delivered his message like a bark. "By order of the *tawananna*, gather your possessions and leave the city." Just as abruptly, he turned and walked away with the sun flashing like mirrors on the studs, buckles and blades of his uniform.

"Wait! Who? What is this?"

The guard continued several steps more before he turned and walked back. By then Ras's mother had joined him.

"Please, Jeran," she said. "Come in. A moment, please."

The guard's expression softened, possibly from the use of his name.

Ras didn't care. He moved eye to eye with the guard. "Where's the proof my father was a spy? Where was his trial, his opportunity to explain why he left the city? Where is his body?"

"My orders were to deliver the queen's order, nothing more," he said, holding his ground. His tone was wooden.

As far as Ras was concerned he might as well have been announcing a street cleaning. He watched the guard retreat along the terrace for several moments until he closed the apartment door.

"Are we never to know what happened? Should we go to the Magistrate and demand to know why my husband is . . . was a traitor?" Azzia choked and couldn't continue.

"Queen Resat!" Ras spit the name like he'd tasted something vile. "She's behind this and I doubt the Magistrate will tell us anything. But I'll find out . . . somehow."

His mother shook her head and Ras could hardly stand the pain he saw on her face. "Where are we to go? Jeran didn't say how long we have. It's . . . it's too much," she said, stumbling to her bedchamber.

Ras balled his fists and felt his heart beating in his ears. He paced the floor, stopping to listen at his mother's door each time he passed. He thought she might have gone to sleep until he heard her sobs. It was more than he could bear. On his next pass by her door, he tripped over the soft leather boots he wore for racing in the games. They lay askew, worn from years of running. But they'd been with him in good times. They knew him and fit him well. Like grasping an old friend, he lifted them in his hands, kicked off his felt shoes and put them on. By the time he finished dressing in old clothes, he felt his body's eagerness. He could either run or kill someone. He closed the door softly behind him.

After the Lion Gate, he doubled his speed on the downward slope, taking long, leaping strides. As he hoped they would, his body and mind loosened. What was Takana repeatedly telling him? *Anger accomplishes nothing.* For as long as they'd been friends, Ras wished he could approach his problems with Takana's slow, steady resolve. His present circumstances needed that kind of approach. His head understood this but his heart, and ultimately his fists and feet, responded to other forces. Cool down. Take it slow. Not yet!

He would begin by questioning Takana. The ways of the royals were carefully cloaked, kept purposefully from the rest of the people, but Takana might know something. Was his father wrongfully accused? Did anyone consider that perhaps he'd been threatened and was carrying the tablet to safety? His father was gone, but his good service and reputation could be restored. He wouldn't rest until they were.

At the athletic field, Ras was disappointed to see so many runners using the track. He'd wanted to run, screaming at the top of his lungs if he wanted to. But when he saw Angulli among the stragglers, he resigned himself.

"Is Takana here?" he said, shortening his stride and surprising his friend.

" Ras! No. To tell you the truth, I don't understand why *I'm* here. I've never been so scared. I thought our lives were over. I thought the gods . . . I don't know what I thought. Why do you think the Sun Goddess abandoned us?"

Ras didn't respond. It was hard to breathe. He forced his legs to move with shear will, but after several laps, sharp pains shot through his chest. He left the track and loped to the shade of the trees, swung his head and sent a spray of sweat from long coils of coppery hair.

Angulli stopped next to him. "Hey, why stop now? I'm just beginning to warm up."

Without answering, Ras bent and placed his hands on his knees to hide his face. How could his friend understand what he himself did not? He'd left his mother at home with her grief when he should have been at her side. He stared at the ground and shook his head slowly from side to side.

"Are you ill?" Angulli said.

Ras walked away and fell to his knees. "My father's been executed for treason. I'm going to kill the bastards. I'm going to clear my father's name." He raised his arms and raised his voice to the sky. "My king, send me your strength!"

Angulli gasped. "What? That's ridiculous. Who told you that? Maybe you misunderstood."

Ras opened his mouth to call his friend a fool, but changed his mind.

Angulli moved around to face him. "O gods, if that's true it's horrible, unbelievable. But, you can't handle this yourself. Listen, your father had allies. If he was charged and executed unjustly, they'll find out. Promise me you'll seek them out first."

Ras swallowed his anger, looked into Angulli's guileless face and forced a smile. He brushed the dusty coating from his knee-length tunic. Angulli, he recalled, had once allowed a mosquito to drink its fill of blood and fly away rather than crush it. *She needs to live,* he'd said, scratching. In all the years Ras called Angulli his faithful friend, they'd never faced a serious challenge. But they were no longer children. They were men among men and sometimes it was necessary to fight for justice. Would Angulli raise a sword if needed? He hoped it would never be necessary. Could Angulli be right? Could his father's friends in the acropolis already be working to clear his name?

Ras glanced across the field where someone was shouting his name. It was Urhi, Ibiranu's son, who'd adopted his father's sneer when he was no taller than a broom bush. While Ras, Angulli and Takana strengthened their friendship over the years, Urhi, emboldened by his father's appointment to chief, drew together his own band of malcontents. Three of them moved in behind Urhi.

"Those loyal to the kingdom are finally moving to make our Hittite world strong again," Urhi said, striking a pose. His big dark eyes were heavily lidded, covering his menace with a false appearance of boredom. The four stood with hands on hips, chins canted forward and smirks on their sweaty faces.

"You're a liar. No one listens to what you say," Ras said, moving alongside Angulli and bumping Urhi's shoulder as he passed. They walked away, but Ras imagined that smashing Urhi's face into the earth would be far more satisfying. When they were beyond Urhi's hearing, Ras confided his thoughts. "Chief Ibiranu was most likely the one who'd escorted my father to the scribe's chamber to transcribe the king's last words. It was his job to protect my father."

"Uh, I guess," Angulli said.

Ras bit his lip. He kept the rest of his thoughts to himself. No sense confronting Ibiranu. But Takana was a different matter. He'd been absent from the city, benefiting from the clarity distance often creates. And now that he was back, Ras believed his royal friend might know something. Yes, he had questions for Takana.

"Do you think what happened yesterday was because of your father's execution?" Angulli said.

"It was proof to me of how the gods watch over us."

"But—"

"I don't care what anybody else says, the gods saw King Suldana leave us and then they saw Ibiranu execute my father. The Sun Goddess of Arinna knows my father was innocent. She was sending Hattusa a message. And I believe she'll help me to clear his name."

Angulli didn't say anything and Ras thought that was just as well.

They climbed the steep embankment that led to the Lion Gate in the southwestern wall. The land continued to climb through the Upper City until it leveled off and dropped into the Lower City. The acropolis anchored the east end of the highest point and the Temple of the Storm God marked the west end. Both were impressive monuments, both sparkled in the sun. For the moment they offered Ras something to focus on, anything to distract him from the burning in his chest.

Although Ras had not traveled far beyond the city, his father had filled his imagination with stories and visions of faraway places. Angulli, on the other hand, often accompanied his father and brothers to Babylon and Egypt to purchase horses. Each time, he returned insisting Hattusa's temples were superior, but Takana and Ras both believed their friend's provincial bias trumped reality.

The gleaming temple soon disappeared as the high stone walls loomed ahead. At this southwestern expanse, the wall was twice as high as elsewhere. Two rectangular towers flanked the entrance, a passage marked by exterior and interior portals. Each was fitted with a pair of heavy wooden doors, the outer one sheathed in bronze. The highest point of the wall was strengthened by a broad rampart with a parapet for bowmen to use if the city were threatened.

Two massive stone lions, with teeth bared in their wide-open mouths, faced outward on either side of the imposing outer portal. They appeared to roar a challenge: King Suldana II's royal symbols, reflecting the monarch's willingness to pounce if provoked. But, as Ras' father once pointed out, the Hittite lions were tame compared to the vicious stone beasts standing guard at the wall surrounding Luwadna Land, many days east of Hatti.

Ras' chest burned again. There would be no relief until the truth was known. He turned his attention to the gate ahead.

"Why are they questioning everyone?" Angulli said.

Ras shrugged but agreed it was unusual, especially when most of the people were recognized citizens who used the gate regularly. The sentries, on the other hand, were not the only security forces present. Three of the men were part of the king's royal bodyguards, distinguished by their elaborate uniforms, scale armor and broad swords. The conical bronze helmets, shining in the morning sun, were worn only by the king's *mešedi*. There had to be a reason why they were stationed at the gate.

Finally, Ras and Angulli got the signal to pass. The inner courtyard was thick with dust kicked up by horses and people. Soldiers were everywhere. Something was wrong. The guards, usually attentive to the passing of pretty girls and not much else, moved quickly to force Ras and Angulli against the wall.

"Go home, Angulli," one of the guards said, giving him a shove.

Ras watched Angulli walk away until the guards surrounded him and obscured his view. He knew these men. They'd been mentors during training. They were the fathers of his friends. Is this how it was going be? Was his every movement, every word going to be suspect? Ras searched their faces. One of the guards took his arm, pulled him aside and leaned close. "Go home quickly and help your mother. Guard your footsteps. Talk to no one." He gave Ras' arm a squeeze and used his chin to point the way to the acropolis.

"My mother? What about my mother?" His guilt at leaving her alone ramped up. But the guard had already turned his attention to the next group in line.

He walked briskly, noticing soldiers standing in clusters everywhere. People's faces peered from windows and through partially open doors. The sun was directly overhead and the cobbled streets, usually filled with playing children, were vacant. Hushed, disembodied voices floated in the dusty air. At the acropolis he took the central stairs two and three at a time, climbing past the terraces and running through the connecting colonnades until he reached the third privileged level below the king.

Up ahead royal guards were making piles of furnishings, kitchen items and clothing—*his* furnishings, cooking items and clothing. Just inside the door, Royal Guardsman Jeran loomed over his mother. She was pleading with him. Ras' eyes adjusted to the diminished light inside their spacious apartment and when they did he was shocked by his mother's appearance. Her eyes were swollen and rouge was smeared across her face.

He'd never seen his mother other than poised, well groomed and in control. She was distraught. Nearly all of their possessions were piled out on the terrace and there was nothing he could do about it except clench his fists until they ached for lack of blood.

She looked shrunken. Her green dress hung awkwardly on sagging shoulders and dimpled on her felted shoes with their upturned toes. Her beautiful hair, usually brushed until its copper highlights shone, hung in disarray, slipping from the combs that normally fastened it at her temples.

Jeran had been in their home many times to accompany his father on his missions. How many times had his father praised the guard for his service? And now this!

"By law, by King Suldana's decree, this home is ours for life," she pleaded.

"Azzia, my orders are from the queen. Hapati's entourage was intercepted by the royal guards in the Easterly Valley, six miles from Hattusa. He was accused of treason and when he resisted, execution was carried out on the spot. What reason other than treason would have him so far from Hattusa when the High Priest was waiting for the tablet?"

"My father worshipped the king. He would never . . ."

His mother covered his mouth with her hand. "Where are we to go?" she said.

"Nowhere in the city," Jeran said. He turned his back to the door where other soldiers awaited his orders and lowered his voice. "Listen, Azzia, I was there when the queen went to the Old Woman to ask for confirmation that you and Ras should die also." Azzia's hand flew to her heart. "She set a snake free in a basin of water. It swam past Sin, Death, Temple, House, and Prison. It stopped and circled in the area of Life.

"You see how fortunate you are? No one would dare to argue with the Old Woman, but I saw the queen's face. It was crimson. Remove yourselves from her line of sight. She seeks to dispose of anyone the king loved. And, please tell no one what I've told you."

Ras nodded his understanding but bile burned his throat.

His mother ran from the room and Ras turned to go to her but hesitated when a chariot pulled up outside. Inara, Master Palla's wife, stepped out. At the sight of her, Ras brightened. Master Palla had trained his father and was a close family friend. More than that, he seemed always to know the mind of the city. Perhaps she was bringing information, perhaps a reversal of the order. He moved closer to the door to listen to what she was saying to the guard.

"You know very well the gods demand cleansing rituals." She pulled a small scroll from under her cape and Ras saw the Old Woman's black seal on the document. There was writing on the tablet, but the seal was all the guard needed to see. He turned to leave but Inara grabbed his arm.

"Tell your chief this absurd action has upset the entire city. People are frightened. Look around. They've cleared the streets and pulled their children from their play. Throwing a family—particularly a family of the royal court—out into the street affects everyone. They don't understand this. Your chief's reaction is to flood the gates and streets of the city with guards. They're making it worse. Tell him!"

He left without comment, taking his men with him.

"Come, Azzia, Ras," she said, closing the door and pulling them into the bedroom. Already his mother's aspect had changed.

"Is Palla coming? We need him to speak for us, to speak for Hapati. He trained him. Of all people he can vouch for my husband's faithfulness to the king."

"He tried earlier but was overruled. He sends his heart to you both"

"The queen wants us removed from the city, but what if we move to a far corner away from the acropolis?" Azzia said. She sat heavily on the room's lone bench.

Inara frowned. She loosened the pale blue scarf draped over her head and gathered it to her chest. "You needn't move immediately. The Old Woman has ordered a cleansing for a small house outside the walls and the *tawananna* cannot interfere with this. Besides, there is a favorable side."

"Favorable? Outside the walls? All our friends are *here*." Azzia leaned forward and held her face in her hands.

Inara motioned to Ras to pull a remaining floor cushion to the front of the bench where she dropped and pulled her skirt around her legs. "It should come as no surprise to you that power drives the royal court. The queen knows who can hurt her. Palla has many friends in high places. She cannot touch him, at least for now.

"He wants you to know he is using every means to protect you. Of course he's made it clear to the queen that treason, especially a scribe's treason, had to be dealt with quickly and severely. But, I assure you, he knows Hapati never had a treasonous thought. Still, the queen must be convinced of Palla's full support on this issue. You understand?"

Ras and his mother nodded but without conviction.

"When Prince Setmel is crowned, she will be quick to eliminate anyone whose loyalty is in question." Azzia stood and paced to the other side of the room as Inara continued. "We must wait out the prescribed days of mourning and allow our beloved king to wander in the Afterlife paradise before he takes his rightful place among the gods.

"In the meantime, the owner of the little house I mentioned has recently died—a good reason for a cleansing ritual which will take some time."

Azzia nodded and her head sunk like a heavy weight against her chest.

"Stay out of sight as much as you can. The less you are seen, the slower the queen will be to act against you. She will be distracted by the rituals and the public platform it offers. Pretending she will miss her husband will consume all her energy."

Azzia smiled weakly but Ras saw no humor in Inara's words. He felt the walls closing in on both of them. Suddenly his hand bounced at his side as if he expected to find a sword. "Nothing about this makes sense to me. I swear I will find some answers."

A blast of wind blew the window shade horizontally and a loud crack of thunder shook the room. Azzia screamed. "The Storm God has heard you, son. Say no more. Oh, our belongings will be ruined." She ran from the room.

But Inara's servants had already begun to carry the furniture inside and everything was indoors before wind-driven drops splattered on the stone terrace. Furniture was stacked in the center of the room. Baskets had spilled their contents and shards of shattered pottery were scattered everywhere. Rain drummed on the walls, the terrace outside and the wooden shutters over the windows.

The roar was calming in its own way, like a cleansing, washing the dust from the air, drowning out the sounds of soldiers' boots, pushing aside the wild confusion that had consumed Azzia and Ras. They sat quietly together on cushions next to red embers glowing in a brazier. Inara held Azzia's hand in her lap.

"Do you see how the Storm God is with us? I feel it. Listen, I have more to tell you," Inara said in a low but urgent tone.

Palla, she said, had been listening for months to rumblings in the court while the king's health declined. He felt an evil circulating, creating doubts about Hapati's loyalty. Palla never doubted the king's resistance to the rumors, but his disease was taking a toll. That's when Palla began making plans. Inara said he withheld his plans from her for her own protection, but she knew he had them.

"There are men in the royal guard who oppose the queen and have pledged loyalty to Palla. They will be near you to watch for trouble."

"And if there is trouble? What then?" Ras said.

Azzia opened her mouth but Inara smiled and raised her hand. "Your father's spirit rises stronger than ever. He, too, was a warrior for justice. He was always thinking ahead, to be ready for anything. Palla is the same. Have you forgotten he trained your father? I beg you to trust him."

While the rain assaulted the apartment, Ras walked outside to a large brick fireplace against the wall where a wood fire produced embers for inside the apartment. He used tongs to fill a bucket, then carried them inside to a stone-lined alcove and placed them in the brazier. He stirred the embers to increase the heat before settling back on his cushion to watch his mother's face. The glow cast shadows in the hollows of her eyes and along the edge of her aquiline nose. She appeared more relaxed and Ras felt she'd accepted her friend's words, even if he had doubts. His thoughts focused on a way to clear his father's name. Yes, he was like his father—passionate and loyal to the ones he loved.

"You have a few days before the cleansing—" Azzia slumped against her. "She is spent. Let me put her to bed."

Ras left the room. Moments later Inara joined him in the gathering room. "You wear your questions like armor, Ras, and your mother will feel them as every mother feels her child. If you give in to them, you give her more worry." Ras nodded and she continued. "I will make preparations for the cleansing and call for you when they're ready. The Old Woman said you will live and so you shall."

When Ras closed the door behind her, he tried to recall the hope he'd felt with her arrival, but it had vanished.

CHAPTER SIX

THE THIRD DAY OF MOURNING

The High Priest of the Storm God prays:
"Allani, Sun-Goddess of the Earth, Sun God of Heaven,
Ancestors, receive King Suldana II's Spirit. See, O Gods, the chair
that holds his bones."

TAKANA

Takana, Ras and Angulli dripped with sweat. They'd met before the sun rose, ran for two hours and finished up with a sprint into the forest's cool shade. But before they left the road, they heard someone approaching. Urhi.

"I'd like to crush him like a bug!" Ras said with his face turned aside.

"It's good to see you practicing after yesterday's lackluster performance. Something bothering you?" Urhi said, sticking his thumbs in his waistband.

Takana saw Ras spring forward and caught his arm before he reached Urhi. "Don't let him provoke you. On your worst day, you're a better runner than he is and he knows it."

"You weren't here yesterday, Takana. He quit after one length." Urhi turned to Ras. "You're slipping. Perhaps you should drop out now. I doubt there will be a place for you anyway, now that your traitorous father is dead."

"My father was no traitor, you donkey's ass!" Ras said, lunging for Urhi.

Takana grabbed him again. "Don't waste your energy on him. His opinions are worth no more than he is."

Urhi stuck his chin forward. "Ha! You've been gone so long, you're out of touch. It wouldn't surprise me if *your* time in Hattusa is limited. You just don't know it yet." He stepped away.

"Are you saying you know something I don't?" Takana said, grabbing Urhi's tunic.

Urhi yanked himself free. "You've always had your way around here—the king's favorite, and all that—but you're not our future king's favorite. That spot belongs to me, and when he's crowned, you'll see changes. I'm thinking Harmesh might soon look very good to you."

Takana moved away, pulling off his soft leather boots as he went. He tied the leather strips together, slung them over his shoulder and cocked his head to his friends. They walked away together. When Takana looked back, Setmel had joined Urhi and they were deep in conversation. It occurred to him that Setmel had suggested the confrontation.

"Will you go back to Harmesh?" Angulli said.

Takana glanced at Ras's face before answering. His head was down and curly hair covered part of his face, but not enough to hide the sadness. It twisted Takana's heart. With a few words he could lift his friend's anguish but did he dare? Palla had cautioned him and he'd agreed Ras was unpredictable. Takana eased his conscience with an idea that might lift the spirit of both friends.

"To tell the truth, I'm conflicted. Not happy about what I see and hear in Hattusa, and I don't doubt it will be worse with Setmel on the throne, but . . . Look, there's something else, something I want to tell you about Harmesh."

They came to a fallen tree. Takana set his shoes on it and sat beside them, wiggling his toes in the tall grass. Angulli and Ras stretched out nearby.

"It's eight suns' travel from here, that's all I know," Angulli said, trailing his hand through the grass.

"There are talented people there with new skills to teach. In the last few months I've been working with some chariot designers," Takana said. It surprised him to feel so positive about a place he used to think of as a prison. "We've been working on a chariot that will hold three men instead of two. Think about it. As it is, when either the driver or the bowman is incapacitated, the chariot is useless. If a third man acted as a protector, our casualties would drop."

"Don't forget the horses. They're lost too," Angulli said. "I like your idea."

"So why should that interest us?" Ras said.

"I hoped you'd both be interested enough to go to Harmesh with me and work on them. Even Setmel would recognize the advantage this would give our warriors in battle."

"That's tempting," Angulli said, bouncing to his knees. "But, wait, what about the extra weight on the horses? Wouldn't that cut down on their speed and maneuverability?"

Takana enjoyed seeing Angulli's face light up when talking about his life's work. "If the floor of the chariot is reinforced and the axle moved to the center of the floor as opposed to the rear, the weight would be shifted away from the draught pole and yoke supported by the horses," Takana said. Angulli nodded thoughtfully and seemed to be picturing the design in his mind. He turned to Ras.

"Not interested. I'm not going anywhere until I clear my father's name."

"Understood. We all want to see that happen, but it's not going to happen tomorrow. It's going to be . . . Listen, Ras, wouldn't you like to get your mother out of this troubled city. Harmesh is—"

"Harmesh is what? Some unknown something or other. Means nothing to me!" Ras threw up his hands, then rolled onto his side and faced away.

"Would it be an exaggeration to say you don't know much about it?" He took a breath, realizing his tone would add to Ras' anger. He started up again, slowly. "Let me tell you, Harmesh pays a tribute to the kingdom well beyond any other vassal state." Takana was encouraged when Ras sat up and faced him. "The land is rich. Sweet water is everywhere. The ports along the Black Sea receive ships from places you've never dreamed of and the goods . . . well, things you've never seen. Besides, the population almost doubled in the two years I spent there. It's an exciting place." He paused to note Angulli's imagination was working full blast.

"Maybe you have a point about my mother. I'll mention it to her. But I'm not leaving my father's proof of innocence to anybody. It's my job, my responsibility. You two do what you like." He rolled back onto his stomach.

"Well, as I said," Takana continued, "I'm conflicted. Leaving Hattusa when I know, at least I *think* I know, what's going to happen. That feels wrong. Maybe I wasn't born a Hittite but when my father's kingdom was destroyed and he was killed, my mother and I escaped here. King Suldana was like a father to me. Leaving makes me feel disloyal to his memory."

"I understand that," Ras said. "The king played a part in my childhood too. I wonder what he thinks of what's happening here and what he'll do about it when he becomes a god." He flipped over again and searched the sky.

Angulli turned to Takana. "How old were you when you came to Hattusa?"

"Five or six, I think. I don't remember much about the battle, just being scared to death. I barely remember my father. The best years of my life were with King Suldana." He lapsed into old memories.

The forest sounds filled the silence—the rush of wind against the clinging dried leaves, the tap-tap of woodpeckers on the trunks and the thunk of heavy, round seed pods falling from the plane trees. Ras added his drumming foot.

Suddenly Takana jolted upright. "God in Heaven, look at the sun! The funerary rites. I forgot." He waved and kicked up his heels, shouting they should think about what he said. He could only hope their decisions would be made before Setmel made life unbearable. But as he considered this, a new thought niggled its way into his mind.

What if the people rebelled, who would take the throne? His next thought stopped him in his tracks. The *tawananna* resented his closeness to the king. Did she think the king . . . ? He raised his head to the heavens to ask for . . . what? He shook his head to clear it and set himself in motion again toward Yazilikaya. He walked through the city but once he was outside the protective wall, he broke into a run for the rest of the way to Yazilikaya. For a change, he welcomed the ritual as a distraction.

The feasting and sacrificial rites had begun when Takana arrived at the sacred grounds. He slipped in next to his mother. Nearby, the king's bones were piled on a chair like ivory trophies after an elephant hunt. Earlier in the day, the Old Women had sifted through the ashes and lifted the king's bones with silver tongs. They'd been dipped in oil and polished.

Tables for the gods, some with statues, others with sacred symbols, were set around the perimeter of the *hekur*-house. Loaves hot from the oven were piled like small aromatic hills. From time to time someone carried a dripping morsel, a piece of meat covered with sizzling fat, to one of the gods. As the morsel was placed, the subject murmured a supplication before returning to his seat.

The High Priest ordered cups filled and everyone toasted the honor of the deceased three times. The savory fragrance of roasted meats mixed with the smell of sweat, excrement and blood settled on the crowd. Takana had forgotten the contrasting odors of funereal rites and how they twisted his stomach. He reached in his pocket for a mint leaf.

He followed his mother's lead. She was deft at bringing empty fingers to her mouth again and again when she had no desire for food. While he faked eating, a minor priest paraded back and forth with items the king would need in the Afterlife—a piece of turf to symbolize the pasture where the king would live, broken farming tools, and freshly sacrificed cattle, sheep, horses and asses. It was a ritual that would continue for days until the king's bones were laid to rest.

The Third Day of Mourning was marked with specific beverages and Takana counted the empty jugs lined up behind the tables. There were ten jugs of beer, ten jugs of wine and ten empty jugs of the ritual beer called *walhi.* The last set had been used to douse the fire at the critical moment when the flesh was burned away but the bones were still intact.

Across the table, Takana saw the *tawananna* looking at him . . . but differently. There was something familiar about her expression and for a brief moment he remembered. He was six years old and she was watching him and Setmel playing a game on the floor at the palace. He'd just arrived in Hatti, still quivering inside from the blood and fear of war. He hardly knew what to make of his new, unfamiliar home in the Hittite acropolis. Her smile was warm and inviting.

Takana felt a sudden, deep sadness for her, as though she too might be remembering an earlier time in her life, a time when she was content with simpler things. Then, just as abruptly, she looked away. What forces were at work in her? He knew only that evil had resulted, and it would be foolish to drop his guard. The Queen Resat he remembered was gone, replaced by a ruthless, power-driven despot.

He doubted she was consumed with grief. It was more likely she was planning her next move. An uneasy feeling in his stomach led him to think it would come swiftly after the rites were completed. He had to make his own plans sooner rather than later. He whispered to his mother and, without waiting for a response, left the table.

Steps from the table, a fat priest in a long flowing robe presented a perfect cover for him. Takana moved in the priest's shadow until he was clear of the main crowd. He asked a royal guard for a horse and left the burial grounds. A quick glance at the sun told him he had a few hours of light left. He nudged the horse to its fullest stride and when they reached the city wall he guided the horse along the northern edge, searching for a tree he knew that brushed the city wall. As a small boy he'd used it to avoid the guards, always on alert for mischievous young boys. He tethered the horse to the trunk, jumped to the first branch and climbed. At the top of the wall, he patted the bark like an old friend and dropped down on the inside.

Takana reached the *eduba* without seeing anyone and slipped around the building to the partially shuttered window of Palla's office. Since their last meeting, his respect and appreciation for the old man had grown. It comforted him to know Palla worked behind the scenes to protect King Suldana's legacy from the queen and Prince Setmel's poison. Once the crown was placed on Setmel's head, only the will of the people could make a difference and bloodshed would be inevitable. Takana shuddered at the thought, but he would be part of it. Of that he had no doubt.

Through the window, he saw Palla facing his shelves of baked tablets, fingering them and moving some from one spot to another. Someday Takana would ask the master to teach him to read, but that would come later. In their current situation, the thought seemed trivial, even silly. There were far more important things. To begin, he yearned to know more about Hapati, where he was, and how he'd been rescued. He wanted to know more about all the things Palla had set in motion to protect Hatti. He needed to draw on the man's wisdom and resources, to probe the mind and heart of a true patriot. Most of all he needed hope.

Takana breathed deeply and admonished himself. His needs could wait. It was time to dedicate himself to serve in whatever way Master Palla suggested. He tapped lightly on the window frame and held his face where the light would catch his features.

The old man smiled broadly at the sight of him and moved quickly to open the door. "I was hoping you'd come. We must get to work before it's too late."

"Yes, I feel it too. Something dark is closing in on us." He felt the urge to ask the old man if he knew the king's mind before he died, but the very thought seemed audacious.

Palla crossed the room to pull a reed shade down over the window. "Your mother? How is she?" He motioned for Takana to sit opposite him in a chair with a woven cane seat.

Through the open office door, Takana could see the large classroom across the corridor, still in disarray from the day's classes. Wooden benches were strewn with tablets—wax and clay—and styluses of various sizes. Short, three-legged stools were stacked in a corner. Palla's office, on the other hand, was dominated by a wide-mouth oven with three shelves inside to hold the tablets. Red embers glowed in the dark recess.

Palla closed the office door and repeated his question. "Your mother?"

"Sorry. She's composed but just below the surface I can feel her anger and fear—worried about me. I know she's unsettled about the future—like all of us—but there's little I can say to help.

"Tell me, how was the *tawananna* able to move so quickly against Hapati? Ras says he wants to clear his father's name, but revenge is closer to the truth. He's going to get himself killed."

"I know. I'm doing my best to see their acropolis apartment is watched by royal guards I can trust."

"We owe you our gratitude, Master Palla. I can't believe how quickly the city's fears are growing. The dark day was a warning for all of us. Things are not as they should be and everybody knows it."

Palla shook his head, giving flight to his long, fine strands of gray hair. His skin hung loosely over his bones, but energy and strength, topped with fierceness in his dark eyes, were his true essence.

Still standing, he poked Takana's chest with a bony finger. "We must do something to restrain the queen before the mourning period is over. As it is, she thinks she's untouchable and can do whatever she desires. Her move against Hapati is an example."

"Maybe the gods will take pity on us and spirit her away."

"Ah, yes, but the people and the gods will demand a cleansing first, a cleansing only truth can produce."

Takana jumped to his feet. "A cleansing of her spirit! That would be something! It would take magic!"

"I don't need magic, just a powerful secret." Palla moved over to listen at the door before he continued. "Setmel is *not* the king's son!"

A flush traveled the length of Takana's body. He was shocked but, at the same time, Palla's words struck a chord in his subconscious. "I knew it! Somehow I knew he was no part of our king. Who spawned that evil?"

"Twenty years ago King Suldana sent the queen with a treaty to King Amilla of the Kingdom of Kazaram. Its purpose was to strengthen trade between our two kingdoms, but she went with her own agenda to convince Amilla that with her support he could move against Hatti Land and win. To seal the bargain she bedded him many times during her visit. It's their venomous mix that flows in Setmel's veins."

A sound— half laugh, half choke—left Takana's throat. "You have keen eyes and ears, Master Palla, but did you conceal yourself in Amilla's bedchamber?"

"Do you think mine are the only eyes and ears loyal to King Suldana? Queen Resat's words and actions were tolerated for the king's sake, but never misunderstood. Because she believed the king was weak, she gathered her own expansionist followers and gradually rid the palace of those who supported the king—not all, but a goodly number. Would you doubt she's been building alliances beyond our borders?"

"Kazaram, obviously, but how could she get away with this? And if you knew about it, didn't others?

"Ha! Consider this: it's not only for the king's sake that the queen's actions were kept secret. Are you not amazed at how our great king held women equal to men? He heeded their counsel and insisted the courts protect their rights. But he was no fool. Queen Resat made the mistake of believing benevolence and diplomacy are weaknesses, when in fact they require a type of strength and skill she's incapable of understanding. I'm sure you've figured out how shrewed our king was when he sent you to Harmesh." Takana's eyes widened and he nodded.

"There are secrets in the palace just waiting to be used at the right time. Be comforted, I've built my own group of loyalists."

Takana, even as a growing boy, was aware of the then-youthful scribe's fierce loyalty to the king. It extended to the whole royal family. Master Palla also made no secret of his fondness for Takana, but at that moment Takana saw more. Trust? Pride? What other secrets were tucked away in the old man's mind?

"Do you think the king knew about the *tawananna's* unfaithfulness?"

A veil seemed to fall across the scribe's features and he took several moments before he answered. "I've wondered about that myself. I know he was a man who placed the kingdom above everything else, even his own happiness. Our beloved king was also a man of order. He loved The Law and believed it was our greatest protector. I'm counting on that for our own safety."

It was an unsatisfactory answer, one that filled Takana with renewed sadness for his uncle. He sighed and returned to Palla's plan. "What you've already done is remarkable, old friend, and all of Hatti will be indebted to you. But will the forces you've gathered be strong enough to stop her?"

"No, not alone." He poked Takana's chest again. "If you have the courage, I have a challenge for you."

"I'll find the courage. What is it?"

"Your uncle, King Naram-Suen of Luwadna, could be our secret weapon. I'm thinking his military strength and blood tie with Hatti would be enough to stop any ambitions Amilla might have to make a move."

"Hmm. I see what you mean. The alliance between our two kingdoms protects us from aggression. Amilla should know Hatti and Luwadna would use their combined strength if Kazaram threatened."

"If Amilla were driven by logic, I'd agree. As it is, I'm not sure. So many things I'm not sure of." He sighed and seemed lost for a moment, before he raised his head and fastened on Takana's face. "That aside, will you go to your uncle?"

"But even with the fastest horses, if memory serves, it will take sixteen, maybe eighteen suns to reach Luwadna. By then Setmel will be in command."

"What if I told you your uncle is already on his way?" Palla said. "And his is not the only foreign kingdom drawing near."

"Who else?"

"I'm not sure, but possibly King Amilla."

"You're saying my challenge will be to meet up with my uncle to warn him, correct? I'll leave immediately." He moved to the door.

"Wait! Are you Ras? It's not like you to move without thinking."

Takana nodded and sat down again. "Yes, of course. Forgive me. I can't go alone and my mother . . ."

"Exactly. Listen, I was so sure of your response, I already have the perfect companion for you, a capable man. Your mother won't want you to go, but I believe her loyalty to the kingdom and her brother's legacy will help her see the necessity. You must take a letter from her to her brother-in-law and sister. I'll prepare it quickly. As for King Amilla, even if he reaches Hattusa beforehand, I doubt he'd make a move before Setmel has the throne."

The burden was etched on the old man's face. Takana nodded and squeezed his narrow shoulder. He stepped outside, welcoming the cool breeze against his skin. He couldn't deny the chance to leave the city was also welcome. He was ready for a challenge. The only thing that would give him more pleasure would be the chance to sit quietly with the old king to ask if he knew Setmel was not his son. Sadly, that chance would never come.

CHAPTER SEVEN

THE FOURTH DAY OF MOURNING

The hasawa speaks:
"Great and Powerful Gods, drink! Spirits of the Afterworld, eat!
All Powerful Gods of Sun and Moon, Mountains and Plains,
King Suldana comes to you. Accept him!"

ANGULLI

Horses woke Angulli with sound and vibration. Without opening his eyes, he knew they congregated at the farthest edge of the vast horse reserve before racing to the feeding troughs—his signal to pull on his boots and a warm fleece vest. But Angulli was reluctant to leave the dream he was having of a woman in the tack shop who made his heart quiver.

It was late in the day. He'd been running and just managed to reach the shop before it closed for the night. Inside, he searched for the bushy-haired, bent old man who could barely walk but who knew exactly where to direct his customers to the goods they needed. "I need reins," he called. No one answered but there was a rustling sound at the back of the store and a small figure moving toward him. She stopped short. Long dark eyelashes fanned out on her bronzed skin. Highlights of amber rippled on the waves of hair that curled upward on her shoulders. "My father keeps reins along that wall." She pointed without looking at him. He allowed his eyes to follow the curves of her round breasts straining against her linen dress. He imagined his hands easily spanning her tiny waist. "Can you show me?" he said. She raised her warm brown eyes to his . . .

"Ah! What a stupid dream," he said to the wall. He could think about women all he liked but that didn't make him a man.

He reached for the cord that raised the woven reed window shade above his bed. The horizon was a thin red line dividing earth from sky, and in that emerging light a hundred horses were galloping on hard, dry ground. As a tot, the sight frightened him—huge beasts running full out, exploding toward him with thundering hooves and shrill sonance. With more experience, he understood the horses ran together to celebrate the joy of the herd, their oneness. The leader, a brown stallion with a black stripe along his sides, had earned their obedience. He was intelligent, courageous, fast and clever and possessed a long memory of past successes and failures. Angulli spent many days studying his movements and the ways in which he communicated with his band.

He sat on the edge of his bed and watched them. The stallion ran out in front, testing the herd and himself. His tail fluttered like a flag waving to those he enticed to follow. They would run until he stopped.

Angulli dressed, moved quietly through the house and jogged to the main corral. His breath left his mouth in small clouds. The horses had just disappeared over the rise where he knew they would whirl around and return. He straddled the wooden fence to wait.

"I thought you would sleep later, son."

Startled by his father's voice, Angulli jumped inside the corral. "I, I didn't hear . . . You inspected the fence, father?" He kept his head down as he climbed back over the fence and hoped the scant light masked his embarrassment. "It's my job; I'm sorry."

"No, no, the walk was good for me. How was your time with Ras and Takana?"

"It felt like no time at all. They're . . . I don't know, maybe unsettled is the best way to describe them."

"We're all unsettled."

"Yes, but we're out here," he said, making an arc with his arms, "and they're . . . I'm afraid for Ras. His anger twists his brain. And Takana . . . he makes his appearances at Yazilikaya for his mother's sake, but every day he's more wary. Just yesterday Urhi, Setmel's close buddy these days, hinted Takana would not be welcome in Hattusa for much longer. I think he should return to Harmesh now, but I doubt he will."

"Before the rites are complete? Before the Coronation? No, no, son. That would turn the royal court against him. If he has any hope of returning to Hattusa, he must first fulfill his duty as the king's nephew."

Angulli smiled weakly. His father's understanding of politics was as keen as any city dweller, even if Takana and Ras thought otherwise. "Takana is encouraging Ras and his mother to go to Harmesh with him."

"Harmesh? And what does Ras say to that?"

Angulli shrugged. "All I know is Urhi said Ras may not be invited to participate in the Coronation games because of his father's . . . well, you know."

The herd approached and small stones fretted at Angulli's feet. He welcomed the rising sound and the distraction. Explaining his friends' troubles made his head ache. The lead stallion crested the hill and sped toward them. Moments later Angulli and his father were engulfed in dust. When it settled and the sound abated, his father asked, "How's your experiment working?"

It was a question Angulli's father and brothers asked often. The question didn't bother him but the mild mocking tone his brothers used did.

"I'm making progress. Do you want to see?"

"See what? You have my blessing, but I must say I don't understand what you're trying to do."

"I hope to prove to you that you'll have better results with the horses if they *choose* to do what you want." Angulli heard his father sigh. Clearly his father's blessing was nothing but an indulgence. "Will you take a moment to watch?"

His father nodded and climbed the fence to perch and wait.

The horses stopped and milled around beyond the troughs. Five or six young colts continued to run but never far from their elders. They would approach when the food was distributed.

Angulli stepped onto the lowest fence railing, placed his fingers in his mouth and whistled. At the long, shrill sound, a trim, pale brown mare separated from the herd and trotted toward him. Angulli stepped inside the corral, away from the troughs, turned his back on the mare and waited. He watched his father's eyes grow larger as the horse came up behind and nudged his shoulder.

Angulli turned and blew into the horse's nostrils. The mare snorted and nodded her head several times. Angulli scratched and petted her neck, sides and rump. Then he walked along the fence. The mare followed, and she continued to follow as Angulli walked forward, backward, side to side and finally back to the fence. By this time he noticed the smile growing on his father's face. But there was more he wanted to demonstrate.

Angulli grabbed the horse's stiff, black mane and swung himself across her back. The horse remained still until, with hands spanning his thighs, he moved his legs slightly and she walked forward. It was a performance and she seemed to know it. She turned, trotted, galloped and walked backward, all with the nudging of Angulli's legs. Finally, he dismounted and smacked her rump and she returned to the herd.

"Do you see her willingness to please me?"

"I see you've made a friend, my son. But I wonder how such training helps when your mare is yoked to another to pull a chariot?" He ruffled Angulli's hair and walked to the house.

Angulli's face burned. No one in his family doubted the horses were important but they believed they were incapable of improvement—unlike the chariots and the men who operated them. His father's question confirmed this. Angulli also knew it was why his friends thought him naïve, untested in the ways of grown men. There was some truth to their assessment. Unlike most of his contemporaries, he hated fighting, politics, and one man thinking he was better than another because of birth. He should have been born a horse, he thought, then laughed out loud.

That wasn't entirely true. He accepted his role as the youngest in the family, but it came with constraints. As long as he was cast in such a role, he'd never get permission to go to Harmesh with Takana. He replayed the chariot design in his mind.

It was a simple but brilliant idea, the kind of innovative thinking Takana had shown over and over. He had no doubt his family would recognize the importance of the idea, just as he knew they'd never see the value of winning the horses' trust. Clearly, his focus was the horse's welfare, not its warfare. Unless he could find a benefit to the warriors, his work would remain unimportant in their eyes.

He whistled again for the mare and she trotted to his side.

"I know you want to serve. I can feel it," he said, mounting her. Angulli kicked her sides and she galloped, following the pressures of his legs to go left and right, slower and faster. As the wind whistled in his ears and the herd watched, Angulli imagined himself in a battle, maneuvering the horse to engage. Suddenly he shouted at the top of his lungs. "Weapons! My arms are holding weapons!" He halted the mare. "*This* is the value of training a horse to obey the pressure of my legs. It leaves hands—both hands—free to use weapons!"

His heart was pumping so hard he couldn't help glancing at his chest to see if his tunic moved with the thumps. He laughed out loud, jumped down from the mare and walked toward the house where he knew the morning meal was waiting for him. He was bursting to tell them his thoughts. He also wanted them to know Takana's invitation to go to Harmesh was for him as well as Ras.

But a few strides from the door, he hesitated to say a prayer to the gods for their guidance and to give his heart a chance to beat normally. Over his head a russet bird landed on a tree branch and looked at him, cocking its head from one side to the other.

"No?" Angulli said. "No?" Then he laughed again. Maybe he was giving too much credit to the animals in his life. But maybe the gods guided the bird to him. He turned around and went back to the corral fence.

Behind him the door opened and slammed shut. His middle brother joined him.

"You missed a good laugh," he said. "And if you don't hustle, you'll miss your favorite barley porridge too."

"I could do with both," Angulli said. "What was so funny?"

His brother stood back, looked at the horses and back at Angulli. "You and your love affair with a horse."

"What? When did hard work become something to laugh at? Get out of my way." Angulli pushed past his brother and walked toward the house. Half way there he looked back and took a moment to enjoy the surprise on his brother's face.

Again the door slammed behind him but was immediately reopened by his brother. They exchanged sour looks before Angulli's brother walked to a corner and sat on the floor. Their mother frowned at both of them and the room became suddenly quiet.

"I'd like to know why you find my work with the horses deserves a laugh," Angulli said.

"I'm sorry, son, but we can't help but think it's a waste of time." It was his father's voice and everyone else in the room sat a little straighter.

"You're wrong about that. I'm working on something. I'm just not ready to talk about it yet. But there is something I want to tell you. Takana has an idea I think you *will* appreciate." It wasn't lost on Angulli that the mention of Takana's name got their attention. It boosted his confidence.

While he considered his words, he walked to the brazier with a bowl. He bent to sniff the bubbling porridge of roasted barley grain, filled a bowl and reached for a handful of dates and figs. Before sitting he eyed a platter of small loaves, regretting his hands were too full to grab several while they lasted. But his mother had been watching and she scooped up three loaves and a cup of milk and set them next to him. Then she filled a bowl for herself and took her usual place near the window to watch with satisfaction while the men ate. Angulli, too, surveyed the room. His father and brothers were rough and sometimes insensitive, but their love was constant. It had been enough until now. Now he wanted respect too.

On a routine day, his father and oldest brother spent most of their time working with officials of the military, often late into the night. They took orders for horses trained to pull chariots or to accept a single rider. They attended to the horses' wounds and illnesses, and when their attempts failed, they put them down, a task that saddened the whole family. Fortunately, the birth of leggy new colts balanced their spirits. After a birth, which they all attended when possible, they held a friendly competition of guessing the colt's attributes, everything from intelligence to sexual appetite. Knowing their guesses were ridiculous never impeded the enjoyment of the moment.

Angulli's middle brother was the trainer. He had an uncanny talent for spotting which of the horses was best suited for riding and which would work best with a partner pulling a chariot.Angulli's responsibilities were less focused, filling in wherever he was needed. In addition to feeding the horses, he assisted his middle brother. Nothing would change this until his father and brothers were convinced he was ready for more responsibility. That time had come. The challenge was to build a logical argument that demonstrated to his family he was ready and also that his ideas would be valued by the kingdom.

Angulli wrestled with his thoughts. He'd already heard indulgence in his father's voice. As head of the family, his brothers would fall in behind him. They saw him as a novice who needed more experience. Takana was twenty, only a year older, and they respected him. Perhaps Takana was the way to his family's heart. Angulli scraped up the last bit of porridge in his bowl, looked up and waited for his father's eyes to meet his.

"Takana's been experimenting with a new chariot design," he said.

"What's wrong with the one we have?"

His oldest brother mumbled something under his breath and bent back over his plate.

Angulli addressed his father again. "His design supports three without adding stress to the horses."

"Not possible. It's been tried. The base becomes unsteady," his father said in a tone that indicated the conversation was over.

But Angulli pressed his point. "He moved the axle from the rear to the middle and strengthened the flooring. Think of it! Adding a warrior to protect the driver and the bowman from horsemen and foot soldiers with spears will save our men and our horses."

His middle brother was the most wary of change and Angulli could see him getting ready to ask another question.

"Oh, and another thing," Angulli continued, "moving the axle to the center distributes the weight of the men across the draught bar and not onto the yoke." The look on his brother's face couldn't have made Angulli happier.

There wasn't a sound in the room. Even his mother had stopped her work at the hearth. This wasn't sufferance, they were listening.

"Can we see one of these chariots, brother?" his oldest, most practical brother said, looking at his father for approval.

"Yes, but for now only in Harmesh. When Takana returns there, he wants me to go with him to help build them."

"I forbid it," his mother shouted. Her hands flew to her mouth, shocked by her outburst.

Angulli's father rose from his seat, walked to his wife and placed his arm around her shoulders. It was a rare show of affection, although Angulli had sometimes glimpsed playful pinching and kisses when they thought no one was watching.

"I have confidence in the young prince," his father said. "His heart is Hittite through and through. Do you want to go?"

Angulli exhaled slowly when he realized he'd been holding his breath. Did he? He was excited about the idea, felt the pull of patriotism, but he hadn't dared to give the idea serious thought. "I do," he said softly, surprising himself a little.

Early in the afternoon, two servants from the temple of the Storm God came a second time to cut a piece of turf from the fertile farm land on the eastern side of the horse corrals. He watched the reverence of their movements, their grave attention to each detail. When they left, Angulli searched the eastern sky where Yazilikaya's black rock formations embraced the fearsome spirits of the Underworld. Somewhere under the canopy of clouds, prayers were being made to Istustaya and Papaya, the Underworld goddesses who spun the thread of a mortal's life span. They were spinning the king's years on this Fourth Day of Mourning, recounting the king's good deeds. Angulli imagined the aroma of fresh-baked bread and the savory smell of roasted meats. He envisioned the piles of broken tools and the sacrificed animals. The two goddesses were known not only to provide the offerings to the gods, but also the livestock the king would need in his new world.

Though barred from the rituals, Angulli felt it had been a remarkable day. He'd taken some new steps. Some were taken with confidence, others, like preparing a demonstration of how the horses' training would help the warriors, required careful planning and hours of work. But he was resolved to do whatever was needed to prove himself worthy.

Out in the corral, the mare moved with determination through the herd until she stood side by side with the stallion. They were beautiful together, perhaps mates? Nothing was impossible.

CHAPTER EIGHT

THE FOURTH DAY OF MOURNING

URHI

Urhi tramped through the streets mumbling to himself. His legs felt weak, his breath came in short bursts. Anger simmered in his belly but it would work against him if he allowed it to show. Twice he'd asked his father to meet with him and twice was refused. Yesterday, again, the guard at the barracks said his father couldn't be disturbed. But Urhi persisted, telling himself he was worthy of his father's attention.

"Tell my father, my future is at stake. Tell him I will meet him midday tomorrow at The Blue Inn." Somehow urgency found its way to his voice and won the guard's consideration. He swore the message would be delivered.

Now as Urhi neared the inn, he pictured his father waiting for him. He recited the main points he wanted, needed, to convey. He'd tell his father he knew he hadn't attained the highest levels, but he'd never quit, never stopped trying. Most important, he'd explain how much Prince Setmel depended on him. It was, he knew, a patriot's duty to seek improvement at all times. Then he would ask his father to give him an opportunity. But when The Blue Inn came into view, he stopped and leaned against a waist-high wall. He fixed his father's face in his mind—a face smiling with pride—before he could get his feet to move again.

The Blue Inn, situated behind the city's busiest commercial center, was always full of people. Though Hattusa was dotted with small taverns that catered to local, repeat customers, the inn provided something extra—a large space with tables and benches and small nooks at the back of the room for privacy. Unlike other gathering places, The Blue Inn clientele included traders from other kingdoms, travelers needing room and board, and local businessmen. It had been built to accommodate their needs.

Overall the yellow glow of oil lamps created an atmosphere of relaxation and comfort, and, most of the time, a background hum of friendly voices. But there were times when rumors agitated the citizens and men left their seats to debate. As such, the inn was valued not just for camaraderie, but as a place to hear the unguarded opinions of the people. Uhri knew that was why his father liked it.

He had to survey the room twice before he saw his father in one of the private spaces. Ibiranu was out of uniform, looking like any other man having a drink at the end of a busy day. He sat alone in one of the nooks with a cap pulled down over his forehead. Urhi walked around the edges of the room to reach him.

"What's so urgent you had to use one of my men to bring me a message?" Ibiranu said, hunching low. "You couldn't wait until later at home?"

Urhi bit his tongue. Neither he nor his mother had seen him since the king's death. He'd made a point of telling them he would stay in the barracks in the event he was needed. At any given time, he'd explained, the queen might need an escort to Yazilikaya.

Urhi didn't miss his father's company. He'd never gotten used to it. When his father was at home, it was to complain about his mother's social ineptitude. He'd heard it so many times he knew the words by heart. *If not for you I could be chief of the king's royal bodyguards, leader of the mešedi, closest to the king. Why couldn't you entertain occasionally? Men with wives who could impress with fine food and entertainment advanced faster than those without.* In this dynamic, Urhi was invisible. He kept his thoughts to himself and attracted friends who admired him for being the royal guard chief's son. Lately he found himself wanting more.

"I'm ready for a position of importance, father. Soon Setmel will be king and he'll be making changes in the kingdom." He was encouraged by his father's attention and what appeared to be a slow-growing smile. "I'm ready to give more to the kingdom." He straightened in the chair—proud of himself—and fixed his eyes on his father's face.

"This is good, very good, but a position of importance? On what basis? You think because you're my son, you deserve it?" The smile was gone.

"Well, no, but I thought you might send me to a vassal state to test my skills. That's what the king did for Takana and it earned him respect. I want the respect of my peers, men like Takana and his friends. I'm sick of their attitude toward me. At the races recently, they threatened me, father. Takana thinks he's better than me."

His father searched his face until Urhi felt heat rising from his neck to his ears. Beads of sweat started to form on his forehead. It occurred to him nothing good was going to come of his request. He placed his hands on the edge of the table and began to rise. Ibiranu stretched his arm out across Urhi's chest.

"I have a better idea," Ibiranu said, looking over his shoulder as Urhi settled back on the bench. He seemed satisfied no one was within listening distance and leaned closer to Urhi. "Tell me more about Takana."

Urhi swallowed. It was the first time his father had ever spoken to him like a confidant. He was thrilled. He searched his mind for information about Takana and found that just the mention of the name filled him with hate and resentment. Could he tell his father how many times he'd been shoved aside, kept at arms' length? Was he a leper? Maybe he wasn't as swift as Takana and Ras in the races, but he'd outrun Angulli many times. Yet Angulli, too, ignored him. He took a breath and leaned forward until his nose was within inches of his father's. "As your son, I'm as good as he is. Yet they never include me in anything they do. Did you know that?"

Urhi saw his father raise his eyebrows. He pressed on, pleased to have his full attention. "Think of it, father, there's no reason for their attitude except arrogance. Didn't the king send Takana away? Isn't Ras the son of a traitor? And Angulli spends his time with horses—stupid, four-legged beasts! The three of them act like they're better than me. I'm asking you to help me show them how wrong they are."

His father frowned. "Yes, yes, very interesting, but not what I need. What do you know about Takana's movements?"

Urhi squirmed. "Ah, not much, but I can find out. Is that what you want?"

His father's frown deepened. Urhi searched his mind for anything that might fit his father's expectations, but when nothing came, anger filled the void. If he'd been given opportunity to hone his skills like Takana, he had no doubt he'd be his equal. Why hadn't his father found a way to advance him? Why hadn't he asked him to be his apprentice, helping to keep the city safe, traveling around the kingdom and meeting important people? Did anyone know his father even *had* a son? Bile was rising and burning in his throat. But such thoughts could be dangerous and he quickly composed himself. The last thing he needed to do was anger his father by pointing out his negligence, implying he might have faults. "Give me a day, father, and I'll bring you information."

Ibiranu shook his head. "Not yet. I want you to do something now."

"Just name it, father, and I'll do it."

"Look around this room. What do you see?"

"Men."

"Is that the best you can do?" Ibiranu splayed his hands on the grease-stained table and tapped his fingers impatiently.

Urhi looked around the room again, more slowly. "I see men talking together. I recognize some of them. Shopkeepers and messengers and, oh, there's a group I recognize from the forge." He was pleased he recognized so many.

"That's better. But what are they talking about?"

"Huh? How should I know?"

Ibiranu answered with a disgusted expression that made Urhi's stomach clench. What did his father want? He got up from the table and walked slowly around the tables. He stood for several moments, picking at his nails, then moved to another group and did the same. He could feel his father's eyes following him. If his actions displeased his father again, he would have no recourse but to leave, return home and never raise the subject again.

When he'd circled the entire room, he returned to the table to find his father leaning forward, expectant. "And now?"

Urhi flushed with excitement. It was clear he'd done the right thing. He proceeded to pass along the snippets of conversations he'd heard.

"Complaints mostly. They think Setmel will raise taxes to build a larger fighting force and move against some of the troublemakers nibbling at our borders. They named the Kaskans in particular. That man, the one with the scarf wrapped around his neck, said more territory means more taxpayers sharing the load. They laughed at him.

"That group of blacksmiths," Urhi indicated with a flick of his head, "think Hapati's execution was a mistake. They said he should have had a trial and been hung in a public place as a lesson for others. But those two men, at the table nearest the door, said they don't believe Hapati was a traitor."

Ibiranu took his time to respond, making Urhi question himself. He watched his father study the men. Finally, he said: "This is information I can use. Good. You may have a talent for listening."

For a brief moment Urhi was elated, but he quickly sobered. "Listening and bringing you what I hear? You mean, like a spy? How will my friends know? I want them to give me respect. Who would respect a spy?"

"Have you been living underground like a blind mole? Gathering information is important. Make your decision. Do you want the rabble's respect or mine?"

Urhi was confused. It wasn't what he'd hoped for, but this was an opportunity to work with his father. In time it might lead to other things—a place in the royal guard or a position on the king's court. His parents would be in a position to acquire a bride from an important family. "What can I do to help?"

Ibiranu smiled broadly, set his elbows on the table and let out a slow breath. "The queen has charged me with smoothing the way for our future king. She suspects Takana and his friends will not be supportive when the crown prince takes the throne. The king must have the confidence and admiration of his people."

"Yes! Believe me, Takana and his friends treat Setmel like they treat me. I can give you as many examples as you want. Every time we're together they make it clear how they feel."

Ibiranu sat straighter, lifted his head. His chest seemed to expand. "The queen wants me to get rid of them. Maybe you can help."

"Me? How?" He leaned back, feeling mildly fearful of his father's words. But his father's smile was so warm he began to realize how confident his father must be to ask for his help.

"Do you see how you're in a unique position to learn their whereabouts, perhaps their plans? If I knew they'd be away from the city, together or separately, my men could carry out the queen's wishes without an audience. Could you do that?"

"Yes, yes, easily."

"You've pleased me with your eagerness. Let's have a drink to celebrate working together for the new kingdom." Ibiranu motioned for a server.

While they waited for a jug of beer, Urhi acknowledged the loosening in his chest. His muscles ached from the hours of tension. His hands warmed. He'd never felt closer to his father. He felt strong and able. His mind was already working on a plan to lure Takana, Ras and Angulli away from the city. He imagined how attractive a friendly competition would sound to them. He would tell them it would get them ready for the races following the Coronation. It would work, he was sure of it.

A server arrived with a jug and filled two cups. The golden liquid bubbled, danced its way to the brim and overflowed. Urhi grabbed his cup and emptied it in one long swallow, oblivious to the foam seeping through his fingers. He hardly tasted the sharp wet brew, but as he placed his empty cup on the table, his eyes met his father's.

"Tell me," Ibiranu said, filling Urhi's cup again.

"Huh?"

"What were you thinking? Obviously, not about the beer." He snorted.

Urhi flushed, wiped his fingers on his tunic and emptied his cup again. "Ha, thirsty, I guess." He flipped his hands over several times. But when his father neither smiled nor commented, Urhi shifted in his seat and considered whether or not he should share his idea. It would be best to think carefully and avoid having his father find flaws. He filled his cup again, this time drinking slowly and going over the plan again in his head.

"Ah, well, you know we run together. There will be races after the Coronation and I thought I could suggest a special race."

His father's eyebrows sent their second signal of pleasure. "Yes, good. What else?"

Urhi pressed on, describing a forest clearing they could use, but his father's expression suddenly drained his confidence. "Father," he said, rising, "this must be planned carefully. I'll work out every detail and meet you later." He backed away from the secluded nook, retracing his steps to the inn's main door, unable to disengage from his father's frown. But as he passed one of the tables, he collided with a man who got up suddenly. They spun together and hit the floor hard enough to draw everyone's attention.

The man rubbed his head and looked at Urhi on the floor. "Stupid pup! This is no place for you."

Urhi rolled onto his knees, looking up at the thick expanse of the grinning man standing over him. "Do you know who I am?" Urhi said, through clenched teeth.

"A fool who should look where he's going." He offered a hand to Urhi.

Urhi ignored it, struggled to his feet and yanked down on his tunic. He glanced around the room self-consciously and was glad to see most of the men had looked away . . . but not all. The eyes of Master Palla, seated in the nook next to the one he'd vacated, were staring intently.

Suddenly strong arms closed around Urhi's chest from behind and pushed him to the door. He struggled against their hold until he recognized the ring on his father's finger.

CHAPTER NINE
THE FOURTH DAY OF MOURNING
RAS

Ras opened his eyes to a colorless, predawn light. Through the open window above his pallet, he smelled the rain-soaked earth and imagined a mist floating through the narrow streets like a ghost stream. He closed his eyes and let his mind take him out the door, down the terraces to the street level. There he stepped into a thigh-high mist and imagined himself lifted by an unknown god who propelled his torso magically through the streets, out through the gate and into the forest. He fantasized that seeing such a legless sight, a small child might tell his mother about a new "god of the mists" who roamed the streets before the Sun Goddess of Arinna dissolved it with her fiery breath.

Normally, the world of fantasy and imagination provided hours of pleasure and release to Ras' mind. There were stories of talking animals, secret hiding places and adventures in far away places—all tucked away for a day when he could watch his children's eyes light up with joy. When, as a family, they could sit around glowing embers, wrapped in love and security. Someday . . . some future time. For now, why indulge in fantasy when truth itself was so unreal?He pulled off his night tunic and dressed. The felt shoes he'd last worn were across the room where he'd kicked them aside in frustration, but as he bent to slip them on, his eyes fell on the soft leather boots with curled toes his father had given him and chose them instead. As he fastened the laces around his calves, Ras felt the pull of memories gathering. He shook his head to rout them. Such thoughts would further diminish his energy and he needed some fresh air before the Old Woman arrived to escort them to the cleansing. Again, he shook his head. This time to dispatch the temple messenger's admonishment to *Stay in your quarters.*

Why? The arguments spun in his mind, not the least of which was the fact that before the day passed, he and his mother would be forced from the only home he'd known. Secrets! Orders! Ras was sick of them. What else could be taken from his family? It had been three days and no explanation for his father's treason had been given. Now they were ordered to leave the city. It wasn't right they were excluded from the ceremonies, left to imagine the pageantry, unable to publicly express their love for King Suldana II.

Ras remembered his father's tears when he described the king's compassion for a courageous old woman who sought forgiveness for her quarrelsome son. The king forgave the son's outburst in the royal temple—he'd merely been overeager—and substituted a year of servitude for a year in prison. The occasion resulted in a long lecture from his own father to control his hotheaded temperament. "Sorry, father," he whispered, "not this day!"

Ras finished lacing his boots, closed the door quietly and asked the gods to keep his mother asleep until he returned. Slipping down less-used streets and avoiding the gated areas of the city, Ras came to a secluded portion of the Old Women's temple, near the eastern edge of the city wall, north of the acropolis. He slowed to a walk, unable to resist another childhood memory. He and Angulli once had climbed the wall to spy on the rituals being performed inside. They saw the Old Woman remove the white hood that always obscured her head and almost fell off the wall when they saw she was young and comely.

The pleasure of the memory was too much to resist, especially with the uncertainty of his future. Who knew if the opportunity to spy would ever come again? He felt mildly giddy at his childishness but not enough to deny himself. He started to climb.

Once over the temple wall, he climbed until he reached the roof over the main chamber. He felt huge and exposed against the whiteness as he crept higher. From there he lifted himself over a small opening, a smoke hole, one of many encircling the temple's main altar below.

He peered downward. At first the torch lights around the circular altar were all Ras could see. But then, gradually, he saw figures moving. The Old Woman stood in the center. Two temple servants appeared from one side, pulling a goat whose eyes were white with fright. A blade was quickly and smoothly drawn across its throat and two servants moved forward to lift the hind legs, while a dark stripe appeared in the stone channel at the base of the altar—blood. The Old Woman caught it in a large pitcher and the goat's spasms slowed, then stopped.

Temple servants, bare-chested and wearing short linen kilts, carried and stacked wood in layers under a narrow platform. They placed the goat, with legs and head dangling, above it. Immediately a low, guttural sound vibrated in the chamber. The sound, unlike any human voice, came from the Old Woman. She carried a lighted torch to the stacked wood. The last thing Ras saw before the smoke billowed through the hole was the Old Woman pouring blood on the heads of the servants standing around her.

He loosened his grip and slid down the wall, grasping the seams between the polished white stones to slow his downward pace. He was about to drop onto a narrow ledge when movement below caught his eye. A royal guard was watching him. Embarrassment was quickly replaced by cold fear. He froze when the guard lifted his arm. Ras expected he was reaching for his bow, but the guard was urging his quick descent.

Words of regret rehearsed in his head. He pictured the guard at the door of their apartment delivering the news of his death to his mother. His tunic caught on rough mortar between the smooth stone blocks and threads pulled, snapped and tore. One more level and he'd be face to face with the final moments of his life. What was the guard waiting for? With a final hop, his feet squared in the dirt—lean runner's legs opposing dark leather straps tied fast to thick muscled limbs.

The sun's rays, just rising, glinted on the guard's helmet and a wide leather chin strap dug into his clean-shaved face. He took a step forward. His nose touched Ras' and his eyes were so intense Ras believed he felt heat. "Go home and stay there." The words were emphatic, but the guard's lips barely moved.

Ras backed away with a whispered prayer of thanks to the gods and ran. He'd barely closed the door of their apartment when his mother walked in the room. Simultaneously, horse hooves sounded outside on the terrace paving. Azzia flung the door open and they stepped out to see the Old Woman just turning the corner. Her chariot led a horse-drawn wagon laden with rags, silver urns, brushes and brooms. Four empty wagons followed. A fifth wagon carried six temple workers. Their long hair was plastered to their heads, not with the blood he'd seen earlier in the temple, but with water. They stopped at the door. Ras and his mother took the moment to look back and absorb the details of their home for the last time before stepping aside.

While workers poured into their apartment, Azzia and Ras acknowledged their neighbors gathering for the second time to see their acropolis apartment emptied of their belongings. Necks craned to see whatever would give them the necessary clues as to why the wagons had come. No proclamation had been made. It was not a day dedicated to special rites. Every citizen of high or low rank knew the specific days set aside for offerings and supplications to the gods of every rock, mountain, tree, spring and river. This wasn't one of them—therefore, an omen.

Azzia and Ras, along with their neighbors, eyed the wagons, particularly the one filled with silver urns. They knew the silver to be a conscious living force endowed with human emotions. From the earliest awakening of their spiritual awareness, every Hittite knew the Storm God and the Sun Goddess of Arinna were intricately woven into their daily lives. Divine wrath would fall on anyone who failed to appear for supplication on every specific occasion. What occasion was this? An offense?

They waited, lips moving with prayers for protection from the worst possibilities. Pestilence? A warning from the Oracle? Frowns and fear etched their faces. Mothers pulled their children close. Ras and Azzia understood. These were their neighbors, fellow members of the royal court, but they expected no words of comfort. Years of friendship evaporated in the aura of fear.

The spacious apartment had taken years to fill with comfortable furnishings and precious artifacts. It seemed to take mere minutes to empty. Two guards from the last wagon escorted Azzia, wrapped in a drab cloak, and Ras, erect and expressionless, to seats alongside them. The Old Woman raised her arms, pulled her white hood forward, and the people bowed to receive her words.

"O gods! Cast your eyes on Azzia and Ras. Though they move from one place to another, we ask you to follow. They remain your faithful servants wherever they go. They worship you wherever they are. Do not lose them. Listen for their voices of praise and supplication for they will never stop. Watch for their faithfulness. They will keep their eyes on you, O mighty gods."

Her words hardly eased the people's fear, but Ras latched onto the idea of the gods' presence wherever they went and took comfort from it. Then the Old Woman grasped the sides of her chariot and her driver led the caravan down the terrace levels. When they reached the bottom, the procession moved through the Acropolis Plaza, made a wide bend past the Storm God's temple in the Lower City, moved into the Upper City and exited through the Lion Gate. Along the way Ras watched the city inhabitants join the privileged acropolis tenants. But when a former neighbor waved to his mother, Ras saw her shift her eyes straight ahead. By nightfall their humiliating experience would be retold as a rare spontaneous event happening to someone else. In time the "someone else" would disappear from their lips forever. Their former status as the family of the king's royal scribe would be wiped from memory, not by time alone but by fear of association. These were bitter thoughts and Ras turned away, too, and watched the Old Woman's commanding figure.

The caravan of wagons moved along the main road until narrower paths branched off in many directions. The Old Woman's chariot took a right turn into the forest where small homes were scattered among the trees. They stopped at a small white building with a roof of wood planks and tree branches. The walls were whitewashed bricks. A fire-place of red bricks rested against the wall at the side of the door. Leaves and branches were piled inside, an indication no fires had been set for some time.

Temple servants, balancing urns of water on their heads, jumped from the wagons and carried rags and brushes into the house. Ras and his mother were left to stare at the humble rectangle and a few high, narrow windows.

"Well," Azzia sighed, "I rather like the pattern of light and shadow created by the mortared bricks, don't you?"

Ras stepped back, shocked by his mother's comment. But when he read the expression on her face, he smiled and nodded, grateful to know her spirit had not been broken.

They stared through the open door as the sun dribbled through the overhead canopy of evergreen pines. A breeze moved the branches and Azzia pulled her cloak closer.

"1 like the blue door—meant to keep out evil spirits, I hear," Ras whispered. His mother responded with a disparaging sound in her throat.

The Old Woman moved from her chariot to stand on a slight rise. She raised her head to the heavens. She prayed, asking the Sun Goddess of Arinna to fill her with greater power. When a ray of sun caught on her neck medallion, Ras believed it was a heavenly signal her message had been received. As remote and formidable as the Old Woman appeared, Ras felt she was sympathetic, even sorry for their troubles. She'd spoken no words of actual comfort but something, a feeling, the tilt of her head . . . something.

As everyone watched, two workers scrubbed their way toward the door. Brushes scraped and water sloshed to the last and finally they stepped outside and stood on either side of the door. Two servants erected a canopy bearing a coiled green snake, carried it to the Old Woman, raised it over her head and escorted her to the door. She halted at the threshold, looked inside and spoke. Only the vibration of her voice carried outside and onlookers were left to imagine what she said and what was happening inside the small mud-brick rectangle.

A moment later the two remaining temple workers, glistening with water and sweat, emerged carrying silver urns of muddied water. They filled the wagons with the urns, bowed to the Old Woman and walked to the wagons filled with furnishings. As the Old Woman led the remaining group to a nearby stream, Ras and Azzia turned back to watch the workers carry their possessions into the house, like ants returning to their underground hole.

At the stream two workers dug a shallow ditch. They filled the depression with tiny silver and gold boats. Then one by one the urns were emptied into the ditch, carrying the little boats into the clear, churning waters of the rocky stream. Gradually the water ran brown from edge to edge. They waited, and when the stream ran clear again and the boats could no longer be seen, the Old Woman walked to the water's edge, emptied a small vial of fine oil and honey into it and raised her arms.

"Just as the river has carried away the ships and no trace of them can be found anymore, whoever has committed evil word, oath, curse or uncleanliness in the presence of the god, even so let the river carry them away. And just as no trace of the ships can be found anymore, let evil word no longer exist for my god; neither let it exist inside the walls of this house. Let roof, walls and floor be free of that matter."

Her eerie voice floated in the air around them long after she returned to her chariot and drove off, followed by the wagons and the people of Hattusa. Insead of following his mother into the house, Ras stood in the doorway watching the retreating crowd. No one turned to look back.

Inside, they shifted baskets and furnishings into some semblance of order until Ras, noticing his mother's labored breathing, stepped outside to place several logs over the dried leaves and branches already in the fireplace. He pulled a small piece of flint from his pocket and struck a spark to ignite the dried leaves. Moments later flames ignited the branches and licked the logs. He found comfort in the leaping flames and growing heat and called to his mother to join him.

"How well do you know the Old Woman who performed the cleansing rite?" Ras said, pushing a log into the hot center of the flames.

"They don't form personal relationships as a rule. But, now that you ask, there was something about her . . ."

"Yes. That's why I asked. She seemed . . . well, not her words exactly, but somehow she was sympathetic."

"I don't know, Ras. Maybe we feel so abandoned we're imagining what we desperately need."

Ras nodded. "Let's go in and light every clay lamp we can find. It won't be long before I can pull some embers from this fire for the brazier inside."

As Ras lit the lamps and Azzia found their sleeping mats, he noted the interior was divided into three separate rooms. Two would provide separate spaces for sleeping. They placed cushions around the brazier in the remaining space, and when Ras filled the brazier, the added light, though minimal, added enough illumination to chase the darkness. Before long heated air moved about the room and Azzia sighed. Her body slumped, heavy with the exertion and emotion of the day.

To Ras it seemed their possessions reflected their own situation—tossed, bruised, unsettled. The smell of damp earth added its own message. They were reduced to the lowest possible level, stripped of any semblance of their former selves. It would take many fires and sun-filled days before the water-softened bricks were dry enough to hold the weight of their personal adornments. Until then the drabness of their new home would match the colorless future Ras envisioned. Azzia kissed his cheek, got up with difficulty and walked to the room where she'd padded the mud floor with reeds and bedding.

Alone, Ras studied the embers and watched the sun's movement through the narrow window until it disappeared completely. Memories of his father and sad thoughts about the future were unbearable. What of tomorrow? What would he do? Could he still participate in the races? Would his friends who lived inside the walled city welcome his friendship or would they fear being tainted by his father's so-called treason? It hurt to think some might believe it was true. He knew he had to move on, not just for his mother's sake but for his own. And for Hatti.

Move on? The thought surprised him. How could he resume his life? He had to understand why his father was taken from them. He wasn't the only one who believed that treacherous lie. According to Urhi, Takana and his mother were out of Prince Setmel's favor. Now he and his mother were removed. It felt like another kind of cleansing was taking place. It made him shiver. He stared at the red glow, realizing his anger had just fused with fear. Is that why Takana suggested Harmesh? Would Setmel threaten them when he became king?

There was a soft knock at the door. In his present state of mind, Ras felt a sharp pain shoot through his body. Neighbors wouldn't call after dark, would they? If they wanted to be welcoming, wouldn't they have come as soon as the Old Woman left? The knocking persisted until Ras got up and asked who was there.

"It's Angulli, you goat. Open the door."

His friend's embrace made his eyes sting and he held Angulli overly long.

"It smells like a swamp in here," Angulli said. But when Ras glared, he added, "By tomorrow the fire and sun will have done their work.

"How did you know where to find us?" Ras said.

"My brother and I were delivering horses to the stables when you passed by the Temple of the Storm God. I watched the whole cleansing procedure and waited until everyone left," Angulli said. "I figured by now you might be ready for a change of scene. Can you take time for a run? You know, keep up your speed for the games? It's only ten days until the Coronation festivities."

"It's dark," Ras said.

"Maybe here in the forest, but not on the road. There's still enough light left."

"You think I'll still be welcome at the competitions?"

"With your record of wins? Besides, it will send a message to Urhi that his barbs have no sting," Angulli said, heading for the door. "That reminds me . . ." He turned back to Ras. "Did you happen to see what Urhi was doing yesterday at the athletic field?"

"I try *not* to look at him," Ras said. "I did notice Takana wasn't there though. Do you know why?"

"No. It's nothing new. We can't always know what's going on with him. Besides, everything's weird in Hattusa right now. I'll admit I'm . . . Anyway, I saw Urhi twice huddling with some royal guards and then talking to Setmel. When I walked by I heard Takana's name mentioned. I know that sneak is up to something. I can't help it. Then when Takana didn't show up yesterday . . . I'm worried about him, that's all."

Ras was tempted to tell Angulli he was beginning to think his father's so-called treason wasn't the only reason they'd been forced out of the city. Urhi, after all, was a minor player. There just had to be stronger, more powerful forces at work. He wanted to tell him about the royal guard at the Old Woman's temple, too, but why worry Angulli. Instead he grabbed his soft boots from a corner near the brazier. "Well, since we don't know where Takana is, we can't do anything about it."

"We can keep our eyes and ears open." Angulli said.

Ras didn't miss the frustration in his friend's voice. Nor did he doubt Urhi was up to no good—he always was—but he had enough on his mind.

"Come on," Angulli said, moving toward the door again. "I have wings on my feet today. You'll have trouble keeping up with me."

Ras laughed in spite of himself, while he wrapped the thongs around his legs. By the time he reached the doorway, Angulli was almost at the stream. A moment later he was next to Angulli, sharing his pace. He'd think about sharing his new fear later.

CHAPTER TEN

THE FOURTH DAY OF MOURNING

TAKANA

Takana had a favorite spot at the northern end of the acropolis terrace. Looking west, the rising sun in the east caught the highest points of the white temples and displayed them against the deep green of the forest beyond. To the north, the trees with vibrant colors were fading. Takana imagined the trees transferring their energy inwardly to prepare for winter. He never tired of the constantly changing and evolving view. In many ways it was like his life. Though, unlike the trees, he needed all his strength now.

He was battling with himself. He felt the strong pull of friendship in regard to Ras. How could he best support his friend until the truth about his father could be revealed? It pained Takana to know that a few words from him would give Ras and his mother peace. On the other hand, Master Palla's challenge ignited his duty to the kingdom and his king's legacy. His words carried wisdom and weight, and more often than not, inspiration.

How had the old scribe accessed privileged information and gathered men and resources around him? It was a mystery, yet it didn't surprise him. It made him proud to know there were many loyal men in Hatti, willing to risk their lives for the peace and security of the kingdom. That thought gave rise to another—death awaited them if their efforts failed.

His attention shifted to his own responsibility. It was time to see Palla and pick up the tablet, but it occurred to him the streets would be filling with people and the royal guards would be on full alert. The last thing he wanted was to cast any suspicion on the old scribe.

Without returning to his apartment, he descended the acropolis terraces to reach the street level, then followed a little-used path along the back. Up ahead he focused on a roof close to the fortified wall, where it dipped from the height of three men to two. It was his plan to use the roof to reach the city wall, follow it north and drop down behind the *eduba.* But before he got there, someone called his name. Urhi.

"What a coincidence. I was on my way to see you. I have a proposition," Urhi said.

"Proposition? Not now, I'm on an errand for my mother." It was close to the truth and Takana hoped it would suffice.

"I should have said *invitation.* Look, just because we don't have practices doesn't mean we have to stop running. I'm concerned about our team, especially when I see Ras slipping and you missing altogether."

"Did I miss an announcement? Have you been promoted to wet nurse? My royal duties transcend all others. You should know that."

Urhi's upper lip twitched as it always did when he didn't know how to respond.

"Isn't this a bit out of your neighborhood? You wouldn't be spying on me, would you?"

"Well, not spying, but I have been watching for you. I make it my business to look out for our kingdom's best interests. Sometimes I wonder about your loyalty, Prince Takana."

"Loyalty? You and I could have an interesting debate on that subject. But another day." Takana could feel his irritation mounting and started to walk away.

Urhi stepped in front of him. "I'm sorry, that's not what I meant to say. We don't agree on much but I don't question your loyalty. In fact I've been watching for you because I want to suggest a special practice for our fastest runners. We must keep our skills sharp for the Coronation games. Don't you think it would be challenging to be pitted against the best of our team?"

Takana pressed his lips together. Only curiosity kept him from leaving.

"I was hoping you and Ras could meet me and a few others at first light in the wide forest clearing just beyond the north wall."

"Urhi, I'm struggling as it is to complete my duties to my mother, the royal court and . . . I don't have time for this. Move!" Takana stepped away, only to find Urhi at his side again.

"Do I have to humble myself? You are greatly respected among the runners. We look up to you, take our inspiration from you. Please come, and bring Ras with you," he said.

Takana sighed. Urhi had a look of desperation about him that softened Takana's impatience. He knew very little about Urhi, except that he was Chief Ibiranu's son— that alone deserved sympathy. On the whole, though, it was Urhi's sarcasm and posturing that caused Takana, and others, to avoid him. He managed a smile before he answered. "Well, you seem to have the team's welfare at heart, Urhi. I'll do my best. Now, may I go?"

Urhi nodded and Takana was shocked to hear him giggle like a girl as he turned his back. He seemed stranger every day.

When Urhi was out of sight, Takana climbed to the roof of the house, jumped onto the wall and followed it to the rear of the *eduba*. He heard Palla's voice when he reached the window outside the old man's office. Two other voices, ones he didn't recognize, were in the mix. One thing was certain, Palla was angry.

The argument continued and made him edgy. He was about to leave when two men, a royal guardsman and a citizen, strode out the back door and separated. Some of Palla's rebels? It would be a comfort to know who the old scribe's loyal royal guards were.

As Takana approached the back door, he collided with the old man and for a brief moment they twisted together into the building.

"Uff!" Palla said, stumbling backward. He righted himself against the door frame.

"Takana! The gods have sent you. I was just about to look for you at Yazilikaya to tell you the message for King Naram-Suen, is ready."

"I heard you arguing. Trouble?"

"Not really. Call it eagerness. Some want to move now against Setmel. But I convinced them otherwise.

"Aren't you late for the rites?"

"I know. My mother's there representing both of us, but I felt an urgency to see you."

"Is something wrong?"

"Just edgy, like something is hovering . . . I don't know exactly."

Palla walked with him to his office and closed the door. "You're not alone. All of Hattusa is unsettled and with good reason."

There was a scratching sound on the window shutters and Takana jumped.

"Pah! It's just the dry leaves. But those feelings? You may be more intuitive than you know. Perhaps what you feel is the presence of strangers."

Palla sat in the nearest chair, curled his heavily veined hands on his lap and took a settling breath. "Sit down. I have so much to tell you. I've confirmed that large groups are moving this way. Maybe they're Hittites coming for the Coronation, but there might be others with less friendly intentions. It's unnerving."

Takana jumped up. "O gods! It just occurred to me. Think of this, Master Palla. That's what turned light into dark. The Sun Goddess of Arinna was trying to warn us. I must report to the barracks. Ibiranu will be assembling the army."

Palla grabbed Takana's tunic. His eyes were burning, his body controlled but suddenly alive. "No! Leave that to others. Use this distraction to go to your uncle. This is your best chance to leave the city without raising questions. Did you tell your mother what you plan to do?"

"No, not yet." Takana's head was spinning. "No matter. My mother will agree with your strategy, I'm certain. You have the—?"

"Yes. Stay here while I find your escort."

Palla was out in the corridor before Takana could suggest that he go alone. He reasoned his chances of slipping by the army would be easier alone. But Palla, carrying a helmet and warrior's outerwear under his arm, was back with a royal guardsman in tow. He handed over the gear while introducing Gille.

Takana measured the man who stood stiffly before him. He looked vaguely familiar, perhaps they'd passed each other during royal guard activities. He matched Takana in height, but he was wiry and his body radiated energy. When their eyes met it was with tacit approval—at least for the moment.

"We should leave now. I brought horses. Tied behind the building."

Takana felt his eagerness, but the lack of information about Gille's experience gave him pause. Doubt faded when he looked back at Palla. The old master's face was lit with admiration. Somehow the guard was involved with Palla and had earned his trust. Takana forced a smile and noted the relief on Gille's face, along with an understanding of Takana's hesitancy. That kind of intuition had its own value and Takana relaxed a bit.

Palla thrust a carefully wrapped bundle at Takana.

"The tablet with my mother's letter? Tell me what it says."

Palla shook his head and edged them toward the door. "No time."

But Takana held his ground. "Someday you must teach me to read and write."

"You have no idea what it takes to be a scribe. You haven't the time. You have another calling," Palla said.

But Takana pushed the tablet forward again. "Tell me what it says."

Palla resigned himself. He peeled away the protective cloth, held the newly-baked clay tablet to the oil lamp on his desk and read aloud:

"To my esteemed brother-in-law and beloved sister: Our brother and your faithful friend, King Suldana II, has joined our ancestors in the Afterlife. Only the thought of him walking with the gods lifts our grief. Soon he will protect us from heaven as he did when he walked among us. Until then, dear family, will you lend us your strong arm? We fear Kazaram's King Amilla will strike while we are frail and absorbed in the days of mourning. Please send your forces with Prince Takana to present a united force should he attempt a strike against us. Your faithful and loving sister, Patupa."

While Palla held the tablet, Takana pulled a lightweight textile armor over his tunic, buckled on a broad sword and dagger and eased on the helmet. "Do you think we'll reach him before the Coronation?"

"I don't know, but all the more reason to go now."

Takana nodded, took the padded bundle, slipped it between his skin and tunic and signaled his readiness to Gille.

"May the gods protect both of you," Palla said, grabbing Gille's arm to emphasize his words.

Gille winced and jerked his arm away.

"Are you all right?" Palla said.

"A cut but it's healing nicely, just a bit tender."

"Let me see."

Gille raised the sleeve of his tunic to reveal a long, red gash. "It's better, almost healed, see?"

"How?"

Gille looked from Takana to Palla and back again.

"Takana knows everything I know, Gille. How did you get that wound? Trouble with Ibiranu? The royal guards? You're not leaving here until I know everything. You have a dangerous mission ahead."

"I needed blood to convince Ibiranu I'd carried out his command."

Palla understood immediately and a moment later Takana nodded. "Thank you, Gille. I'm grateful to have such loyalty at my side."

As they moved to the door, Palla stopped them. "Something just occurred to me, Gille. How will you explain your absence? Ibiranu will—"

"Don't worry. My squad leader sympathizes and will cover for me, as I would for him if the need should arise."

Palla exhaled audibly and placed his hand on his heart.

They left the *eduba*. Outside, the wind had picked up and the air was filled with rustling leaves still maintaining their grip on the overhead branches. They moved quietly through the streets, leading their horses. When they reached the first small gate, they saw that the guard was standing some distance away talking to a servant girl. They slipped through without being seen. To their relief no troops were in sight and once they reached the forest's edge they mounted and trotted side by side, using short bursts of conversation to decide on an obscure route to Luwadna Land. Gille, it seemed, was already briefed about their purpose. What else did this royal guard know?

"Have you heard if Ibiranu is rallying the army?" Takana said.

"Yes, and you feel you should be with them."

"To be honest, it crossed my mind."

"You're doing the best for Hatti by going to King Naram-Suen," Gille said, spurring his horse.

Takana's curiosity increased with Gille's authoritative tone. If not for his total confidence in Palla's judgment, he might have felt some resentment. But he set his questions aside and gave Gille the leadership the young guard clearly felt was his. They rode hard, staying parallel but clear of roads and avoiding contact with people. Before long the Sun Goddess would sleep and a merciful moon would provide shelter for their journey. Takana imagined the army, supplemented by the royal guard, was busy gathering people within the walls and sending search parties beyond the city. It was the latter they needed to avoid. His mouth opened to share the thought with Gille, but changed his mind. Why tell him something he would know? Humility didn't come easy but Takana knew its value.

The forest opened up a few miles from Hattusa. They entered the rich farmland that supplied fruits, vegetables and spices almost year round and supported large herds of cattle, woolly lambs, goats, pigs and several types of game. Takana thought he smelled apples and his stomach twisted with hunger. He spurred his horse and came alongside Gille.

"We have a long ride ahead of us. Let's pick some apples."

Gille reached behind and lifted a pouch from inside a folded cloak. "Take what you need, I've eaten."

Without looking, Takana reached inside and pulled out a handful of nuts and dates, standard traveling food for soldiers, although the ration was greater than normal. Gille, he decided, had planned for both of them.

Gille looked back and laughed at Takana's cheeks, stuffed like a squirrel's.

Thunder sounded and both men searched the sky. But it wasn't an approaching storm. It was the pounding hooves of horses. Takana's reaction was to move deeper into the forest, but Gille restrained him.

"They've already seen us." Before the soldiers reached them, Gille shouted. "Squad Leader, we've seen no one. What about you?"

The leader's face went rapidly from suspicion to surprise. He came to a stop. The soldiers, well behind their leader, kept their distance but slowly fanned out around Takana and Gille. Their horses snorted and sidestepped. Gille nodded greetings to soldiers he recognized and Takana breathed easier.

"Prince Takana! I wasn't told the royal guard had deployed scouts ahead of us." A frown was etched between the dark eyebrows that formed a shelf over his deep-set eyes.

Gille inched his horse forward. "Excuse me, Prince Takana." He turned to the squad leader. "The royal guard doesn't need permission from the army to fulfill its mission. I have been instructed to escort Prince Takana to his uncle, King Naram-Suen, to garner the support of Luwandan forces to protect us during the days of mourning. We are not to engage the enemy but to go directly to Luwanda." At that point Gille smiled broadly and moved even closer. "In my opinion, squad leader, these divisions between royal guard and soldier mean little when the kingdom is in danger, so I am glad to share information with you. We've been traveling the forest edge from the east side of the city to this point and we've seen no one."

"Very well. Safe journey." He nodded to Gille. "You might mention the value of shared information to your chief. May the gods protect us." The squad leader bent his head respectfully and waved to his men. In moments the soldiers were back on the road, disappearing behind a wall of dust.

"I'm beginning to understand Palla's confidence in you," Takana said.

"Actually, wouldn't you have been disappointed if we hadn't been stopped by our warriors?" Gille's face became stern. "I'm more concerned about the area beyond the hills ahead. The Luwadnans will be as protective of their land as we are of ours. When they question us, *you* will be the one to answer." He nudged his horse forward.

"Wait!" Takana moved to his side. "When he gets back to the barracks, Ibiranu will know our mission."

"No, he won't. The squad leader is one of Master Palla's faithful. He will cover for us, and the others couldn't hear what we were saying."

Gille was a puzzle to Takana. True, he'd been away in Harmesh for two years and his visits to Hattusa rarely included contact with the royal guard or the army. His assignment in Harmesh excused him from duties in the capital city, and Gille, to his knowledge, had never brought messages to the vassal state where he and his mother lived. Perhaps he was the son of a powerful citizen. Or maybe his father was an officer in the army. Whatever the case, Gille already had proved his intelligence and the ability to apply it effectively.

Daylight was receding rapidly. They moved out onto the road where a sliver of pearly moon provided illumination. It appeared that decades of carts shuttling commercial trade between settlements and chariots carrying the wealthy had polished the surface until it shone like a silk ribbon. Narrow footpaths paralleled the road on either side, marked occasionally with piles of rocks whose purposes were long forgotten.

Takana watched the moon peeking at them through the trees. He felt the presence of the Moon God Arma and quickly acknowledged her place in the pantheon of Hittite gods. Although weaker than the great Storm God, her traveling companion was a lion, and Takana gave thanks for them. He asked her to sweep away any clouds in their path so she would not lose sight of them until she was certain the Sun Goddess of Arinna could take her place as their guardian. His tension drained away in the soft moonlight and he moved his horse alongside Gille.

"It's been years and I was very young," Takana said, "but I seem to remember higher ground not far from here."

"Foothills. We'll spend the night east of the higher rises to avoid routes that might be used by the Kazaramites, who are not our friends."

But blood relatives to some, Takana thought.

CHAPTER ELEVEN
THE FIFTH DAY OF MOURNING

The High Priest of the Storm God prays.
"O Gods of the Heavens, O Departed King Suldana. We offer hot
loaves for breaking, wine for toasting. See King Suldana's image
formed with figs, olives and raisins. Enter our presence."

TAKANA

Takana woke as the stars faded. The sky overhead was cloudless, still an ash gray. At the higher elevation frost clung to the few shriveled leaves and grasses that gathered in clumps on the hardened ground. No tall trees grew in the area, only low slung oak, stunted by long winters and thrashing wind. He got up, rubbing his side where a rock had made its mark while he slept, too tired to move. Gille jumped up and pulled his sword before he saw Takana standing. His sheepish grin made Takana laugh. At the same time he was grateful for Gille's reflexes. They quickly checked their horses, shared some nuts and dates and left the area.

For what seemed an endless time, they climbed rise after rise and descended into grassy meadows with swift running streams. Surprisingly, not even a rabbit scrambled away from their intrusion, a potential problem if they needed to hunt for food. Occasionally, in the distance, lamplight suggested a cluster of homes. It reassured Takana that perhaps one of the rural farming communities would offer the opportunity to replenish their food supply when Gille's pouch emptied.

Gille slowed his mount until they were side by side. "See that line of tall trees in the far distance?"

"Probably follows a stream."

"That's what I'm thinking. It'd be good to reach it before dark and build a lean-to. The air carries the smell of rain.

Takana sniffed, but only the fragrance of sun-warmed grass filled his nostrils. He followed Gille at a quickened pace and in the absence of conversation, he fell into speculation. What was happening in Hattusa? How soon would they meet up with his Luwadnan uncle and what reaction would he have to their request? But neither of these mind wanderings brought any satisfaction to his curiosity or worry. He concentrated, instead, on the landscape, remembering Master Palla's reminder to be alert. But though the tall grass, huge clusters of boulders and evergreen trees might provide opportunity for an ambush, he soon fell into the rhythm of his horse and relaxed.

By the time shadows lengthened, they reached the stream and hobbled the horses so they could graze close by. They built a lean-to with branches cut from a few of the smaller trees, exchanging few words as they worked together. Takana found himself enjoying the guard's company as one shared task was added to another. But then Gille began to gather firewood.

"Wait! Should we call attention to ourselves?"

"You mean by building a fire? We've nothing to hide from anyone. We are on our way to visit King Naram-Suen to seek his support."

Takana's face flushed momentarily. "I guess the tensions in Hattusa are still with me," he said, but Gille had turned toward the stream.

"I'd like a fish supper. How about you?"

Takana was about to ask how that could be managed, when Gille pulled a length of string from one tunic pocket and a carved bone hook from another. "See if you can find a stout branch about the length of your arm," he said over his shoulder.

Moments later, supplied with a branch, Gille fastened the string to it and shoved it into the soft ground. Then he proceeded to kick up the damp earth until he bent down and pulled a worm from a clump and fastened it to the hook. He tossed the hook and string into the deepest part of the stream.

Takana laughed. "I don't remember that from warrior training."

"No, I learned to do this long before training. When you're hungry enough, you learn to feed yourself."

Takana wanted to probe but thought better of it.

Three cooked and consumed fish later, Takana and Gille stretched out next to the fire. On their first night together, followed by the long distance they'd just covered, there had been little conversation. Takana assumed Gille enjoyed silence. Besides, the result was a relaxation of his own tensions. But the fire and the end of a long second day produced feelings of fellowship, and he decided to attempt some conversation. He'd know soon enough if his traveling companion preferred silence.

"If you're not too tired, I'd like to hear about how you learned to fish."

Gille studied Takana's face for several moments before he nodded. "I was about ten complete seasons and an orphan." He sat up straight and held his hands to the fire. "One day my parents were with me, the next . . . I never knew what happened to them."

Takana took a moment to imagine what that must have been like. Even when he lost his father, he had his strong, capable mother. And then there was King Suldana . . . "Other family?"

Gille shook his head. "We lived far from other people. I've come to believe my father liked it that way—independent. He taught me how to take care of myself. I've sometimes thought maybe he knew I'd need to know someday." He added a log to the fire.

"How did you end up in Hattusa?"

"I was caught stealing." He turned to see Takana's reaction before continuing. "The people I stole from didn't take me to the Magistrate. I guess they felt sorry for me. But they put me to work, hard work. I proved my value so well they recommended me to a friend in the army when I was fifteen. I worked my way into the royal guard the same way, showing them what I could do. I've been in the royal guard for six years."

"A hard life," Takana said, taking in the fact that Gille was a year older than he was.

"A satisfying life. Serving King Suldana was an honor. I hate what's happening now. I know you agree or we wouldn't be on our way to King Naram-Suen. What about you? I know you've been in Harmesh. Do you have a wife there?"

"Wife! No!"

Gille smiled and gave Takana a sideways look, which Takana took as a tease. If there had ever been a barrier between them, it had just been breached. He was enjoying the conversation. But wife? The question burned and his memory raced back to Harmesh, to Elin. He'd spoken to no one about her, but somehow the stars overhead, the sound of the stream, the rustle of leaves and the feeling of anonymity with Gille loosened his tongue.

"What do you do when you meet someone you can never have?"

"You're a prince. You can have whoever you want."

"Come on, now, you know how it works. My mother will choose a wife for me. Besides Elin, a woman I met in Harmesh, is a peasant girl and I'm stuck with having to marry someone royal."

"Oh, well, with that reasoning I'm stuck with having to marry a peasant girl, so we're even."

"Reasoning? It's the law, sent to us from the gods. I believe they know what's best for us."

They fell silent. Takana stared into the fire's embers long after Gille started to snore, evidently not the least bit bothered by The Law or The Gods. As for him, he was wide awake and surprised at the depth of his excitement at the mention of Elin. Now, he couldn't think of anything else and asked the gods to forgive his weakness. Finally, he edged her out of his mind by thinking of Queen Resat and what foul deeds were fermenting in her head. He fell asleep hoping Gille was right when he said his mission to Luwadna was the best he could do for Hatti.

CHAPTER TWELVE

THE SIXTH DAY OF MOURNING

High Priest of the Storm God prays.
"Spirits of Heaven, the house of stone is ready.
The couch to hold our king's bones is ready. We light the lamp
with our finest oil,
and we offer an ox and a sheep to the honor of
our beloved King Suldana II."

TAKANA

"Are we still in Hatti Land?" Takana asked midmorning the next day.

"For at least three more suns. Why do you ask?"

"Master Palla believed my uncle would have left Luwanda as soon as word spread of King Suldana's failing health. I think today is the Sixth Day of Mourning. I just hope we can get back to Hattusa for the Crowning."

Gille abruptly pulled his broad sword from its sheath and slowed his horse.

"What is it?" Takana said, shifting around to see.

Suddenly, as they moved around an outcropping of rock, a dozen cavalry men came barreling toward them. Luwadnan warriors! Swords, helmets, harnesses and buckles flashed in the morning sun. In moments they were completely surrounded and Takana braced himself as arrows were pulled from quills. He threw up his hands.

"I am Hittite Prince Takana, nephew to King Naram-Suen," he shouted. When no one moved, he shouted again. "I bring an urgent message from my mother, Queen Patupa." Still, no one moved. He glanced quickly at Gille, but there was no facial message. Was he indicating his complete confidence or something else? Takana nodded, remembering Gille's earlier words: *The Luwadnans will be your problem.*

A horse moved behind him and Takana turned.

"What proof do you have?" a soldier said, coming closer.

Takana looked into a scarred face, cold eyes and a formidable body. His quiver held arrows with serrated metal tips and sent a chill up Takana's spine. Any attempt to remove such an arrow would mangle a man's flesh irreparably. The soldier's black hair hung to his shoulders and was threaded with silver. He needed to convince this seasoned warrior quickly.

"Here, this is the message for your king," Takana said with force. "Must I waste time with a history lesson? Our two kingdoms are bound together by blood and treaty. My mother is your queen's sister! Your king's sister-in-law! I am your king's nephew! Let us pass quickly, our message is urgent."

The officer seemed unimpressed by Takana's speech. He took his time searching the etchings on the tablet, though Takana doubted he could read. Finally his eyes rested on the official seal at the bottom. He looked up with a friendly smile, returned the tablet and nodded."We will see you safely to our king."

The squad leader rode ahead, six others flanked Gille and Takana and the rest followed behind. When they crested the hill, the land sloped downward gradually and soon they left the high meadowland behind. Huge round boulders dotted the landscape, some piled as high as a house. Within a few moments low-slung tents became visible as far as his eyes could see.

They rode slowly among the boulders and tents, watched by heavily armored soldiers who stopped their tasks to watch them pass. Up ahead the squad leader stood at attention while a tent flap swung open. The soldiers dismounted and fell to their knees as King Naram-Suen and Queen Alina emerged with wide, welcoming smiles. Takana dismounted and knelt, but the queen reached for him. She looked like a slightly older version of his mother.

"My darling boy, how wonderful to see you again," she said, raising him with her hands on his shoulders. "You've become a man! Could it be so long since our last meeting?" She threw her arms around Takana's neck before he stretched to his full height. Gille, at his side, remained on his knees, looking sideways with a grin.

"Welcome to Luwadna Land, Prince Takana," the king said. His voice seemed to bounce off the boulders and Takana dropped to his knees again. "We wish your mother could have come with you," he said, directing him to rise. Unlike his aunt's spontaneous affection, the king placed his hand on Takana's shoulder and studied his face. "You've come with urgency, I think, eh? Come, sit with us." He led the way back through the tent flap.

Takana followed his aunt and uncle inside the tent, but not before he took a quick backward glance at Gille.

He seemed to have quickly made himself at home and was walking away with the small squad of warriors.

Aside from rich fabrics on the sleeping pallet, the tent's contents were sparse. There were cushions tossed about and it was to these the Luwadnan king guided Takana. Two men stood in the far corner of the tent—one held a tablet, the king's scribe. The queen turned to the other man and ordered drinks before she sat. Then their eyes, full of anticipation, fastened on him. Takana swallowed. Everything depended on him now and he said a prayer to the Almighty Storm God that his words would convince his uncle of their need. The queen was talking to him, asking about his mother, her health, and his schooling. Takana responded until he could no longer hold back.

"Our king is dead! We hear warriors may be on their way to Hattusa! We fear an attack while we are in mourning!" Takana said without breathing.

King Naram-Suen pulled his cloak over his legs and searched his wife's face before speaking.

"We are on our way to you with all good intentions, my boy." The king's words were spoken with a smile. "Be assured of our support."

Takana quickly nodded and felt heat rise on his neck. "Forgive me. Hatti is grateful to have you as our ally. Our concerns lie elsewhere."

"Yes, we want to help in any way necessary," the king said, as a servant set three filled cups on a small wooden plank. "But, as to your sad news, we had hoped to arrive in time to say our farewell, but . . . We've been on our way for fifteen suns, but still too late. I'm sorry."

The queen hung her head and the king encircled her waist with his arm before he continued. "We continually lift prayers to our gods for your king and for your people, nephew." He shook his head slowly side to side. "We grieve knowing we will not see him again until our own time comes. Of course we accept we must be ready to face the Underworld at any age, yet he should have had many more seasons."

"I prayed that the gods would not let him suffer," Queen Alina said.

"He was at peace. My mother and I arrived from Harmesh just in time to see him whisper some words to Hapati, but then he closed his eyes for the last time. The *hasawa* assured us everything had been tried. He left us in peace, I'm sure of it."

"Thank you."

Takana pulled the tablet from under his tunic and the king beckoned to his scribe, a young man whose squinty eyes darted up and down the tablet before he read aloud. When he finished he quickly tucked it under his arm and retreated to the corner.

"The Tablet speaks of Kazaram's King Amilla. But that's laughable! They have no chance against the combined might of Hittite and Luwadnan forces," the king said. His eyes danced at the thought. "Are these the concerns you speak of?"

"Uncle, there are many in the kingdom who are opposed to the *tuhkanti* and—"

"Are you and my sister safe?" The queen's voice quavered.

"There's great unrest among the people. Many fear the kind of king Setmel will be but for now we're fine. Some members of the royal guard have pledged allegiance to Master Palla. They watch over us."

"Palla, the master scribe? I remember him well. My brother loved and trusted him for his wise counsel," Queen Alina said.

"As I recall his interests always reached well beyond the *eduba,* but he is long past leadership, I think."

"You might think so," Takana said, "but there is fire in his belly for Hatti. He sees forces inside and outside that threaten our kingdom. Many of the royal guardsmen want no part of what's happening in the acropolis. They remain loyal to the course set by our King Suldana. When Setmel takes the throne, those loyal to the *tawananna*—soldiers and other high-ranking officials—will set neighbor against neighbor. And it won't stop at our borders, I fear. All of the mutual benefit of trade relations and peace will be swept away by their ambitions. That's why Master Palla sent me to you."

The king was suddenly animated. He set his cup on the table absently and it rolled to the ground. The servant sprang forward to retrieve it. "I see. If Kazaram, by some miracle, joined forces with power hungry Hittites . . . But you said you have other concerns? You may speak freely without worry of being overheard." He pursed his lips thoughtfully and shook his head. "You said forces within and without threaten the kingdom."

"Evil! There's no other word for it. Hatti is besieged by evil!" Takana could feel his heart beating in his ears. His goal, he repeated to himself, was to assure Luwadna's military support, but suddenly—whether it was the effect of their unconditional love or because of his pent up anxiety—he could no longer hold back. Palla's caution to guard secrets flashed in his mind, but Takana saw no danger in revealing everything he knew. In fact, he believed such knowledge would strengthen his uncle's desire to help. "Many fearful things have happened in the capital since the king's death."

The queen motioned to her servant to refill Takana's cup. "Please, dear one, you must unburden yourself. Drink! Calm yourself. Then tell us everything. All of Luwanda is at your disposal."

Takana drank and wiped his mouth with his hand. The look of concern on the faces of his aunt and uncle touched him to his core. Without a spoken word from them, Takana's tension dissolved and in its place was a sense of security he hadn't felt in a very long time. He wanted to share all he knew with his family. "I thank the gods for Master Palla," Takana began. "He has uncovered shocking evidence of evil deeds."

For the next few moments, Takana recounted Hapati's reported treason and execution and his ultimate rescue.

The queen's hand flew to her mouth and the king frowned. But before either of them could comment, Takana told them what Master Palla had uncovered regarding Prince Setmel's parentage."

The king was first to recover from the shock. He became thoughtful and said: "I believe I understand why the Sun Goddess closed her warm and watchful eyes. Such deeds! Punishment will fall like rain!" He fell silent again but his eyes darted back and forth and Takana imagined his mind was sorting out the steps that must be taken to make things right in the Hittite Kingdom. Takana knew Master Palla and everyone in the realm would welcome such help.

Suddenly, the king's face reddened and he rubbed his hands together. "That poisonous viper! Her ambitions pose a danger to all—not just the Hittite Kingdom but the entire region! If not stopped, the *tawananna* has the power to accomplish our worst nightmare."

They sat quietly. Only the sound of the king's hands rubbing together as he sat staring from the tent walls to Takana's face. "My boy, have you not considered that *you* might be the king's choice?"

Takana bounced on his cushion. "No. I'm not ready for such a position. I believe the king saw promise in me and that's why he sent me to Harmesh. Would he have done that if he thought I was ready? No, no, once this mess is cleared up and Setmel and the queen are exposed, the High Priest of the Storm God will speak for the gods and we will have a divine choice for the throne."

"A divine choice . . . Yes, this is how it will be." The king rose and shouted to the royal guard standing by the door. "Send for the Chief of the Royal Guard and take our guests to a tent where they can rest.

"My boy, for many suns we have been aware of King Amilla's army. They have been west of us and I'm sure they are tracking us as well. So you see he already knows better than to make foolish moves. The danger lies in his troops merging with others. We leave at first light."

As the encampment welcomed a new day, sounds of men and horses on the move wakened Takana and Gille. They received fresh clothing and servants delivered wine, platters of cheese, olives, a variety of fruits and steaming bread on a long plank. Gille's eyes, not yet completely opened, popped at the sight. Neither spoke until the wine was gone and the platters nearly empty, except for the handfuls of nuts and fruit Gille stuffed into his pouch. He gave Takana a sheepish grin.

The appearance of a guard brought them both to attention. "King Naram-Suen is ready," he announced.

Takana leaned close to Gille. "How many soldiers are here?"

Gille shrugged.

They followed the guard through a wide path between the tents. Even before they reached an area enclosed by boulders higher than a man, the sounds of eager men and horses was swelling.

The king shouted above the din. "I have sent a messenger ahead to King Amilla. His notice of my imminent arrival will raise a rash on his skin. By the time we arrive, he will have scratched himself raw," he said, laughing at the image in his head. He threw his leg across the back of a dark stallion. Silver medallions attached to the horse's leather reins flashed in the sunlight and he led the way.

A warrior walked forward with Takana and Gille's horses. They'd been cleaned and brushed. Their tails had been braided and their stiff black manes tied in bunches. The flourishes completely changed their appearance. Takana thought they held their heads higher than before. The idea made him smile and he lowered his head to hide it.

Looking at the mounted men, Takana wondered if they were not underestimating King Amilla. Surely, the *tawananna* would have sent him word of the king's death. It would be a signal to prepare his strike, if that was her intent. His heart thumped suddenly. Of course that was her intent! He had no doubt of it. Perhaps King Amilla was already surrounding Hattusa. Why had he not thought of this before?

"Uncle," Takana said, moving alongside, "what if the Kazaramites are already surrounding Hattusa?

The king twisted and faced Takana. "They haven't. While you slept, half of my army moved ahead. They will stay out of sight and await my orders to proceed to Hattusa, if necessary."

How were these messages conveyed with such speed and over such distances? He longed to know and tucked away the question for another time. Takana looked at Gille, who rode slightly behind him. His companion's eyes were busy observing everything. Takana's heart beat even faster and his muscles tightened. War! And he was in the midst of it, surrounded by King Naram-Suen's army. Why weren't the horses charging ahead instead of their steady walk? But as he glanced at the controlled expression of the king's face and body, he took a deep breath and followed his lead. If he did not feel the king's calm, at least he could pretend. But before long the calm had worked its way through his body, and Takana realized the king's posture had not only affected him, it sent a message to his warriors. *I, your king, am confident. I know exactly what must be done. Place your faith in me and follow.*

King Naram-Suen was the kind of leader he wished to be.

CHAPTER THIRTEEN
THE SEVENTH DAY OF MOURNING

The hasawa prays.
"Ancestral Spirits, Allani, hear our prayers and incantations.
Hear our music. Bless King Suldana II as he approaches."

PALLA

Palla did not attend the fifth and sixth days of mourning. His conscience pricked but he felt driven by increasing dread. Now, with the dawn of the seventh day, he prepared to visit the settlements outside Hattusa. He wouldn't be missed. Abundant feasting attracted bigger crowds each day. Still he hoped he would return in time to make an appearance before the rites concluded. And in case someone inquired, he left word at the *eduba* he would be examining potential students outside the city. That was not his primary intent but one that would satisfy the curious.

As he left the city behind, he rehearsed the qualifications he'd set over the years. Competition for the coveted career was fierce for boys of every economic level, yet the sons of wealthy families held the advantage. Their language skills, a necessary qualification, outstripped the sons of the poor who had little exposure to commerce and little or no social refinement. But sophisticated language alone did not qualify them. They needed to display endurance and sufficient dexterity to wield the wedge-shaped stylus required for cuneiform. Most boys, unfortunately, were returned to their homes in disgrace within the first few weeks.

Those who remained received the old scribe's intense scrutiny. The proficient progressed to copying religious texts and great literary classics like the epic of Gilgamesh. They learned not only Nesite, the official Hittite language, but also Akkadian, the international language of diplomacy. As their cuneiform progressed, Palla added instruction in the cultural traditions of Hittite society. Finally, he tested their integrity and dedication to duty by sending each student away on an internship. His methods were successful. He had every reason to believe parents would be eagerly waiting for his arrival.

Palla wished he had equal confidence in the other reason for visiting the villages. The time had come to rally the support of the village leaders in the event of a rebellion following the *tuhkanti's* crowning. Over the years he'd heard murmurs of opposition against Prince Setmel and the queen, not only in Hattusa but in the surrounding villages. Palla did his best to keep them informed and they said they trusted him. Now he would test that trust. Now he'd explain the steps he'd taken with organizing sympathetic members of the royal guard. Now was the time he needed to know the amount of silver shekels and the numbers of men their village would commit.

Palla rode five miles outside Hattusa and made a wide circle to visit three of the largest villages. By late afternoon he stopped to feed his horse and review his findings. First, there was no shortage of eager young men aspiring to be scribes. And, second, he was gratified to know manpower and resources were available. He mounted his horse to visit one more settlement before heading home.

The surrounding hills turned persimmon in the setting sun. Between the long shadows, the warm sun caressed the old scribe as he led his horse to the road. Buoyed by success, he increased his mare's pace and soon approached a familiar tavern at the edge of the village. He waved a greeting to three familiar men seated together. They returned his wave but not the smile he sent their way. Was he unwelcome? He prepared himself for a challenge.

"Stirring things up, we hear," one man said, as Palla approached a weather-beaten table.

The old scribe pursed his lips and surveyed their faces. He'd dealt many times with these men—two were merchants, the other a farmer. "Do you have spies in every village?" He spoke with good humor, hoping to see a change in their expressions.

"Better," the farmer said. "We have *business* in every village. You speak of fearful things, Master Palla, and such speeches make the people nervous."

Palla pulled a stool close and leaned in. "As we've discussed before, if the *tawananna* and *tuhkanti* have their way, our kingdom will change in ways that should frighten each one of us, our wives, sons and daughters."

"Get to your point. We understand the dangers. A rebellion, eh?" The deep voice belonged to a copper mine owner.

"I'm sure of it. The time for thinking and anticipating is over. I've gathered forces in the city, but we need every

Hittite who will act to protect the kingdom. So I ask you, how many men are willing?"

"A better question would be: Who has nothing to lose and who has too much to lose? Our wealthy citizens believe it best to wait until Setmel is on the throne, to let the natural succession take place," the copper mine owner said. He spoke slowly, aware of his authority, of the power he wielded.

"I tend to this view myself," said the other merchant, a dealer in metals. "Perhaps the weight of the crown will give the *tuhkanti* the courage to silence his mother. God knows she has pulled his strings long enough. My bet is he's sick of it. Can you say such an eventuality is impossible?"

Palla turned to face the farmer, a man he'd met on many occasions and knew to be strongly opinionated.

"I see your points," the farmer said to his friends. "I might even agree with you if I sat in an office with a door closed until someone came carrying a bulging purse. But I see the young men who work the fields to provide food for their families. They need us and we need them. With Setmel, I'm convinced our young men will be snapped up for the army. You've heard the same stories I have about his cruelty. His mother doesn't ride with him; he makes his own way in the skirmishes along the borders. Let your purses deny that."

Before Palla spoke he let the three men toss their thoughts back and forth until he understood every nuance. When they quieted, he said: "Not one of you has been successful without careful planning, is that not so?"

"Ha, it took me a year to sign a contract for your copper," the metals dealer said to the miner.

Palla stood up, placed his hands on the table and moved his face as close to the three as possible. When the three men likewise closed the distance between them, Palla whispered: "Then let us be prepared. Let us be ready to protect our future. Let us dedicate ourselves to Hatti, our sustainer. Will you gather the men and be ready if Hattusa is threatened?"

The men breathed a deep sigh as they nodded, their jaws clenched and their eyes shone with steely determination. Palla was grateful for such men.

It was dark when he steered his horse toward the eastern wall of Hattusa and then turned sharply north on the road to Yazilikaya. He wished he could give Takana and Gille the good news about support in the outlying villages. As soon as he could he'd pass the same encouraging news along to the royal guards who were in harm's way under Ibiranu.

Once inside the sacred grounds his thoughts turned to King Suldana II. The funeral rites were winding down. He left his horse with a guard and took a seat at the nearest table. The *mešedi* were lifting the king's oiled bones onto several large brass trays. They formed a single line and walked up the black steps carved into the *hekur*-house where King Suldana II would be laid to rest. Behind them were the High Priest of the Storm God, the *hasawa*, the *tawananna*, Prince Setmel and Queen Patupa. Palla, unable to enter, closed his eyes and imagined the prescribed ritual.

In his mind's eye he saw the *mešedi* use silver tongs to place the bones on a couch prepared in the tomb where the king was laid to rest. A lamp with fine oil was placed before the bones. An ox and a sheep were offered to the soul of the dead. While all stood by, the Old Woman offered prayers and incantations and then led the procession from the tomb. Women began wailing. Horns and drums played a slow dirge while servants carried a final serving of food from table to table.

Palla walked quietly back to his horse, feeling the exhaustion of his travels. But as he passed the gate to the funeral grounds, someone called his name.

"Master Palla, my lady Queen Patupa is desperate to see you. I have looked everywhere for you. See, there," he said pointing, "she is leaving. She will await you at the acropolis."

In sympathy for the young servant, Palla handed him a coin with the promise that he would go immediately. He knew his horse was tired so he kept a slow but steady pace. Along the cobbled streets a few merchants remained, clearing away their wares, tying down tent flaps and loading carts and asses for the trip to their homes or drinking establishments. Women and children had long since returned home to prepare for the evening meal. Palla, too, yearned to be home with Inara.

Queen Patupa's summons was no surprise. In fact he'd been expecting it, knowing Takana hadn't prepared her for his departure. He braced for the sting of her anger and fear. He felt suddenly heavy and weak, or—May the gods forbid!—guilty of placing everyone in grave danger. What if he'd miscalculated or exaggerated the dangers? What if word of his plotting behind the scenes had reached the *tawananna*? How could he approach her in his present state of mind? How could he help her when he felt uncertain? Should something else be done? No, he knew fear clutched the throats of many citizens. He could only hope the plans he'd set in motion were the right ones. To bolster his courage, he spoke out loud, "I am a citizen of a great kingdom. O gods, protect your people and give me strength."

When he entered the apartment Queen Patupa was sitting in a straight-backed wooden chair. His guilt deepened at the sight of her. At the rites, she had worn a hooded robe. Now he could see she was gaunt and frazzled. A patterned wool blanket was tucked around her legs. Her eyes were swollen and bloodshot. Her thick, black braid of hair had lost its shape and shine. She threw the wool aside, jumped up and walked forward, pointing her finger. "My son is missing. I've been out of my mind with worry. I know he's been in contact with you so you must know something. We're already uneasy because of Hapati's execution, and now my son . . . Do you know anything?"

"There was no time to tell you. Takana felt sure you would understand, as did I."

"What? What am I supposed to understand? Have you put him in danger?"

"Your son is a loyal Hittite and he is on a mission of great importance. He and I both knew you would agree our kingdom is worth any sacrifice."

"So, you admit you've sent him away. Where?" She sat down, whether from exhaustion or surrender, Palla didn't know.

Two servants moved forward to attend her but she waved them away. They looked at Palla and, with long practiced sensitivity, read his tacit message, nodded and left the room.

Palla took a seat next to her. For a brief moment he considered telling her Hapati was safe and about the steps he'd taken to protect her brother's legacy. She, after all, was strong and politically astute. But he decided against revealing such details. She was a woman and needed to be protected. In time she would understand everything. "He has gone to your sister and brother-in-law, King Naram-Suen. I've known for some time they were on their way to Hattusa, so it's possible they are already together."

Her shoulders relaxed somewhat but something in her eyes gave him pause. This was a woman who'd lost her husband, sensed their future was in jeopardy and escaped to assure the safety of her son. Now he was endangered again. How could Palla know the present state of her mind? He watched her face change, saw the tilt of her chin and read strength, even aggression, despite her weary eyes.

"There's reason to believe Kazaram might strike us while we mourn our king," Palla said.

Her eyes widened momentarily but then registered understanding. "Just tell me Takana is not alone, Palla."

"With a trusted and able guide and defender," Palla assured her. "Very soon, if not already, he will be in your sister's safe, loving arms. King Naram-Suen will know exactly what to do. He will honor his treaty with us. Amilla may be hungry for power, but he's not stupid. Your son carried a letter from you to ask King Naram-Suen to warn Kazaram of the consequences of interfering with Hatti."

"What? From me? Without my seal? You are bold, Palla, bold indeed." She walked to a cabinet, opened a small box and pulled out a cylinder seal. "Ha! Very bold." She waved the cylinder in the air. "You used a counterfeit seal, didn't you?" She threw up her hands. "Oh, well, no matter. I understand the necessity."

"Just as your son said you would."

The worry had not left her deep brown eyes but her pride was palpable. She understood loyalty to her country. And, though Palla recognized her instinct to protect Takana, the time had come for her to accept his growing independence and she knew it. Leadership and courage were his birthright, after all. Whether he tested himself now or at some future challenge, it was inevitable.

"When do you suppose he'll return?" she asked. Palla opened his mouth but hesitated when she took a deep breath. "Takana will return for the Coronation. I'm certain of it."

"Yes, that would be my hope," he said. Again he noted the thrust of her chin and pressed forward. "Queen Patupa, your brother was greatly loved by all in Hatti Land and not least of all by me. I know you've heard there is concern about the *tuhkanti's* ability to rule."

She nodded.

"I fear a rebellion among the people," Palla said.

"What? To overthrow Setmel?" she said.

"Yes, it grows even in the outlying villages."

"It will be crushed by the royal guard and the army. Queen Resat would see to it." She shimmied forward in her chair, sparkling with excitement. "That is unless you have a sufficient rebel force. Do you? And who would take the throne?"

"If joined by the Luwandnans, I believe we have. As to your other question, all I can say is I have confidence in the Hittite people."

"I've been selfish. I've prayed only that my son was safe. Now I will send my prayers to the gods, asking that power be sent to our people."

Again, the old man considered, and then decided against telling her what he knew about the queen's fornication and Setmel's true parentage. All would be known soon, he reasoned.

Palla rode along the streets to the *eduba*. He paused to let his horse drink at a well while he recalled his conversation with Queen Patupa. What still troubled him was that others—the *tawananna*, Ibiranu and King Amilla—were shaping their own agendas. Of the three, the queen was key and she was unpredictable. As *tawananna*, she could call on the royal guard and the army if she suspected any threats against her son or disruption of the Coronation. Spies were well paid and abundant.

Kazaramite spies surely reported King Suldana II's death. What if the Kazaramite army launched a surprise attack during the Days of Mourning without the *tawananna's* knowledge? It might be just the kind of show King Amilla would love to perform, not only for the chance of success but to impress the queen. Palla's head was spinning with doubts again. His reunion with his wife would have to wait.

He approached the *eduba*, noticing a light coming through the window shutter in his office. Palla tied his horse in the back, walked around to the lighted window and peered inside. His assistant, Brocas, had a man by the shoulders and was shaking him violently. Palla jumped back briefly to consider what would elicit behavior he'd never seen before from his assistant. Brocas was a quiet, patient teacher, who handled unruly boys with ease while performing his duties with precision and thoroughness. He was unflappable.

He pushed the shutter open and leaned in. Brocas was startled but he moved to the window without loosening his grip on Mutwalli. Suddenly Palla recognized the face of the former student he'd suggested to Gille for Ibiranu's dirty work.

Brocas, with Mutwalli in tow, opened the door. "Master Palla, I've wondered all day if you'd returned."

Mutwalli yanked himself loose and ran for the door, but Brocas dove for him and set his knee on the man's back, pinning him to the floor until he had a firm grip on his arm.

"I heard him bragging in the courtyard about how he'd served as Prince Setmel's scribe, how he was going to be a wealthy man and live in the palace."

Mutwalli scowled and stamped hard on Brocas' foot. Brocas reacted by lifting him off his feet in a bear hug. Mutwalli's legs flailed like a roach set on its back.

Palla went to a corner cupboard and pulled out a length of rope. Together, they tied Mutwalli tightly to a chair in the schoolroom and the old scribe spoke for the first time.

"Now, tell me what this is all about. You've already succeeded in showing me a side of you I never knew existed."

Brocas laughed. "You've never spoken to my sons. Can we go in another room? Don't move, Mutwalli, I'm not done with you."

Behind the closed door of the adjacent room, Brocas said: "He's already told me he made a tablet for Ibiranu. But I want to know why he thinks Prince Setmel is going to reward him."Brocas cracked the door enough to see Mutwalli struggling ineffectively against the rope.

"I don't think Setmel knows anything about it. It's the queen's doing," Palla whispered. "Her lackey ordered Gille to find him a scribe to forge King Suldana's final Proclamation. Gille knew none of our enrolled scribes would perform such a task, but he had to follow Ibiranu's orders. I recommended Mutwalli because I suspected he'd be willing to break the rules. May the gods take pity on his weakness and on me for placing him in temptation's way.

"Actually, Brocas, he's to be pitied. He did well here at the *eduba* until I sent him to do a business contract for a young businessman who couldn't afford his own scribe. Mutwalli disgraced himself by touching the man's young son. Mutwalli swore the boy seduced him. Nothing could be proved so the town's magistrate let him go. When Mutwalli returned to the *eduba*, I overheard him recounting his 'encounter' and I dismissed him."

Wonder showed in Brocas' eyes, and he headed for the classroom. "I want to know what's on the tablet."

"No! No! No! Go no further! You have done well to reprimand Mutwalli for the forgery. Disgraceful behavior, to be sure, but forget the rest for my sake. Such knowledge could be a danger to you."

Brocas agreed hesitantly and followed the old man back into the schoolroom where he untied Mutwalli.

"You," Palla said, pointing, "are a disgrace! You know the rules of the *eduba*: Only a graduate may act as a scribe. You are barred from ever re-entering the *eduba* and the records will show why. Also," he said, inches from Mutwalli's arrogant face, "I'm writing a complaint against you for the Magistrate. He will be given a complete report of your weakness and potential for criminal activity. Don't be surprised if the Magistrate takes action against you. At the very least, you'll be watched. Now, leave here and never come back."

Mutwalli looked like he was about to protest, but Brocas whirled him around and kicked him in the buttocks. Mutwalli stumbled out the door and Brocas closed it behind him. When he turned back to Palla, anger had changed to sadness. "What possessed him to do such a thing?"

"I fear for him. He has no idea what he's gotten himself into."

The master scribe sat in his office long after Brocas left. He pulled a clean, soft tablet from its moist wrapping and picked up a wedge-shaped stylus. The woodpecker-like jabs quieted his mind, slowly loosening the knot in his chest. His *eduba,* his tablet house, existed on its reputation to graduate men who were not only accomplished but who excelled in the cuneiform script. It was his life's work, his identity.

The training was necessarily arduous. Discipline was harsh, often including beatings for laziness, recalcitrance, or incompetence. Had Mutwalli's failure ruined his self respect? Had it made him vulnerable to corruption? Pity tempered his outrage at Mutwalli's corruptibility but flared again against Ibiranu.

He pushed back his chair, lifted the lantern and walked to the far corner of the room, closing the window shutters as he passed. He reached behind a box of baked tablets used for practice reading and pulled out the wrapped bundle Gille had handed him five days ago. It was still soft.

He set it gently on the floor, settled himself next to it and pulled the lantern close. As he read the tablet, the king's voice filled his head—so unselfish, so loving, so dedicated to his people. His eyes clouded with tears, not only to read his king's last wish, but to know that in all of Hattusa only he and Gille knew Hapati's tablet was safe.

But his next thought made him shiver. Of the two of them, he alone could read the cuneiform. His mind ricocheted in yet another direction: To whom should he give Hapati's tablet? Palla studied the tablet as though it would provide an answer. He clutched the terracotta reverently, grateful for the message but anguished by his impotence. He knew tradition dictated that he deliver the tablet to the High Priest of the Storm God's temple. But years of observing the priests had shown him that not even the High Priest of their most powerful god was impervious to political considerations.

Panic generated another question: What if he was killed? Or Gille? Or Takana? The *tawananna's* plans would go unchecked.

He blew out the lantern but made no move to stand. For the moment he needed the seclusion and the quiet. King Suldana, when faced with problems, sought the Temple of the Storm God, his avowed mentor and the most powerful of all the gods. But the king had been ill for some time and the queen had used the time to plot against him.

What was wrong with him? He'd lived so long surrounded by gods and the superstitions that clung to them that, though uninvited, they slithered into his head like snakes. Publicly he felt pressured to call on the gods, to use the words of supplication and to show up at the temples for rites and other forms of fidelity. Privately he had no inclination to petition them, no desire to throw his problems at their feet and confident he would find the answers he needed without them.

Still, and despite his own inner feelings, he respected the king, whom he knew would have lingered long in the temple, sacrificing precious livestock, ordering his servants to place the choicest fruits, nuts and honeyed cakes at the feet of their statues. It was the way of the Hittites.

He rewrapped the tablet and moved back into the room. Light poured through the window and the room's features took shape. He walked to the oven and stoked the embers, still glowing from the day's tablet baking. Then he closed the oven door to let the heat build. While he waited, he slid the tablet from its sheath, placed it on an iron grill, and read the words again. As a last act of reverence, he ran his fingers around the outer edge to smooth the few dents his handling had caused. He fed the grill to the oven, inspecting the tablet line by line . . . Like a bolt of lightning his eyes fell on the king's sacred seal.

"Of course," he said, closing the oven door, "Hapati's training would have him imprint the king's seal immediately. The king's seal! It was the only proof needed that the tablet in Palla's hands was authentic.

But did Hapati imprint the seal at the king's bedside or when he reached his chamber? Was the seal on his person or was it in his chamber? Could Mutwalli have gotten the seal? Suddenly it was crystal clear what his next move had to be.

CHAPTER FOURTEEN

THE SEVENTH DAY OF MOURNING

ANGULLI

Angulli greeted mornings with awe. The burgeoning light, gentle breeze and smell of damp earth spoke to him of new beginnings. As the herd gathered—stamping and snorting at the fence, waiting for him to unload the feed—their outpouring of energy and excitement was contagious.

"You act like you haven't been fed for days. I'm moving as fast as I can," he said, tossing feed in each of the troughs.

They bent to eat and Angulli turned away to inspect the fence along the western edge of the corral. His stomach growled for his own breakfast. When he turned back he saw that the mare had separated from the herd and was waiting for him. Two others were with her.

"Are these your friends?" he asked, looking them over. It gave him pleasure to talk to the horses, even more to imagine they understood him. In fact, their attraction to his voice was the beginning of his idea that a relationship could be formed.

The three horses stared. Their ears twitched. Were they saying they wanted to be trained? He hopped over the fence and scratched the mare's head, but she stepped back and one of the others came closer. She pressed against Angulli's shoulder and he responded with a pat to her neck and a scratch between her eyes. It was the same with the third horse, a young stallion. His game of understanding their thoughts wasn't working, although they returned his stare. It was so surreal, Angulli burst out laughing. Startled, they scattered and returned to the herd. The mare looked back at him twice. Was she looking for an apology?

Physically, she had the same powerful frame of her kind, including an air of aggression, even arrogance, but tenderness poured from her large brown eyes—at least Angulli believed it did. He'd long ago given up thinking of her as a dumb animal without feelings or thoughts.

"Aku," he said, still laughing. "It's time you had a name. Aku sounds about right."

He turned away, toying with the idea of telling his family he'd named a horse. But he knew how they'd respond. He could almost hear, *You're getting crazier by the minute, brother.* Or, *Horses think of food, security and sex, nothing more.*

They were wrong. Their expectations for the horses were limited to strength, endurance and obedience. They approached each new horse with their long-established goals in mind. The first was to establish supremacy over the horse. After that came a series of sensitivity training exercises. The horses were exposed to noises ranging from human voices to wagon wheels to the sound of clashing weapons and the swish of flying arrows. By the time the moon made three passes, the trainers knew each horse's strength and personality. Decisions could then made about whether a horse performed best as a mount, or yoked to another as a chariot horse.

Angulli couldn't wait to demonstrate how capable they could be in battle. He'd been practicing with weapons and felt ready to show the results to his family. But after his father's reaction the first time, he decided to enlist an ally, a knowledgeable ally. He'd invited Ras. His family, he hoped, would appreciate that Ras was a trained warrior with battle experience.

Now he looked west, waiting. Finally, he saw Ras coming. His friend's copper-colored hair gave him away before his features were recognizable. A moment later he tied Ras' horse to the corral post.

"What's this all about?" Ras said.

"I've been working on something with one of the horses, training her to respond to leg pressure instead of reins. It's—"

"Did I hear you right?" Ras said. "No reins? If I didn't know better, I'd think you were crazy."

"Well, that's what my family thinks. I hope you're going to help me prove them wrong."

They hung their arms over the corral fence, watching the horses as Angulli told him his goal for the morning. "I'm sure there's value in the kind of training I'm proposing, but it'll go a long way with my family if you agree with me. Just because I haven't fought a battle on horseback doesn't mean I don't understand the skills you need. Don't forget I've been throwing spears from horseback at the athletic fields. I'm more certain than ever there's value when you don't have to . . . I mean if your hands are . . . Well, let me get my father and brothers and I'll show you."

Angulli had prepared a separate corral with targets in various positions before he brought Aku from the main herd. She was calm, holding her head high, snapping her tail up and down. She paid no attention to the audience. That alone was testament to the training she'd received.

As Angulli's father and brothers joined Ras, he directed them to stand some distance away from the targets.

He strapped a quiver of arrows behind his back, slid a spear through each side of his waistband, grabbed Aku's mane and mounted her.

He trotted her around the corral twice, picking up momentum until she was galloping at full speed. At the far end he turned her abruptly, pulled a spear out and flung it at one of the targets. Before the spear hit the target, Angulli turned Aku around again, pulled an arrow from the quiver, fitted it to the bow, aimed and hit another target. In the blink of an eye, Aku twisted completely around and another spear flew to a target. Arrows flew one right after the other as Aku galloped, stopped and twisted at Angulli's urging. The dust still swirled in the air when Angulli returned to the fence. Every target had been hit. The look on his family's faces was just what he'd hoped for.

Angulli's father put his hand on Ras' shoulder. "Hardly the chaos of a battle though, eh, Ras?"

Angulli's face fell. He was about to throw up his hands when he glanced sideways at Ras. His friend was smiling.

"No, it wasn't a battle. If it had been, I'd be feeling very sorry for the enemy. That was impressive! Amazing! Angulli, you're a genius!

"Let me tell you, except for the sword in a one-on-one engagement, we must separate from the battle to be effective with arrows and spears, because we can't shoot and guide the horse at the same time. To use those weapons, we drop the reins and the horse runs straight forward or in an arc. A warrior who can guide his horse to do what Angulli just demonstrated would be of great value—and just think of the surprises on the faces of our opponents!

"My commander must see this. How long did the training take?"

"Two, maybe three cycles of the moon." Angulli beamed.

"I'll talk to my commander soon and ask him to come," Ras said. Then he turned to Angulli. "How many people know about this work?"

Angulli understood Ras' question immediately. He never dreamed his insecurity would turn out to be an advantage. "Only those of us present here today."

"Be sure to keep it that way. The city has spies who wouldn't waste any time to make money from our enemies for this idea," Ras said, as he untied his horse and mounted.

"We understand the need for discretion," Angulli's father said. "And if this training is important, we will all learn Angulli's techniques."

Angulli struggled to keep his composure, but chills were running up and down his body. He chose to accompany Ras back to his house, asking him to wait while he picked another horse to give Aku a rest and grabbed some food from the kitchen. As Angulli filled a sack, his father walked to his side.

"You have made us proud today. It seems it takes a fresh imagination to advance our training techniques." He squeezed Angulli's shoulders with his big hands and Angulli felt the warmth of his grasp all the way back to the corral.

He and Ras left the training grounds and rode side by side through the forest far north of the city. He still felt the thrill of Ras' endorsement and wanted to talk about it, but one look at his friend's face told him Ras had retreated into melancholy—one of Ras' two moods of late, the other being anger.

"Have you seen Takana lately? I wanted to ask him why he thought the Sun Goddess withheld her light. I've never experienced anything like that. It felt like the end of the world. What did you think?" Angulli said.

"I'll tell you this, I don't care what the temple priests say. I believe the gods sent us a warning because they see what's going on here. My father's execution is just one of the evils in Hatti. We've got to do something or the gods will do more than take the light from our sky.

"As for Takana, I haven't seen him for four days. He hasn't been to the athletic field."

Angulli's horse was acting strangely until he realized he'd been using leg pressure to direct its movements. The poor horse was confused. Angulli took a firm hold on the reins and felt the horse relax.

"I guess you won't go to Harmesh with Takana after the Coronation," Angulli said.

Ras gave him a look that made Angulli sorry he'd asked. "I'm not going anywhere until the bastards responsible for my father's death pay for it. I'm willing to give my life to clear my father's name. He was no traitor!"

Angulli nodded and let silence clear the air. When Ras' face reclaimed its natural color and his hands relaxed on the reins, Angulli changed the subject.

"Thanks for telling my father and brothers you believe my training has value. You meant it, right?" He regretted the words immediately. His insecurity was showing again. Obviously, he admitted to himself, confidence needed practice.

"Do you think I'd lie about something like that? Fighting is life or death."

They had reached the northern edge of the city and turned sharply west. The ground sloped gradually downward, the forest deepened and almost instantly cooler air refreshed them. The horses reacted with hopping side-steps.

"Let's walk a bit, if you're not in a hurry," Angulli said, lifting his leg over his horse's rump and jumping to the ground.

"Why would I be in a hurry to get back to . . ." Ras stopped abruptly and fell silent for a moment. "Are you going to go?"

"You mean to Harmesh? Well, it's exciting to think about. I've never been on my own. I didn't think my family would like the idea. But then my father said I could go if I wanted to."

"So you'll go."

"Well, everything's changed now. I mean with the horse training. Maybe I'll be training my father and brothers." A chill rippled through his body again. In the space of an afternoon, his whole world was changed. "I can't wait to hear what your commander has to say."

The road to Ras' home was crowded with carts, manual laborers and horses—nothing like living in the king's palace. It showed on his friend's face. Angulli's heart ached for him. With deep sadness he understood that the horse manure clinging in the air they breathed meant one thing to him, quite another to Ras.

In quiet moments, Angulli dreamed of the Mediterranean seaports. Even Harmesh, bordered on the north by the Black Sea, had great appeal for him. If Setmel caused unbearable changes in the kingdom, he would go with Takana to Harmesh. For the first time in his life he had options. He could hardly believe it. Building chariots in Harmesh or new status as a horse trainer wherever he went—he couldn't lose either way.

Azzia greeted them at the door. She looked like she'd just left her bed. Her hair, though tangled, had glimmers of the copper she'd passed on to her son.

"My family sends greetings," Angulli said, tying his horse to a post. "They are eager to know how you are and hope you'll visit soon."

Azzia, with and without Ras, had been a frequent visitor to the horse center. Before her marriage to Hapati, her wealthy parents gave her a horse and lessons, even though it was rare for a woman to ride. Their only restriction had been that she was never to ride alone and never more than a mile outside Hattusa's walls. Her best memories, she'd told them, were of the forest, weaving around the trees and jumping across the streams.

After marrying, Hapati trusted her knowledge to choose the horses for their personal chariot, and Azzia used it as an excuse to visit the herd often.

Angulli noticed the hurt in her pale green eyes and chided himself for making her recall her losses. He chewed the inside of his cheek.

"Please thank them for me but . . ." She lowered her head.

Angulli nodded. When Azzia went back inside, Ras remained with him.

"Ras, have you thought . . . Your mother might welcome a move to Harmesh. It might be good for her."

Ras flinched. His face became thoughtful.

Angulli's spirits began to rise. "You and your mother should get out of Hattusa. Think of how the new chariot will help our warriors. Who knows, everything might change here. Maybe Setmel will accept Takana because of the new chariot design. After all, he'll command the forces.

"O gods, what am I thinking? The very thought sickens me. Maybe you won't want to return at all. But, won't it be easier to decide what to do if you're in Harmesh, away from all this mess? And . . . and . . . think of this, it might be safer to clear your father's name from a distance. Takana would know how to do that, I'm sure of it."

It was the longest speech Angulli had ever made. He surprised himself and Ras looked attentive.

"Every day my mother's spirit fades. She spends hours in bed. She complains about my attitude. What does she expect? What do any of you expect? It's so hard to accept losing my father but to be uprooted from the only home we've ever known . . . Everything is different and I hate it, hate it!" He slammed his fist against the wooden door frame.

Angulli saw Ras' jaws move from side to side and heard his teeth grinding together.

"Let's talk to your mother about it. See what she says. At least we'll be ready to tell Takana what we decided when he gets back from wherever he is."

"Will you go?" Ras said.

"If the horse training thing doesn't work out? Definitely. I've never been on my own. I'm the youngest in my family and have the least say about anything. I'm sick of it. I need a change."It slid between his lips easily. Harmesh, working with his friends—it sounded wonderful. Maybe Takana and Ras would think it was because he felt it was safer in Harmesh than in Hattusa. Maybe they were right. They knew he wanted no part of being a warrior. He cringed at the idea of killing anything. Besides, there was more than one way to serve the kingdom. He could take his mare, maybe the two others, and continue their training—someone would want a horse trained to obey leg pressure. By the time he and Ras entered the house and found Azzia, he was smiling broadly. Every negative thought had been banished.

"Good news? I could use some," she said, inviting them to sit with her.

Angulli looked at Ras, expecting him to explain Takana's proposal to her, but he was staring at his shoes. Would this be his second speech of the day? He cleared his throat.

"When Prince Takana returns to Harmesh, I might go with him. He's been telling Ras and me about a new chariot design he's been working on. It's got the advantage of carrying three men instead of two—a driver, a bowman and a protector. He wants us to help him. My father gave me his blessing."

Azzia inhaled sharply and looked at Ras. "You? Would you leave Hattusa?"

Instead of answering, Ras sprang to his feet and paced the room. His mouth was working but nothing came out.

"By the gods, Ras, is this the life you want? Being angry? Plotting revenge? It's changing you in ways that frighten me."

Angulli was surprised at Azzia's sudden passion.

"Would you come with me, mother?"

"Me? Both of us move to Harmesh?"

"I won't go without you. It would be good for you. And maybe if I have something important to do, this burning in my chest will go away."

"I'll admit I've missed Queen Patupa as a friend. She didn't want to leave Hattusa, but she knew the value for Takana and . . . It *might* be good to go at that. I hate it here and things are only going to get worse. If you want to do this, I'll go with you. Yes, I'll go."

Angulli walked his horse through the bleak streets. Several times he heard the irrepressible sound of children playing, but they were out of sight. Their happy laughter seemed incongruous in the drab surroundings. He thought of his own family. They'd always lived outside the city's walls but somehow it was different. Their lives were full, vibrant and, perhaps more telling, they were valued by the kingdom. He considered himself lucky to share so many things in common with Takana and Ras, even though their lives had grown from different roots. Could he be happy in new soil?

And there were the horses. He loved them for so many reasons: beauty, nobility, cohesiveness. Like him, they were

part of Hattusa but separate at the same time. Angulli imagined that even when they charged into battle, they were focused on the driver and the work they were doing for him.
They remained free of the hate and resulting chaos. Why
couldn't all people live life as they did?

The answer came to him immediately. There was no way
to ignore the evil of some men. There was no way to ignore
the danger his friends faced. He wanted to help in any way
he could.

At the main road around the city wall, Angulli threw
his leg over the horse's back, patted her neck and sat tall.
His life was going to change. He searched his mind for arguments but there were none. Fresh new challenges lay
ahead. Excitement coursed through his body like a stream
about to overflow its banks.

CHAPTER FIFTEEN
THE EIGHTH DAY OF MOURNING

The High Priest of the Storm God speaks.
"Prepare the lush meadow for our king,
where he will live as a god among the gods.
The land is his, just as he gave us land when he
lived and ruled among us."

TAKANA

By late afternoon King Naram-Suen's forces approached the mountain foothills. Following just behind the king, Takana noticed he'd increased his horse's pace and was tilted forward on his mount, his jaw set. His soldiers needed no verbal communication. They took their orders from his body language.

Gille moved up alongside. "Your uncle, I believe, senses something. Keep your sword ready."

Takana's head swiveled from his uncle to the forested hills ahead, where soldiers might easily hide. It was one thing to ride across an open plain to meet your enemy, quite another to be ambushed. His nerves tingled.

Suddenly King Naram-Suen raised his hand and reined in his horse. A lone soldier was coming over the hill—a Luwadnan warrior. He pulled alongside his king and spoke quietly with arms pointing in several directions. Then, as quickly as he'd arrived, he turned and rode back the way he came. The king called for his commander, who listened and then moved back along the line of warriors to convey the orders.

Takana, who rode with his aunt behind the king, longed to know what information had been shared. Had Kazaram warriors been spotted? His speculation ended when the king called to him.

"It is as I suspected. Amilla's troops are strung out many miles west of Hattusa and they're moving slowly east. They'll be stopped by Hittite warriors and will say they are going to the city to mourn the loss of King Suldana and to honor the new king. It's to be expected. Most likely some soldiers were sent earlier to scout in and around the city. I've sent a small group to monitor their movement, but we will camp for the night and move west in the morning."

"Toward the Anti-Taurus Mountains? We will need to cross the Cehan River. I know it well, uncle, and it runs high this time of year."

The king studied Takana's face. "What do you suggest?"

"The land flattens at the upper reaches of the river. There are some places I know where the men, horses and the chariots can pass safely." He was grateful that some of his training had taken place in the area.

The broad crest of a hill was chosen as a campsite and work commenced. Takana used the remaining hours of daylight to stretch his legs. Tents were being erected everywhere and Takana was impressed with the military precision he observed. He still had much to learn and tried to observe as much as he could. At least ninety percent of the king's army had traveled on foot, yet they moved with energy organizing the campsite. In no time horses were relieved of their burdens, gathered into small groups, examined for their fitness and fed.

By the time he'd circled the camp, light was fading and Takana headed back to where he'd dropped his belongings. Fires were springing up and shortly the smell of food filled the crisp night air. Takana's stomach reacted, but the temptation of a warm blanket beckoned. He decided to forgo the meal and pulled a blanket from his pack. But as he wrapped it around him, a young man in a helmet too large for his head walked up to him. He reminded Takana of Angulli, although he couldn't imagine his friend in warrior garb. "Prince Takana, the king wishes your company."

Takana yanked the blanket from around his shoulders and dropped it to claim his space at the base of a tree, still thinking of his friends in Hattusa. He'd left without speaking to anyone, including his mother. Although he couldn't explain how, he felt certain by now Palla had explained his mission to her. He hoped Ras and Angulli contented themselves with speculation.It wasn't the first time Takana had excluded them from his plans. As a member of the royal family, he had obligations and expectations over which he had no control. They understood that, but it didn't mean he enjoyed keeping secrets from them. Thinking of secrets sent his mind tumbling to Urhi. "Ye gods," he mumbled. Urhi would be furious he didn't show up for the "swiftest runners" event, nor had he mentioned the run to Ras and Angulli as he'd promised. Was that four days ago? A lifetime seemed more likely.

The king was waiting for him by a campfire. A tent had been erected just beyond. Inside, a lantern cast shadows on a mat piled with blankets, a makeshift table and several squat stools. Guards were stationed on each side of the tent's entrance. Takana kicked a stone away and sat.

"I've been wondering something, nephew. It's impossible to know what will happen when the truth about Setmel is revealed but let's set that aside for the moment. Will you and your mother return to Harmesh?"

"I don't know, uncle. Harmesh has much to offer, but I still think of Hattusa as my home, even though its future is unknown.

"I believe some turmoil is inevitable given the destructive actions of Queen Resat. Some in the city are angry and suspicious, even if they're unable to name the perpetrators. They wonder why a trial wasn't held. They feel unsettled and fearful. There may be a rebellion regardless of the Proclamation. I know Master Palla fears this and is trying to find the safest solution. It's in the old man's hands and he has my complete trust."

"I can't wait to hear how the old scribe accomplishes that. But we must set this aside and remain alert to dangers at hand. You've carried a heavy burden, my boy. It's a terrible thing to worry about the future of your kingdom and unbearable to suspect that your king's wishes might have been tampered with. This is what you are saying, are you not?"

"I have no proof, uncle, but Master Palla is sure of it and that's why he sent me to you. We fear the *tawananna* and King Amilla have . . ." Takana could not continue.

The king reached over and grasped Takana's arm. "My boy, this is how it is. You have done nothing but bring news of your king's passing. By going to Hattusa, Luwadnans are honoring our joint treaty by standing protectively at your side while you mourn. As King of Luwadna, I will stand as a friend at the Coronation of your new king, whoever he is. Nothing more, nothing less. That is, unless more is needed. Do you understand?"

"Thank you, uncle." He started to rise when the king tapped his arm.

"If you are not overly tired, your aunt asked me to question you on a personal matter." The king rearranged a rug on the ground for his outstretched legs.

Takana moved a little closer to the fire.

"Before we received word of King Suldana's failing health, we expected our next travel to Hattusa would be to attend your marriage." He watched the fire dance along the logs.

Takana swallowed. He hadn't expected this. The topic of women and marriage was tossed back and forth between Ras and Angulli but always with humor and teasing. Of course he planned to marry one day—they all did—but for two reasons it wasn't discussed. First, it was the family's task and second, the travel back and forth to Harmesh hardly lent itself to settling down.

Takana rubbed his chin stubble. "I want to marry, but my mother hasn't mentioned anyone to me and I don't give it much thought."

The king leaned back and laughed heartily. "Forgive me, my boy, but I ask you to remember I was once twenty. As I recall no one had to mention women to me. They swarmed around my senses like bees in a flower garden.

"Listen to me. I'm aware you've had no father to talk to and although distance precludes a daily discourse between us, Alina and I have no children of our own and you are important to us."

Takana shifted his position, though his discomfort was not physical. He often thought his marriage presented a burden to his mother. He was sure she would welcome help from her sister. But that wasn't the entire truth. There was Elin, the woman he'd met in Harmesh. The encounter had been alien to everything he'd expected. He hardly knew what to make of it himself. She'd thrown him completely off balance, but never so far that he'd forgotten her. He let his mind drift among the flames.

Elin was unlike any woman he'd encountered, subject to her own governance and no other. He'd met her while running, which was a surprise in itself. He'd never before known a girl to run. They were far from town, coming from opposite sides of a hill. She said she ran every day because her body ordered it. And, he noted her body had benefited greatly. Everything about her was evidence of freedom—what she did, what she thought, how she spoke.

He was intrigued and thereafter timed his running to coincide with hers as often as he could. They became friends, which he knew was a breach of proper conduct. Then one very warm day, under a cluster of pines where they sat to cool off, she kissed him. His shock was quickly replaced by passion. She pulled him close, so close he felt the warm, soft outline of her body through his tunic. He remembered closing his eyes to imagine how her bare skin would feel against his and, as if she heard his wish, she loosened her belt and pulled her linen dress over her head. He moaned at the sight of her firm breasts, the curving line of her waist that gave way to ample hips and a patch of golden down between. Her hair fell past her shoulders, caught the dappled sunshine and reminded him of liquid gold.

The restraints of his clothing became more than he could bear and he clumsily pulled and unbuckled until she reached out to help. They came together as naturally as one ocean wave folds over another, unaware of their surroundings, touching each other, responding to each encouraging sound. Her ultimate cry satisfied him beyond all imagining. In all his dreams of being with a woman, there was no comparison to what he felt in her arms. And when she said she felt the same, he took his turn at kissing her, but with twice the passion.

Afterwards, Takana feared the consequences and asked how their coupling might spoil her future marriage and children. Her answer stunned him. *The man I want will know my heart and nothing else will matter.*

Takana jumped when the king spoke. "I seem to have tapped a strong memory. Who is she?" he said, chuckling. He snapped a branch in two and fed it to the fire.

"Uh, someone in Harmesh. It should never have happened. I've never mentioned her to anyone, but I can't forget her. It's impossible and best forgotten."

"Impossible? Maybe, maybe not," King Naram-Suen said.

"No, really, it's impossible."

"Well, as you wish."

Takana started to rise. The king's voice led him to believe he'd dropped the subject. But Takana was wrong.

"Did you know the queen and I built an orphanage? It sits next to the palace. Alina and I go there almost daily to walk among those dear children, sometimes to tell them a story. The people think we are kind and generous, but the truth is the children lift my spirits and give me hope. They touch me in a way that makes me humble and taps the best inside me.

"Ah, but I ramble and you must be tired. Nevertheless, your aunt will never forgive me if I can't convince you of our sincerity and concern for you."

Takana nodded and got to his feet. "We all need something that lifts our spirits. I feel better when I run—something about the breeze and freshness, my blood pumping. I can't explain it but it helps when I'm troubled."

"I see. Well, you have years before you need to wed and have children. If you are lucky, as I am, you and your arranged-for bride will find love, which will make you happy beyond anything you imagine," the king said, rising. "Get some sleep."

Takana watched his uncle's back until the tent flap closed. He thanked the gods for his uncle's concern for his and his mother's welfare. When he reached his own campfire and the blanket he'd left crumpled at the tree, he wrapped it around himself and closed his eyes. The silkiness of Elin's skin moved across his fingertips moments later. Sleep didn't come easy.

CHAPTER SIXTEEN
THE NINTH DAY OF MOURNING

The priest of the Temple of the Sun Goddess prays.
"O Sun Goddess of Arinna, My Lady, Queen
of All Countries! Look!
We bring all our King Suldana II will need to work the land
in his new life among you."

PALLA

As Palla approached Yazilikaya he heard the sonorous voice of the temple priest reciting the words to ensure King Suldana II's meadow would be ready for him when he passed from this world to the next.

"And have this meadow duly made for him, O Sun God! Let no one wrest it from him or contest it with him! Let cows, sheep, horses, and mules graze for him on this meadow!"

Palla stopped to listen. When the priest finished, servants placed twelve loaves of freshly baked bread on each table set around the opening of the *hekur*-house. Other servants converged on the tables with freshly-made *walhi*. First used to douse the cremation fire, the new barrel was released to the mourners.

The banquet tables were full, endlessly resupplied by the flaming braziers of roasting meat and the fresh food arriving from the city and surrounding farms. Members of the royal family and court came and went according to their need to return to their homes to bathe, sleep and change clothing. Each day, too, priests representing gods from the various temples took turns at center stage to recite the prayers and supplications of the people.

Except for a few days, Palla stayed only long enough to be noted before returning to the city. Each visit to the burial grounds, each ritual performed, and every priestly message added yet another layer of skepticism to his personal beliefs. What he observed were gods treated like men on a grand scale. Gods lived in palaces, surrounded by servants and plied with sumptuous food. The people were duty bound to obey the dictates of the seasons, to pay homage to individual gods and to show their gratitude with prayers and sacrifices.

Yet when misfortune struck, the priests claimed it was because of the people's lack of observance, improper conduct or violation of an oath. When the High Priest of the Storm God announced that the god had been negligent in his duty to protect the Sun Goddess of Arinna, Palla understood his words were politically expedient. He made the *tawananna* happy, something he'd remind her of when he wanted something. "Pah!" he uttered aloud. He slipped back through the forest and hurried along the path closest to the *eduba*.

It was midday, classes were dismissed and Brocas was removing tablets from the oven when Palla entered the building.

"How did the lessons go today?" he said, slipping off his fleece vest.

"You will be pleased. This is an especially bright class, Master Palla. Oh, yes, Ras was here to see you. He said you sent word. I told him you'd be back at the *eduba* by midday.

"Does he want to learn to read and write? I can make room in my class for him. With a little extra coaching, he'd catch up, I'm sure."

"He hasn't said so. It's Takana who's eager to read and write but . . ." He shook his head. "As for Ras, I'm not convinced he has the constitution for the work. That man is built for action. I want to talk to him for another reason."

Brocas peered into the oven and grabbed a heavy cloth.

"Here let me help you with those," Palla said, wrapping his own hands and reaching for a hot tablet."

One by one fifteen tablets were set on wooden racks to cool. Brocas' class was approaching graduation and their cuneiform was precise. It was the *eduba's* tradition for the proficient students to produce tablets for new students to use to practice their reading skills. Palla paused over each tablet, complimenting the work on one aspect or another. Brocas smiled broadly.

Both men turned when they heard a soft knock at the door. Brocas removed the rags from his hands and walked to meet Ras in the passage between the classroom and office. Once inside Palla's office, Brocas excused himself.

"You look well. Your mother?" Palla said, directing Ras to a chair.

"Our bodies are sound, I'm happy to say. But we feel like strangers outside the city walls. I . . . but you wanted to talk to me," Ras said.

"Yes, I understand. When the city gates close behind you, it's like stepping into a void. We should discuss that someday because Hatti's people, inside *and* outside the walls, deserve to feel the kingdom's arms securely around them. Just seeing the occasional royal guard isn't enough. But another time. I need the king's seal."

"The seal? You think I have it? My father kept my mother and me apart from his work, as much for our protection as his. He told us spies were like pigeons, always pecking about for any tidbit of information they could use—usually for no good." He stood and paced. His face wrinkled with pain.

"I'm sorry, Ras. If I could put this off, I would. But I'm worried the royal seal might be put to evil use."

"I don't understand what's happening to Hatti. It's like my future has been taken away. First our king, then my father . . . I don't know anything about the king's seal. I'm not holding anything back. You don't know me at all, if you can think that!" He leaned against the wall, his face pinched in dispair.

"No, that's not what I think. What I'm wondering is, did your father have it with him or is it in his chamber at the palace, perhaps hidden somewhere?"

"I don't know. I'll ask my mother and get back to you."

"Would you be willing to search his chamber, Ras? You could tell the royal guards you were there to recover your father's personal items." He placed his hands on Ras's shoulders.

Ras's body stiffened under his touch. The old man sat back down and waited. It pained him to see Ras' suffering and imagined Azzia feeling abandoned, lonely and afraid. In six days, he said to himself, just six more days before Hapati would be restored to his family. But at that moment, face to face with Ras, the old man buckled.

"Ras, please sit down. I must ask you to forgive me for keeping a secret that has caused you and your mother great pain."

Ras, still standing, turned a wary face to Palla, who felt diminished next to his youthful power. There was anger playing at the edges of Ras's mouth and Palla reminded himself of the young warrior's volatile nature. But there was no retreat. Palla inhaled and let his breath flow through pursed lips. "Your father is alive and safe."

Ras jumped. His mouth flew open, his eyes popped. His body trembled. "Alive? Where? How?"

But before Palla could answer, Ras collapsed onto the chair, crossed his arms across his chest and wailed.

Brocas ran into the room and, at a wave from the old scribe, retreated. Palla pulled a cloth from a pile next to the oven and gave it to Ras. He wiped his face.

When he'd collected himself he looked at Palla with a mixture of disbelief and anger.

"We thought only of protecting him."

"We? Who else kept this secret?" Ras spit the last word.

"Takana and—"

"Takana! My friend watched my agony and said nothing?"

"That's right. Don't believe for a moment it was easy for either of us. We did it to keep your father safe. We worried about your anger. You were, maybe still are, consumed with revenge. There's so much at stake—more than your father's safety—we couldn't take the chance. I beg you, tell no one but your mother. Promise me!"

"When can I see my father? Where is he?"

"Wait until the Proclamation, just six more days. Everything is carefully planned. You must act as if nothing has changed. For your father's sake, can you do that?"

Ras stared at Palla until the old man turned away.

"I guess I should be grateful . . . well, I am, I am. Takana says I'm too quick to react. I'm sorry." He smacked his hands together. "My father's alive! I can't believe it."

"It's true but you must act as before. Yes?"

"Yes, I will. My mother, she's . . . I can't wait to tell her."
He got up and walked to the door.

Palla stopped him. "The king's seal?"

"Oh, the seal, my father's workroom . . . yes." Ras nodded and inhaled deeply. "When do you want me to go?"

"Now!"

CHAPTER SEVENTEEN
THE NINTH DAY OF MOURNING
RAS

The urge to run home to tell his mother his father was alive was crushing. Several times along the way he hesitated and almost changed his mind. But Master Palla's tone was urgent and gratitude drove Ras to carry out the old scribe's request. Ultimately he turned toward the palace with resolve. Only two or three people were in the plaza, which gave the guard plenty of time to watch his approach. Ras could almost read the guard's rejection in his stiffening posture. With two clipped sentences he said he didn't recognize Ras and without proof he was the son of the king's former scribe, he could not allow him to pass. Ras turned away and by the time he reached home all thought of the king's seal had flown from his mind.

"Mother, sit down, I have wonderful news." He sat next to her and let the story fall from his lips like manna from heaven. Several times his voice cracked as he watched his mother's eyes widen. When he finished she reached out and pulled him to his feet. They clung together and let the tears of joy flow. A moment later she pushed away.

"Is he well? Where is he? Can we see him?"

Ras sat again and his mother followed. "Not yet. Master Palla was very clear that we mustn't give any indication of change. No one must know until the Proclamation. It's all planned."

For several moments Azzia stared into her lap. Ras saw her take several settling breaths, set her jaw and twitch with anger. "How could Palla let us suffer that way? The cruelty of it is beyond anything. All those years of friendship . . . I trusted him completely and he let us believe—"

"If you want to blame somebody, blame me."

"Oh, I know, I know." She shook her head and sent her copper curls flying. "I'm so sorry. I know Palla better than that." She giggled in a way Ras had never heard before. "He's alive. It's so wonderful. I'm so happy . . . Wait, what do you mean you're to blame? That's ridiculous."

"Is it? You know me better than most. Would you say I'm the type to jump into action or to plan carefully?"

Azzia put her hand over her mouth. "Master Palla was worried about how you'd react if you knew the truth."

Ras nodded. "Takana has cautioned me about my temper, but the urge to challenge and fight overcomes me more often than not. It's a flaw in my nature. I must ask the gods for help and I will, beginning now."

A moment later she threw her arms around him and they laughed and cried joyfully. But the moment passed quickly and Azzia sobered again. Her mood changes were unsettling, but Ras had to admit they echoed his own more often than not.

"We thought we'd lost him forever. Six days seems worth the wait, son," she said, wiping her face with her palm.

"Ye gods! I almost forgot. I have work to do, work for Master Palla." Ras explained the need to search his father's acropolis quarters for the king's seal and how he'd been denied entry.

"Hmmm, well, it appears *we* have work to do." Her eyes sparkled as she spoke—a look Ras remembered. She agreed the king's seal had to be secured. "Your father was obsessed with its security. Can you imagine the damage to the kingdom if the king's seal falls into the wrong hands? We must be diligent, Ras." She sighed. "It feels good to know we can be helpful."

"But not as good as knowing my father is alive."

Azzia, with eyes brimming, lowered her head and clasped her hands together. "We should go to the acropolis while it's still light, but let's take a moment to be calm." She moved to fill a pot with water for tea, while Ras carried in a fragrant pine ember. They sat in silence, breathing in the spicy brew that soon circulated in the small room. Worries nibbled in his head but he refused to let them spoil his happiness.

He could see the same emotions playing on his mother's face. Finally, she gave him a knowing smile over her tea cup. Yes, he thought, they were alike in many ways. Yet Master Palla's wife, Inara, said he had his father's spirit, and he believed that to be true as well. So, too, would his children be a mixture of family traits. He closed his eyes and asked the gods to strengthen the good within him and banish the bad, for now and for the future.

They plotted a route to the acropolis, tipped their cups for the last sip and donned warm robes.

"I wonder where he is and if he's alone," she said, in a hushed tone, as they left the brick hut. "We mustn't forget that someone—maybe many people—risked everything for this to happen. I will go to the temple later today to give thanks."

"Better not. Someone will wonder why you're giving thanks when . . ."

"This isn't going to be an easy five days, is it?"

They smothered chuckles, then put on somber faces and passed through the drab streets. As the sun dipped, the earth released a damp exhalation. Lanterns glowed in a few of the homes and the sound of crying babies carried through the air. A large brown dog with long unkempt hair saw them and bounded their way with a wagging tail and a happy yelp. Dirty paws streaked their clothing but they hardly noticed. Nothing could suppress the happy secret they carried.

"I've been thinking," Azzia said, "about how easy it is to become self-absorbed. I've been guilty of that and I regret it. Our family is part of Hatti's history. Don't ever forget that, son. What we do today is important. Let it show through everything we do and say." She gave Ras a wide smile and drew her dark blue cloak around her shoulders.

Ras fastened the closing, kissed her cheek and returned her smile. It had been a long time since he felt so light.

They entered the city under the gaze of the twin lions and Azzia explained their intentions to a guard she was able to call by name. He wished them well, even offered to summon a palace servant to help them carry items if necessary.

"No, our only wish is to find my husband's personal stylus, a gift from my father, and perhaps a fleece he kept there for cold mornings, nothing more," she said without hesitation.

It didn't surprise Ras, just reinforced what he already knew about his mother. She knew how to accomplish any goal to which she set her mind. But knowing that didn't stop the red blush rising at his collar. Fortunately, the guard hardly gave him a glance.

"Let's get this over with," he whispered once they were beyond the guard's hearing.

They picked their way carefully over the slippery, uneven cobbles. Food stalls were still open and children ran to Azzia to hawk their goods. "Rosy ripe tomatoes! Cabbages bigger-than-my-father's-head! Sweet onions!" Two young boys were particularly assertive.

"Maybe when we leave the city, children," Azzia said. They followed anyway.

A cart rumbled past and stopped at a vegetable stall. The driver was the royal family cook, along with a young servant girl, there to purchase the day's needs. The cook's face lit with recognition, but he abruptly looked away and fingered the onions.

"Poor man. We're not the only ones who have to guard our actions. I can just imagine the changes taking place in the royal household," she said.

Up ahead the acropolis overwhelmed the plaza with its size and beauty. The two rambunctious boys, aware suddenly of where they were, turned around and scampered back to the food stalls. Ras and Azzia chuckled before continuing through the plaza where the royal palace guards were already examining their approach.

"I am Azzia, wife of the king's former scribe. My son, Ras," she said inclining her head. "The new king will want a clean chamber for his appointed scribe. We're here to be sure nothing remains of my husband's . . ." She managed to make her voice catch and Ras was quick to place his arm around her waist.

"I recognize you," the guard said in a matter-of-fact tone. "Be quick and return this way." His voice was firm but not threatening.

They climbed the terraces and walked to the second level below the king's private quarters, where the paths were lined with smooth stone columns. No residents were about, no guards stood at the doors anywhere.

"The place is deserted," Ras said.

Azzia nodded. "No doubt the royal occupants are at Yazilikaya. They will have taken their servants with them to help with the food service."

"It always seemed that food and drink were the main event."

"That's no surprise, since you consume so much." She snickered briefly before turning serious. "Today's the day the king's bones are carried into the *hekur* house. It's a solemn time."

"Then why do I remember music and dancing?"

"Because after the *mešedi* move in to guard the entrance and the royal family emerges, the musicians and the dancers begin the celebration."

They reached Hapati's chamber and found it unguarded, but when Ras tried the handle, it didn't yield. His breath caught. "All this way for nothing!"

His mother waved him aside and reached under her cloak for a long, slender piece of metal. She placed it in the lock with a sure hand, jiggled it gently, then turned until the lock clicked and the door swung open.

"Who taught you to do that?"

"Your father, just in case he lost his key. He made two. One he hid here at the palace somewhere. The other he kept with his writing tools at home. The first time I saw it he described how it worked."

Azzia began searching the cabinets and desk drawers. Ras turned and busied himself with checking the walls for loose bricks. He examined the torch light holders, too. When they were certain they hadn't missed anything, they got down on their knees and examined the floor, lifted the rugs and ran their fingers along the molding at the base of the walls.

"Look!" Ras said suddenly. "This seems odd."

With Azzia looking over his shoulder, he ran his finger across the wood molding at the base of the door. A short section in the center protruded slightly above the rest. Ras caught each side with his fingernails and lifted the wooden section. Nestled behind was a small rectangular metal box, three fingers wide and deep and about the length of his hand. The box had no engraving, no identifying mark of any kind. If left out on a table, no one would give it a second glance.

Ras lifted the lid and Azzia gasped.

"This is it!" she said. "You can see the outline of the king's ring seal in the box's soft lining." She drew her finger reverently around the edges."

"But where is it? Do you think father took it with him?"

"You must tell Master Palla right away. He needs to know it's not here, although I can't imagine what he can do about it."

Ras tucked the box inside his tunic where he could feel the cool metal against his skin. He shifted it slightly until it was securely held in place by his belt. Azzia replaced the molding and ran her fingers over the surface. After one last glance around the room, they closed the door behind them and retraced their steps.

The guard at the base of the palace steps nodded respectfully. "Were you successful?"

"There's nothing left of my husband's belongings. They've been tossed away like trash, just like my husband." She squeezed a tear from the corner of her eye.

Ras saw the conflict of emotions on the guard's face— pity for them but awareness of the charge of treason and Chief Ibiranu's orders.

"I'm sorry. I remember him well, but it would be best if you didn't linger in the city," he said.

Ras, feeling like an actor in a drama, walked with his mother for a short distance beyond the Lion Gate. When they were out of sight of the guards, he turned to his mother. "That felt strange."

"Yes, but necessary. Go, I'll be waiting at home. And please tell him . . . Well, you know what to say."

He watched her walk away. There was a bounce in her step but he was sure he was the only one who'd notice it. A chill ran up his spine as he realized how many things are done unconsciously and sent a prayer to the gods to guard them. Knowing how many lives were at stake would help them to be circumspect.

Ras jogged north along the western wall of the Upper City, watching the gleaming walls of the Temple of the Storm God rise above those of the lesser gods. He kept to the wall, running at an even pace as it curved east toward the *eduba*. He felt the pull of friendship knowing the horse compound and Angulli were only a short distance farther north. How he wished to share his news!

His body warmed with the steady pump of his legs and his thoughts turned to those who accused his father of treason. Master Palla probably knew more than he shared, and Ras hoped the old man had a plan for their punishment. For the time being, he was content that he and his mother were part of it now. At the very least, they were providing a piece of information Palla needed. Soon—very soon, he prayed—a more decisive blow would be struck. Those who were behind such evil needed to pay.

Up ahead he noticed a mounted guard passing between two single-level buildings. He slowed to a walk, careful to stay in the shadows of the buildings. The area was dotted with grain silos, closely guarded day and night. Ras had heard the silos led to eleven underground grain pits which held sufficient annual rations for up to 32,000 people—their survival in the event of a siege. The silos were an example of his beloved king's love for the people. Ras reminded himself he was one of those the king loved. Somehow, when King Suldana II took his place among the gods, he would use his power to expose the guilty.

Past the grain pits, he quickened his steps and arrived at the *eduba*. The back door was open, and he heard voices in the classroom at the front of the building. One of the voices was Master Palla's. Ras entered the office to wait, but waiting gave way to worry. What would Palla make of the missing seal?

"The seal wasn't there!" Ras said, startling Palla as he entered the room. "Here's the box that held it."

"As I feared," Palla said pointing him to a chair. "Did you have trouble getting by the guards?" He walked to the window and lowered the reed covering before he sat by a work table. He pushed aside an assortment of styluses scattered across the top and crossed his blue-veined hands in the space.

"No, my mother knew the guards. Actually they were sympathetic and offered to help us. A pleasant surprise."

"That should tell you something important. Even among the royal guards there are those who know things are not right in the kingdom."

"What's to be done about the missing seal?"

"It is just another part of the puzzle I'm trying to work out. Be patient and use your energy to care for your mother."

Ras stood. "I will, but surely there's more I can do."

Palla led him to the door. "Be present at the Proclamation in six days."

CHAPTER EIGHTEEN
THE TENTH DAY OF MOURNING

The High Priest of the Storm God prays.
"O Mighty Storm God, All Protectors of Hatti,
All Providers of Life, All Dwellers of Heaven and
All Spirits of the Underworld. Receive our king
who comes to you from our world to yours. "

TAKANA

The Luwadnan king sent for Takana early the next morning. "I'm thinking of entering Hattusa tomorrow on the Eleventh Day of Mourning instead of the final day. I will seek the advice of my commanders, but I want to know what you think."

Takana hesitated, but immediately saw the wisdom of the king's thinking. "Your presence will lend security in two ways, as I see it, uncle. First, outside the city, Amilla's forces, wherever they are, will see they are outnumbered. Second,

199

the people will celebrate the company of friends. When was the last time Hittites and Luwandnans enjoyed their bond. Ah! And Queen Resat, who is no doubt using the days of mourning to reinforce her own agenda. Why give her the time, eh?"

"But what of Master Palla? You said he has a plan. I wouldn't want to upset what he has put in motion."

"Gille could go to him now and explain your timetable. Besides, what would be gained by waiting here so close to the city just to pass time until the last day of mourning?"

"That was the question that started me thinking. Yes, Gille is the perfect choice. Who better than a Hittite royal guard to travel the roads to Hattusa?"

Back at his campsite, Takana set out his gear in preparation for the morning. He slowly examined the broad sword Master Palla had given him. The nicks and scratches were evidence of its past use. He ran his thumb along the edge and found it sharp and lethal. The last couple of days with his uncle and the Luwadnan forces had sharpened his mind as well. Clearly, building relationships with his men was the key. The king's willingness to listen to his men's opinions allowed them to speak their minds freely. And when he made a decision, they understood he'd weighed their ideas, balanced it against his experience and gave his orders with a confidence that left no room for argument.

Gille had grasped King Naram-Suen's plan and was already on his way. As much as Takana was enjoying the company of the Luwadnans, he envied Gille. He'd be in Hattusa to see the effect of King Naram-Suen's arrival from inside. Oh, to see the faces of Queen Resat and Ibiranu, in particular, before they could regain their composure. They would have some measure of warning but Takana believed the Luwandan forces would dazzle them.

When routine camp activities diminished and the sun was well past its apex, King Naram-Suen gathered his commanders together to prepare for the morning. Thin columns of smoke from the night fires rose like gray ghosts released to new haunts. Takana stood outside the circle of men but close enough to hear the king's words. He was repeating information relayed through the army scouts. Takana's skin crawled when he heard the Kazaram army was merely four miles outside Hattusa, strung out around the city.

"We are within a day's ride to Hattusa's Lion Gate. I have decided to move forward tomorrow. What are your recommendations regarding the Kazaramite army?" King Naram-Suen's voice was grave as he addressed the circle of armored leaders.

On Takana's right, a tall, barrel-chested commander stepped forward. "My Lord, let's move against the Kazaramites now and rout them before they get any closer to Hattusa. Then the final days of mourning can be days of sacred peace for our Hittite friends. Send a thousand to the east and a thousand to the west—catch them in a vise and cripple them." Heads nodded.

"Squeeze them until they surrender," another soldier shouted. Louder voices joined in.

Eyes turned to the king for his reaction, but before he could respond another voice rose above the din. "Would such a bloodbath honor our peace partner, King Suldana II?" The voice belonged to a commander standing next to the king.

Takana didn't recognize the man, despite the days they'd traveled together. He was tall and slender, his voice reedy.

"Kazaram will not initiate an attack, knowing they cannot win against Hittite and Luwadnan forces combined," he continued. "They already know we are here. We can accomplish our goal merely by marching our full force to the main gate and announcing our presence tomorrow. What could the Kazaram do but say they are there for the same purpose?"

King Naram-Suen stood and looked from man to man for their reactions. Some frowned and others appeared surprised, but one by one they nodded in agreement. The king's face lit up. "You are my pride! I feel the gods are with us. Tonight we will make sacrifices to our gods for success and be ready to ride into Hattusa at first light. Prepare yourselves. Sheathe your swords securely. Let it appear you have no need to use them, but never forget they are there."

The men scattered. With the new orders, activity erupted everywhere. At that moment a flock of storks with their white underbellies, black wings and heads, passed overhead from north to south. Takana had been awed by them all his life, not just because they were thought to bring good luck, but because they nested on the roof of his acropolis home in the summer and he could hear the chirping of their chicks. Their activities had provided hours of entertainment for all the children in the palace. Likewise, the sight of the storks in the camp was a welcome distraction from the tension of their mission. All the men were watching their flight, laughing and reveling in the promise of their benevolent presence.

Takana continued to inspect his own equipment until someone called to him.

"Prince Takana, we hear you race in Hattusa's games. Come join us in a foot race."

Glad for the distraction, Takana agreed. As the men lined up, he found himself next to the king at the starting line. He faltered momentarily but soon ran with those in the lead.

He wondered if he should let the king pull ahead, but his body felt light and before he knew it he'd won, leaving the king and fifteen battle-hardened men behind. They surrounded him with laughter and congratulatory slaps. One or two challenged him to a rematch. Takana said he was willing, but the king waved them off good naturedly. "Save your energy for tomorrow! There's no telling what challenges we might face!"

That evening as Takana sat by a fire, the king, looking relaxed in a simple tunic, dropped heavily on the ground next to him.

"You are swift of mind and foot, nephew. Why don't you consider Luwadna as your home? You could have a promising future as a member of our royal court. You are, after all, part of my family. And my wife, ah, she would find such joy to have you and your mother with us."

King Naram-Suen assured him the thought was not a new one for him, certainly not based on the last few days but rather reinforced by them. It had occurred to him long ago, he said, when Takana's father was killed defending his throne. "I know what happens when a family has no man to protect them. We look after our widows and fatherless children, as they do in Hatti, but their lives lose their former quality nonetheless. Obviously, you are a man now, but with the coming changes . . . I always need good men by my side and can offer you a fitting position. You would be respected, your mother protected. From what you say, your *tuhkanti* shows no such inclination."

Neither was this a new thought for Takana. He believed such an idea had crossed his mother's mind, although she never spoke of it. His clue was the wistful look in her eyes whenever she spoke of her sister, a relationship her brother, however loving, could not fill. Over time loyalty to her husband's kingdom had diminished and shifted to King Suldana II and the Kingdom of the Hittites. Takana's memory was of Hatti only.

"You are kind to offer. And the thought has crossed my mind, but Hatti is my home." He reached out to his uncle and set his hand on his shoulder. "More than anything, I want to live in peace and help my kingdom to prosper. If I can't do that in Hatti Land, I will remember your offer. I won't speak for my mother but I know how important you are to her."

"I ask only that you remember my words."

Takana nodded. He lifted a twig from the dirt and poked at the fire. He could feel the king's eyes on him and glanced sideways to see a broad smile on his face.

"Another thing to remember, Takana. A good woman by your side helps no matter where you are. If the woman from Harmesh is your heart's desire, a way can be found."

Takana sputtered and held his hands up. "Uncle, thank you. But I can't think of such things now, not until we see what happens after the Coronation. As long as Hatti is unsettled, how can I make plans?"

The king smiled briefly and turned his face to the fire. Takana followed suit. But he saw Elin's face in the flames and longed to see her again. He sent a prayer to the gods, the only thing he could think to do.

The king snapped a branch in two and fed it to the flames. "Very well, you're right. No rush. In the meantime, enjoy the women provided for your satisfaction. They will teach you things to help the shyest bride melt in your embrace."

"Hmmm," Takana said, remembering the thrill of Elin's enjoyment. He felt a strong urge to ask how Elin, a commoner, could be a wife to him. But he thought better of it.

The king scrambled to his feet. "Well, I'm spent. Think further on this and when you are ready you will say so. Sleep well. Tomorrow we will attend the Eleventh Day of Mourning in Hattusa." He soon faded from the firelight into darkness, and Takana saw the king's tent flap open and close.

CHAPTER NINETEEN
THE ELEVENTH DAY OF MOURNING

The hasawa prays.
"Ereshkigal, Goddess of Death, we appeal to you. Send your gate-
keeper to open the seven doors of your Underworld palace. Give
our King Suldana II safe passage and then send him quickly from
the Dark Earth to his heavenly meadow."

TAKANA

Late morning the next day they entered a wide, verdant valley. The forest thinned and occasional signs of Hatti's population could be seen in the distance. The paths just ahead divided three ways, straight ahead to a mountain pass, left to higher peaks, and right to the area Takana had suggested. The king turned and called him to his side.

"How long before we reach the Cehan River?"

Takana swiveled on his mount and recognized many landmarks. This was familiar territory and he thanked the gods for blessing him with useful knowledge. "Very soon. This right path will lead us to a place where we can cross the river."

For a time, they wove between low hills, where grasses grew tall and slanted together from the force of the captured wind. As they emerged to flatter ground, Takana saw the high peak of Mt. Erciyes rising along the eastern horizon. The sighting told him they had reached the eastern foothills of the Anti-Taurus Mountains. The river was below. As he searched through the trees, flashes of metal caught the sun. Warriors! He kicked his horse and pulled alongside his uncle.

"Uncle, we are being watched! I saw—"

"That should not surprise you. My troops have been watched at every move, possibly while we were still in Luwadna Land. As long as we appear steady and controlled, they will not feel threatened. If their intentions were otherwise, we'd have known by now."

As Takana predicted, the river was easily forded by the horses and wagons. Ahead the land leveled but in the distance was a steady rise and their first view of Hattusa's walls, high and majestic on the crest. King Naram-Suen halted the columns and ordered the raising of the Luwadnan banners.

Well before they started the climb to the Lion Gate, it swung open and seven fully-armored royal guards rode toward them. Takana recognized Ibiranu sitting taut on his mount, eyes fixed on him long before he shifted to King Naram-Suen.

Ibiranu and his men dismounted and knelt briefly. "I am Royal Guard Chief Ibiranu. Welcome, King Naram-Suen." His face sent another message.

The king nudged his horse forward until he was next to Ibiranu. "Chief Ibiranu, I wish to honor the treaty our two kingdoms share by attending the remaining days of mourning and the Coronation of your new king. I request permission to encamp my men around your wall. They are here to ensure the safety of Hatti while you transition with a new king," he said.

"How kind. We are honored." Ibiranu remounted and motioned to his men to do likewise. But before he sat on his stallion's back, he stretched high to see the column of men behind King Naram-Suen.

Takana turned to see for himself and was pleased to note that Luwadnan troops continued beyond sight.

"My commanders will see to it that we cause no disruption. If we don't have space around the city, our remaining men will move into the forest. Please call on us if we can be helpful in any way."

"Yes, yes, of course. How many are you?" Ibiranu said.

"You'll hardly know we are here."

"I will escort you to the palace. The queen is attending the closing of the *hekur* at Yazilikaya, but she will be told of your arrival."

"Thank you. My men will move ahead, but my queen and I wish to express our condolences to Queen Resat and Prince Setmel," the king said. "Prince Takana also is eager to attend the rites."

At the sound of his name, Takana moved forward. Ibiranu, clearly unhappy, nodded. His eyes bore into Takana while the king spoke to his lead commander and the information was conveyed from one column to another. King Naram-Suen and his scribe, who suddenly appeared at his side, Takana, Ibiranu and his royal guardsmen stepped aside as the columns moved forward and then split into two slow-moving groups.

"This is good. Our people should gather more often," King Naram-Suen said, lips spreading to expose large white teeth.

Ibiranu managed a thin smile. To Takana it looked more like a wince.

"This way," Ibiranu said, moving to the lead.

Takana raised his face to the cloud-filled sky. He felt the Storm God himself had spread his spirit over the Hittite Kingdom, as if to say, "All is well." A low rumble and lightening in the distance confirmed Takana's thoughts.

Hattusa's people paused as the group moved slowly through the streets. Their expressions were a mix of surprise and wariness. King Naram-Suen responded by smiling, waving and shouting his greetings. The people caught his spirit. They gathered behind the procession and were quickly joined by others. The mood was almost party-like until Ibiranu led the group out an eastern portal which led to Yazilikaya, a destination no one chose unless protocol demanded it. The people remained behind but maintained their cheers and waving.

When they reached King Suldana's burial site, they handed their horses to waiting servants and walked to a table that was quickly set up for them. Queen Resat, Prince Setmel and Queen Patupa stood at the entrance of the *hek-ur* with the High Priest. It was a highly sacred moment in the ritual.

According to tradition, King Suldana II had already entered his transitional stage between the present world and the next. His spirit was duly prepared for the Underworld. His mortal casing had no further use or significance. Inside the tomb, all the tools, implements and sacrificed animals were secured for him. All that remained was for the family to enter for final prayers. Takana quickly took his place next to his mother, who squeezed his hand and smiled. Together they entered the stone chamber that had been carved to hold the king's bones and his needs for life among the spirits of his ancestors.

At the entrance, the High Priest turned back to the gathered dignitaries and spoke: "O Sun God, let no one wrest from him or contest with him all that is his. Let cows, sheep, horses, and mules graze for him. As he unites with his ancestors, we pay homage to our King Suldana II who is now our god."

It took a moment for Takana's eyes to adjust to the dim insides of the cave and to notice its contents. Walking ahead, the priest threw fragrant herbs ahead of each step into the chamber. Takana soon understood why. The smell of decaying livestock had asserted itself. He saw that a couch had been carved into the soft rock. While they watched, two minor priests spread a white cloth over it. The Storm God's High Priest took silver tongs and lifted the king's bones from the chair to the couch. More slaughtered animals were carried in and placed against the outer walls.

Moments later the royal family emerged, descended the few steps, and watched as two guards rolled a stone across the opening. It fell into a deep groove with a loud crack that echoed against the hills surrounding the burial grounds.

Ibiranu quickly approached the queen who had already spotted King Naram-Suen. Ibiranu bent to speak to her but she waved him away, took her son's arm and walked somberly toward the king and queen.

"Queen Resat, I came as soon as I heard. My kingdom is saddened and will mourn King Suldana II as a great leader of his people." Then he turned to Prince Setmel. "You are the *tuhkanti*," he said with a bow. "My kingdom stands with you as with your father. Our pledge to honor the peace and cooperation between our two kingdoms is strong. Outside Hattusa's walls my army has surrounded you with a protective embrace. Nothing will intrude on this solemn, sacred event or the Coronation to follow, I assure you."

Setmel accepted the king's words and configured his features to convey a noble expression. It contorted his face so unnaturally Takana had to turn away to avoid being disrespectful. Queen Resat maintained her outward sobriety but the gold flecks in her green eyes sparked. To Takana she had the look of a stag already aware of the spear heading for its body.

CHAPTER TWENTY
THE TWELFTH DAY OF MOURNING

The High Priest of the Sun Goddess of Arinna speaks.
"Spirit of King Suldana, you are not alone.
Your ancestors await you with open arms."

QUEEN RESAT, THE *TAWANANNA*

Queen Resat, wrapped in a red fox-lined robe against the autumn chill, reclined next to the bathing pool. Stars twinkling through the opening in the roof mingled with the room's flickering oil lamps on the surface of the water. The serenity did nothing for her mood. Just moments before, the room had been filled with servants, parading back and forth from her dressing rooms with what they hoped would be acceptable garments for the Coronation. But nothing seemed right and she dismissed them.

Choosing among her many gowns, capes and jeweled accessories was one of her greatest pleasures. Having her hair arranged in surprising new ways could change even her foulest mood. But knowing the Luwadnans were just outside the city gates had drained all pleasure from what should have been an evening of magical proportions. Takana had gone too far. What right did he have to announce King Suldana's death? She had ordered messengers dispatched when the king died. No one needed to be reminded of the Fourteen Days of Mourning. They would have calculated the Day of Coronation and proceeded accordingly. Takana's help was not needed.

King Naram-Suen had broken the standard procedures by coming early. His behavior demonstrated lack of respect. Given time she would find a way to express her displeasure but not at the moment. There were other things she wanted taken care of before her son received the crown and took his seat on the throne.

She called for a servant. "Bring me a dressing gown and send word to Chief Ibiranu that I want to talk to him right away."

She walked to a mirror and stared at her image, stirring a bronze bowl of lapis lazuli, amethyst and turquoise with her finger. She tried on each piece and was repositioning a tortoise shell comb in her hair, when there was a soft knock. A servant girl walked timidly into the room, but before she could speak, King Amilla brushed her aside.

"Surprised?" he said with a wink.

"Delightfully so." She turned her back in case her face betrayed her true feelings and walked across the room to a full-length, wood-framed mirror.

He made a noise in his throat.

Satisfied with her appearance, she swiveled on her toes and walked into his arms. "The people will see your presence as a tribute to my husband. But," she said in his ear, "I know you are here for me."

He took her shoulders and moved her away. His face became stony. "Of course you know the Luwadnan army surrounds the city. Did you know they would come with their forces?"

"I knew nothing of that."

"King Naram-Suen. Curse him for his audacity! He sent one of his commanders—I should say one of his *spies*—to tell me he was on his way to assure nothing disrupted the funeral rites. Of course, he said he knew that was my intention as well! He seems to think we're the best of friends. What a laugh!"

The lanky king walked away, sat heavily in a green settee and flung his leather-wrapped leg over the armrest. He sighed. "No, I don't imagine you are any more pleased with his presence than I. Why he couldn't wait until the last day of mourning as decency requires, is beyond crass." He drummed his long fingers on his chest. "Well, what now?" he said, shifting his gaze to the ample bed on his right.

Queen Resat turned away from his leering face, mumbling something about needing to be fresh and rested for the trying days ahead. She walked to her dressing table to finger the jewels again, chose a thick chain of gold with dangling discs of descending sizes and held it to her neck. She set it down and was walking toward Amilla when there was another knock on the door.

Ibiranu. She spun around twice, checking the reaction of one man to the other. She could almost smell the scent of male aggression in the room. "You look like a wild dog. Is this how you approach your queen? As you can see I have a guest, King Amilla of Kazaram, here to pay his respects."

Ibiranu, flustered, fell to his knees. He swiped his face with a small square of cloth, pulled from inside his vest, and ran his fingers through his unruly hair. "Forgive me, my queen. Your maid said . . . I was on my way to the guardhouse to clean up before bringing you a report of my findings when one of my guards said someone was in your chamber. I had no warning you were expecting anyone so I rushed right here."

"Yes, I sent for you, but I'm busy now. At least you're doing your job. I forgive you. I'll send a servant girl for you later."

He bowed and left. Moments later a loud crashing sound came through the door. The queen peeked out into the adjoining room and saw Ibiranu pick up his helmet and slam it against his side. Then she closed the door, heard the crashing again and burst into laughter.

"There goes an impatient man." She smiled inwardly. A little frustration would keep Ibiranu on his toes. If he felt unsure of her feelings for him, the resulting pressure would also work to her advantage. In fact, some jealousy between Ibiranu and Amilla would spur them both to shine in her eyes.

With a sense of satisfaction, she dabbed at her eyes and moved to the mirror again, while Amilla strummed his fingers, this time on the armrest of the lounge. She straightened her hair, feeling his eyes travel over her from head to foot. When she turned around, his mouth was tightly closed but his thoughts showed clearly on his narrow face. Was it suspicion, anger, lust, or perhaps aggression? Yes, he wanted to best her, to take control. Let him try. She untied the ribbon at her neck . . . .

When Amilla finally left the chamber, she dressed and sent a servant again for Ibiranu. She lit several oil lamps while she waited and soon the fragrance of cedar settled over the scent of sex. Ibiranu had hardly closed the door when she began speaking.

"Why wasn't I alerted? He came directly to my chamber. He could have been a murderer."

"This is why I came as soon as I heard. My queen, we are surrounded by Luwadnans and Kazaramites. I was coming to assure you that everything was under control, that my men are stationed strategically in case there is any disturbance. Do you want King Naram-Suen's or King Amilla's access restricted in anyway?"

"No, I don't like being surprised, that's all." She walked to the lounge and sat. "Just keep in mind they're here out of duty and respect. But I must admit it annoys me to learn Prince Takana carried word of the king's death to King Naram-Suen. Such orders should have come from me. Do you see what I mean about him? He seems to think he can make decisions for Hatti just because my husband liked him. He has tried my patience too many times. Besides, Setmel tells me he doesn't trust him.

"You've disappointed me and the time is getting short to get rid of him and any others who will cause trouble for our *tuhkanti*. Takana and his mother have been gone for two years. No one will miss them and the others are of no consequence. If you fail you will be looking for a new post, far from here, I might add." She quickly stood and paced the room.

Ibiranu pursed his lips and moved his shoulders as if to settle them in their sockets. It pleased her to see his unrest, to know he dangled at the end of the string tied to her finger, so to speak.

"My plans are working. You needn't worry. The way for Prince Setmel will be cleared of all detractors before the Coronation, I promise you."

"Good. I want all eyes on my son and me for that sacred event."

She could see she had invigorated him, added some new pressure to his task. Like every servant, he needed incentive. But as she watched his expression, she saw a change taking place. How marvelous! The gods had gifted her with special talents. She could read his thoughts. What she now saw was pleasure. He loved her ruthlessness, her courage. Obstacles were dust mites, easily moved aside with the sweep of her hand.

"To be clear, my queen, we're speaking of Prince Takana, Queen Patupa, Ras, Azzia, and Angulli.

"Angulli? Don't waste your time. He's nothing. The others, yes. Take care of it. They trouble me. My son's Coronation will be the highlight of my life. I'm counting on you to make sure of it."

After Ibiranu left, she stretched out on the lounge by the pool again. She searched the heavens and lifted a prayer to the Sun Goddess of Arinna, at rest, but always diligent. "My Lady, Counselor of My Life, Keeper of My Soul, you know my heart. I fear the actions of others who might twist my words or misunderstand me. My loyalty to the kingdom is a heavy burden. I implore you to raise a strong leader for us. If some must die, your will be done. Without your help, I would be lost. Do not forsake me."

She looked into the dark night sky, already envisioning a glorious Coronation and a new beginning for the Hittite Kingdom. A moment later her mood soured. Why should she expect a glorious Coronation? Her wishes had not yet been carried out. Why should she believe Ibiranu when he said his plans were working? So far he had nothing to show for his efforts. At this late date, she was a fool to place any confidence in him. She needed her own plan.

The faces of Hattusa's power base paraded through her mind. Who stood to receive the greatest gain with Setmel as king? The High Priest of the Storm God? Yes, but he lacked the ruthlessness it would take to eliminate royals like Queen Patupa and Prince Takana. It had to be someone uninvolved in the rituals, someone free to move through the city unchallenged, someone who would do anything for her, someone with the stomach for what she needed done and someone with the resources to make a plan and carry it to conclusion. Amilla.

She called to one of her servant girls, one she'd seen flirting often with the royal guards around the palace. It occurred to her that the girl was daring, an attribute that might be useful. "Do you like this bracelet?" She dangled lapis lazuli beads set in silver bezels on her finger.

"Indeed I do! Will you wear it for the Coronation, my lady?"

"If you do exactly what I am about to ask, you may have it for the Coronation yourself."

The girl was speechless, unable to take her eyes from the sparkling blue stones.

"Ask one of your royal guard friends to bring King Amilla to me."

Queen Resat paced the room, looking out the window to the plaza below each time she passed. The third time around, she saw Amilla striding across the polished stones, where the moon's pale glow cast a ghost-like shadow behind him. She smiled thinking he would need to be a ghost to carry out her plan.

"Miss me so soon?" He crossed the room, placed his hand under her hair and clutched her head. "I've hardly had time to recover, but perhaps if you—"

Queen Resat stepped beyond his reach. "Well, let's just say I've thought of another way you can demonstrate your manly aggression. But perhaps you're too . . ." She walked away, watching his startled expression.

He flopped into the lounge and lifted his leg over the arm. "Stop baiting me and tell me what you want. I'm not a toy you can manipulate and then toss in a corner. I'm always ready for a challenge. What is it?"

She smiled and sat between his legs on the lounge. "Days ago I asked Chief Ibiranu to eliminate some troublemakers, people who oppose the *tuhkanti* and who will cause trouble for him, perhaps even before the Coronation. He just told me he has failed again. I'm desperate for someone who doesn't fail! Someone like you."

CHAPTER TWENTY-ONE
THE TWELFTH DAY OF MOURNING
IBIRANU

Ibiranu slammed the door. As a second thought, he bolted it and tossed his helmet and breastplate on the narrow barracks bed. He was in no mood for company. Queen Resat and King Amilla bobbed and bubbled together in his head like a cauldron of boiling tar—dark and foul. He couldn't say exactly why, which perhaps was most troubling of all. As he saw it, his duties required risk, not only to his position but also to his very life! Yet what guarantee of personal benefit did he have?

Clear the way for Setmel. Remove his detractors. Those were her orders, her expectations. He would obey. But, what then? How would she reward him? Could he become the Magistrate and serve as administrator of The Law, second to the king? Should he have sought some assurance from her before proceeding? He'd never doubted her motives before, why now? His assurance had always come from her willingness to share her innermost thoughts with him. In return he'd kept her confidences, acted discretely on her behalf, done whatever it took to please her.

But something had shifted. He could feel it. The walls of the small barracks room felt closer, the air stale. He pressed his temples and King Amilla's face flashed in his memory—his expression, his leg over the queen's lounge. Such familiarity! Why? Despite the appropriateness of sympathy for the loss of the king, he suspected something else. Had she invited him? How many times had his queen whispered to him about how easy it would be to defeat the Kaska tribes in the north, the Arzawan states in the west and southwest? She swore that if King Suldana had been bolder, he could easily have moved against any number of neighboring territories.

Were she and King Amilla planning to combine Hittite and Kazaram forces? It could be done. Did she want to be King Amilla's queen? What would his position be under those circumstances?

That wasn't all that troubled him. Of course King Amilla's army offered power, but his leg over her lounge spoke of another force altogether. He was too familiar, too comfortable in her bedchamber. Perhaps he should return to the acropolis and demand to know her intentions.

He paced from one side of the room to the other, merely four strides each way. A high window along one wall, a battered chest for weapons, pegs to hold his clothing, the simple bed—all indications of the royal guard's life of service and security for Hattusa. When he stopped pacing, he shook his head from side to side. No, it wasn't time to confront the queen. Not until he had reestablished her confidence in his ability to carry out her order. When the *tuhkanti's* detractors were eliminated, he would be in a favorable position to make his own demands. She needed to know how ruthless he could be when it was called for.

Ibiranu breathed deeply. A weight lifted from his chest. But it was short lived as another thought intruded. What did Setmel think of him? He would occupy the throne, but no one doubted the queen's intelligence and wisdom would be Setmel's guiding force. The *tuhkanti* had been in the royal guard since he could sit a horse and wield a sword. He managed well enough, but his reputation among his contemporaries was less than exemplary. Short temper, pettiness and cruelty were words whispered behind his back.

Instantly his own son's face sprang before him. Urhi, too, lacked the qualities Ibiranu valued. As a youngster he spoke of being a warrior, but he had no fire, no aggression. In size and weight, Urhi equaled most men in the royal guard. His swordsmanship was above average and Ibiranu especially enjoyed watching him compete with bow and arrow. But he lacked cunning and strategic skills and as such would never rise to leadership. No, he would never be more than one of the screaming mass sent forward against an enemy . . . and the first to die.

Ibiranu cursed. Unlike Urhi, he'd had no advantages, yet he quickly advanced up the ranks. Some might credit luck, but he remembered deliberately maneuvering his horse next to the queen's at the Harvest Games in the hope she might notice him. When her horse suddenly rose up on its rear legs, he was there to steady her and take her horse's reins. On that day, her eyes invited him to stay close for the rest of the day.

His queen had reason to be pleased with him. Unlike his own mother. Though she had long ago left for the Afterlife, her piercing dark eyes still haunted Ibiranu's dreams. There was no pleasing her, no way to chase away the deep crease between those eyes. But he never let her see him cry, even as his failures piled higher and his mother's frown deepened. Had she ever smiled at him? His father, too, shrunk under the intensity of her gaze. When his father sunk to the Underworld, Ibiranu imagined him seeking and finding a sanctuary from his mother. It brought a weak smile to his face. He didn't miss either of his parents. Why would he?

Ibiranu steeled himself and opened the door. There would be no sleep for him until the queen's orders were fulfilled. Not that he would have slept in any event. Reasons, more numerous than cats running loose in the city, would have kept him too edgy for sleep. King Amilla's face flashed before him again and his face burned.

Later, after he'd done her bidding, he would confront her. He would accomplish her bidding so perfectly, so completely, she would realize no one could match him for dedication or power. There was nothing she couldn't do with him at her side. But first . . . *Get rid of them,* the queen had said. Her meaning was clear. She was letting him know she had complete confidence in him, that he would carry out her wishes and protect her from any complicity in their deaths.

She didn't need to know about Urhi. How could his flesh and blood be so inept? His son's plan must have failed and, even more telling, he lacked the courage to say so. Perhaps Urhi's wish to be sent away had merit for both of them. He'd think on it later. For now, he had more important matters to attend to.

He closed the door again and turned back to the small room. He stared at his shelf-like bed. He'd been sleeping there for longer than he cared to remember. Just outside the door an eager, obedient servant boy slept on the floor. The boy hung on his every word, but understood nothing. It struck Ibiranu that there was no one to hear his concerns, no one who appreciated the difficulties he faced and no one to lift his spirits.

Ibiranu felt it was a sacrifice his queen appreciated. Admittedly, sometimes his body called out for the soft bed in his home. While not in the acropolis itself, it was close by. Distance, to be honest, wasn't the only reason he chose the barracks. He felt he deserved better than the wife and son he had.

He lifted his head to the gods and prayed that his plans would succeed and open up a new life. He deserved it for the faithfulness he'd shown. He tightened his leather belt, yanked the door open and told his startled young messenger to assemble the guards in the main barracks.

"Will you be going to Yazilikaya, my lord?" the youngster said.

"No. The *mešedi* are in charge for the remaining days. Prayers and feasting continue but I have other orders to fulfill!" he said, moving off.

"But what of the ghosts?" The boy's eyes widened. "My grandmother says this is the most dangerous time. She heard . . ."

The hairs on Ibiranu's neck prickled but he faced the boy. "Get busy with your work and you won't have time to worry about ghosts."

It was true that from the moment the stone was rolled across the king's tomb, security was in the hands of the *mešedi.* But, though the feasting, prayers and petitions would continue until the final two days were completed, the people believed something else was going on inside the *hekur*-house.

The sound of the stone seal was said to herald the arrival of the king's ancestors, led by the Storm God and hundreds of other gods in the Hittite pantheon of sacred ones. They descended into the chamber to accompany the king to his new life. If the gathered spirits sensed an omission or an error in the rituals, a wandering ghost might unleash any number of evils on the people. The *mešedi* were there to stand firm against the ghosts and assure the work of the spirits was uninterrupted. The king's elite bodyguards would remain vigilant throughout the day and night until the new king was crowned and their allegiance shifted.

Ibiranu patted the sword at his side, said a prayer for the *mešedi* and turned his thoughts to his plan to carry out the queen's wishes. He would tell the guards their time had come to secure the kingdom for the new king. That was it! Those were the words! Their time had come! The kingdom needed them!

He strode past the adjacent horse stalls, entered the barracks and slammed the door. Six guards, seated around a table in the gathering room, jumped to attention. He eyed each man, stopping suddenly at Gille.

"The queen has needed my services and kept me from our routine assemblies. I trust all of you have performed faithfully without my close supervision."

Ibiranu followed each man's nod solemnly, stopping again at Gille.

"Where have you been working? It's been days, I think."

A squad leader stepped forward. "Forgive me, Chief, with all of our added security details—the foreign troops and travelers from distant villages here for the Coronation—I neglected to tell you I ordered him to patrol the outer villages. I'd heard a report of unrest regarding disagreements between some soldiers and farmers. Gille is experienced in negotiating and I knew you would want the peace preserved during our time of mourning."

Ibiranu glared at the guard, but thought better of spending time reprimanding him. His queen's orders couldn't be delayed. Instead, he nodded his understanding, turned to the group and gave them a satisfied smile. "Sharpen your blades. We're going hunting tonight."

His royal guards were seasoned fighters, and their sleepy eyes quickly widened with anticipation.

"Chariots or individual horses?" a guard asked.

Ibiranu didn't answer. He was taking his time to examine the men one by one. He had fought with these men. They loved the king and were sworn to protect the kingdom.

"This night calls for soft leather shoes." He pulled his dagger and ran his hand along the crescent handle and then the blade—cold and sharp, a perfect companion for his bold plan. "The Hittite Kingdom is meant for great things. As protectors of Hatti, the time has come to demonstrate our patriotism. Crown Prince Setmel will lead us soon. He has a vision to lift the Hittite Kingdom to greater heights. Nothing and no one must impede him. This is our challenge and we will not fail.

"As unbelievable as it may seem, there are those who are plotting ways to undermine his progress. We are charged with their elimination. We must do our work swiftly and cause no disturbance among the people.

"We will pass quietly through the city, outside the gate to an area that should be unoccupied. You know, however, we are surrounded by the Luwadnan and Kazaramite armies. Their presence may make us uneasy, but it is to be expected. They are here to celebrate the crowning of our new king. If we pass among them, we will be recognized as a normal patrol." He paused to look each man in the eye before he continued. "But our mission is to quietly eliminate troublemakers before they can strike."

"Who are they, chief?" The voice came from the back of the room.

"Prince Takana," Ibiranu said through clenched teeth. "At one time he was a patriot. He was loved by the king. But he's been gone for two years. His loyalties lie elsewhere." His hand reached up to rub the back of his neck.

The men looked from one to another.

Again, the guard at the back of the room spoke. "Others?"

Ibiranu recited the names and noted the fidgeting and glancing around the room. He leaned across the table, a sudden move that captured their attention. "Hapati's treason was a shock, was it not? Did you think he was acting alone? We are surrounded by evil. It must be stopped before the Crowning. We're going to see to it. The kingdom is in our hands."

"You said 'quietly,' chief, but Prince Takana and Queen Patupa are in the palace. They must be lured away somehow," the same guard said.

Ibiranu was pleased with the comment. It meant his men felt the challenge and were thinking strategically. "Good," he said. "Precisely my thinking."

Before they left the barracks it was decided two of the guards would tell Prince Takana and Queen Patupa the Old Woman wanted to see them before the rituals began at Yazilikaya. Two other guards would go to Ras and Azzia with the same message. "Once you have them, dispatch them quickly," Ibiranu said. "Then meet me in the forest beyond the North Gate on the northeast side of the city. We'll bury them well before daylight. Go!"

He pointed to the two remaining guards. "Bring horses and then follow me to where we will wait for the others."

For what seemed an endless time, Ibiranu watched the brightening horizon with rising temper. Many curses burst from his mouth each time he completed another tramp through the grass. Finally, four guardsmen arrived empty handed.

"They've gone. When there was no answer at Queen Patupa's apartment, we broke in, but not even the servants were there."

Before Ibrianu could respond, the other team delivered the same message. "Hapati's family also was gone."

In a fit of frustration and anger, Ibiranu dismissed them with an order to take all but his horse and standby in the barracks. The quiet settled around him. He imagined himself delivering another failure to the queen and felt panic. But, knowing her impatience, it would be worse to wait. He mounted the one remaining horse. At the acropolis, he galloped up the terraces to the queen's quarters, rehearsing his words with each step.

He faltered at the door. A wave of nausea sent him to the edge of the terrace where he breathed deeply until it passed. The outlines of the city were forming against the brightening sky. He yanked on his leather breastplate with resolve and knocked on the apartment door. It was quickly opened. The door to the queen's chamber was ajar, revealing the queen on a cushion by the bathing pool. He sighed. At least he hadn't needed to wake her.

She started speaking before he reached her. "Your face tells all. I can barely stand to look at you."

"One plan has failed, my queen, but I have another." His voice was weak and the queen's face hardened.

"You'd *better* have a foolproof plan. When the High Priest of the Temple of the Storm God reads the Proclamation, I want all of Hattusa cheering for my son. I don't want to be looking over my shoulder at Prince Takana, worrying about future mischief," she said. She lifted her hand.

Ibiranu rushed to help her and then watched her walk to the opposite side of the room and back. She was breathing rapidly, trembling with anger. "There's something else you'd better consider, Ibiranu," she hissed. "There are spies among your royal guardsmen. How else do you think Takana and his mother are suddenly beyond your reach?"

Ibiranu swallowed. Spies among his royal guardsmen? The room spun. He felt suddenly abandoned. His men could never . . . But his thought was interrupted when the queen spoke again.

"Do you doubt for a moment, King Amilla would carry out my wishes if I asked?"

Ibiranu's mouth opened but he couldn't form the words he was thinking. He nodded and left. It wasn't until the chill outside air hit him that he realized he no longer doubted the queen had formed an alliance with King Amilla. What else had she done with him? That slimy-lipped royal!

His anger carried him swiftly down the terraces, while a desperate plan took form. He headed toward his home.

The house was dark except for the kitchen where he heard his wife's shuffling footsteps. He had to admit her faithfulness was beyond imagination. Whether or not he shared her bed, she refused to sleep until she'd assembled breakfast food for him, in case he was called to duty in the night. *Whatever you may face this day, my husband, I want you to have the nourishment you need.* She was turning away from the cutting board when he coughed. She swirled and dropped the platter she was holding. Pieces of fruit, slices of meat and cheese bounced across the polished stone floor.

"Oh, you startled me. But, but there's food ready," she said. Her honey-colored hair was tucked into a cap. Ringlets fell across her forehead and rosy cheeks. She was wearing a simple homespun dress to her ankles and a white apron tied around her small waist.

"Are you completely out of touch with the world? Have you forgotten there's to be a Coronation? I don't have the leisure of sitting at meals. Where is Urhi?"

Her face fell. "His bedchamber, but . . ."

Ibiranu, with his wife's voice trailing behind him, opened the door to Urhi's room. His head was buried in the bedclothes.

"Get up! I'm giving you one more chance to earn my respect."

CHAPTER TWENTY-TWO
THE THIRTEENTH DAY OF MOURNING

The High Priest of the Storm God prays.
"Beloved King Suldana, pity us for we cannot see you. Bless us,
for we will listen to your counsel at the foot of the statues we will
build in your honor and we will worship you."

URHI

After his father left, Urhi stared at the ceiling in his bedchamber. He thought of slipping out of the house and
running so far away from Hattusa no one would be able
to find him. But almost instantly shame struck his gut and
then fear. What if he was found? He threw back his bed covering, dressed and left the house.

For a time, Urhi wandered through the silent, dark
streets. When he reached the temple area, he leaned
against the wall of a small house. His heart beat wildly,
his head ached and he struggled to breathe. Nine days

had passed since meeting with his father at The Blue Inn, and with each day a clammy grip had increased around his chest. He tried to gather the courage to tell his father he'd failed but each time he faltered and his stomach unleashed whatever food he'd eaten. Nights brought no relief. Conflicting thoughts sparred like swordsmen and kept him awake.

He'd avoided the barracks when he knew his father was there. What could he say? He'd failed to deliver Takana and Ras as promised and time was running out. Now his father was challenging him again. What made him think he still could be successful? Takana's mark was not on the royal guard duty roster so there was no way to track his movements. He thought to find a secluded spot where he could watch Takana's acropolis apartment, but he hadn't followed through. Why? Why? Not his father's wrath, but something even more frightening had stopped him: He felt *relief* when he failed. Was he going mad? How could his mind wish for Takana's death and life at the same time?

Urhi could hear his father calling him a coward, even a traitor to Hatti. But there was a counterpoint to the indictment—the memory of Takana's smile and praise the last time they met. If there was a chance Takana and his friends might someday welcome him, he would sacrifice anything. If he pleased his father would it bring him love? If he advanced in the ranks, he thought, he wouldn't need his attention. On the other hand, if he had the support of loyal friends . . . Ha! Little chance of that! On and on it went.

Up ahead a young girl carrying a basket of bread came his way. He recognized her as the baker's daughter, beneath him socially, but attractive nonetheless, and friendly.

"Are you on patrol, my handsome protector?" she said. She set her basket on the cobblestones.

"I'm on a special assignment for my father." He shifted his shoulders and placed his hands on his wide leather belt. "Hmmm, smells good."

She reached down and tore a small loaf in half and handed it to him. "Fresh from the oven. My second delivery to the *hasawa's* temple today. I imagine they have either added new servants to the temple staff or their appetites have exploded. Do you like my bread?" She moved closer and Urhi could smell baked goods in her hair.

"Umf," Urhi said. His mouth was too full to open, but he nodded enthusiastically. He'd had no breakfast and it was nearly midday. Suddenly, he choked and waved his arms wildly.

"Something wrong? Let me get you some water."

Urhi swallowed with effort. "No, no, I just thought of something, that's all. You're probably right." His mind raced with the idea of extra people in the temple. "We depend on the Old Women for many things. Their work is interesting, don't you find it so?"

"Oh, yes. Just this week an Old Woman helped with the birth of our neighbor's daughter. And they are back and forth to Yazilikaya for the rites every day. You should see the carts piled high with food offerings for the gods."

Urhi reached into his tunic for a cloth to wipe his face. "Thanks for the bread," he said, turning toward the Temple of the Old Women. But several steps later he stopped and walked back. An idea was developing in his mind and one more piece of information, if she could give it, would complete his thought.

"Do you know which way the carts travel to Yazilikaya?"

"It's the strangest thing, now that you ask. I've wondered the same thing because I've seen the carts being loaded at the back of the temple and then pulled inside. I've never seen them travel on the streets, but once I saw a loaded cart outside the north wall. How it got there mystifies me."

He smiled at her puzzled expression and ran home. The exhaustion, headache and chill were gone.

CHAPTER TWENTY-THREE
THE FOURTEENTH DAY OF MOURNING

The hasawa speaks.
"Come forth, Deities of the Underworld.
Drink the blood of our sacrifices! Sip the
honey and milk, wine and water!
Give our beloved King Suldana safe passage to
the heaven he deserves."

THE *HASAWAS*

At midnight, as the people of Hattusa slept, the senior *ha-sawa* walked among the trees in the temple atrium. Her spirit was aflame with messages born of whispering breezes and the scratchings of night-prowling creatures. She heard cries, felt fear, witnessed hatred and saw plots unfolding, earth opening and blood spilling. She was not alone in her agitated state. All around her, lamplight streamed from the temple bedchambers. She left the garden and knocked on the doors. One by one the *hasawas* filed silently from their rooms into the courtyard.

"Do you feel the stirring of the city?" she said, pulling long red hair from her neck to release it over the back of her white robe.

"And the trembling of the earth as well," several *hasawas* responded.

"The gods are sending us a warning. Murderous bands are walking Hattusa's streets. I sense some are foreigners, but others are our own people. Do you see the same vision?"

The senior *hasawa* watched their faces as each acknowledged the same omen. "Quickly! To the roof as the sun rises! We must send our voices to the gods and ask for their protection!"She led the way up a winding staircase, where she took a position near a slender column of smoke rising from the altar fire below. At her direction, the others formed a circle at the outer edges of the temple roof, facing outward. In one purposeful movement, they raised their hoods.

A tremulous humming ensued from the hooded recesses until the air vibrated, grew in strength and moved out across the rooftops of Hattusa. Images blurred, marking its passage. Near the horizon, clouds parted, and Moon God Arma looked back to wait for the message from the *hasawas* before slipping away to rest from her nightly patrol. A hush, deeper than silence, made way for the senior *hasawa's* words.

"O Mighty Storm God, My Lord, Preserver of Order, Supreme Overlord, Protector of the Land of Hatti, Just Lord of Judgment, King of the Universe! O Sun God of Heaven, Shepherd of Mankind! O Goddess Lelwani, Queen of the Gods of the Infernal Regions! O Moon God Arma, before you sleep, listen! O Sun Goddess of Arinna, Giver of Life, rise with your golden glory to hear our prayer! Gather the gods! Call them with your mighty voices! Let no god ignore our plight! Your people revere your special powers and in this new day all are praised, all are needed.

"Do you hear my voice?"

The *hasawas* waited for a sign the gods were listening, knowing no voice would speak again until assurance was received. The moon dangled by half. Then a ray of sun shot across their bodies, standing like white columns, part of the building itself. It was the sign they needed.

"O Holy Gods! Our beloved King Suldana II, soon to join you in the Heavens, loved his people. We prospered and you profited from our wealth. We gave you the best of our livestock, our prayers, our obedience and our devoted service, remembering every holy day, every word of praise for your goodness.

"O Holy Gods! Protect us! We are afraid! Words of hate fill the air we breathe. We see hands ready to open the earth so they can hide their monstrous deeds. O gods, pay attention, confuse the plots of those who would murder! Twist their tongues! Block their understanding! Send your power to wipe harmful intentions from their thoughts! Protect us!"

They waited, watching the sun embrace the city, knowing that, along with the light, the gods were gathering everything into their protective arms. When the senior *hasawa* pulled back her hood, they did likewise and followed her back to the courtyard below.

"Now we must do our part to help the gods," she said, as they sat huddled together on the garden's several benches. "We must make little dogs of tallow and place them near or on those who are plotting murder. The gods will reward our efforts to make their work easier. Do you have a clear vision of the ones we must seek out?"

One voice spoke. "On the roof, I saw a banner of Kazaram colors. Do you agree that King Amilla and his men are plotting to kill?"

"Your powers are keen. Yes, set your animal image in his pocket or near where he and his warriors are gathered. The gods will take care of the rest. Does anyone else have a clear vision?"

There was a soft rustling as the *hasawas* looked back and forth at each other.

Another voice spoke. "I saw Chief Ibiranu's black stallion. Do you think his horse has sent us a message?"

"Animal spirits are strong observers of good and evil. Take the black's advice. He will guide you to the chief."

Another voice spoke. "*Hasawa!* In my vision there was a young colt with the stallion. What do you make of that?"

"It means Chief Ibiranu has infected his own son with his venom. Place the little dog on or near him and trust the gods to know what to do." In an instant she recalled Master Palla's concern about Urhi. He pitied him but conceded that the boy's ineptness might lead him to success in carrying out his father's wishes.

The Old Women ran from the courtyard, darting in different directions, while the senior *hasawa* watched the heavens for signs. White clouds moved swiftly across the pallid sky, chased by a line of larger gray bodies. A strong wind dipped into the courtyard and shook the upper branches of the trees. The senior *hasawa* raised her arms. "O My Lords. I feel your hands at work."

She lowered her head until the sound of shuffling drew her attention. One *hassawa* carried a large bowl of soft, warm tallow. Others carried crushed herbs, small seeds and fine sand—elements to add greater effectiveness when mingled with the tallow. Each *hasawa* dipped into the wax and deftly shaped a dog small enough to fit into her palm. They held the tiny effigies in their outstretched hands briefly, and when the dogs were firm, they stood to indicate their readiness.

The senior *hasawa* gathered them and spread her arms, and though she could not span the circle, each Old Woman reacted by pulling up her hood in readiness.

She dispatched them. "Go! You are protected by the gods. Have no fear."

As they left the temple, the *hasawa* walked into the central chamber and climbed to the raised altar. She ordered wood added to the embers and an unblemished lamb for slaughter. While she waited, she bent down and dipped her hands into the bowls surrounding the altar platform. She lifted handfuls of green leaves over her head and threw them into the air. Some were caught in the rising flames, others floated off to the sides on the moving warm air, and the cleansing smell of eucalyptus and mint filled the room.

She lifted her hooded head and waited. The lamb bleated. Blood filled the stone channel at the base of the altar. Slowly amid the flames, the *hasawa* saw the Old Women spreading out along the streets of Hattusa. One stopped to speak to a royal guard, who bowed before her. She placed her curled hand on his quiver of arrows and when he stood she placed her open hand on his chest.

At the barracks, just north of the acropolis, another *hasawa* circled the building before going inside. Moments later she emerged from the stables. Her hands swung open and free at her sides. A circle of *hasawas* gathered briefly at the Lion Gate. They spread out and raised their arms in blessing, first facing into the city, then outward toward the woods.

Several times the senior *hasawa* ordered her servants to stoke the fire. She tossed more herbs into the air. When the fire reached again to the roof she stared into the flames again, transfixed.

She saw two *hasawas* circle a house not far from the barracks. They circled three times, then one placed her dog at the front of the house, the other at the rear. Almost immediately the flames shot up fiercely. When they died down, she saw the *hasawas* clustered together just outside the temple door. She climbed down from the altar and walked to the door to greet them. But as she stepped outside, they were still gathered in a tight circle. She joined them.

One *hasawa* spoke. "We must seek the gods' counsel again."

Another spoke. "We have failed."

Another spoke. "We could not complete our task. I fear something has been neglected. Perhaps the gods need something more from us."

She turned back to the temple, urging them to follow. The massive door closed behind the last *hasawa*, and without a word all eyes were drawn to the fire. It had flared beyond the opening in the roof, something they'd never witnessed before. The senior *hasawa* climbed again to the high altar and they surrounded her at its base. The roar of the fire was the only sound. The *hasawa* bowed her hooded head. Her arms drooped at her sides. They waited.

Some time later she descended and led them out into the atrium.

"You have not failed. The gods have heard our prayers and have done what we asked."

One *hasawa* spoke. "But we failed to find a pathway to Urhi."

"Yes, I know. The gods examined him but found no hatred, only a desperate need to please his father. His destiny will play itself out. There is nothing more we can do."

CHAPTER TWENTY-FOUR
THE FOURTEENTH DAY OF MOURNING
PALLA

A t the *eduba* the old scribe shuffled from one task to another, accomplishing nothing. So many things could go wrong in the next couple of days and though he'd been over and over his plans, he was afraid. It was as though an invisible spirit whispered in his ear, making the hairs on the back of his neck stand on end.

He felt intuitively that his discomfort had nothing to do with planning but something spiritual perhaps. He walked to the window. Across the narrow road, a young boy was struggling with a large box which was obviously too large and heavy for him to carry. Like a flash, his mind reached back to The Blue Inn and the exchange Palla observed between Ibiranu and Urhi.

How ridiculous that he should be thinking of Urhi in view of all of his other concerns. But it wouldn't go away. Perhaps it was the result of working for years with hopeful, eager young men, that he was drawn to the conversation between Urhi and Ibiranu at The Blue Inn. He'd watched

Urhi's eager expression turn to distress and then to fear. It had troubled him at the time but with the press of other concerns, he'd tucked it away.

It was no secret Urhi was scarred by an uncaring father and his interaction with his peers seemed only to attract those who used him for their own gain. So what was Ibiranu up to with his son? Whatever it was, Palla was sure nothing good would come of it.

Once again he pushed Urhi from his mind and shelved some newly-baked tablets, but moments later he called to Brocas to say he was leaving on an errand. No need to tell his assistant it was an errand to find some peace of mind. In times past, the senior *hasawa* had served this purpose. Despite the spiritual world in which she functiond, she was firmly grounded in practicality. That was precisely what he needed now. The days ahead would require clarity and courage, both of which were slipping from his grasp. He tossed a robe across his shoulders and left the building.

At the Temple of the Old Women, Palla took the steps two at a time. He asked the servant who met him at the entrance to beg an audience with the *hasawa*. As the servant's footsteps faded, Palla succumed to . . . he hardly knew what to call it. The air moved softly but enough to deliver a shushing sound to his ears. The fragrance of flowers mingled with herbs, found their way into his senses and released the tension in his neck. He was a man who needed logical explanations for everything, but this time he needed more. He needed the *hasawa's* very special gifts.

She approached him in a long, spotless linen robe and a smile. Her luxuriant red hair flowed to her shoulders and spilled over her breasts. Her black eyes were ringed with ash, making them appear sunken and empty, skull like. People feared her and, having sought her counsel many times, Palla knew she liked it that way.

"Good," she said, "You heard me calling. I'm glad."

Palla felt no need to doubt her ability to reach his spirit wherever he might be. She stared at him momentarily, somehow understanding his need without asking. He watched as she whispered instructions to a servant standing at her side. Moments later he pulled a stone plug from a water spout left of the altar, while two more servants approached, one carrying a deep bowl, the other a green water snake, held behind its head with the servant's thumb and index finger. When the bowl was half full, the snake was introduced.

The *hasawa* pulled a hood over her head and invited Palla to join her on the altar. Together they watched the snake circle the bowl three times. Finally it curled tightly over one of the symbols along the sides of the bowl. She nodded and a servant retrieved the bowl, lifted the snake from the water and kissed its head. As they retreated, she stepped to the center of the altar and raised her arms.

The room vibrated as sound erupted from within the *hasawa's* hood. "Almighty Gods, your Divine Will has been delivered. The snake says that he who receives the crown will bring prosperity to Hatti.

"Our devotion knows no bounds for your kindness and your care. May we please you with every word of praise, every sacrifice made and every duty performed."

She lifted her white hood with long tapered fingers, settled it on her narrow shoulders and stepped down from the altar. She left the temple's main room, indicating with her hand that Palla should follow her. When they reached the garden atrium at the back of the temple, she stopped and turned around to face him.

"Now, Master Palla, the message I pronounced was for my servant's ears, or any others who might be wandering in the temple. I'm well aware you have no interest in snake oracles. Now, your stress is obvious. Tell me what you need."

A crooked smile, which seemed out of place on her face, emerged and her eyes moved from their depth to dance on the surface.

A strange sensation pulsed through him and he felt himself pulled into her eyes. There in the dark void something moved through his mind, and when he returned to his body he felt that everything he knew—every fact, fear and secret—had transferred. He was still staring into her eyes and incredibly Palla thought he could see everything reflected there. Yet instead of feeling violated or fearful, he was relieved, unburdened, peaceful. She was smiling in the most curious way and Palla could do no more than return her smile.

Finally he coughed and raised his hand to his mouth. "Ah, oh," he stammered. "True, your snakes don't interest me. I came because I am plagued with doubts. I thought perhaps . . . I've witnessed your wisdom and kindness many times." He paused, irritated that he sounded unsure of himself.

"So? Wisdom I've heard. Kindness? I'd be interested to know what you think you've witnessed."

Her answer surprised him, almost made him laugh. Too, it had the effect of focusing his thoughts and for that he was glad. For all the mystery surrounding the work of the Old Women, her question was revealing, even touching.

"You were the one who sent your servant to tell me about the house for Ras and Azzia. Its location couldn't be more perfectly situated for my loyal guards to keep watch over it."

The *hasawa* raised her eyebrows.

"And you were the one who called for a cleansing to give them time to prepare to leave the acropolis."

"Hmmmm, you can think what you like. These things were a matter of practicality, nothing more. By the way, your 'loyal guards,' as you call them, are risking far more than my servants. Still, we must do what we can to ward off whatever evil is to come. I believe we can."

"I'm not sure. Something I observed at The Blue Inn troubles me. All together I feel confused, helpless in the face of what's to come."

"Helpless is hardly a word I'd use to describe you. But, yes, confusion is all around us. The people whisper, the warriors strut about and our leaders' hearts lack love for anyone but themselves."

They walked to a bench and sat. The *hasawa* leveled her face to his, waiting as if to capture each word as it fell from his mouth. Her skin was youthful and glowing, reminding him that the ages of the so called Old Women ranged widely. Some very young girls entered the ranks if they demonstrated the spirituality and talents needed.

"Chief Ibiranu plans to kill Prince Takana, Queen Patupa and anyone else who might resist her son. Ras, Azzia and Angulli are also in danger because of their closeness to the prince."

"Yes? Something more?"

"I believe Chief Ibiranu has recruited his inept son, Urhi, to help. The idea is so far fetched . . . but I fear he may be successful precisely because he is so incompetent."

"The gods have him in their sights," she said.

Palla looked at the Old Woman with amazement. She was more than a woman with great powers of discernment. Now he pondered her ability to leave her body and travel even to places like The Blue Inn. Pah! She had spies! Or could she?

"I won't ask how you know these things, but something must be done to protect them. My feeble efforts may not be enough." Anxiety coated his words but he couldn't help it.

"It's true Ras is impetuous, perhaps vulnerable, but I sense new forces at work in him. Angulli is driven by love for his friends. Possibly vulnerable, too. But Prince Takana? He has intuition even he is unaware of. It grows within him as he calls on it. I've known such men. They're rare. King Suldana was one of them.

"Come with me," she said, rising. "I believe I can ease some of your worries, dear Master Palla."

He followed her light-footed gait into the temple, making so many turns Palla was disoriented. The building's exterior gave no hint of the labyrinth within. They descended one staircase after another, each level branching off into several corridors. At the base of the third staircase, Palla followed the *hasawa* through a tunnel of stone. At the end she hesitated in front of a large, wood-plank door. She knocked.

Palla's mouth dropped open at the sight of Ras, and on large cushions behind him were Takana, Queen Patupa and Azzia. He clutched his chest and unsuccessfully tried to hold back a sob.

"How? When did you . . .? I thought . . . I imagined . . ."

Azzia jumped up and embraced the old scribe. "There are no words to thank you for all you've done. Hapati, alive! Ras has told us what you did. We're grateful, joyful . . ." Her voice caught and she returned to her seat.

Takana pulled a cushion close for Palla and Azzia handed him a cloth.

Palla dabbed his eyes and looked around the large room while he caught his breath. The room was brightly lit by oil lamps on several tables and brackets along the walls. Four sleeping pads were partially hidden behind draped fabric. In another area, large platters held the remains of a meal.

"We all owe you a debt of gratitude," Takana said, grasping the scribe's hand. "The gods have used you for the good of the kingdom and for that we thank you.

"Let me tell you about the—what can I call it?—the miracle our *hasawa* has performed. As we were preparing to sleep last night, two young children came to our door and said the *hasawa* was calling for us and to bring what we needed for a few days. Soldiers were everywhere, but they were not looking for a family with children and we slipped right by them," Takana said.

"It was the same for us," Azzia added.

"Never doubt the gods watch over us. You were not stopped because their eyes were clouded by the gods," the *hasawa* said. She turned to Takana. "Listen carefully to me. Soon I must leave for the final rites at Yazilikaya. I believe we have a way to get you to the last day of mourning safely, but it will not be without risk."

"I can guard them," Ras said, jumping up from his cushion.

The *hasawa* studied him carefully, frowning and smiling alternately. "Yes, but stay hidden unless you're needed and return with the wagon and my servants. Promise me you will follow these instructions."

Ras nodded.

She continued, addressing Takana and Queen Patupa. "Each day a covered wagon leaves here for the forest to gather wood for the temple fires. This afternoon the wagon will carry you to the forest edge near Yazilikaya. A chariot will take you from there to the final ritual. At the conclusion, I, along with the temple priests, will lead the *tawananna* and the *tuhkanti* on the last procession from the burial ground. Your chariot driver will take you to a well-hidden tunnel outside the wall. Only the *mesedi,* the king and priestesses of the Old Women's Temple know it exists. It leads to this sanctuary where you will be safe. I must go now to prepare for the ritual."

"I will pray to the gods for your safety," Azzia said. "It's bitter to be barred from honoring the king with our attendance but—"

"A great injustice has been done to you," the Old Woman said. "Perhaps I can help."

She asked Azzia and Ras to kneel and empty their minds of all thought. She placed her hands on their heads. Almost immediately a rush of wind swept through the room and a voice poured from within the Old Woman's hood.

"Lelwani, Queen of the Dead, you dwell with the wicked, but soon you will open the portals of the Underworld so those who live in your infernal abode can come forth to partake of the offerings of the people. For the sake of justice for Azzia and Ras, show them to us now so we might feel their goodwill, so we might know they will ensure fertile soil, new growth, new life and new leadership for Hatti. Open the portal and come now, Deities of the Dark Earth."

The wind whipped harder and harder, raising a sound that seemed to make the stone walls shake. Then the Old Woman released their heads.

Azzia and Ras grabbed each other, clearly shaken. "I, I saw the High Priest of the Storm God draw a dagger from under his robe and dig a pit," Ras stammered. "Servants filled it with sacrifices—a sheep, bread, beer and wine. Then I saw . . . I saw the gods of the Underworld eat and smile before they returned to the river."

"Thank you," Azzia said, clutching her chest and struggling to catch her breath.

Ras, still shivering from the experience, nodded his head.

"What? I saw nothing. I heard a rushing sound, but that's all," Takana said.

Palla's mouth was agape. He bowed with respect.

"You will be safe here," the Old Woman said to Azzia. Then she addressed Queen Patupa, Prince Takana and Ras. "The temple servants will come for you when it's time to attend the final rites. In the meantime, ask the temple servants for whatever you need. Tonight we will make plans for tomorrow's Proclamation. Now I must go."

"I will see you at Yazilikaya," Palla said, following the *hasawa* out of the room.

Once outside, not even the brisk air broke the spell of what he'd just experienced. He knew he was moving toward the *eduba* but he was oblivious to everything around him. His thoughts were filled with amazement. He wondered when the *hasawa* had entered the temple to begin her training with healers, midwives and mystics. He knew she had to memorize hundreds of rituals, prayers and incantations, arduous work but necessary since she had to be ready at a moment's notice to perform. He raised his eyes to the heavens and thanked the gods for her, recognizing the irony of his action.

Back at the *eduba* Gille was waiting for him.

"Ah, it's good to see you, Gille. Have you resumed your duties? No problems with Chief Ibiranu?"

"No. As I hoped, my squad leader told him I was sent to an outlying village to settle quarrels between a group of farmers and some soldiers.

"The chief is frantically searching for Takana, as we are. I'm worried, but if Takana has avoided Ibiranu's hounds, I'm glad."

Palla motioned to Gille to sit while he walked to the window and pulled the reed shade over the shutters. "The Old Woman has them at the temple."

"Ah! Bless her! The perfect place. I will report back to the barracks to keep an ear for information we might need."

Master Palla lowered his voice further. "If you can, keep a watch on the north wall when the people make their way to the rites at Yazilikaya."

When the sun reached its zenith, Palla walked his horse through the gate to the sacred burial grounds. He handed the reins to a servant and walked to one of the tables, noticing that Takana and his mother had arrived safely. Flutes and drums began to play and the high priests from every temple processed to the clearing inside the circle of tables. Each priest carried a statue of the god they represented. They circled three times and then carried their statues to individual tables overflowing with flowers and vines around the perimeter of the *hekur*-house. Servants placed bread and sizzling meat fat among the flowers, while other servants delivered heaping platters of roasted meat, vegetables and bread, first to the table of royals and then to the others.

The bench Palla was sitting on suddenly bounced. He turned to see a smiling King Naram-Suen.

"Ah, welcome to Hattusa! I heard you were here."

"We're not the only ones, as you also may have heard."

"Yes, although the other presence is less welcome. We must pray the gods will be attentive in the next few days.

"But not all my thoughts are gloomy. I imagine you and Queen Alina had a warm reunion with Prince Takana."

"He is like a son to us, Palla. We sorely regret our long absence from him and Queen Patupa. My wife and I have been wondering—"

A temple servant reached between them to place a platter on the table and both men pulled apart momentarily. After the servant passed, the king leaned close and lowered his voice.

"My nephew carries a heavy burden of worry over the future of Hatti. More importantly, he fears for his life."

The old scribe started to tell him Takana and his mother were safe for the time being, but the king interrupted.

"We have asked Takana to return to Luwanda with us. My queen yearns to have her sister close, of course. And

I can offer Takana a position of importance in a nation of peace. But he's conflicted by loyalty to King Suldana's memory. He believes he's needed here.

"What do you think? Will you encourage him? He respects you. I'm convinced your encouragement would convince him of the value of my offer."

The musicians approached the table, making it difficult to hear. Palla took the hiatus to quiet his own selfish conflict. Not knowing what the next few days might present further complicated his thoughts. He raised his eyes to the heavens and sighed.

The music had moved off and Palla shifted on the bench to look squarely at the Luwandan king. "I believe Prince Takana has not only the intelligence but also the right to make his own decision."

The king pulled back and looked disappointed. But a moment later he nodded, smiled and put his arm around the old scribe.

CHAPTER TWENTY-FIVE

PROCLAMATION DAY

ANGULLI

Angulli carried a flaming torch to the long stone building where the hay was stacked. Just inside the door, he set the torch securely into a leather cone and lifted a heavy, homespun apron from its hook. He reached for a pitchfork. His movements were rhythmic, imprinted by practice, and the hay was quickly transferred from the stacks to a wheeled cart. Outside, the horses were already lined up along the narrow trough where he spread the fresh hay. Angulli smelled their breath mingling with the cold morning air and he breathed deeply to make himself one with them. He wondered if they could feel his joy. Did they know he would be training more of them to respond to leg pressure?

For seven days he'd been waiting to talk to Takana and Ras about the new options in his life. He felt like a new person. First, if he wished, he could accept Takana's offer to go to Harmesh. Second, he could remain at the training compound with responsibility for his own special method. He had to catch up with them today or he was sure he'd burst.

He heard the scuff of leather shoes on the packed earth and turned to see figures approaching. Even in the dark, Angulli recognized his father and brothers by the shape and movement of their bodies. They'd assembled earlier in the warm gathering room as usual where their conversation, normally loud and full of playful teasing, had felt tense. Angulli guessed no one was willing to speak from the heart, yet their worry was palpable. Their world was about to change. With Setmel as king, there would be more horses to train and more chariots to build to support a greater fighting force. Did he want to be part of that? He cursed under his breath. The blood of men and horses would soak the earth, sacrifices to their leader's ambitions.

"We've been talking about leaving early for the Proclamation and Coronation," his father said, bending to gather up hay that had fallen and tossing it into the trough. "Your mother and I will be as close to the west side of the Temple of the Storm God as we can—if you want to find us, that is."

"Don't bother looking for me," his oldest brother said. "I plan to see the city sights."

"That'd be the closest barrel of beer now, wouldn't it?" snapped his middle brother.

Angulli set down the pitchfork he'd been leaning on. "I'm hoping to see Takana and Ras before the king's Proclamation is read outside the Great Temple. I still haven't told them my news."

"Yes, well, there are other issues to be settled today. Don't be disappointed if yours has to wait a bit," his father said.

"I guess." Angulli looked at his feet, thinking his own thoughts. If the kingdom changed under Setmel, Harmesh offered an alternative—maybe for his whole family. That was a new thought, but today, despite his questions, he imagined nothing was impossible.

They walked off to the horse stalls and Angulli bent again to his task. He reached to scoop the last bit of hay, thinking of their conversation. Why did his father think he might be needed? True, word had spread throughout Hattusa that the Luwadnan and Kazaram kings had come to attend the crowning and their armies encircled the city. Some, he heard, welcomed the security but others were uneasy to be surrounded by strangers, armed ones at that. He vaguely remembered Takana mentioning he was related through his mother to the Luwandnans, but he knew nothing of the Kazaramites.

A soft nicker and warm breath made him look up. Aku was staring at him and chipping the earth with her right front hoof. He took it to mean she wanted something and since she'd already eaten, perhaps she was eager for some exercise or training. She'd never been beyond the compound, but it suddenly seemed like a trip to the city was a perfect opportunity to expose her to new circumstances and test her reactions. Increasingly, the mare seemed to relish every new move, even the most challenging ones. He was amazed at her quickness. It was almost like she anticipated his commands before he gave them.

He opened the gate and she followed him to the stalls. As she often did, she stood by his side and leaned into him. Angulli, who'd observed the horses in the corral stand body to body, understood his mare was enjoying the closeness. He pressed his cheek against her neck and felt the steady beat of her heart. Since she was never first to move away, Angulli wondered how long was long enough. But today was not the day to test his question. He slapped her rump softly.

Stepping behind her, he began to braid her tail and fasten the end with a slender leather strip. Next, he threw a bright blue blanket over her back and reached for reins hanging on a hook at the end of a stall. But then he stopped. She had no need for reins. She turned to look at him and nodded her head several times. "That's right, I don't need them." He hung up the apron and picked off the few pieces of hay caught in the waistband of his leather kilt. He mounted Aku and left.

Darkness was lifting as Angulli rode along the northern side of the city before rounding the western side. When the Lion Gate showed ahead, he turned sharply away from the wall and toward the sprinkling of shabby homes where Ras and his mother lived. Why wouldn't they want to leave Hattusa and start a new life in Harmesh?

He reached the stream and followed it to the house. A dog in the adjacent yard barked an alarm and Angulli smiled at the face that appeared in the window. He tied Aku securely and knocked at the door. When there was no answer, he knocked a second time. Perhaps they left for the city early, he thought, and turned back to Aku.

The man leaned out the window. "They left the night before last with two small children."

"Oh," Angulli said, with a wave.

"You're the second caller today," the man continued. "A royal guard, a young lad with big, dark eyes was here with four others. Are my neighbors in trouble then?"

"Wha . . . ? No, I'm sure not. Thank you." Angulli frowned. Big eyes . . . Urhi! What did he want? A cold chill traveled through his body.

To be doubly sure, he circled around to the back of the house, thinking he might find a clue. Fear for his friends built with each step and before he returned to his mare, he picked up a spear that was leaning against the whitewashed wall. He jumped on his mare and rode again to the northern edge of the city, glancing occasionally at the shaft in his right hand. It had a familiar feel, but the thought of aiming it at a body and not a target was beyond his imagining. Still, if his friends were threatened . . . He swallowed and squared his shoulders.

Angulli hugged the northern edge of the forest, moving slowly. The sky was brightening and he could see the tips of the Lower City temples catching the light. A snapping branch called his attention to the trees and Angulli thought he saw shadowy movement in the deep shade. He squeezed his legs and the mare stopped. He thought perhaps the movement was his own bouncing on her back, but men on foot were beginning to emerge. Royal guards! They were focused ahead, and when Angulli followed their line of movement, he spotted a wagon.

Almost simultaneously, the wagon sped up, moving east and bouncing wildly. The men started to run, raising their bows and reaching for arrows. A cover flew off the wagon and two men stood. When Angulli recognized Takana and Ras, he kicked his mare into a full gallop and raised his spear. Horsemen came from nowhere, circling the wagon, forcing the bowmen away. The wagon stopped. Takana and Ras jumped down with swords drawn. Bodies converged and swords flashed everywhere.

Angulli urged his mare closer to the wagon where he saw Queen Patupa peek from under the cover. As he raised his eyes, he saw a bowman taking aim at Takana's back. He urged Aku ahead and she lunged forward. Angulli launched his spear and the man fell. In the same instant, another spear thrown from behind him found its mark—a guard heading straight for Angulli. When the spear thrower reached Angulli's side, he shouted his thanks. By this time Aku had rounded the wagon and Takana saw Angulli, but before they could acknowledge each other another royal guard dashed between them and tossed a spear to Angulli.

He was confused by the guards' actions but there was no time to think. To his right a guard raised his spear on a direct line to Takana. Again Angulli urged Aku forward, raising his own spear. He found his mark but to his horror the guard already had launched his spear. It landed deep in Aku's neck. Angulli was tossed, barely missing the wagon.

He managed to find his footing and was almost at Aku's side when a man jumped in front of him. It was Urhi, sneering and holding his sword in the air. But just as Angulli raised his arms to protect himself, strong arms grabbed him around the waist and slung him onto the rear of his horse.

Angulli struggled to get loose but the guard held fast to his belt until they were clear of the battle. "What are you doing? Go back," he said, finally breaking loose and sliding to the ground. He turned and started to run back to the wagon but the guard stopped him with his horse.

"Go to the Great Temple, Angulli. We'll escort Prince Takana and Queen Patupa there for the Proclamation as soon as Ibiranu's guardsmen are taken care of," he said.

"What? What's going on here? Aren't you a guardsman?" Angulli said.

"I am but I no longer follow Ibiranu's orders."

Angulli stared wide-eyed, trying to make sense of the words. "It's like the gods performed a miracle. I just happened to be passing here on my way to the Temple of the Storm God. But you? How did you know they were in danger?"

"Some of us have been working with Master Palla to protect Prince Takana and Queen Patupa. This morning he told us to hide in the forest along the north wall and watch for the chariot coming to escort them to the Proclamation. How Urhi and Chief Ibiranu's royal guards knew they'd be there, I don't know. We have watched him, but he's slippery as a snake. You can be sure he will be questioned, along with others. A thorough cleansing will be needed when this is over." He looked toward the wagon.

"Look, the battle's over."

From where Angulli stood, he could see the dust settling. Horsemen moved slowly around dark forms on the ground. They looked like rocks, but Angulli knew they were fallen men. "I must go back for my horse," he said.

"Horse?"

Angulli knew that expression. It was the attitude of most people, soldiers in particular. Horses were the means to get someplace faster than walking, nothing more. He flushed with anger. "That mare would give up her life for me. Her value is well beyond transportation. I'm training her in special ways. Take me back, maybe I can save her."

The guard stretched out his arm. Angulli grabbed it and threw his leg over the horse's rump. Up ahead he saw the mare's form on the ground where she fell. There was no movement, not even when Angulli ran and dropped at her side. For several moments he rested his head on her neck, hoping to feel the beat of her heart and knowing he wouldn't. Two pairs of boots appeared next to him and he raised his head. Takana and Ras. He dragged himself to his feet and leaned into his friends' arms.

All around them bodies were being picked up and loaded into the wagon. Queen Patupa stood, averting her eyes from the bloody scene.

"One of your horses?" Takana said.

"The best of my horses."

"She took the spear meant for me," Takana said. "I honor her for that. And you, too, Angulli. You came out of nowhere."

"I was looking for you, Ras. I thought we could go to the Proclamation together. Your neighbor described a royal guard who was there earlier. It sounded like Urhi and I didn't like the sound of that. Then I saw the wagon and the guardsmen." His voice fell to a whisper as he looked over the fallen bodies. "So many dead."

Takana put his arm around Angulli's shoulder.

"Urhi's dead," Ras said.

They walked together to his body. Urhi's arms and legs were splayed, his face turned to the sky, his big dark eyes staring. The sneer was gone. In its place were the soft features of the man he could have been.

CHAPTER TWENTY-SIX
PROCLAMATION DAY
TAKANA

As bodies were loaded into the cart, Takana and the others huddled together, dazed, speaking in half sentences, trying to make sense of what had just happened.

"I never want to fight a battle like that again," Takana said. He held out his sword-bearing arm. It was shaking like the rest of his body. "There was no way to know who the enemy was! I could have killed a friend!"

"Did I see royal guardsmen fighting against each other?" Angulli said. "I think one tried to kill me, but I know another helped me. I don't understand. Urhi was never a friend but . . .

"And, I might never have been here, but I was looking for you, Ras." Without waiting for an answer, he turned to Takana. "Where have you been? I don't understand this. They were trying to kill all of you, weren't they? Why? Who were they?"

Ras said he thought it was Urhi's doing.

Queen Patupa said she couldn't imagine Urhi had the authority to organize the royal guards. "Yesterday, the Old Woman's plan to get us to the last rite worked perfectly. I guess we'll never know how Urhi found out."

A rumble interrupted their speculations and they swirled around to see a royal guard arriving with a chariot. Angulli stood looking puzzled as the group brushed off their clothes and ran fingers through their hair.

"We'll see you at the Proclamation, Angulli," Takana said, stepping into the chariot with his mother.

Next to him, Ras climbed onto the side of the cart. "I'll get my mother and we'll return to the *hasawa's* temple."

Takana started to pull away but stopped when he saw Angulli's pained face. A guard that Takana recognized as the one who'd pulled Angulli from the fight walked up with a horse and gave Angulli the rains.

"Here, take this one," he said. "She won't make up for your loss, but she'll get you to the Proclamation."

"You're okay then?" Takana said.

Angulli nodded and forced a smile. Takana reluctantly signaled the driver and the chariot headed for the North Gate.

Bright sun hadn't reached the streets but the rooftops were lit. Takana glanced at his mother, next to him on the chariot. It was clear she was still thinking of the battle and was just as shaken as he was. But as they reached the city wall, sounds made it clear the city had cast aside its mourning mantle. They heard music and high spirited voices and, when the gate was pushed aside, they saw that the streets were flooded with people. Butchers were lighting their braziers and royal guards in dress uniforms were maneuvering their brushed and braided horses through the streets, attempting order. Seeing the people happy lifted their spirits. For the moment at least they'd set aside their fears.

Men and women returned from the forest with ever-green branches and began weaving them together to festoon walls and buildings throughout the city. Musicians gathered in small groups with drums, wood flutes and horns to practice the pieces they would be called on to play for the dances and games following the crowning. And from each of the temples clustered in the Temple Plaza, smoke was rising from burning sacrifices. Merchants barely opened their shops when they were besieged by customers, especially women buying fabrics woven with silver and gold threads to catch the sun and later the torches.

The henna booths turned out women whose hair, hands and feet were decorated with reddish-brown designs. Young girls shrieked with delight as they compared one original design with another.

But when the trumpets blew from the Temple of the Storm God, commerce ceased and the Hittite people ran to the Temple Plaza. Takana drove across the city and took a position near the King's Gate, where he knew the procession of royals would begin. There was a strict order to the proceedings and Takana waited. They were no sooner in place when the sound of horses' hooves came from along the eastern wall and entered the city. He recognized many of his neighbors from the acropolis, but his chariot driver held back until just before the *tawananna* and *tuhkanti*, last in the procession.

Some of Hattusa's people had waited at the King's Gate so they could follow the procession through the Upper City and into the Temple Plaza in the Lower City. All along the way people squeezed against the buildings to allow chariots carrying the people of status. Once inside, they stood in relative quiet, packed closely together at the outer edges, glancing from time to time at the grandest temple door of all—the one that housed the Exalted One, Preserver of

Order in the Cosmos, Supreme Overlord and Protector of the Land of Hatti—the Temple of the Storm God.

At the temple, Takana helped his mother from the chariot and they waited by the stairs under the menacing statue of the Sacred Bull. Hatti's citizens crowded in but left a corridor open for the royal family, who had slowed their chariot in order to make a grand entrance. While they waited, the people shifted from place to place to find the best view. The lucky ones would be close enough to hear the High Priest read King Suldana's Proclamation, the naming of his successor.

On Takana's right, something was causing a disturbance. It was Chief Ibiranu and two of his high-ranking royal guards, elbowing a path through the people. When they reached the base of the temple steps, Ibiranu looked left and right, made eye contact with Takana and quickly turned away. Takana wondered if he knew his son was dead . . . and if he cared.

The crowd quieted, the bronze doors of the Temple of the Storm God swung open and the High Priest emerged. The queen's chariot entered the plaza, pulled by four matched black stallions draped from neck to rump with gold embroidered black silk. Hammered gold discs hung from their leather reins. The chariot's frame was covered with gold leaves to reflect the sun at every angle. The chariot driver wore a black tunic, a pleated black kilt and a festooned helmet of polished brass. Queen Resat, resplendent in pale silk and a jeweled crown, took Prince Setmel's arm and stepped from the chariot. The crown prince looked uncomfortably rigid in a tunic of woven gold threads and a robe of embroidered red fabric draped across his shoulders. They stood briefly at the base of the temple under the gaze of the High Priest and then ascended the steps to the portico.

Next Queen Patupa and Prince Takana, showing no obvious evidence of their earlier ordeal, took their place behind the queen while leading nobles gathered at the base of the stairs. Though her back was to Takana, he saw the queen turn her head and scowl at Chief Ibiranu. Takana stole a look at his mother. If not for her respect for the event, he thought she looked like she wanted to deliver a pointed shoe to the queen's rear.

One by one the chariots were dispatched to make room for the people. King Naram-Suen and Queen Alina came into view. As dignitaries of a foreign kingdom, they rightfully occupied space directly below on the left side of the temple entrance. Takana caught his uncle's eye and the barest nod of his crowned head. Their brief time together had renewed not only the family bond but also the importance of allies. His fireside talks with his uncle were still very much a part of his thoughts. They would be until he had a clearer understanding of the future. For the present, it was enough to know he could serve Hatti whether he remained a citizen or became an ally in Luwadna.

At the edge of the Temple Plaza the people were moving aside for another chariot. It carried King Amilla with two high-ranking officers running alongside. Happily for Takana the shuffle revealed Ras' copper curls. He was bending slightly and speaking to someone next to him. Takana hoped it was Angulli.

Quiet settled over the plaza again. The High Priest stepped to the portico's center, turned slightly toward the Sacred Bull, and raised his arms in supplication. "Mighty God of Thunder, withhold your lightning and storms this day. Pour down your blessing on this sacred rite. Grant our departed King Suldana II a place of honor beside you. Hear his words!"

As the High Priest accepted the tablet offered by his attendant, Takana heard mumbling in the crowd. Three hooded men were threading their way through to the base of the steps. When they were directly under the High Priest, Master Palla threw back his hood. "That's a false tablet!" he shouted and pointed to the figure next to him. "Here is the one King Suldana dictated to Hapati with his dying breath."

All eyes turned and gasped when Hapati, pulling back his hood with one hand and holding a tablet high with the other, ascended the stairs and handed the tablet to the High Priest.

Swift movements came from several directions. Takana saw Queen Resat step back and move behind Setmel. Her hands grasped her throat. At the base of the stairs Chief Ibiranu was backing into the crowd behind him. To the right, a totally different scene was taking place. Ras, Azzia and Hapati were exchanging smiles and mouthing their greetings. It filled Takana with momentary satisfaction. But the tension in the entire plaza was mounting and Takana felt his heart accelerate.

The High Priest stared at Hapati for several moments before taking the tablet from him. "Are you a ghost?"

"No. I am flesh and blood, saved from death to bring you King Suldana II's final words."

The Priest looked from one tablet to the other with total disbelief registering on his wizened face. "What am I to think? Both tablets bear King Suldana's official seal," he said, handing them to his aide. "This is an offense to the gods," he said, visibly shaken.

Master Palla ripped back the hood on Mutwalli and pushed him up the steps to stand before the High Priest. "Confess your forgery, Mutwalli!"

"It was Ibiranu! He forced me!" Mutwalli shook so badly his tunic rippled.

"And it was Chief Ibiranu," Hapati added, "who dragged me from the palace with the king's tablet, accused me of treason and asked his royal guard, Gille, to kill me," Hapati said.

All eyes searched for Ibiranu, finding him as he tried to bolt. But he was restrained by Gille, who'd worked his way close to the chief.

"I was doing my queen's bidding!" Ibiranu shouted, pointing to the wide-eyed queen, who'd retreated further behind Setmel. The stunned prince was twisting furiously to see his mother.

The people erupted in protest. Some looked confused, some pumped their arms in the air with anger, while others fearfully pressed their hands together and shouted supplications to the gods. A few, like Azzia and Ras, held their positions, just waiting for the opportunity to run to Hapati. Takana pitied them. They could neither run to him nor expect him to come to them.

At the High Priest's order, the trumpeter called the people to order and when quiet was restored, he moved to the edge of the portico. "According to the Law, I am the Storm God's earthly voice. I must seek his counsel.

"Go to your homes. Purify yourselves and pray to the gods." Then he turned and ordered his attendants to escort those involved to the Audience Hall and to hold them there until he performed the necessary sacrifices and prayers.

By midday the High Priest arrived at the masssive Audience Hall in the interior of the acropolis. Hattusa's senior Magistrate, in a long black robe and a tall conical hat, followed close behind. Takana and his mother followed them to the base of the dais, but for a moment both the High Priest and the Magistrate seemed puzzled. The priest whispered to the closest temple servant who immediately pointed to a distant wall where Queen Resat and Setmel stood. Ibiranu and Mutwalli stood in a corner on the opposite wall, and Master Palla, Hapati and Gille were pressed against a third. At a signal from the High Priest they gathered in, although still keeping a distance from each other.

Just as he was about to begin, the hall door opened and a temple servant stepped in tentatively with Azzia and Ras. The High Priest nodded and Hapati ran to join them. For several moments, the priest fussed with his robe, glancing up occasionally to wait until Hapati managed to pull himself together.

The High Priest, presiding as the god's emissary, climbed the few steps and sat in the king's throne. He stared at the floor for a time, then he coughed and invited the Magistrate, who was holding both tablets, to speak.

"Let us begin with you, Hapati. We will hear from you what transpired after the king dictated his last words."

Hapati recounted how Ibiranu came to his chamber after the king's passing, took him to Yazilikaya, accused him of treason and ordered Gille to kill him and bury him behind a ruined *hekur*. But instead, Hapati told them, Gille instructed him to wait there and he would be taken to safety.

"After Gille left, three men arrived on foot. They took me through Yazilikaya—" Hapati shuddered while the emotions replayed. "They took me to a tall stone hill where they rolled aside a large stone. It was dark, a cave, until they lit a torch. I've never seen the like, my lords. Carved in stone was everything I needed for comfort—a bed, a bench and stool. They provided oil lamps, and firewood for warmth. Openings in the stone ceiling carried light to me during the day and escape for the smoke from the lamps and a small fire at night. Every day they brought food and wood and when they left, they rolled the stone across the entrance to hide me from prying eyes. I thank the gods for their kindness."

Azzia looked into her husband's face. "I will praise the gods forever."

"You dared to disobey the Chief of the Royal Guard?" the Magistrate said, turning to Gille.

Ibiranu suddenly shot forward. "Not only has he disobeyed me, he and other disloyal guards have killed my son! They must be punished!"

The Magistrate ordered Ibiranu to step back. "I will deal with you later. Go on, guardsman."

"I did disobey, my lord. My loyalty was to the king. Even before he died, the queen was working to reverse his orders. Ibiranu was sworn to obey the king's orders yet he allowed the queen to change them. It was she who ordered Ibiranu to kill the king's loyal scribe. When I pretended to carry out the chief's order, Hapati made me promise to give the tablet to no one but Master Palla and I swore on my life.

"When I returned from Yazilikaya, I gave the tablet to Master Palla, and when I told him Chief Ibiranu wanted another tablet made, he suggested Mutwalli. He'd failed to graduate from the *eduba* but he could read and write."

"Tell me more of the royal guardsmen," the Magistrate said.

Gille went on to reveal the growing division within the royal guards themselves and how Master Palla rallied guards to protect Queen Patupa and Prince Takana. "Chief Ibiranu told us our duty was to clear the way for the *tuhkanti.* He said the queen had ordered the deaths of anyone who stood in the way of Setmel's path to the throne—Prince Takana, Queen Patupa, Ras and Azzia."

"Yes, you see! It was my duty to obey," Ibiranu shouted.

The Magistrate listened to everyone, holding the queen and Ibiranu back despite their protests. When, finally, he called on the queen, she took several steps forward and raised her chin.

"I am blameless in this! I am surrounded by incompetence, helpless to fulfill my duties as queen. Chief Ibiranu, who is charged with protecting me, is an idiot who has misinterpreted my orders more than once. I dare to say he answers to troublemakers in the kingdom. There must be an investigation!"

Ibiranu's mouth flew open. His face glowed red and he tore his tunic from the neck.

The queen shifted to Setmel, hung her head and stifled a sob. "I weep for my son. I had such hopes for him but . . . He suffers from unbridled ambition. He has taken advantage of my grief and weakness to reach for power well beyond his abilities."

Setmel lunged for her, but a temple servant wrestled him to the floor.

Queen Resat gave him a look of disgust, grabbed her skirt and, with a flourish, turned back to the Magistrate. "Now, in the safety of this room, I will tell you what fear has prevented me from revealing before now. Beware of King Amilla!"

"King Amilla? King of Kazaram? What of him?" the High Priest said, jumping to his feet.

The queen's hands flew to her throat. "He said he'd kill me if I . . . I mean, if my son, when he became king that is, if he didn't join forces with him and move against Luwadna."

Her aspect suddenly changed. She looked feverish and her eyes bulged from their sockets. "Don't you see this is what's behind everything? How could I do the things they accuse me of? Yes, I'm queen, but I'm just a woman."

The Magistrate appeared untouched by her speech. He turned to Hapati. "Which tablet is your work?" the Magistrate asked.

"The one that says, 'Setmel is son of King Amilla . . . unfit. I proclaim Prince Takana.'"

"Me?" Takana stepped back and his mother grabbed his arm.

Setmel screamed hysterically. The queen threw herself at Takana's feet. Heads swiveled from one to the other and mouths stood agape, until all eyes all settled on Prince Takana.

"Read the tablet," the High Priest ordered, handing Hapati the tablet.

"That *is* all. Those were the last words he uttered before he breathed his last."

"The king was *cuckold* and he *knew?*" the High Priest said.

The queen, with her arms around Takana's feet, sobbed and begged for forgiveness. Prince Setmel wrenched himself free and stood over her, screeching. "My Coronation is ruined! You've ruined everything!" He looked around the room from face to face in complete disbelief, then stepped forward, raised his chin and shouted. "I am the *tuhkanti*, the crown prince, the next ruler of the Hittite Kingdom. I demand your respect or I'll order the royal guards to stake your heads on the gates—even yours, mother."

The queen jumped to her feet and grabbed his robe. "You ungrateful child! You'd be nothing without me."

From the top of the dais, the Magistrate addressed Gille. "Take him and his mother to their chambers in the acropolis. Place guards on their doors. Put Ibiranu and Mutwalli in the guardhouse. Go!"

He turned, then, to the High Priest. "My Lord, a suggestion?" The High Priest, looking exasperated, nodded. "May I suggest we ask King Naram-Suen to provide warriors to assist Master Palla and Gille in separating the royal guards? We must know their loyalties. They are not to be blamed for their actions. All will be given a chance to swear their loyalty to the new king when the time comes."

Again the High Priest nodded and once more the Magistrate spoke. "How do you suggest we handle King Amilla's part in this?"

The High Priest frowned. "This is a political matter. If King Amilla plotted with Queen Resat to overtake Hatti, he already knows their plot has failed. Besides, can we believe anything she says? No, we must make no aggressive moves against the king of Kazaram. Perhaps King Naram-Suen's men could keep a watchful eye on his movements?"

The Magistrate caught Gille's eye and received an assuring nod. "Good. See to it," he said.

When the door closed behind them, the High Priest sat down with a heavy sigh and grasped the arms of the chair. His knuckles turned white and he stared at the floor. The others waited in silence, barely breathing.

Finally he raised his eyes and addressed them. "We must finish our work. The people are waiting. Prince Takana?"

Takana was vaguely aware of the orders and movements of the last few moments. His heart felt ready to burst. With a nudge from his mother, he nodded.

"Magistrate, recite the punishment for the queen's treason," the High Priest said.

"The law is clear. She has committed treason against the king. Her sentence is death."

Again the High Priest stared at the floor before he stood up. "Our laws come to us from the gods who live in the heavens. Their ways are not our ways, yet they are all knowing. They alone have full knowledge of heaven and earth. They bless us with all we need and for this we honor their guidance.

"The voice of our Most Holy Storm God comes to me and I speak the words he gives me. Therefore, on the day following the Coronation, Queen Resat will be put to death for treason. Ibiranu will be banished from Hatti Land. Likewise, Setmel will be banished from the kingdom. Mutwalli will serve as a slave to Master Palla for five years, after which time Master Palla will decide his future."

Each sentence was like the slice of a sword. Takana's head was reeling. King? King of Hatti?

The Magistrate descended the steps, but the High Priest turned to face Takana. "You must open your mind, resist uncertainty, receive that which is mobilizing for you. Our Mighty Storm God is gathering the gods together. By the time the crown is lowered onto your head, their spirits of wisdom and courage will become an inseparable part of you.

"Now, I must go. The people are waiting. Once I've spoken to them, I will seek our Storm God's direction. Magistrate! Draw up a document of punishment to be read before the Proclamation." He left the Audience Hall with the Magistrate on his heels.

Takana blinked. His mind and body had frozen. The room fell silent and Takana welcomed it, not just to hear the words again in his head, but to react to his own reality. He studied the faces around him, saw his mother watching him and Ras together with his parents again. Moments later they were all looking at him.

He took a deep breath. "I'm not worthy of this. How can I be king?"

"Who better than you?" Ras said. "We've just heard the voice of our Storm King. We listened with the ears of mortal men, but we mustn't question his judgment."

It didn't sound like Ras and he searched his friend's face. Wasn't this the impulsive, explosive man of action? When had he ever bowed to someone else's words, even a god's? When had he ever used words like "mortal men?" Ras didn't think in such ways, at least not in his presence.

Ras didn't flinch from Takana's stare until Takana's mother interrupted.

"I confess to you I've thought of you in this way for many years. If not as Hatti's king, then king somewhere else. You are a king in every way, my son," she said.

Takana touched his chest. His heart felt ready to burst.

Master Palla walked over and grasped his shoulders. In all the excitement, Takana forgot the old man was in the room.

"Today I can still hold you as my friend. Tomorrow I will kneel before you as my king and my heart will be bursting with joy."

"I'm not prepared. I'm not," Takana said, shaking his head. "I feel King Suldana's presence with me so strongly but . . ."

"But?" Palla said.

"Perhaps I can learn to be king, but order the queen's death? I can't, I can't."

"The Holy Priest and the Magistrate will order it before you are crowned, I'm sure," Master Palla said. "The High Priest speaks for the king in his absence."

"No," Takana said. "I must speak to him now." He straightened his tunic, ready to bolt, but Master Palla gripped his arm. "Your wishes must wait, my prince." The urgency in the old scribe's voice worked and Takana nodded. He led the way to the chariots waiting for them outside.

CHAPTER TWENTY-SEVEN
TAKANA

A s their chariots entered the Temple Plaza, the trumpets
continued to blare from the portico of the Storm God's
temple. Master Palla took a place at the base of the steps
while Queen Patupa and Prince Takana climbed to take their
places. The High Priest stepped through the huge bronze
door, giving them a nod that conveyed confidence and command. Against the polished granite stone of the temple, he
was luminous in a fresh white tunic and a wide swath of dark
fabric held fast by a burnished metal disc at his shoulder.
Takana watched in awe, knowing that when he spoke to the
people, they would be assured his words came directly from
their All Powerful Storm God.

They waited together, watching the people spill into the
plaza, eager no doubt to hear what order the gods would
bring to the disruption of Proclamation Day. Whatever they
were doing when the trumpets sounded, they'd scooped
their children into their arms and came running. Takana
saw merchants still wearing blood-stained aprons from preparing sacrifices, carpenters with sawdust in their hair and
children still clutching their toys. A squad of royal guards

took their places around the perimeter of the plaza and guided the people methodically, and to Takana's eyes, sympathetically. Hittites, after all, were people of ritual and order. Their Day of Proclamation had dissolved into chaos, trusted leaders had betrayed their trust, and, perhaps equally forbidding, was the thought of their beloved king who witnessed everything from the heavens. What was to become of them? They lived at the mercy of the gods. What price would they demand for such disregard for the law?

Soon the shuffling stopped and faces fastened on the High Priest. He stepped forward with his arms stretched out to them. Silence and stone-like stillness responded to the Storm God's earthly emissary.

"Blessed be our Mighty Storm God, Protector of the Land of Hatti, Guardian and Enforcer of the Law. Comfort us! Evil deeds have been done! Those we entrusted to govern and protect us have betrayed us and sought to destroy our kingdom and the blessed memory of our King Suldana who dwells among you in the heavens.

"Help us! What is wrong must be made right! Guide us! Until our kingdom is set right, we dare not welcome our new king, the one proclaimed by our beloved King Suldana II. We must bring the wrongdoers to justice.

"Loyal Citizens of Hatti! I declare this a Time of Preparation. Be diligent! Trust that the gods *will* guide us. Raise your voices in praise! Be generous in your sacrifices! When the Mighty Storm God pronounces his punishments against those who have betrayed the kingdom, the trumpets will sound. Until then, may the gods watch over us."

As the crowd dispersed and the High Priest retreated into the temple, Takana walked with his mother to the chariot, hesitating to give a quizzical glance to two royal guards standing on either side of him. Instantly, they bowed deeply. Bodyguards? He rolled his eyes and spied Ras and

Angulli waving. He waved back, adding a signal to wait for him, while he spoke a few words to his mother. By the time he finished they were at his side.

"What a day this has been," Angulli said. "Ras told me what happened in the Audience Hall. I guess I should kneel, but it's still a secret, eh?" He beamed and then covered a chuckle when he noticed the two guards.

Takana nodded. "Yeah. Look, for now I'm still me! To tell the truth part of me doesn't want to think about it, but there's something I've got to tell the High Priest. Can we run later? It will help clear my head and there's so much I want to tell you."

They agreed to wait for him at the North Gate. Takana sighed in gratitude and climbed back up the temple steps two at a time. Already the air was becoming suffused with the smoke from sacrificial fires and Takana imagined the urgent incantations of the priests in the surrounding temples. As he pulled the bronze temple door aside, the guards posted themselves on either side. His protectors, he conceded, but he was annoyed nonetheless.

Inside the door of the temple, Takana asked a servant to announce him to the High Priest, and while he waited he pressed himself against the granite wall and prayed.

Gods, Ancestors, hear me. I would give anything to feel the certainty of this rock at my back. As you are now a god, My King Suldana, help me.

His eyes sprang open at the sound of a timid cough. It was a temple priest, as wide as he was tall, struggling with a goat while trying to open the door. He fell to his knees.

"No! Please! I'm not the king yet."

News travels quickly among the temple servants, Takana thought. He smiled, glad for the comic relief, and held the door for the confused priest waddling after the escaping goat. Everything was becoming too serious too quickly.

At that moment, the servant returned and asked Takana to follow him.

It was rare to see the inner spaces of the High Temple, a maze of corridors with painted reliefs of the Storm God in various poses—a lightning bolt in his hand, his hair and robe rippling in the wind, and one showing his arms reaching out to embrace the people. When Takana was sure he'd never find his way back to the entrance without guidance, the servant opened a door. Just beyond, the High Priest was standing waiting for him.

"Holy One, I don't wish to begin my reign with the death of the queen." He hadn't intended to blurt his words but the revelations of the last few hours had dulled his judgment. Each passing moment seemed to evoke new questions, new consequences. How long had devious minds been at work to usurp King Suldana's leadership? How deep into the royal court did it reach? It was evident that such plans had been fermenting for years before they exploded in the Temple Plaza.

Takana realized he was pacing, absorbed in spilling the words he'd come to say. He quickly turned to the High Priest and read patience and pity in his expression.

"She must be punished. She put her own desire for power above the king's and above the interests of the Hittite people."

"Yes, it's The Law, I know. But I believe there's a better way, a way which may show her the error of her ways, perhaps even redeem her."

Though the High Priest looked skeptical, Takana continued. "King Suldana understood human weakness, yet whenever possible, he punished with mercy. We always felt safe under his rule, didn't we?"

The High Priest waved him to a corner of the room where two ornately carved chairs with leather-woven seats faced each other. Takana, eager to make his case, perched on the edge. The High Priest crossed his legs. Except for an expression of curiosity, there was an unmistakable air of dismissiveness about him.

"It is well known you spent time with your uncle, evidently sufficient time for the king to weigh your worth. He has named you his successor because he understood you to be a lawful man. As such you must accept what has been handed down to us. The Law is clear, my prince, death is the punishment for treason."

"Yes, Holy One, I spent most of my years close to the king and I know he respected The Law, but I also observed his actions. Listen, please, our sovereign knew the queen resented the time I spent with him. And as Setmel and I began warrior training together, I admit I found it difficult to hide my growing disrespect for him. The queen never hid her rancor. I've had sufficient time to conclude that's why the king ordered my mother and me to Harmesh. He removed the thorn from the queen's side and, at the same time, gave me the opportunity to develop and mature, to learn more about the people outside the city and discern how best to serve them. I'm a better leader because of his wisdom," Takana said, desperately swallowing the lump in his throat. "You see how he sought solutions that preserved over those that destroyed. His action preserved peace for his queen and education for me."

The High Priest shifted in the chair, uncrossed his legs and placed his felted feet firmly on the polished stone surface. Takana braced himself, expecting the priest to repeat The Law. Instead, a smile took over his normally stoic expression. "What is your suggestion?" he said.

"Servanthood, Holy One. Strip her of all power, of all opportunity to manipulate. Symbolically, it is the death of a queen, isn't it?"

"Interesting." He paused. "I'm not convinced she can change her ways. Besides, who do you suggest as her master?" The High Priest crossed his legs again.

Takana fidgeted. He hadn't considered that. His thoughts were of an earlier time when the queen was a loving mother and aunt. Who had the patience and wisdom to remold her? The question was just the trigger he needed to reveal the answer.

"My aunt and uncle, Holy One."

"The King and Queen of Luwadna? Hmm, a curious idea. What makes you think they would even consider this?"

Takana explained what he'd begun to think of as destiny, the hands of the gods on him as he traveled and spoke with his uncle. At the time his uncle's description of their love for children and the orphanage they'd set up made little impression on him other than to confirm their compassion. Now it seemed the perfect solution. He described the orphanage to the High Priest and how the children had the natural talent to change character and spirit.

"Holy One, the queen's heart was not always black. We know the king respected her counsel. He loved her! Something happened to her over the years. I remember a time when she was good and kind. I believe my uncle and aunt can use her with the children in the orphanage. When she is stripped of her present situation, I think the children can restore her."

Takana sat back and placed his hands in his lap, suddenly aware of his aggressive posture and wildly gesturing hands. His breathing slowed while he imagined the High Priest examining his idea carefully. As he studied the priest, Takana began to understand why King Suldana sought his counsel in times of trouble. True, he could be politically expedient, but his loyalty to the king and the people of Hatti was sincere. Finally the priest stood and placed his ringed hand on Takana's arm.

"After what we learned today, she is no longer queen. She is an ordinary citizen. As such she can be made a slave and given to the Kingdom of Luwadna. I will call for the Magistrate immediately and we will draw up the necessary contract as soon as King Naram-Suen gives his assent. Would you like to speak to your uncle or . . . ?"

'I'll go immediately and return with his answer." Takana turned to leave but the High Priest spoke again.

"I have already pronounced banishment for Setmel and Ibiranu, as you heard. The sentence is fitting for both. But, I've been thinking . . . Setmel belongs to King Amilla, does he not?"

Takana caught the High Priest's meaning immediately. "Yes, of course, and I have the same hope, although we can make no suggestion. Banish him from Hatti and let the King of Kazaram do as he will. Setmel won't survive alone, that's for sure. Good," Takana said. "And Ibiranu? He is responsible for his son's death, though he did not wield the sword that cut him down. He ordered Hapati's death and fortunately was unsuccessful. Banishment from Hatti Land seems to fit his crime as well. I hope the gods will hound him for the rest of his life until he understands his errors."

"I will add my own prayers to yours. Your mercy will be shouted from the rooftops," the High Priest said.

Admiration from the most powerful priest made Takana squirm, but he nodded solemnly, thanked him and moved away. But he stopped.

"Something more?" the High Priest said.

"I mean no disrespect, Holy One, but I'm not yet king and there are two royal guards. . ." he said, hoping he was not overstepping his prerogatives. "Those who would do me harm are under guard, secured behind locked doors, right?"

"Until the Proclamation. In the meantime I will pray and watch for signs. We must allow time to hear the will of the gods and restore order to the people. But then, Prince Takana, you must accept the necessity."

Takana set his jaw and nodded.

He left the High Priest in the quiet, shadowy innards of the temple, walking slowly through the corridors in counterpoint to the rush of thoughts in his head. When the doors were pulled aside, a temple servant was speaking to the guards. Takana hesitated before descending, and when he did there were no footsteps behind him. Here and there he saw people gathered in small animated groups, presumably still trying to make sense of the disrupted day. He rehearsed his words as he jogged across the Temple Plaza to the acropolis where his uncle and aunt were quartered.

But just as he approached the gate to the palace, a bass voice called his name and he turned around to see a chariot with a familiar banner. He realized his mind still lacked clarity because it took a moment for Takana to recognize the colors of Harmesh. He jogged to shorten the distance between them and stopped dead when he saw the vassal lord he knew so well. Seeing him in Hattusa was surprise enough, but it was the girl standing next to him that made him catch his breath. Elin. What was she doing there? Here?

"My Lord Odepinu?" Takana said, reaching the chariot.

"Prince Takana! We were hoping we'd get to see you. We've come for the Coronation, but there's some confusion. Do you know what's going on?"

The question hardly registered. He was too astonished by Elin's broad smile to answer. She looked happy, while he was befuddled. Befuddled, yes, but his heart bounced as well.

"This is my daughter, Elin, but I understand you already know each other very well," Odepinu said. "Come. Join us.

We've been assigned an apartment in the acropolis. Do you have time?"

Takana's mouth was dry and Elin was still grinning. "Uh, yes, there's been some confusion but . . . yes, I'll come, but I must . . . I have . . . I can't now, but soon, I promise."

The lord nodded but Takana could see he'd added curiosity to his confused expression. Takana gave him a smile and leveled a frown at Elin before he left them.

His legs felt weak, wobbly, and excitement was quickly replacing the shock and annoyance that had briefly passed through him. Not now, later, he said to himself, and he nudged Elin's face out of his mind. It proved difficult. Her beauty and so-sure-of-herself manner refreshed him in a way he didn't quite understand, though he liked it. She was never an open book, too insightful and intelligent to be taken at face value. Those were just some of the reasons she excited him, challenged him. She'd never be possessed by anyone, but he wanted her anyway. But not now—later, he said to himself again.

Inside the Acropolis Plaza, Takana watched Lord Odepinu's chariot pull around back to use the ramps to the upper terraces. He took the steps in front, slowly, not only to collect his thoughts before talking to his uncle and aunt about Queen Resat, but to avoid seeing Elin again until he could control the excitement he felt. He reminded himself he was angry. Why had she never mentioned who her father was? How did he miss seeing her all those times when he met with the vassal lord? She had some explaining to do.

His aunt answered the door on the first knock.

"Takana! Come in. We've talked about nothing else but what happened today. What's being done about the false tablet?"

His uncle's booming welcome interrupted his answer until they were seated and Queen Alina brought a tray of cups filled with fruit juice. Takana took a long swallow and explained what had happened, but he stopped short of telling them his name was on the king's true tablet. His uncle turned his face sideways and squinted. Suddenly he turned to the servants and ordered them from the room.

When the room was cleared and Queen Alina was giving her husband a stern look, he spoke. "*You* are King Suldana's successor to the throne!"

Takana felt heat rise from his neck to the top of his head and knew it pulsed red.

The king threw his head back and laughed. "I knew it! I knew my brother-in-law would do what's best for the Hittite Kingdom."

They pulled Takana to his feet and embraced him.

"I don't quite believe it yet," Takana said as they sat down again. "But already there are decisions I have to make and I've come to ask for your help."

He described his desire to maintain the quality of mercy established by King Suldana. His aunt and uncle exchanged glances that spoke of their memories of his generous spirit.

"The queen will be banished and become a slave," Takana said.

"What? I understand mercy and the need to temper revenge and vindictiveness. But, Queen Resat? After what she's done, after what she *planned* to do? Not sentenced to death? She has committed treason!" the king said. "The people will demand it!"

But when Takana said nothing in response, his uncle placed both hands on his knees and lifted his head. "Tomorrow the Magistrate will pronounce the punishments and it will be settled. He is Keeper of The Law."

"My heart says otherwise," Takana said. He described the queen he knew as a boy of six. "She was a loving mother to me and Setmel in those days. I witnessed her devotion to the king and his for her. I don't know what happened to change her into the black spirit we know today, but I believe goodness may still be there, deep inside."

He looked directly at his uncle, the Luwadnan king. "Do you remember what you said about the children in your orphanage, how they lift your spirits and draw out the best in you?" The king nodded but a frown knit his brow. "I would like to give Queen Resat the chance to redeem herself, to see the damage she has done to Setmel and to herself, to learn to use her intelligence and passion for good again. Would you accept her as a slave to help with the children?"

The king and queen exchanged a long look. And, while the king shook his head and rubbed his hands together, the queen spoke. "You want to offer her a second chance."

"Yes," Takana said.

Queen Alina turned to her husband. "Do you remember watching the change take place in the children we found huddled in the streets? They bit and scratched, cursed and spat at our servants when we tried to bring them to the orphanage. Do you remember how quickly they became happy, loving and playful when they were secure and loved?"

The king's eyes became glossey and his face softened. The queen continued with a trill of laughter, so like his mother's.

"We'll watch her like a baby duck venturing into deep water for the first time. We won't let her drown but we'll insist on hard work until she functions as she was meant to. Hopefully, the shock of cold water will awaken the good in her," the queen said.

The king laughed at his wife's analogy. "And if she doesn't function as she was meant to, we'll drown her!"

"So you'll take her with you?" Takana said.

Suddenly serious, the king spoke again. "Hear me. If she doesn't convince us she understands the evils she perpetrated and will devote herself to goodwill, we *will* end her life."

"The Magistrate will prepare a document of ownership. You'll have the right to do whatever you want with her," Takana said.

"Then we accept the challenge," the king said, and the queen added her agreement.

Takana felt dizzy as he took the steps down to the plaza. The feeling was familiar, like when he'd run faster and further than he planned. He was exhausted but his day could not end, not until he reported to the High Priest. He walked to the Temple of the Storm God through relatively quiet, empty streets. He hoped the gods were bringing peace and comfort to the citizens. Maybe later he'd feel them come to him, come and deliver the relief his mind and heart needed. The sky was expressing its own disposition as he drew near the temple. Clouds were rolling in, crowding out the sun. Let me have time with my friends before this day ends, he prayed.

When Takana was led inside the temple, he found the High Priest waiting near the altar. "Are you still firm in your decision, Prince Takana?"

"The King and Queen of Luwadna have sealed it for me. They will receive our former queen and await the pleasure of the gods for her redemption, if it is to be. If her dark spirits cannot be vanquished, they will execute her as they would any disobedient slave under their laws."

"Very well. I will call for the Magistrate immediately to prepare the documents. Listen for the trumpets and we will put this mess to rest. I will declare continued preparation until The Law is carried out and the gods have restored peace to the hearts and minds of the people.

"Heed your own preparation, Prince Takana."

He knew the High Priest meant he should prepare for the Proclamation, but his heart was tugging him to the North Gate.

CHAPTER TWENTY-EIGHT

TAKANA

The sight of Ras and Angulli waiting for him at the North Gate put wings on his feet. They took off together without words, enjoying the rhythm of their feet on the hardened path. North of the city wall the land sloped gently downward and in no time at all the cool, moist air of the forest reached out for them. Once under the dense shade of the evergreens, only an occasional shaft of the descending sun kept the path visible. Well-worn by Hatti's citizens and marked with cart wheels, the footpaths fanned out in many directions, most leading to homes nestled in the landscape here and there. Takana purposefully avoided them and led the way to a favorite secluded spot where they could sit and talk undisturbed.

Without exchanging a word, they increased their speed. It brought a smile to Takana because it told him they were as eager to enjoy some private time as he was. Out of the corner of his eye Takana saw Ras shoot ahead, giving Takana a provocative look as he passed. The competition was on! Angulli laughed out loud and slowed down, aware he'd be rapidly outdistanced. And by the time he reached the familiar flat boulder overlooking a wide valley, Takana and Ras were sprawled out and gasping for breath.

"Well, which one of you two idiots won?"

"I did!" Ras sputtered.

"By the gods, you did not!"

"You're both idiots anyway." Angulli grew sober and shook his head. "It just occurred to me that this may be our last run together *and* the last time I'll call you an idiot without being dragged off to a cell in the guardhouse."

Takana's eyes stung and he quickly lowered his head. He'd been thinking the same thoughts. It was true he would not run in the Coronation games, nor could he take off and run through the forest whenever he wanted. And he knew everyone would guard their words in his presence. But just as quickly he remembered his uncle running with his troops, joking and laughing with them. Somehow he, too, would find ways to refresh his spirit and search out private moments in what he imagined would, for the most part, be a very public life.

Ras made a noise in his throat. "Angulli's right. It's not going to be the same," He sat up, ripped out a bunch of grass and tossed it in the air.

Takana heard him, but his mind had jumped ahead— ideas, like quickening seeds, were bursting with new life. His head snapped up, followed by the rest of his body. He left the rock and paced back and forth, searching for the words he wanted. There were questions he needed to ask, but only one answer he could accept. Instinctively, Takana knew the more important the question was the more time should be spent in preparation. But there was no time! Ranting was Ras' style. It gave his friend release, but ultimately ended in confusion. And Angulli? In his eagerness to please others, he'd had little experience with decision making. Finally, Takana positioned himself firmly.

"My uncle, King Naram-Suen, said something to me. At the time, it didn't register but now . . ."

"Are we supposed to know what you're talking about?" Ras said.

Angulli looked bewildered but he got up to stand with Takana. Sweat was running on his face.

"My uncle said, 'Maybe, maybe not.' He was saying something that seems impossible, might not be."

"Huh?" Ras twitched with impatience.

"You want something that's impossible?" Angulli said.

"We were talking one night about our marriage customs," Takana said. Their eyebrows shot up and they stared at him with identical expressions, something akin to fear. He quickly waved his hands in the air and laughed. "No, no, that's not what I want to talk about. My uncle's message was that we shouldn't give up on anything we want badly. And what I want is for our friendship never to change."

"I'm afraid it's going to. You'll be king!" Ras said.

A distant rumble drew their eyes to the sky. No clouds were visible, but the sun was decidedly dipping toward the horizon and clouds were rushing in to take its place. The Sun Goddess needs her rest and so do I, Takana said to himself, but not before I speak what's on my heart. He set his shoulders.

"Right! I'll be king! Responsible for the kingdom! I'll need others to help me, people I trust, people who have the same hopes for the kingdom that I do. People like the two of you." His stance felt suddenly awkward and he dropped his arms at his sides. Ras' jaw dropped and Angulli choked.

"You heard me. I want both of you close to me. Here's what I've been thinking: I have great confidence in Royal Guard Gille. I want him to replace Ibiranu. Ras, I'd like you to become one of his commanders. I know Gille well. He'll appreciate your loyalty and passion. And from him you'll learn patience, timing and decisiveness."

Ras, blinking and sucking in his breath, dropped to his knees. "I'm honored. I won't let you down. You have my promise."

Takana closed his eyes. Had the trauma of losing and regaining his father awakened something latent in Ras? Twice in recent days his friend had surprised him with the responses of a man whose world had stretched beyond his personal boundaries. He opened his eyes and smiled. It was going to be satisfying to watch Ras grow.

He turned to Angulli, who had frozen except for widening eyes. When had his gentle friend *ever* put his own desires before others? He abhorred anything unjust, hateful or cruel. Yet despite his mild manner, Angulli had responded with striking courage when it was needed. It was time all of Hatti recognized him as the best of Hittites.

"What you've done with horse training is remarkable and shows great inventiveness and perseverance. I believe your family has already accepted your new ideas and will work with you, right?" Angulli's head bobbed up and down like a spring. "But there's the chariot idea we've talked about, too. I want you to oversee the design and manufacture of a new fleet of chariots to carry three men. How does that sound to you?"

"Like heaven on earth!"

Ras wrapped his arms around Takana and Angulli. "Maybe some things will change, but we'll be working together for the same cause. What happens next?"

Before answering Takana cocked his head toward the path and broke into a slow run. They jogged abreast, threading their way through the trees.

"What's next? So much happened in the Audience Hall. I remember the hair on my arms standing on end. The accusations, the anger, the fear. It was awful, but I believe the High Priest said he and the Magistrate would prepare the official punishment documents and then make a public announcement to the people."

"That shouldn't take long. The laws are already spelled out," Ras said.

Takana opened his mouth to respond. He wanted to say that life and death decisions should never be made quickly, but an internal voice interrupted. Was he going to be the kind of king who struggled to make the hard decisions? He remembered the decisiveness of King Naram-Suen and the admiration he felt for him. Yet there were times when his uncle withheld his own thoughts to consider others. Both skills had their place, he determined, with a tacit nod. I will never sentence anyone to death unless all other alternatives are exhausted. Sadly there will be those whose lives threaten the peace and safety of the people, and then, with the help of the gods, I will have the courage to do what must be done. He looked up, hoping his unspoken words had reached the gods.

"I have faith in our laws, Ras. But those who are responsible to carry them out must consider mercy and justice. It's not a simple task, but it was King Suldana's way. We'll know when the trumpets call us.

"You heard the High Priest declare this a Time of Preparation. He knows we've been damaged by evil deeds and the people need time to heal and prepare for a new beginning. The reading of the punishments will come first, and when the kingdom is shed of those who would do us harm, the gods will respond to the prayers and sacrifices and heal the people. Then, the Storm God will speak through his High Priest and call for the Proclamation."

No one spoke. Takana imagined he wasn't alone in thinking of the sober scene they would soon face: Queen

Resat and Setmel, Ibiranu and Mutwalli displayed in disgrace before the people. No one could know what would happen. Would the people agree that the punishments were just?

As if he could leave the uncertainty behind, he pushed ahead into a full run and shouted over his shoulder. "I need to talk to my mother before this day ends. There's something I'd like to settle before I'm crowned." The words still sounded strange and sent a chill to his bones.

Takana was no sooner in the door to his apartment when his mother jumped from her chair. "Where have you been?" She had bathed and changed into her sleeping gown. Everything about her was crisp and fresh, not a sign of fatigue, but she seemed anxious.

"Enjoying my last hours of freedom with Ras and Angulli. They want to be part of building the kingdom, mother. I'm grateful." He smiled and she responded with her own. "It's late, mother, but I want to talk to you about someone. He took a breath and prayed that the time was right. "I met old friends. Here for the Coronation," he said.

She seemed oblivious and continued to chatter. "You know, I once doubted the gods could possibly care about each of us individually. But today's events make me realize everything has its purpose. First we were safely dispatched to Harmesh, away from the queen's deadly purposes. I hated it at first, but I learned how alike people are no matter what their station, no matter where they live. I saw you grow, my son. The gods were preparing you. Do you see?" she said.

"More than you know." She was about to speak again and Takana lost his patience and interrupted. "Mother!" Her eyes widened with his strident tone.

"I know it's our custom that you and father, if he were with us, would find me a wife to share my life. But the gods brought someone to me in Harmesh and she's here for the Coronation."

"What are you talking about? You never—"

"No, I never told you about her. I didn't know how our marriage could be arranged. I loved her from the first, but we were just beginning to know each other when we were called back here. I know we've been rash. She's not a traditional kind of woman but she's wonderful. Does this hurt you?"

"Why would you ever think your happiness could hurt? You say she's here for the Coronation? Does she know how your circumstances have changed?"

"No, not yet. She's here because her father is Vassal Lord Odepinu."

"Elin? Elin is the girl you just described? I know Elin," the queen said.

"You know her? Why did you never mention her to me?"

"I did, at least I think I did. You were busy with your chariot designs and other things. You didn't seem interested. And she was always away in the country, with her aunt, I think, involved with various charitable projects, as I recall. Oh, this is wonderful! All the time I was worried about not fulfilling my responsibilities to find you a wife and you and she were taking care of it yourselves."

She stopped and looked thoughtful. "It might be best if you didn't tell anyone. Let me drop a fact or two into the right ears and let nature take its course. A hedge against those who would criticize me, you understand? Oh, this is marvelous—a daughter and grandchildren in my future."

"You don't see any problem, mother?"

"Problem? You'll be king."

Where had he heard that before? Was being king the answer to everything? No, not everything, he admitted to himself.

CHAPTER TWENTY-NINE
DAY OF PREPARATION
TAKANA

Takana woke with a start. He was naked, except for his boots. The last thing he remembered was leaning over to loosen the laces. He reflexively pulled on his sleeping tunic which lay rumpled next to him. But when he leaned forward to stand, his legs were not ready to respond. It had been too long since he'd slept so soundly—maybe his legs needed more. He stretched and rubbed his scalp, luxuriating in a sense of wellbeing. The knot in his stomach, the throb behind his eyes and the ache at the back of his neck were gone. He felt a leveling off, a balance taking over the emotional seesaw of the recent past. Yes, the kingdom was suffering and it would take time to regain the confidence of the people. But Hittites were a strong, resolute people. They were innovative and clever. Indeed, clever and ambitious! Therefore there would always be those who hungered for more. But he would worry about such things later.

The unmistakable sounds of his mother's movements seeped through his bedroom door. He wondered what new thoughts might have sprung to her active mind overnight. What did she think of Elin? She was so sure nothing would stand in his way once he was king, and she'd always thought he'd be a king one day. No problem! All was meant to be! In time he hoped her certainty would become his. Nor could he tell himself she was a woman given to fantasy or delusion. She was a queen, experienced in social graces and diplomacy. She was intuitive and resilient and wise. He didn't remember witnessing her interaction with his father—he was too young—but it was easy to imagine how he would have depended on her for level-headed counsel.

He pulled aside the heavy window covering and opened the shutters, still reflecting on her words. Was that why, unlike him, she was not shocked by the king's proclamation? While he busied himself with doing the king's bidding, did she intuitively understand King Suldana's motives?

The window framed a rectangle of brilliant blue, and he watched a cloud pass across like a ship on a placid ocean. It made him think of the gods living in heavenly glory, ever diligent to protect and intervene.

He fell back on his bed and stared at the ceiling. Several times he blinked as the grain in the wood planks shifted and outlined an image. King Suldana? He rubbed his eyes, questioning if he was fully awake, but when he looked again new images came and went: Master Palla, Ras, Angulli, Gille and, suddenly masses of faces—men, women, children. He bolted upright, his ears filled with long, shrill sounds, and then knocking.

"Are you up? Takana! The trumpets have sounded. " His mother's voice was nearly as sharp as the trumpets.

"Yes! I'm coming," he said, yanking off his sleeping tunic. He glanced again at the ceiling but it looked like what it was—wood. He sighed, neither accepting nor rejecting what he'd seen. No reason to make sense of it. The message was clear. He would be king, king of a strong and talented people. He fastened his leather belt, set his shoulders and left the room.

"No time for breakfast," his mother said, indicating a platter of fruit and a steaming kettle hung over the glowing embers in the brazier. "Oh! You look much better today, I'm glad to say." She handed him an apple, pulled the kettle from the embers and they stepped outside to a waiting chariot.

Doors throughout the acropolis slammed, voices called to one another and feet scuffed on the terraces. It almost seemed as if people had been waiting behind their doors, listening for the sound. Now, like racers at the starting line, they were dashing toward the finish at the Great Temple.

"The High Priest of the Storm God is waiting for you to join him at the temple," the driver, a temple servant, said. He bowed deeply.

Without hesitation Takana's mother stepped into the chariot and Takana followed her, but not without the same irritation he felt about the bodyguards. Wouldn't the people notice and wonder why a temple servant was sent with a chariot? Can't I have one more day without fanfare? He grumbled to himself. But as the chariot eased its way into the serpentine mass headed into the Temple Plaza, there were no questioning glances. The people seemed focused on getting to the Storm God's Temple and nothing more.

It was sad to see the houses still dressed in green garlands, sad to recall the excitement, the music and the henna designs on the young women. What should have been a celebration had become a day of betrayal and shame. Takana wondered how the people would react to the Magistrate's reading of the punishments. There was a good chance they'd demand blood. Thinking about it made him shiver.

Out on the street, the chariot and the rushing people were stalled and stretching their necks to see why. Not even Takana, from his slightly elevated position, could see the cause. They moved ahead like slugs over the cobblestones, accompanied by increasingly louder complaints. Finally, as they moved into the Temple Plaza, the reason became clear.

Four prisoners with bound arms and legs stood in individual wooden carts at the base of the temple, under the stern countenance of the Sacred Bull. Hattusa's people fell silent and crept slowly forward to look askance at Queen Resat, Prince Setmel, Royal Guard Chief Ibiranu and Mutwalli, the false scribe. If not for her haughty bearing, the queen was hardly recognizable in a coarse, ankle-length gown. Her auburn hair, normally upswept and secured by jeweled combs, fell over her shoulders in the common fashion of the women, who now, overcoming their fear, looked up at her in amazement, some with satisfaction.

The pall that fell over the plaza made the hair on Takana's neck prickle, and once he and his mother stepped out of the chariot, he climbed part way up the steps to survey the plaza. People were still entering from the outlying network of streets and, though they were unable to see the carts with their bound occupants, they caught the somber tone of the crowd. As a mass, the crowd shifted slowly around the plaza in an unspoken agreement to allow everyone to see the spectacle.

Takana searched for Gille and other royal guards, mildly curious not to see them. His uncle? Luwadnan soldiers? When Master Palla, too, was nowhere to be seen, his curiosity grew. Where in the world . . . ? Then he saw King Amilla standing close to the plaza entrance, no doubt distancing himself purposefully from the queen. Several of his high-ranking officers surrounded him. But Takana's speculations stopped when the door of the Great Temple swung open and the High Priest walked out onto the portico, the senior *hasawa* and the Magistrate following in his wake. Takana moved down and joined his mother as the High Priest raised his arms in supplication to the gods and then lower to draw the attention of the people.

"Citizens of Hatti Land! We are a people of The Law. From Labarna, our first monarch, in the first days of the Hittite Kingdom, The Law has kept order. King Hattusili I and Mursili I, now among the gods, look down on us and smile with pleasure to see our respect for their lawful contributions. We are not like other kingdoms whose laws terrorize their people, whose strict adherence to words on tablets leave no room for mercy or justice. Our laws give us the means to protect the rights of the people, to seek compensation for those who suffer at the hands of others, to aid the widows and orphans so that all Hittites may live full and happy lives. And always, always, People of Hatti, our laws have existed for the sake of justice, balance and order—never for vengeance. Though we punish wrongdoers, we do so with mercy and the hope of restoration. We take care to administer justice fairly and impartially, not favoring the strong over the weak. We protect the vulnerable against their powerful neighbors. We do what is just!

"The Law keeps order throughout the kingdom. In each village, no matter how far from Hattusa, The Law . . ."

Takana, though grateful to hear how the High Priest was preparing the people for the punishments, turned his thoughts to the crowd. He saw respect, even reverence in most faces, but here and there, mostly among the men, there was skepticism and not a few furrowed brows. Did they want release for their anger? He scanned again for Hittite soldiers, guards, his uncle and his Luwadnan troops, but found no more than a sprinkling, inadequate to quell an uprising. His heart beat faster.

"O Mighty Storm God," the High Priest continued. "Almighty Lord and Protector, Sun God, Supreme Deity of Justice, in your journeys through the heavens you have heard our prayers and smelled our sacrifices. We have implored you to call on all the Gods of Heaven and Earth, All the Divine Assembly, to attend to us. A powerful evil has fallen on us. We sought your guidance and offered our sacrifices and you have responded with the words of justice. Your commands have been heard!

"Citizens of Hatti Land, listen as the Magistrate, Dispenser of The Law, speaks."

The Magistrate stepped forward and Takana noticed the *hasawa* edge toward the Sacred Bull, hidden from the people but visible from his position. He saw her reach up and pull her white hood over her red hair. Hardly perceptible at first, but growing in intensity, a vibration traveled out across the plaza like a soft wind moving over the surface of still water. There was a low hum but audible only if one stopped listening to the voice of the Magistrate. If Takana hadn't witnessed her past behavior—the raising of her hood, the vibrating sound—he would have been unaware of the benevolent projection she was sending. He looked out across the plaza to see if the people were affected. It was then he noticed many Old Women dispersed along the outer edges. Had he missed seeing them earlier or was it because their hoods rested on their shoulders? Whatever they were up to, he knew the *hasawas* worked for the good of the population.

The Magistrate's voice lacked the oratory skill of the priest, but the people listened, impatient, he thought, to know that treachery came with consequences. After all, they had prayed, sacrificed, performed the rituals, obeyed, respected their masters and followed The Law. Those who didn't deserved punishment. It was an opinion he understood but overruled, he hoped, for the right reasons.

"Queen Resat," the Magistrate thundered, "is no longer queen. She is banished from the Hittite Kingdom which she has betrayed. She is stripped of the privileges of position. She becomes the slave of the King and Queen of Luwadna."

There was a stunned silence and then several men rushed at the cart, shouting "death!" and "kill her!" They grabbed the side and rocked it until she toppled and disappeared from view. Only when two royal guards, stationed with the carts, pulled their daggers and pressed their sizeable bulk against the men, did they back off. No attempt was made to help her, but Takana heard her moans. When no others came to shout their protests, the men turned away and faded into the crowd.

"Prince Setmel," the Magistrate bellowed, "is *not* the son of our beloved King Suldana and therefore no heir to the throne. He is not one of us! He is banished from Hatti forever."

Takana's head snapped up to see King Amilla's reaction, but he and his men had gone. His attention was drawn back to the people—shocked and bewildered. The Magistrate's announcement hung in the air until its meaning took hold and they understood the ugly revelation. Consternation began as a low buzz, but quickly became angry shouts aimed at both Queen Resat and Prince Setmel. Calls of "shame," "bastard" and "whore" echoed all around the plaza, to which Setmel shouted back, although it wasn't clear what he said. Finally, Setmel, his wet lips hanging open, searched the crowd with an expression of disbelief, as if comprehension had just taken hold in his mind.

All eyes shifted to Chief Ibiranu, knowing he was next to hear his punishment. Until the announcement of Setmel's ineligibility, his stance was proud, even arrogant. Now he looked back and forth from Queen Resat to Setmel, yelling something inaudible, until he fell to his knees and put his head on the floor of the cart, where he remained as the Magistrate stated his punishment.

"Royal Guard Chief Ibiranu used his position to harm those to whom he had sworn protection. He ordered those under his command to kill loyal Hittite citizens. He is banished from Hatti Land forever."

Takana felt a pang of pity for him. He'd been the witless pawn of a ruthless woman, abandoned his wife and brought about the death of his only son. Takana instantly realized Ibiranu's wife's predicament. She would not be a widow, but the effect would be the same, and she had lost her only son. She was a woman without resources. If he could, Takana thought, he would seek compensation for her.

The Magistrate continued. "Mutwalli has disgraced himself by impersonating a scribe, a position he has not earned. He knowingly produced a false Proclamation tablet. He has damaged the reputation of the *eduba*. He will serve Master Palla as a slave for five years, after which time a judgment will be made of his character."

Heads swiveled, undoubtedly to see Master Palla's reaction. But there was no sign of the old scribe. The people were quickly distracted but Takana's worry increased until his attention was drawn by movement. Gille, filthy and breathing heavily, was weaving through the crowd, headed toward him.

"Master Palla . . . sent . . . me."

Takana placed his arm around Gille's waist and together they slowly edged around the side of the temple. No one seemed to notice except Takana's mother, who frowned but remained where she was.

"What about Master Palla? Where is he?"

"A large force of men from the outlying villages arrived shortly before the trumpets blew, and before Master Palla could get to them, they began battling with the foreign forces surrounding the city."

Takana stretched to search the crowd. "My uncle, he—"

"Yes, that's what I came to tell you. King Naram-Suen and his forces have rallied to contain them. He and Master Palla are working together, but King Amilla is—"

"Take me to my uncle," Takana said.

They slipped around the back of the Temple of the Storm God where Gille had tied his horse. Riding together, they exited through the Lion Gate and rode for the forest. Ahead, Takana saw his uncle in animated conversation with a Kazaram commander. He jumped from the horse and rushed to join them.

The commander was explaining how they were attacked. Master Palla countered with an apology and an appeal to the Kazaram officer's sense of fairness.

"These are men from our rural provinces. What else could they think when they saw their capital city surrounded by foreign troops? How were they to know you are here as an ally? Are any of your men injured?" Master Palla's voice was calm, reasoned.

It worked on the commander. "Fortunately, no. Consider yourselves lucky that my men have shed no Hittite blood. It would be wise if your men left the area and allowed us to do what King Amilla has ordered."

"And what would that be?" Takana said, stepping closer.

"Prince Takana! I welcome your authority in this matter. Our orders are to be a protective shield for your capital city until your new king is in full charge. We were informed about the Luwandnan warriors, here to protect as well, but then this sudden attack. You see how it is. Let's be done with this misunderstanding," the commander said.

The scene crackled with tension. Luwadnans stood nose to nose with Kazaramites. Hittite citizens, still brandishing weapons, mixed with Hittite troops who stood at the ready behind them.

"Your training serves you well, commander. Our men will withdraw and you have our thanks for your restraint under the circumstances," Takana said.

The men moved and separated into their own groups, and soon only the normal sounds of men outfitted for battle could be heard. The tops of the trees rustled as a wind moved over the area like a breath, its energy never reaching the ground. Takana joined King Naram-Suen and Gille, while Master Palla went to talk to the men from the outlying villages. When they were well beyond the hearing of the foreign soldiers, Gille tapped Takana's arm.

"The commander has told you a half truth," he said. "Follow me."

They walked to an area where large boulders formed a wall high enough to hide a man. Behind it, a royal guard stood guard over a seated Karazam soldier. Gille yanked him to his feet. "Repeat your orders and you will be allowed to return to your squad. If not, consider that no one will miss you until they return to Kazaram and by then you'll be part of the earth under our feet."

The frightened young man's uniform had the markings of a squad leader, although Takana guessed he was new to leadership. The soldier held his helmet in both hands at his chest and sweat dripped from his loose dark hair. He chewed his lower lip before his words came. "King Amilla ordered my squad to follow the carts carrying Queen Resat and Prince Setmel until they are a good distance from the city. We are to intercept and take them with all haste to Kazaram." He looked anxiously from Gille to Prince Takana to King Naram-Suen. "Can I go now?"

"We'll keep our promise," Takana said. "But first, a slight change of plans. You may take Setmel with you to Kazaram, but Queen Resat must be left with the Luwandnan guards." Takana put his hand on his sword as he waited for the soldier to agree.

He nodded.

"To make sure you do exactly what we ask, I'll alert my men. They'll be watching and you'll be the first to feel Luwadnan arrows, if you don't," the Luwadnan king said.

The menace in his uncle's voice sent a chill through Takana's chest. He could only imagine the effect it had on the inexperienced soldier.

Master Palla joined the group as they watched the Kazaram soldier retreat.

"The villagers?" Takana said.

"Their blood has cooled. Once I told them they no longer needed to worry about Setmel taking the throne, they cheered. Of course, they want to know who will assume the throne, but I told them the High Priest has declared a Day of Preparation. Until the Holy One feels the people are ready, Proclamation Day is put off. We must wait to know the wishes of our departed King Suldana. But I assured them their hearts should be easy because our beloved king will place us in capable hands. They're on their way to the Temple Plaza to hear the punishments. Hopefully they're not too late."

"The Magistrate was all but finished when Gille came for me, but they might still see the prisoners. They'll get some satisfaction from that, I should think."

Suddenly the sound of galloping horses interrupted. Through the trees, they could see the Kazaram forces moving south away from the city.

Takana whipped around to face Gille. "Do you think they're moving to another part of the forest?"

Before answering, Gille glanced at King Naram-Suen. "Our men report that, except for a squad of Kazaram warriors moving east of the city, the bulk of the Kazaram army is on its way home." The king added his assent.

The wind had increased and a wall of dust, kicked up by the horses, enveloped them for several moments. Takana turned his back, pulled a square of fabric from his belt and covered his nose and mouth. In the settling dust, he thought he saw a horse draped with Kazaram colors—King Amilla's stallion, followed by five, high-ranking officers. When he turned back, his uncle and Gille were exchanging smiles.

A royal guard offered Takana a horse and with a quick nod of thanks, he mounted and they rode back to the High Temple.

The scene hadn't changed. The carts were still lined up at the base of the temple stairs, although each prisoner now was held by a guard and forced to face the crowd. Takana and the others dismounted and moved to the base of the High Temple steps, where they received a welcoming nod from the Storm God's High Priest. He moved forward on the portico and signaled the cart drivers.

A path opened between the people and their eyes moved from one prisoner to the next as they passed. One shout was joined by others, one raised fist followed another, and by the time the last cart filed out of the plaza, the sound pounded against the city walls until the Temple Plaza gate slammed shut and Hittites gave their attention once more to the High Priest.

"Citizens of Hatti Land, thank the gods! We are cleansed and delivered from evildoers.

The Kingdom of the Hittites awaits its new king! When the Sun God and the Sun Goddess of Arinna come to us again, we will gather to hear the Proclamation of our beloved King Suldana's successor. Listen for the trumpets! Prepare for a new beginning!"

A new sound filled the plaza, this time one of celebration. Mothers let go of their children's hands and they burst away like multi-colored butterflies freed from their chrysalides to spin and twist together. The women sought out their friends and laughter bounced off the temple walls. Even the men threw their arms around each other's shoulders and many turned to the right outside the Temple Plaza in the direction of The Blue Inn.

Gille and Master Palla excused themselves and King Naram-Suen said he felt the need of his wife's company, some quiet and a nap, in precisely that order. Takana thanked them all and looked around for his mother. He scanned the plaza and located her, then gulped when he saw her talking to Lord Odepinu and Elin. They were watching him as he walked toward them. His stomach fluttered with each step.

"I sense great relief in the people. Do you feel it?" the lord said.

Had he? It seemed so in the Temple Plaza but those assembled were a small part of the kingdom. How soon would the carts be intercepted by Amilla's men? Would restraint prevail among the forces in the forest surrounding the city? Word of the skirmish would soon spread. What would the people make of it? At that moment, the Day of Preparation felt like limbo.

"It's been wonderful to see you," Takana's mother was saying. "But I feel the need of a soft cushion and quiet. The chariot is waiting just there," she said, pointing. "Again? Soon?" There was a lilt in her voice, a knowing smile on her face and her hand rested briefly on Elin's arm.

When Takana turned back, Lord Odepinu was beaming. Elin? He hoped it wasn't just his imagination, but he saw excitement and eagerness. It set him on fire.

"Yes, there was relief, at least here in the plaza," he managed to say. "They don't know who their new king will be, but at least they're optimistic, or maybe they're just relieved to see the last of Queen Resat, Setmel and Ibiranu. I hope the rest of the kingdom will follow."

King Odepinu spanned his belly with his large, ringed fingers and shook with laughter. "Rest assured, they will. Harmesh is part of the kingdom, are we not?" He waved and walked away.

Takana forced a smile. "I'd like to talk to you," he said to Elin. She had not moved and her eyes were shining. "Early, before the sun is high? I believe the High Priest will give the people time to rest before he orders the call to assemble."

"Yes."

If he could, he'd have pressed her to him because that's what he was sure she wanted.

CHAPTER THIRTY

PROCLAMATION DAY

TAKANA

He was fully dressed, sitting at his bedroom window, waiting for the sun to announce the new day. The birds were first to respond with their cheerful songs. Soon the rumble of wooden wheels on the uneven cobblestones—the merchants making their way to fresh merchandise waiting at the city gates—would follow. Hattusa's people would then add their own cacophony of animated haggling to the areas around the gates. These were sounds he loved, symbols of life and prosperity. But for the present only the sounds of nature reached him high on the acropolis.

Takana moved around the apartment quietly. Had his mother awakened before him, she would want conversation and food. He would have found it difficult to share the thoughts that had stirred his mind all night, keeping sleep at bay, and his stomach was warning him not to eat. He slipped out of the apartment and walked across the terrace and down three levels.

He faced Lord Odepinu's door with expectation. If Elin was as excited as he was, she'd be waiting. But there was no answer to his first soft knock. After a moment he rapped sharply with his knuckles and heard the reassuring sound of footsteps. Elin.

They exchanged simple words of greeting and she indicated a circle of large pillows.

"My father is bathing. How is your mother?"

"I left her sleeping. The last few days have been trying." He made a sound of exasperation and held out his hands. "Listen, we—"

"I know you're surprised," Elin said. "Please don't be angry. It was such fun to have an unencumbered relationship." She grinned.

"Unencumbered? Is that the way you'd describe us?" Takana said. "You're the vassal lord's daughter? Why didn't you tell me?"

"I didn't want to, isn't that reason enough?" Her grin had gone completely, replaced by a clenched jaw, an expression he'd never seen on her face before. He decided he didn't like it. Still, she was as beautiful as he remembered and those memories were vivid. His spirit soared in her presence and there was nothing he could do about it.

"I'm just surprised, that's all. How could I have missed seeing you when I met with your father—so, so many times?"

"I was fourteen when you arrived in Harmesh and father thought I should be with a woman. You know, to learn about the changes in my body and, well, other things. I was living with my aunt in the country when I met you."

"Fourteen? How old were you when we . . . ?" Takana fidgeted in the chair.

"I was sixteen, old enough to know my mind. Do you doubt that for a moment?"

A large blue-eyed cat jumped on Takana's lap. She put her face directly in front of Takana's and mewed. Elin had asked a question and it seemed the cat asked again.

314

But before Takana could ask Elin if her cat was always so bold, Lord Odepinu joined them. From their first meeting, Takana felt he'd found a friendly ally, as eager to tackle difficult problems as to drink beer and enjoy the company of others. Despite the problems at hand, Takana felt relaxed in his presence—he had from the first. He reminded himself they were in Hattusa for the pageantry, not the politics. Or so he thought.

He admired Odepinu's ideas about freedom of mind and heart. He remembered having the same exhilarating experience with Elin, who'd extended those beliefs to her body as well as her mind. He just never put the two of them together. And why had he never noticed their identical eyes, not green, not blue, but somehow both?

Servants brought large ceramic cups of beer and the lord took several long swallows before he spoke. "You must be relieved to be rid of the queen," Odepinu said.

"Politics attracts some ruthless people. I'm certain you've heard rumors in Harmesh, but it can't be the same as looking over your shoulder every day. That's how it's been here."

The cat had moved from his lap but was still looking at him and when he looked her way, she mewed again, as if to say she was still watching him.

"Do you think because we live in a relatively small kingdom, we don't deal with politics?" Elin said. Her tone was challenging, nothing he didn't expect from her.

Takana looked at the ceiling. He didn't want to watch the change in their relationship that was sure to come the minute he explained. He took a breath.

"There's so much to tell you," he began. He recounted the earlier events, ending with King Suldana II's Proclamation that he was to be king. He held his breath when the words left his mouth. Elin gasped and followed her father who fell to his knee and saluted him with his arm across his chest. The cat jumped and walked to a far corner of the room.

Takana reached out, one arm to each. He looked around the room and was relieved to find it empty. "You're not the only ones who are shocked. It still feels unreal to me. But I'm not king until tomorrow. Please give me just this day to be an ordinary person, your friend and nothing more."

Lord Odepinu rose slowly and returned to his seat. "I understand, but you ask a great deal of us. Let me tell you, Takana, I never considered you ordinary, as you say. From the first day you and Queen Patupa arrived in Harmesh, your talents and bearing set you apart. I pray to the gods we will always be friends. And let me say, the gods have chosen well."

Elin had returned to her seat but her face was devoid of expression. It made Takana wary. The cat, too, took some tentative steps before jumping to Elin's lap and burrowing into the folds of her gown, the color of spring leaves.

Lord Odepinu slapped his knees, stood and turned toward the door. "Well, I expect you two have much to discuss. Tomorrow will be a glorious day." He placed a hand on his heart, walked to another room and closed the door.

"I don't know where to begin," Takana said.

"Begin by telling me you're not angry anymore," she said.

"Well, no, I'm not. But I'm already feeling the changes in how people treat me." He sighed. "I've kept things from you, too—not about me specifically, but about Hatti. I'd like to tell you now, if you'll listen."

"I've missed the sound of your voice, Takana." She stroked the cat's silvery coat, her hand following the lithe curves of its body.

"I ask you to believe I've shared myself with you completely, but there are things about Hatti no one knows outside the kingdom. Even before the king's death, evil plots were being shaped by power hungry people inside and outside the kingdom. If they get their way, we will be fighting wars at every border."

The sun, rising over the tops of the city's buildings, was sending bright beams through the window's reed covering. They spread out on the floor and the cat, unable to resist, jumped from Elin's lap to tap the beams with her paw. Takana watched her antics briefly before raising his eyes to Elin. Her expression was the same one she always wore when she was listening.

"I know," she said.

"What?" His mind had relaxed along with his body. He shifted. "Oh, sorry, yes, the rumors."

"We've known for a long time that Queen Resat was plotting against the king. Our forces have been ready to join others to ensure she would fail. We didn't just come to Hattusa for the Coronation, Takana, we came to meet with others and make plans for war," she said, with pride.

What a fool he was! Had King Suldana wasted his time with him? Sending him to Harmesh was supposed to broaden his understanding of the kingdom, but he had to question its success. Thank the gods for people like Lord Odepinu—and, yes, Elin, too—who would remind him that distance didn't mean ignorance, nor did it mean the people there had some kind of diluted patriotism.

"I don't doubt your loyalty. But I guess I'm surprised at how much you know. I apologize and I'm gratified. You've reminded me Hatti has allies everywhere!" he said. Suddenly he remembered. "I hate to leave you, but the trumpets will call soon. My mother's waiting for me." He leaned in to kiss her, but she stopped him.

"Your life is going to change, you know." She sat upright with her legs crossed and her fingers laced together on her lap, a look of resignation on her face. He preferred her earlier expression.

"A king can marry, Elin," he said.

"Yes. Still, you have no idea what it's like to be king."

"Yeah, that's true. I'm already feeling the heaviness, but having you here lightens everything. Does your father know how we feel?"

"From our first meeting in Harmesh."

Takana's ears burned. "Everything?"

"He's everything to me—teacher, counselor, my best friend. My mother died as I was born. He hired women to care for me when I was little and I spent long periods of time with my aunt, like I said. But whether I was with my father or not, he was always open with me. He made me feel I never had to keep secrets from him. Between us there's never been anything but complete openness and honesty."

"He's a fine man. I count him as a friend already and it can only get better."

"Nothing would make me happier. But, you're to be king of Hatti and that changes things."

"Hatti deserves a happy king," Takana said, pulling her to him.

"Indeed, above all," Elin said, wistfully. Her hand kept a distance between them.

They parted with a quick kiss, but not so brief that Takana couldn't feel her reticence. He held her shoulders and gave her what he hoped was a reassuring smile. She struggled to return it but failed.

It was not the response Takana had expected, not the one he wanted. Thoughts of the day ahead filled him with apprehension. He'd wanted, needed, Elin to be his one sure thing. He ran his fingers through his thick hair and stepped away from her. "I've got to go," he said, moving swiftly to the door.

Trumpets sounded from the top of the Storm God's Temple. Takana opened the door for his mother and saw that the same temple driver and chariot were waiting for them on the terrace. A royal guard stood at attention nearby. Takana raised his eyebrows but this time he stepped up without resentment or hesitation.

He leaned close to his mother. "Do you think the High Priest fears I will run away?"

Instead of the snicker he expected, his mother responded soberly. "The people don't yet know who their king is, but he does."

Theirs was not the only chariot on the acropolis ramps and when they reached the plaza, people were pouring out of the lower terrace levels—slaves, servants, cooks, housemaids, gardeners, every palace occupant. Likewise, the streets were packed with Hattusa's citizens, moving quickly like a swollen creek after a heavy rainfall. The celebratory mood of the day before was enhanced, reflected in more colorful clothing—little girls with flowers woven in their braids and women in bright, ruffled pinafores. But it was the men who by their expression and appearance best reflected the significance and impact of the occasion on the kingdom's future. On this day their tunics were spotless and felt shoes with upturned toes covered their feet. The buildings had received fresh garlands of evergreens and, when they turned into the Temple Plaza, Takana saw groups of musicians gathering in animated groups. Columns of smoke from sacrificial fires glowed rosy in the sun and looked like fluttering flags.

The High Priest and the Magistrate were waiting just outside the temple door, waiting for Takana and his mother. The *hasawa*, Hapati and his united family stood at the bottom of the steps, along with Master Palla and Gille. Takana acknowledged their happy faces before searching the crowd for Angulli. He was ready to accept that his friend was hidden somewhere in the mass when Ras turned and made room. A grin seemed to take up Angulli's entire face.

New banners waved high above the crowd, evidence that more dignitaries from surrounding vice royal kingdoms had arrived to celebrate. Among them were relatives Takana had never met—distant first, second and third cousins who'd been sent to rule at the edges of the kingdom. Some who'd distinguished themselves on the battlefield, others who'd won the king's gratitude and respect with their diplomatic skills—men whose names were worthy to be on the king's proclamation. No doubt some had come with that very anticipation.

The High Priest stepped forward, raised his arms and silence fell over the plaza. "People of Hatti Land . . ."

Takana held his breath.

The Storm God's spokesman raised the tablet high and projected his voice to the outer edges of the plaza. "I proclaim Prince Takana!"

Flowers and hats were tossed in the air and voices shouted Takana's name. Musicians paraded forward to the High Temple. Royal guards suddenly appeared at the base of the steps to hold back the crowd and allow the elite access to the newly proclaimed king: his mother and the King and Queen of Luwadna. Takana breathed and fought the tears that sought release. He stretched his neck to give a triumphant smile to Ras and his family, Angulli and Master Palla, and as he turned he saw the *hasawa* standing with the Sacred Bull, her hood was raised and her arms extended to all the assembled.

CHAPTER THIRTY-ONE
CORONATION DAY
TAKANA

Takana had forgotten to close the drapery and the room was bathed in brilliance. He knew he'd had dreams that kept him from restful sleep. They were shapeless but disturbing, of that he was sure. As he lay there, bits and pieces of conversations, especially with Elin, replayed in his head but a sharp rap on the door and his mother's voice brought him to his feet. Coronation Day!

He splashed his face, rubbed it dry and used a frayed stick and a paste of mint leaves to rub his teeth. Then he ran a comb through his hair, watching every movement in the polished obsidian like he was spying on a stranger. Would his next look in the mirror show him differently? He reached for the tunic of natural fabric, delivered by a temple priest the day before with the pomp of a religious rite. Since then it had lay stretched out on a bench by his pallet like every other piece of clothing he'd worn since learning to dress himself. But when he tossed it over his head, it covered his arms and fell to his ankles and his skin reacted with a shiver. He took a deep, ragged breath, and walked into the gathering room.

His mother was waiting for him by the door to the terrace where he saw the chariot waiting. Her eyes were glistening, her chin resolute. No words passed between them as he bent to kiss her on the cheek.

He stood behind the driver, clasping the sides of the chariot and looking at the plaza below with his not-yet-king's eyes. At the bottom level, people were waiting silently to watch him pass, people to whom he would soon be responsible. For the rest of his life they would look to him for security, sustenance and leadership. If not for the trust he saw shining from their faces his thoughts might have crushed him. Instead he felt filled with power and confidence. Finally, the chariot slowed and stopped before the steps of the Storm God's temple. He stepped through the door knowing that from that point he would be alone. The thunderous slam of the door behind him provided emphasis.

A semi-circle of white-robed priests, bearing large vessels of water, quickly moved around him. As they settled in position, the High Priest, who stood on a slightly elevated ramp in the center of the room, lifted his palms to the Storm God's stone likeness.

"Welcome, welcome, O Mighty One. Come, come. Receive your servant, Takana. He is loved by your heavenly companion King Suldana II. He is loved by the ancestors who live and walk with you in the celestial places. His head is bowed before you. Your thunder and lightning sent the waters he now receives for purification."

One by one the priests circled around him, filling pitchers from a channel that flowed from the back of the temple. They poured the contents slowly over Takana's head. Four times the vessels were refilled and poured out until he was thoroughly drenched, every thread of his garment saturated. Once between the pouring pitchers, he opened his eyes and saw the Old Woman. She was standing on a pedestal above with the palm of her right hand outstretched toward him. Something was moving from her hand to his chest— nothing he could see, nothing he could explain, nor was it anything he could deny. He knew only that they were joined.

With his eyes tightly closed and the water cascading over him, he felt lifted, airborne.

He saw himself lowered onto the bank of a river. It was flowing very fast, so great and powerful that he was afraid. His knees buckled. He fell and grasped the earth, but it melted away. He felt the water surround his body, pulling him away. Then a voice spoke to him: The river has its destination. Let go of the shore, push off into the middle, keep your eyes open and your head above the water. Look around. See who is in there with you and celebrate. He looked. Many more than could be counted were floating confidently with him. Elin was there, closest to him, smiling.

At this time in history, the voice continued, take nothing personally, least of all yourself. For the moment that you do, your spiritual growth and journey will come to a halt. Gather yourself! Banish the word 'struggle' from your mouth. All that you do now must be done in a sacred manner and in celebration. You are the one Hatti has been waiting for.

As quickly as the vision had come, it ended. Then at a signal from the High Priest, towels were brought to blot away the water. Two priests pulled open the High Temple doors, Takana stepped out, and the crowd roared.

He was grateful water still dripped from his hair. It covered the tears flowing down his face when he looked at those closest to the temple—his mother, Ras and Azzia, King and Queen Naram-Suen, Master Palla, and slightly beyond he saw Angulli, jumping up and down to see over those in front of him. To the far right, Elin stood next to her father. She brought her hand to her face and curled her fingers, a wave meant for him. Someday soon she would stand with him. He had no doubt.

Takana closed his eyes momentarily to lock the image in a place he could recall again and again. For another moment, he pictured his uncle, King Suldana II, smiling and happy.

With trumpets blaring from the rooftops, the High Priest escorted Takana back into the temple where, in an anteroom, he was stripped of the wet clothes and dressed in a feather-light, ankle-length tunic. A purple robe was fastened with a gold disc at his right shoulder. A leather belt with a large gold medallion encircled his waist and purple felt shoes with curled toes covered his feet.

He stepped from the Great Temple again to the roar of voices and descended the stairs where a chariot was waiting. Other chariots were lined up around the outer edges of the Temple Plaza. The people circled in the plaza's center, cheering and waving banners, and when the chariots moved out, they followed behind. They processed through the city streets, accompanied by trumpeters, drums, singers, acrobats and dancers.

When they reached the Assembly Hall inside the Acropolis Plaza, the chariots bearing the High Priest and Takana halted. Four *mešedi*, who would protect him for as long as he lived, came forward and escorted him inside. The crowd outside fell silent. Once inside the hall, Takana was taken to a room behind the raised dais. There he was dressed again, this time in a white linen robe, woven by women whose only task was to prepare the Coronation Robe. It was pulled across his chest and back and knotted at the shoulder. Gold earrings were clipped to his ears and gold slippers were placed on his feet. Fingers arranged his long damp hair.

Takana flinched, unused to others handling his body. He felt suddenly strange, separated from himself, yet full of something that had not been there before. He could feel the presence of King Suldana, his ancestors and all who'd served as Hittite kings before him. His body tingled—the spirit of the Storm God moving inside him. Hands steadied him on both sides and he realized he had closed his eyes and swayed.

The High Priest stood directly in front of him and studied his face. Takana smiled, took a deep breath and followed him out into the Assembly Hall to the dais, where the people had crowded in and stood waiting in silence.

"Divine Lords," the High Priest began, "Our king! We are satisfied with him in life and peace! He is your son, of your form, your vigorous seed. You provided him with your Power, your Influence, your Magic and your Crown when he was still in his mother's womb.

"The land and the mountains belong to him, everything which the heavens wrap around, everything which the sea encircles. Give him dominion over the lands in peace. Give him all life and good fortune, all food and all sustenance. He is the Head of All Living Spirits forever and ever."

A white-robed priest handed a gold crown to the High Priest, who held it over his own head before he turned and placed it on Takana's. "Welcome, welcome, O Son of Our Beloved Storm God. Behold your law and order in the land. You arranged it. You make right what is faulty and declare it perfect.

"We acknowledge the descendant of him who created us. Your soul is created in the hearts of your people and the gods love him. He shall be called King Suldana III."

The thunderous cheer of the people seemed to deliver the final, decisive message and Takana, maybe for the first time, fully understood what the words meant: He was the union of two dimensions—the Living and the Divine. With his eyes on the people, he followed the High Priest down the stairs, where he watched his mother fall to her knees, followed by everyone in the hall.

The chariots filled again and moved in a serpentine procession through the Lion Gate in the west, along the city wall past the Sphinx Gate in the south, and back inside the city through the King's Gate in the east—the same procession taken by Hittite kings for five hundred years.

EPILOGUE

Takana unfastened the shoulder clasp and let his robe slide into the arms of the servant at his side. He shrugged his shoulders and sighed with relief, glad to be relieved of the heavily embroidered fabric. Glad, too, to watch the Assembly Hall doors close behind the last petitioner. Was his first day typical of the days to come? As if reading his thoughts, Master Palla, standing at the base of the dais, chuckled and the High Priest and Magistrate smiled.

He lifted the crown that had etched a halo in his hair, handed it to the *mesedi* at his side and rubbed his scalp vigorously.

"My Lord, the sun has come and gone many times since the last audience. Furthermore, our people prefer to present their pleas to their king and not to me as Magistrate. So . . ."

Takana nodded slowly, still hearing the voices echoing in the massive hall. Had his decisions satisfied? Did he have the confidence of the people? He imagined them returning to their homes, walking along the streets and sharing their stories of the new king's manner, of his decisiveness or lack of it. Did they feel the presence of King Suldana II? Of the Divine Will of the gods? Did he?

The High Priest raised his arms. "Gods of the Heavens, Protectors of Hatti Land, we give thanks to you for King Suldana III, who this day—"

The doors of the Assembly Hall burst open and Royal Guard Chief Gille burst in, ran to the dais and dropped to his knees.

"My Lord, King Amilla's troops ambushed the carts carrying Queen Resat and Setmel. Our men were ambushed, outnumbered and overpowered. They must have had a reserve squad east of the city. They're gone. We tried to follow but they split up into several groups and we couldn't . . ."

Takana, joined by the High Priest and the Magistrate, descended the stairs and motioned the distraught Gille to stand. Pity for his newly-appointed chief flooded his thoughts and he squeezed Gille's arm. He searched the faces of the men around him, his spiritual and earthly companions.

"This is the will of the gods," Takana said. "There was nothing you could have done, Gille. For some reason, the Kazaram have invited evil into their kingdom. Time will show us how it manifests itself.

"I understand Amilla's desire to have a son, but the treachery our former queen is capable of . . . She will use his kingdom for her own selfish purposes. What possible good can come from taking her in?"

In the shrinking light Takana saw the shock leave his friends' faces, replaced by sober thought. Master Palla broke the silence.

"It could be that *she* will be the one to feel the pain of betrayal. King Amilla can match our former queen treachery for treachery. His is not the only alliance she formed, and he knows it."

The End

AUTHOR'S NOTE

In 2004, while researching in Turkey for my first novel, I spent a few days in Cappadocia. The unique rock formations in this area are the result of volcanic eruptions 30 million years ago. I learned that over time the outer layers of this rock hardened but the interior remained soft. The Hittites, who occupied this area from 1900 to 1200 B.C.E. were the first to carve into the rocks to use them as sacred burial places. People are still living in these carved-in-stone dwellings, now furnished with windows, modern kitchens and bathrooms. As fascinating as it was to see these homes, I couldn't shake my curiosity about those first carvers. I started digging too.

The Hittites are mentioned briefly in several books of the Old Testament. Reading them, one might draw the conclusion they were a small Canaanite tribe living in Palestine. In 1834, however, new information surfaced through the work of Charles Texier, a French adventurer-explorer, and suddenly the world of the Hittites was exposed to deeper scrutiny. As it turned out, the Hittites were masters of a great empire, occupying an expanding and contracting area from roughly the Black Sea in the north, the Mediterranean in the south, the Aegean in the West and the Euphrates River in the East. They were amazing people.

Text books by Trevor Bryce supplied information about scribes, warriors, chariots, gods, cures, rituals, marriage, laws and more. It didn't take long for a storyline and some Hittite characters to take residence in my head. Without a degree in ancient history, it has taken me four years of research to make <u>Carved in Stone</u> rich with details about the lives of the Hittite people.

Historical fiction, I've learned, is broadly defined. Some authors adhere strictly to historical events and actual characters. I have not. It is true that the capital city of the Hittite Kingdom was Hattusa and a study of the ruins hint at where the acropolis, the temples and the gates were. It is also true that the Old Women, the *hasawas*, were deeply imbedded in the culture as healers and diviners of divine will. And the Hittites did indeed design a three-man chariot which gave them great advantage on the battlefield.

My goal was to take you into the Kingdom of the Hittites to sense what their lives were like. That's where Prince Takana, Ras and Angulli took shape and became my teachers. There is more waiting to be discovered about these remarkable people. I hope you enjoy this brief glimpse.

Thank you for your interest in my writing.

Fran Marian

ACKNOWLEDGEMENTS

Characters and what happens to them are what give me creative satisfaction. In the case of *Carved in Stone,* the setting—1400 B.C.E—was the challenge. Consequently, research was a four-year-long course in ancient history without professors or the ultimate parchment. Instead, my teachers were the following textbooks: O.R. Gurney's *The Hittites;* Trevor Bryce's *Life and Society in the Hittite World* and *The Kingdom of the Hittites;* K. Bittel's *Hattusha, the Capital of the Hittites;* and *Bronze Age War Chariots* by Osprey Publishing. Also helpful were C.W. Ceram's *The Secret of the Hittites, the Discovery of an Ancient Civilization;* Johannes Lehmann's *The Hittites;* Paul Brewer's *Warfare in the Ancient World;* S. Bertman's *Handbook to Life in Ancient Mesopotamia;* Itamar Singer's *Hittite Prayers;* and REVAK's Cappadocia. The internet, too, has supplied many helpful tidbits.

Absolutely, this informal education has its value. But it's my everyday life that makes writing pleasurable and rewarding. I'm deeply grateful to Linda Johnson and Bonnie Klahr who read early drafts of the story. Carlene Jones provided invaluable help with plot and flow, asking questions that inevitably led to improved writing. Many thanks, too, to Barry Webb, who writes of ancient Babylon, and Stephen

Anderson, who writes about the world of illuminators of ancient texts, for their helpful critiques and encouragement. Terry Medaris, once again, contributed his artistic talent to the book's cover with the usual beautiful result. Mechanical Engineer and friend Bob Stauffer helped me to understand the improved chariot design credited to the Hittites—a topic way beyond my skills. My thanks, too, to the kindness of those who have invited me to their book clubs in Tucson and Philadelphia. Finally, to my family, there are no words— just love and gratitude.

OTHER BOOKS BY FRAN MARIAN

The Rug Broker
Nora Reardon and her Turkish agent, Muharrem El Habashy, travel Turkey's rock-strewn rural roads to purchase rugs. Not just any rugs. Her eyes are searching for colors leeched from desert beetles, patterns that flow onto the loom from ancient memories to calloused fingers, fibers washed in the streams and dried in the sun—the kind of Oriental rugs preferred by her discriminating East Coast clients.

Nora is driven by a passion for the rugs and a need to be independent of her conservative, Lebanese brothers who, since her husband's death, insist her place in is Philadelphia with her five-year-old son, Skipper. That's not what Nora wants.

She struggles with her business and a desperate desire to bond with her son. When she meets Carlos Ghazerian, an Ankara-based broker of antique Oriental rugs, he guides Nora to financial success, until she is thrown into a Turkish prison and her son spirals into a suicidal depression.

The Chinese Silk (sequel to The Rug Broker)
Nora Reardon, a Philadelphia rug gallery owner, built a successful career searching for the Middle East's finest hand-woven rugs. Unfortunately, success has come at the expense of her young son, Tom. Frustrated and angry with her inattentiveness, Tom has turned to Muslim friends for companionship, and when Nora finds a hidden prayer rug in Tom's room, she reacts with fear and prejudice. Her new husband, Carlos Ghazerian, raised as a Christian among Muslims in Turkey, has no problem with Tom's new-found Islamic faith. He accuses Nora of intolerance.

Desperate to unite her family, Nora encourages them to join her in the annual Festival of a Thousand and One Nights in Paradise, New York. But the event is a disaster, friends die, rugs are destroyed, and Carlos and Tom are missing. Nora blames herself.

But guilt, destruction, and death are no match for the power of a centuries-old Chinese silk rug as it weaves its way into Nora's life and proves that love between a parent and child can withstand even time itself.